PROOF
POSITIVE

ALSO BY ARCHER MAYOR

PROOF POSITIVE

A Joe Gunther Novel

ARCHER MAYOR

Minotaur Books
New York

PROOF POSITIVE. Copyright © 2014 by Archer Mayor. All rights reserved. Printed in the United States of America. For information, address St. Martin's Press, 175 Fifth Avenue, New York, N.Y. 10010.

www.minotaurbooks.com

The Library of Congress has cataloged the
hardcover edition as follows:

Mayor, Archer.
    Proof positive : a Joe Gunther novel / Archer Mayor. — First edition.
        p. cm.
    ISBN 978-1-250-02639-2 (hardcover)
    ISBN 978-1-250-02640-8 (e-book)
    1. Gunther, Joe (Fictitious character)—Fiction.   2. Murder—
Investigation—Fiction.   I. Title.
    PS3563.A965P78 2014
    813'.54—dc23   2014016729

ISBN 978-1-250-07033-3 (trade paperback)

Minotaur books may be purchased for educational, business, or promotional use. For information on bulk purchases, please contact the Macmillan Corporate and Premium Sales Department at 1-800-221-7945, extension 5442, or write to specialmarkets@macmillan.com.

First Minotaur Books Paperback Edition: September 2015

10 9 8 7 6 5 4 3 2 1

ACKNOWLEDGMENTS

As always, I am indebted to many generous people for the meat and substance of these stories. They have the knowledge, experience, and insight that I often lack. That is indeed often why I pursue the topics that I do—so that I can interview them and enrich my brain with just a fragment of what they so willingly offer. To them, and to so many others as well, my thanks.

Margot Mayor

Ray Walker

John Martin

Chelsea and Greg Kline

Greg Davis

Bill Schur

Neil Schur

Roberta Zeff

Ernie Conover

Wednesday Night Dinner

Scout Mayor

Julie Lavorgna

Gail Steketee

Shane Harris

Judith Forman

Castle Freeman

Fran Plevinsky

Steve Shapiro

CHAPTER ONE

It was the time of year when New England wobbles between fall and winter, as prone to Indian summer as to sudden, short-lived snowstorms.

It wasn't snowing tonight, but it was cold, and Jason Newville was regretting that he'd only worn a sweatshirt. Nerves played a part. Unlike some, he tended to cool down when he was on a job, instead of working up an adrenaline sweat. But as with most things taken for granted, he hadn't considered it when he set out, and was paying the price now.

It wasn't unbearable. He was born to this weather, and in line with southeastern Vermont's being mockingly labeled "the banana belt," it did run warmer here than in the rest of the state. He'd survive. Besides, he had things to keep him occupied, like the whereabouts of the crazy old man who lived here.

Jason stepped out from behind a large maple at the edge of the darkened property and studied the layout by the light of a full moon. This wasn't his first visit. He'd been here twice before over the past week. There'd never been a change. The house remained still and as black as a tomb. Just as it was tonight.

But instead of lending him confidence, the silence only bred foreboding.

Jason had been burglarizing homes for three years, time enough to have developed a balance between caution and foolhardiness. He had an instinct about most places—an inner radar, as he saw it—that had helped to keep him out of jail, so far.

But that radar wasn't working here. He was as keyed up as during the first time he'd crept from the woods that girdled the house.

It was a rambling spread, once entirely agricultural, with barns, sheds, paddocks, and a centrally located family house. With time, most of the fields had been abandoned or sold off, and each structure at the farm's core—depending on its original sturdiness—had fallen into disrepair, or to the brink of collapse. The one sign of expansion—at once attractive and daunting to Jason—was the steadily accumulating piles of looming, jagged scrap. Depending on their nature and/or size, they bulged outward from every orifice of every building, or seemed to erupt from the earth as semi-mountainous heaps of mechanical debris.

Balers, tractors, combines, tedders, conveyor belts, pickup trucks, generators, and more—ghostly, hulking, rusty, and inoperable monsters teetered drunkenly under the bright moon like otherworldly space junk gleaned from the night sky in the sweeping gesture of an invisible hand. It was an entangled collection of such enormity that it staggered the imagination, and—its scope magnified by the steely-sharp lunar lighting—ignited in Jason's chest an instinctive fear about what or who, besides him, might also be silently lurking among the riot of sharp-edged shadows.

He knew of the crazy guy who lived here—Ben Kendall. A loner, an eccentric, a hoarder of vast appetite. He was a local fixture, keeping to himself but roaming constantly around the neighborhood, his ramshackle open-bed truck swaying under a precarious tower of mostly metal debris. Hand-lettered wooden panels along both sides of the truck advertised KENDALL'S SCRAP & RECYCLING, although everyone suspected that the "recycling" remained mostly in Ben's mind. No one that Jason knew had ever seen that truck leave Ben's property other than empty.

Jason stepped from the trees, not running ducked over as he had the first time, but with trepidation nevertheless, seized by the place's malevolent quality.

As often occurred in the mythos surrounding hoarders, neighborhood rumors of treasure residing in the heart of Ben's possessions had curled like smoke tendrils. There was no evidence of it. Ben displayed no proof of wealth anywhere. But word had reached Jason's ears a month earlier, and prompted his initial reconnaissance a few days ago.

He hadn't stayed long that time, mostly touring the property's perimeters, like a wolf rounding the edges of a sheep pen. As with tonight, there'd been no movement or sound. He'd tried peering through windows, to find every view blocked, and had opened the occasional outbuilding door, to meet a wall of objects standing against him. But no dogs had barked, no lights had come on, and Jason had begun thinking of the place as an unheard-of possibility: a bottomless well to revisit time and again.

His second foray had therefore been bolder. He'd driven here in a borrowed vehicle, bringing two duffel bags. As before, he'd met no resistance or opposition, but he'd been infected by a cloaking eeriness, and at the last minute, opted to stay outside. He'd foraged among the precariously balanced pyramids for the odd piece of salvage that he could extract with minimal noise, and left largely empty-handed and stymied.

Because that was the irony, even to him: While all this was far from any road or keen-eared neighbor, and had never shown signs of life during his visits, Jason couldn't shake the feeling that he was being watched. Like a hypersensitive rodent recognizing the trap while mesmerized by its contents, Jason kept tentatively reaching out, convincing himself that his desire would eventually overpower his dread.

Tonight, he'd told himself, he was going inside.

Because those rumors had to be true. How else could Ben survive, unless he had a ready supply of money? This was a big property, even if in decay. For Jason, whose past homes had been trailers, flophouses, and other people's couches, Ben's spread was an estate. And estates had to be paid for.

Jason approached the farmhouse's front door, set back under a sagging porch roof and guarded by sentries of cordwood, lawn furniture, rusting grills, bicycles, car fenders, and bald tires. He placed a foot carefully on the first stair tread, and pressed down, as he might have in testing the buoyancy of a floating dock. Surprisingly, it remained solid, not emitting the merest creak, as if the wood had been compressed beyond complaint by time and neglect.

He continued, his hands out unconsciously, atop an invisible tightrope. To either side, the dark hedgerows of Ben's belongings closed around him as he neared the door, silent and still.

He placed one hand on the knob and used the other to extract a flashlight from his pocket, suddenly unsure whether he should use it now, or wait until he'd opened the door. Yielding to fear, he hit the switch before pulling the knob.

The door opened reluctantly, rubbing against the inner floorboards, its hinges complaining without conviction. The inside air spilled out, wrapping him in a fog—warm, fetid, cloying, almost alive. He felt the entire house had just released a deep, internal sigh.

"Oh, God," he barely whispered, knowing that the slightest unexpected sound or motion now would be enough to send him flying.

But, as always in his experience here, there was only the silence accompanying the absence of life, or the holding of one's breath.

Timidly, he played his light along the floor ahead, and off to both sides, taking in not a room, as he'd expected, but the narrow confines of a tunnel formed of densely packed newspapers, magazines, and boxes, reaching up to the ceiling.

Scowling, his breathing shallow and rapid, Jason eased by the doorway and entered the rough-walled shaft, his flashlight setting off an endless shifting of shadows. The thick air around him closed in.

Fifteen feet along, he came to a widening, where the clutter lowered enough to allow him to see farther afield. He was standing in a four-foot-deep foxhole, peering out over an undulating landscape of newspapers, files, furniture, catalogs, and paper products. The beam in his hand brought to mind a battlefield searchlight, crisscrossing a no-man's-land in search of movement. In the distance, the tops of doorways indicated paths to adjoining rooms, with overhead clearances of a couple of feet. He had no notion of what the original purpose might have been of the room he was occupying.

Sweating now, light-headed in the rank atmosphere, Jason wiped his forehead with the back of his sleeve, wondering what to do, where to start. Surrounded by more than the plenty he'd dreamed of, he was stuck.

Reluctantly, he climbed from the trench and crawled onto the surrounding rubbish, unsure of what rotting object he might encounter by chance, or even if the unstable surface might suddenly give way and swallow him whole. Fueling his concern, the commingled layers beneath kept slipping as he moved.

He headed for the nearest crawl-space doorway, feeling increasingly trapped and hopeless, telling himself that not every room was the same as this one, and that he was bound to discover some order that made sense.

"I just want to steal something," he murmured as he went, not reflecting on the absurdity of either the statement or his predicament.

In fact, there was a change after he slithered under his chosen door header. From his perch there, he found the room beyond filled more with mechanical objects than with paper. There were appliances and large woodworking equipment intermixed with books, operator manuals, and piles of broken or rusty hand tools. Depending on the spot, he could even see the floor.

Still, he hesitated atop the doorway's steep slope, surveying the chaos ahead with growing frustration. Again, he could see nothing of value, and too much of everything. His head was pounding, and he was getting angry.

Hungry for any success, he finally swung around and slid down the embankment like a kid on a toboggan, skittering paper to both sides and arresting his descent by jamming his boots against a three-legged drill press.

That was the end of all stealth. The drill slowly toppled, smashing into its metallic neighbor and throwing dozens of items into the air.

Jason covered his head against the shower of hardware, throwing out a hand for balance. As he'd been dreading from the start, his fingers closed on something cold, soft, and damp. He screamed in horror, dropping his flashlight in the process.

Scurrying backwards, rubbing his palm obsessively against his pants, he retrieved the rolling light and aimed it at the offending object.

Caught in the bright halo, peering from under the avalanche like a discarded animal carcass, was a partially decayed human face.

CHAPTER TWO

"Vermont Bureau of Investigation. Joe Gunther speaking."

"Hi, Joe."

At the sound of Beverly Hillstrom's voice, Gunther removed his feet from the windowsill and turned around to face the empty squad room, resting his elbows on his desktop and cradling the phone more comfortably. Hillstrom was Vermont's medical examiner—tough, disciplined, and scrupulously thorough. More important to Joe, she had recently become his sweetheart—if, for the time being, a quietly acknowledged one.

"Hey, there," he said. "How's the light of my life?"

"I like that," she laughed. "You're sounding sporty."

"You interested?" he asked. "I could get there in two hours."

"My sofa has recovered from the last time," she told him. "But I'm not sure I want to explain a locked office door in the middle of the day."

"Ah. No guts," he accused her. In the minute pause that followed—and to move them off the subject smoothly—he added, "But you probably didn't call for that, did you? Have we sent you someone I don't know about?"

Her voice took on the professional tone he knew so well. They'd been a romantic couple for a short time, but colleagues for decades.

"It came in as a natural or an accidental," she explained. "I'm still determining that—probably a cardiac event brought on by the stress of an accident. But it's not a criminal case. At least, not based on state police findings."

"Oh?" he prompted her, his interest piqued. Beverly was not one to make chatty shoptalk. Something was afoot. "Where did this come from?"

"Your neck of the woods. Dummerston."

That was near enough, being the township just north of Brattle-boro, where Joe's office was located.

"You have suspicions?" he asked.

She hesitated. "I do," she finally conceded. "And there's a complication. The decedent is related to me."

That caught him by surprise. "Oh, Beverly. What happened?"

"His name is Benjamin Kendall. We were first cousins. He was found at home, under a pile of personal effects, and at first, it seemed reasonable that he'd fallen prey to a domestic mishap."

Joe was used to her almost antique English, but here, it was the substance rather than the delivery that caught his attention. "Reasonable?" he countered. "That a pile of . . . what? Personal effects? *Fell* on him?"

"He was a hoarder," she elaborated. "It's not as far-fetched as it sounds. His environment was literally a series of precarious stacks and archways—books, newspapers, decades'-worth of randomly acquired . . ." Here, even she appeared at a loss for words, and fell back upon, "Stuff."

Trusting that the story would gain clarity, Joe moved along. "You're thinking that's not what happened?"

"He exhibited multiple nonlethal injuries," she went on. "All of them more or less consistent with being pinned under a heavy weight. But it had been days, and his tissues had degenerated, making things harder to sort out. My deputy did the autopsy, per protocol, but I couldn't not come in for a consultation. That being said, a cardiac event seems like the most credible finding—his heart was in poor condition. But it's just not sitting right with me. We're leaving it open at least until the toxicology comes back."

She stopped there, although he knew that she had more to tell. Beverly Hillstrom's autopsies, even if conducted by a deputy, were not going to be anything but in-depth analyses. But she was on tricky ground. This was a Vermont State Police investigation. Joe was VBI—also a state agency, but restricted to major cases—and generally activated only by direct invitation from the lead investigator, which was not Beverly.

He tried easing her distress. "Beverly. I'm really sorry this happened. I didn't even know you had a relative in Vermont, aside from your daughter in college. I thought you were a Philly girl. If you'd like, I'd be happy to call whoever caught this case, just to delicately check his homework."

Her relief was palpable. "Oh, Joe. Thanks so much. I wasn't sure what to do. Ben ended up in Vermont because of me, and I took care of him as much as he'd let me, which wasn't much. To be honest, we'd only recently gotten in touch because of Rachel—the one at UVM. She was looking for an art project—a documentary for credit—and I introduced the two of them just a couple of months ago. It's all so sad and unexpected. I'd really appreciate your giving this a look."

Gunther was teeming with questions, but decided to bide his time and make his approach from the outside in. He reached for a nearby pad. "Give me the lead's name, would you, Beverly? I'll make a phone call and find out what I can."

Brattleboro, Vermont, is in the state's lower right-hand corner pocket, assuming that you envision a trapezoidal pool table with seven urban pockets instead of six, and that you allow for a spine of mountains to run down its middle. The state capital—the seventh pocket—is smack in the table's middle. The others, starting with the lower left, are Bennington, Rutland, and Burlington up the western side, and St. Johnsbury, White River Junction, and Brattleboro down the eastern.

Once dependent on waterways, like most older New England hubs, Brattleboro is fed by the first three northbound Vermont exits of Interstate 91—the paved slab that had completely replaced the Connecticut River as a source of commercial vitality. The interstate showed up on maps like a chain saw's scar, severing the town's once bustling western extension and transforming it into an emotionally disenfranchised entity called West Brattleboro—or, more colloquially, "West B."

That's where the VSP barracks had been built, in an unfortunate example of 1970s architecture, the only advantage of which was its proximity to the Chelsea Royal Diner, just across the road.

Joe parked in the barracks lot, walked up the handicap ramp bordering the low building's oppressively bland exterior, and was met at the door by a square-built young man wearing a dark blue shirt and matching tie. Cops find it hard to resist discounted tie-and-shirt bargains at Sears and Penney's.

"Joe Gunther?" the man said, extending a broad and powerful hand in greeting. "I saw you drive up. I feel like I'm meeting a legend. This is a real honor. I'm Owen Baern."

"Hardly a legend," Joe told him, admiring the young detective's distinctive head of curly hair—an unusual feature in a profession renowned for crew cuts and flattops. "More like a guy who never learned to quit."

Baern escorted Joe into the building, through the secure lobby, and back into the core of the barracks. "That's not what I've heard. You're like the most famous cop we have."

"How long you been at it, Owen?" Joe asked, as much to change subjects as out of modesty.

"Seven years. I've only been working plainclothes for a couple of months, though, so anything you can give me will be much appreciated. I need all the help I can get."

They'd worked their way down a long central corridor, and now entered a small office equipped with two desks. "We talking in general?" Joe asked. "Or the Benjamin Kendall case I mentioned on the phone?"

Baern pulled out a guest chair for him. "Both, maybe. That's up to you. You want some coffee or a soda?"

Joe sat down. "I'm good, thanks."

There was a moment's pause between strangers at a loss for words. Joe's host settled hesitantly behind his desk.

"Why not start with Kendall?" Joe prompted. "How did you catch the case?"

Gratefully, Baern turned to his computer and began reading from the screen. "Came in as an anonymous tip. We chased the cell phone data upstream and pinned it to a guy named Jason Newville, DOB: 7/30/84. I know him from my days on the road. He's a regular when it comes to B-and-Es, selling stolen copper, ripping off car stereos, even shoplifting. And of course, the standard pissant drug deal to see him through the weekend. He targeted Kendall's place because he heard it was a gold mine and Kendall hadn't been around lately."

"Was that common?" Joe cut in.

Owen looked at him. "That Ben disappeared now and then? Just the opposite. He was a local fixture—him and his truck. You know about him?"

"I heard he was a hoarder."

"Yeah. Amazing place. I never saw anything like it. Jammed, everywhere—floor to ceiling. I wouldn't have anything to do with it. My dad was a pack rat. I hated it. Stank, too. But for the Jason Newvilles of the world? That's the smell of opportunity."

"You interviewed Jason," Joe stated, assuming it was a given.

"Yeah. In the long run, he didn't steal anything that I could tell— not that it'll make much difference to the judge. Finding Ben creeped him out. He literally fell over him, according to his story, hightailed it out, and then couldn't figure out what to do next."

"So he called it in?"

Baern shook his head. "I know. Crazy enough to make it believable. Don't know what to do? Call the cops, even if they'll still arrest you for burglary."

"You believe him?" Joe asked. "Newville?"

Owen absorbed the question before readjusting himself in his chair, thinking for a couple of seconds. "You know? I do," he admitted quietly, as if fearful of being called out on it.

"The medical examiner phoned me," Joe explained. "Ben was her cousin, it turns out."

"Ouch," Owen said, although clearly relieved to gain some insight on why Joe was there. He leaned into the computer again, checking its contents quickly. "The ME sent me a preliminary finding. I didn't think there was anything suspicious, or that I'd dropped the ball. Just a heart attack and some minor trauma related to the landslide."

"Undetermined for the time being," Joe clarified. "You ever meet Hillstrom?"

"The chief up there? I heard about her. She's not much fun, supposedly."

"She can be driven," Joe specified. "With Ben, she's saying she wants to wait for the tox results, but that's because she has no hard evidence of a straight-out coronary. This one is bugging her."

"He was family," Owen suggested.

"True," Joe agreed affably. "But that should sharpen everyone's game. Not just hers. Most people have family somewhere."

Baern looked down at the desktop, abashed, before looking up and raising his eyebrows. "You want to see the place? Where we found him? I wouldn't mind a second pair of eyes."

Dummerston is typical of many communities across Vermont, less an actual town than a collection of sub-villages. There's an elementary school at one location, a church and municipal offices at another, the meeting hall and the primary fire station at a third. It's largely a spider-web of roads, dirt and paved, including the longest covered bridge within Vermont proper. But its spread-out quality notwithstanding, the people who live in its embrace are more interconnected than residents of the average urban apartment building. Visitors—and locals— sometimes poked fun at the layout, referring to the homegrown as "woodchucks." Joe Gunther, however—a native of a similar town, farther north—knew better. These communities could come close to being disjointed families, along with a vitality—and a level of caring—that most neighborhoods could only envy.

Owen Baern drove an unmarked four-wheel-drive vehicle to the end of a badly rutted, overgrown dirt road that finally ran out of ambition at a clearing on the edge of Ben Kendall's property. It was past the foliage season, and what leaves were slated to fall had done so, leaving a skeletal superstructure of stark and empty hardwoods crowding in from all sides, as well as a dark blanket of rotting vegetation underfoot. To Joe's eyes, it set the perfect backdrop to the bleak, time-pummeled collection of aging buildings before him, guarded by a thrown-up palisade of twisted and rusting machine parts that made the totality look like some sole survivor's last stand in a postapocalyptic wasteland.

"Wow," Joe commented, stretching his legs beside the car as he got out, and trying to read the lay of the land.

"That's one word for it," Owen agreed. "You can see the challenge to conducting a by-the-book scene survey. It reminds me of one of those man-against-the-machines movies, where everyone lost."

"That it does," Joe muttered, choosing a deliberate course between the obstacles, heading for the compound's main house, and fighting the notion that one of the bristling metal haystacks might suddenly stir to life. It also didn't help that, typical of this time of year, the low sky was bruised and menacing.

Baern fell in beside him. "Not hard to figure what Jason found attractive. When I interviewed him, he admitted that before he knew Ben was inside, dead, he didn't know where to start. There was so much to choose from, he wished he'd stolen a flatbed truck first."

"Tell me more about Jason," Joe requested.

"Meaning might he have killed Ben in exchange for all this?" He waved an arm at the piles they were skirting.

"Maybe if he got surprised?" Joe asked.

Owen gave it some thought before shaking his head. "Never say never, as they say, but I don't see it. Beyond a totally nonviolent rap sheet, I don't think it fits his personality. He's a schmoozer, and probably a bit of a coward. Plus, he did make the phone call, which speaks of somebody seriously out of his element. And let's not forget that the body was already decomposing."

"Good point," Joe agreed.

They reached the door, which had been sealed with yellow tape and a NO TRESPASSING order. Baern pulled out a knife and cut through it, explaining, "We might not've done this normally. But with the autopsy still pending, and no other residents, I figured it couldn't hurt. . . ."

"Sure," Joe said. "You put a man out here?"

"The lieutenant said it wasn't warranted. The tape's to discourage more Jasons from crawling out of the woodwork for a shopping spree, but the budget couldn't handle a babysitter." Owen yanked open the door, adding, "Prepare yourself. It don't smell pretty."

It didn't, despite the removal of Ben's body. It was also no brighter inside than at midnight, every window being blocked by possessions.

Equipped with flashlights and breathing with their mouths open, they retraced Jason's journey through tunnel and over dunes, to where the funeral home and others had excavated around the landslide's foot, mostly by throwing heaps of material across the room. Joe could only imagine the disgust that had accompanied the clearing process.

"You were here when he was removed?" Joe asked.

Owen was looking around, playing his light across the landscape. There was an overhead bulb burning, here and there, but to little effect. "Yup. Took pictures, too. Believe it or not, it seemed tidy compared to this. Everybody was in a rush to get him out."

Joe was trying to reconstruct the scene as they'd found it. "You never suspected foul play?"

Baern sensed where this was headed. "Honestly? No. I know what you're thinking: that we just wanted to get the hell out of here. I've asked myself that a dozen times already, especially since you walked into my office. I swear to God, between how we found Ben and what I found out later about Jason Newville, I can't see anything here beyond a really sad accident."

"So, how's that work?" Joe asked him. "Ben was walking by the doorway and everything from one room suddenly caved in on him?"

Baern fidgeted with his tie. "That's the way it looked at the time. Things have been moved—"

"Not *that* much," Joe pointed out. "There's no place *to* walk by. You either approach the pile head-on, from this direction, or you slide down it the way Jason did, from the other."

Owen became a little defensive. "There are other rooms where it's not a pile that spills into the next room, but a stacked wall. I was thinking the same was true here, and that maybe he was standing in front of it, maybe looking for something down low, when he destabilized the whole thing and it crushed him. I mean, it looks like the side of a hill now, but it might not've been that way originally."

Joe was nodding. "Okay. I could see that. Do you remember—was he mostly pinned by tools and hardware, or magazines and boxes?" He gestured toward the rest of the room. "Like what was thrown off to get to him afterwards?"

"Softer stuff," Owen said. "Why?"

"I haven't seen the autopsy photographs yet, and I know he was partially decomposed, but from what you told me, he was kind of beaten up—scratches and bruises and whatever."

His younger colleague pondered that a moment before conceding, "Which is a little unlikely from a pile of paper."

Joe faced him encouragingly. "Not impossible, but 'unlikely' is a good word."

CHAPTER THREE

Joe was sitting in a booth at the back of an out-of-the-way restaurant in Burlington when a woman slid onto his bench, pressed herself up against him, and delivered a kiss. He responded by infiltrating her unbuttoned coat with his hand and caressing her flat stomach and the underside of one breast.

Beverly Hillstrom broke away only long enough to murmur, "Special Agent Gunther. What do you think you're doing?"

"Taking advantage of a consenting adult, I hope," he said, kissing her.

She slid back out to remove the coat, hung it on the booth's outer post, and took the bench across from him. Her arrival made the air around them smell of the cool, fresh outdoors.

"This okay?" he asked, indicating the seating.

"Wonderful," she said, as she reached out to take his hand, "And it's not that I don't want to be seen with you."

"No, no," he almost interrupted. "I totally understand. It makes life easier for the both of us, to be honest."

She laughed then. "You should know, your ex-girlfriend being the current governor of Vermont. That has to have been awkward on occasion."

He allowed for a rueful smile. "It had its moments when it was news, but no more. Thank God we weren't an item when she got elected. Not that dating the state's chief medical examiner is a step down."

Her eyebrows shot up. "Perish the thought." She gave his fingers an extra squeeze as she said, "I love that you drove all the way up here to see me. You are something else—one of the most thoughtful people I know."

"It's my pleasure," he assured her. "I'm just sorry about the circumstances."

"It was a little disconcerting to see my own cousin on the table," she allowed. "Did you get to meet with the VSP investigator? His name didn't ring a bell with me."

"He's new," Joe told her. "Owen Baern. Solid guy. He'll get the hang of it faster than most."

"And you found nothing suspicious about Ben's death?"

Joe tilted his head slightly. "I'm not saying that."

Their waitress arrived and took their drink orders. Joe waited until she'd left to answer Beverly's question. "It's a given that every investigation has a few questions you can't answer. The trick is to ask if you can live with them. Right now, I can't say that. I'll need some more facts before I'm happy with a finding of 'Accidental.'"

Beverly took a sip of her drink before saying, "Fire away."

He tapped his finger on the menu. "First things first. Otherwise, she'll just keep interrupting."

They therefore dealt with their orders before Joe asked, "Tell me about Ben. You said he moved to Vermont because of you. What's the story there?"

"We were all brought up in Philadelphia," Beverly began. "I come from quite the clan—what you might call Brahmins of the Main Line, not that the phrase means anything around here. The Main Line is a string of suburban towns running west of the city, alongside the primary tracks of the old Pennsylvania Railroad: places named Lower Merion, Villanova, Gladwyne, Bryn Mawr—where I attended college—and several others."

"I was down there on a case," Joe said. "Some pretty fancy houses—not that you can see them too well."

"I should say not," she agreed. "Several of those towns are among the priciest in the country, as they were in the late 1800s. People pay to be invisible from the road—unless, of course, they're showing off."

"That explains the Ferrari dealership I saw," he suggested. "New Money versus Old?"

"As always," she said. "Anyhow—full disclosure—your latest girlfriend is a hopeless blue blood."

"I'm shocked."

Her voice became nostalgic. "I know. That's actually one of the reasons I became a physician—because I was told I didn't have to. All such stuffy idealism aside, however, being a kid down there in those days was pretty magical, as un-PC as it sounds. We had a wonderful, pampered, catered-to childhood, which even then—in my defense—I knew not to take for granted. My parents had figured out that much—they made sure we appreciated how advantaged we were."

"This included Ben?"

"Yes, although from a different angle, and in less than ideal circumstances in the long run. Ben's mother and mine were sisters. They were inseparable as children—my grandmother used to say they were like twins. But my aunt married for love at too young an age, and it didn't turn out well for her. Ben was the result, and in the early days, when things were still happy—he was just part of the gang. But later, his father started drinking, made a string of bad investments, and alienated everyone. They moved away, refused to keep in touch, turned down offers of help. By the time Ben was a teenager, his mother had died and he was living with a drunk. I always thought that was one reason he turned to photography—to put a camera between himself and the world."

"That must've been hard to watch," Joe said supportively.

Beverly leaned toward him. "It should have been, and I have beaten myself up for most of my adult life because it wasn't. Shameful as it sounds, Ben's departure from our special kingdom barely caused a ripple. My mother took it hard. It changed her to have lost her sister. But we kids paid little attention. We were busy having fun and growing up like royalty and going to all the right schools and parties and what have you. It left me with a feeling of lapsed responsibility that I will take to my grave."

Joe took one of her hands in his, stunned by how her own self-doubt was so at odds with his respect and admiration for her. "Whoa. Beverly. Slow down. How were you supposed to know what was going on between the adults? Much less take on the burden of what happened? This kind of crap happens in every family, from the Cabots down to the street sweeper."

She was already shaking her head. "I realize that, Joe. You know me. I've put it all under a microscope—the scientist in the lab coat. You think I am unaware that half the cops in Vermont refer to me as the Ice Queen? That's my armor, and what happened to Ben plays a big role in it. I let him down when he needed me, even if he didn't know to ask for help, and I will never let that happen again. I will be just shy of fanatical in speaking up for the people who appear on my autopsy table—not to mention friends and family."

They paused as their waitress returned and served them their meals.

"It wasn't just that Ben fell off the radar when his parents left Philadelphia," she resumed as they began eating. "I probably could have remained clueless and guilt-free if he'd just grown up to be another banker or insurance salesman or even a passport photographer, for

God's sake. It's what did happen to him that fused with the family's earlier sins, and made me feel that I should have paid closer attention."

"What happened?" Joe asked.

"In a word, Vietnam," she said.

"He served in Nam?" Joe blurted out.

"Yes. It didn't sound too threatening at first. He shipped out as a Signal Corps photographer. He'd married and tried to find work, but without much luck. The army was recruiting, making all sorts of promises, including that you could pick your job and not be sent to Vietnam—both of which were usually so much hot air. But he actually landed one out of two. We were worried for him, of course, but amazed that they'd recognized his skill with a camera and put it to good use. So, despite his being sent to a war zone, we were hopeful that he'd be kept away from any direct line of fire."

"I take it that didn't turn out well."

"No. You remember those days—nightly reports of body counts and defoliation and hearts-and-minds rhetoric and soldiers putting Zippos to thatch-roofed shacks."

"They called them hooches," Joe said quietly, his own memory reaching back all too easily.

"Yes," she recalled. "Well, it was also a PR battle against the protesters the world over, and Ben was caught up in the middle of it. He was photographing appalling things and then being ordered to cull through them so that they looked like the U.S. was winning the war. The letters he wrote home that his wife shared with us became darker and darker. He wrote that he began carrying two cameras—the army's and his own—so that he could document what mattered to him. The irony is that those pictures mostly showed scenes and people that look unaffected by the war, as if he was using the second camera to distance himself from the horror." She sighed and fiddled with the salad that, so far, she'd barely touched.

"Did he suffer from PTSD?" Joe asked.

She looked up from her reveries. "Oh, much worse than that. I mean, yes, he did, but the bullet he stopped with his head did the real damage."

Joe stared at her, his mouth open.

She scowled at her own dramatics. "I'm sorry. That was a little much. Guilt is so hard to keep in perspective."

"Isn't that a contradiction right there?"

She laughed, if only briefly. "Granted."

"So he was sent home," Joe brought her back on track.

"He was. In a coma. He'd sustained critical damage to the frontal lobe, and stayed in the hospital for almost a year, after which he did all he could do to essentially disappear, including ending his marriage."

"That when the hoarding began?"

"Not immediately, but soon thereafter. Personality changes are not uncommon in traumatic brain injury."

Joe took a bite of his burger. Not as distracted as she was, he was hungry. "What happened to his pictures?" he asked.

She placed her cheek in her hand, making him think that she might start to cry. A seasoned listener, he was struck by how affected he was by her distress, and was thereby reminded—yet again—of much she'd come to mean to him.

"I should have known that you'd go to the heart of it," she said. "That's why I called you about this."

"The photographs?"

"Indirectly."

He didn't show his utter lack of comprehension. "So, tell me," he urged instead.

"He kept quite a few," she began. "At least, the ones he was allowed to—the ones he took for himself."

Joe waited, continuing to eat.

"Of course, he was unconscious when he came back. The army just collected his possessions, including what he was wearing when he was shot—which again sounds peculiar, given these days of blood-borne pathogens—and shoved them into a trunk and shipped them home. And those films sat, probably for years, knowing Ben, until he began getting back into photography."

"Where was he living by then?" Joe asked.

"Here," she said. "In Vermont. I'd moved up to take the medical examiner's job—fresh from a fellowship in forensic pathology at the City of Philadelphia ME's office. I'd been here a little while, and had met and married Daniel, when Ben told me that he also wanted to 'live in the sticks,' as he put it. I helped him find the Dummerston property. Technically, I guess you could say I bought it for him, since I was the mortgage holder. But he paid me rent, the first of every month."

"Huh," Joe said. "I had no idea."

She smiled sadly. "I know what you're thinking. It didn't look like it does now. It was nice—a true picture postcard. By then, Ben's father had died, he'd inherited a modest amount, the military was paying him disability, and I helped out with the bigger bills, if I thought he'd accept it."

"Did he? Beyond the house?"

"Hardly ever. We'd gotten back in touch after he left the hospital. It wasn't as it had been when we were kids, but there remained a genuine closeness. In fact, until he met Rachel, I was the only family member he'd speak with. And I think he was grateful for my finding him a corner of the earth in which to hide—not that he ever admitted it."

"That makes sense," Joe said. "How did Rachel get involved?"

"She was struggling to find a suitable subject for a video documentary, and I told her that Ben might be both appropriate and approachable. I knew he was a hoarder, and that the topic is popular right now. I was hoping he might help her along. Of course, I had an ulterior motive: I'd always wanted to draw him out a bit more—he was outwardly gregarious, but remained inwardly guarded—and I also wanted him to meet at least one of my daughters and perhaps form a friendship."

"I take it that worked," Joe suggested.

"More than I'd dared to hope. They hit it off. It took a while. Hoarders are not generally open to scrutiny, and certainly not fond of people invading their inner sanctum. They are at once embarrassed and possessive of their supposed riches. But Rachel was clever enough to show up first without her camera, and to keep private what she thought about his lifestyle. She's a canny young woman."

"Not unlike her mother."

Beverly accepted the compliment. "Thank you. In any case, she eventually made it a habit to drop by Ben's every few weeks, and he became a virtual tour guide of his world for her. You can see the footage—in fact, you'll probably want to. He reminded me of that appropriately named idiot toady, Robin Leach—who hosted *Lifestyles of the Rich and Famous* years ago. Ben would hold up random scraps of junk and go into their histories and provenance as if they were objets d'art. Of course," she added, backpedaling a little, "they were valuable to him, I guess, so I shouldn't be judgmental."

"Did Rachel finish her project?" Joe wanted to know.

"No. Actually, the story becomes a little more tangled. The project expanded as a result of finding Ben's photographs. She stumbled across hundreds of portraits that he'd taken of his piles of possessions, almost as if they were family photos. She was astonished, of course. I'd told her that he'd been a photographer, but even I hadn't realized that he'd kept it up. He'd exchanged the photojournalism of his youth for these abstract images of all sorts of—" she hesitated again. "—things."

"Anything good?"

Her face brightened with pleasure. "They are amazing, Joe. Truly beautiful. When Rachel brought them home, it felt like she'd uncovered the lost masterpieces of some extraordinary artist. It was such a gift. They immediately made me think of past masters like Weston and Steichen, but with a style all their own. Some are so detailed, and almost voluptuous, that they look three-dimensional—reminiscent of those famous nudes and bell peppers that always appear in art books. But Ben's extend even further, lending the same sort of sensuality to objects most of us regard as trash."

"You have them?" Joe asked, surprised.

"Yes. That also took some doing. Hoarders are not prone to letting go. But given that it was Rachel, and that she promised to return them safe and sound, he finally came around. It didn't hurt that she got the college museum interested in displaying them in a one-man show."

Joe's brow furrowed slightly. "How did they find out about him?"

"She showed her advisor some raw footage from her video project, including a couple of Ken Burns–style slow pans of Ben's photographs. The advisor showed it to the curator, and then urged Rachel to convince Ben to share his work with the rest of the world.

"The irony was," Beverly added, "that in the end, the abstracts weren't the exhibition's sole focus. Once again, the war came back to haunt, as Ben put it. Scrounging through the collection, Rachel discovered some old Vietnam prints. They were completely at odds with most photographs of that time and place—which always zeroed in on the violence. Like the abstracts—which are really still lifes—these were so compelling and unusual that the museum wanted them, too."

"How did Ben feel about that?" Joe asked. "Sounds like he wasn't too happy."

"In many ways, my cousin was a fatalist." Beverly continued, "He knew in his heart that he could never be free of Vietnam. But, to answer your question, this is where Rachel got really creative. At first, she was merely surprised to have found the Vietnam pictures. She never knew Ben had been over there. But when she returned to Dummerston to tell him of the museum's excitement, she was completely unprepared for his reaction. He had a meltdown, and refused to be any further part of her plan.

"But don't forget that by now, she had physical possession of the entire archive. It was at my house, where most of it still is. That gave her the leverage to slowly work him around to agreeing to have all of it displayed, albeit anonymously, and with only a token showing of the war images."

"Nobody knows who shot it?" Joe asked.

"That was the deal. If the Vietnam pictures were included, they were to play a minor role, and there was to be no credit given."

"Is the exhibition still on?"

"Not only on, but it's one of the most popular the museum has ever mounted. *The New York Times* ran an article about it in their Sunday edition. It turns out that a reporter from the magazine section was in Burlington, visiting relatives, when they decided to see the show. Now everyone's flocking to see it."

Joe smiled slightly. "I take it Rachel got a passing grade."

"Not yet, but this certainly won't hurt. Remember, the video assignment is still unfinished," Beverly replied. "And sadly, everything's been tainted by Ben's passing. There are so many odd aspects to the timing of his death. That was one of the reasons that I reached out to you, Joe. There is possibly so much more to it than what's appearing on the surface."

"Where's Rachel now?" Joe asked.

"Burlington. She lives in one of the dorms, and I've already asked her if she'd be willing to speak with you. I hope you don't mind. She'd very much like to, if you're interested."

"I am. I'd also like to see the photographs."

His two statements cheered her considerably. "As I mentioned," she said, "the exhibition is still up, but I have copies at home—along with hundreds more—if you'd like to see them."

He waved at the waitress, commenting, "I thought you'd never ask."

Hillstrom lived south of Burlington, on the edge of Lake Champlain, in what, to Joe's eyes, was a tastefully understated mansion. Her ex-husband, Daniel Reiling, was one of the city's more successful lawyers, and Beverly's income as chief medical examiner for over twenty years was substantial. Even before Joe had heard about her moneyed background, he'd felt that she was well off.

They arrived in two cars, since neither one of them ever knew when a pager call might summon them to their separate duties, and began the second half of their evening in the kitchen, standing by the fridge and eating ice cream out of its container with a shared spoon.

Joe took advantage of their proximity to lean over and put his cool mouth on hers.

She chuckled as they kissed, lightly licking the vanilla from his lips. "This is where it began in earnest," she said softly, reminiscing about an earlier late-night snack in this same kitchen.

He laughed. "That's right. The famous midnight bowl of soup."

"I couldn't have you driving all night without dinner," she protested.

"I remember getting more than dinner that night," he said, kissing her again.

She dropped the spoon into the container and placed it onto the nearby counter before draping her arms around his neck and kissing him deeply. "I am so glad you accepted my invitation to drop by."

He stroked her back, his fingers gliding across her figure, gathering up the fabric of her blouse until he'd pulled it free of her slacks. "I'm glad I happened to be working a case so nearby."

She stiffened with a moan as he slid his hands up along her spine and unhooked her bra. Her fingers buried themselves in his hair. "There's a sofa I'd like to show you, just through that door," she murmured.

He reached around to cup one of her breasts. "I'd like to see it."

In a slow shuffle, punctuated by dropped clothes, they worked their way out into the living room.

The ice cream was left to melt.

Ben Kendall's boxes of photographs looked out of place, piled in the corner of one of Beverly's immaculate guest rooms. They were old, discolored, dented, and scarred by a lifetime of being shoved about from one spot to another, and then—finally—abandoned in the heart of a hoard.

"Was he taking pictures up to the end?" Joe asked as they stood side by side, wearing long, belted bathrobes—after visiting the downstairs sofa and then using one of the largest shower stalls Joe had ever seen.

"No," she said. "From what Rachel and I could determine, he gave it up about ten years ago—maybe longer. When she first found the still lifes, she told me that Ben seemed genuinely surprised, as if he'd completely forgotten they existed."

"That seem likely?"

She pursed her lips before responding, "It's possible. Hoarders covet their belongings while forgetting what they've got. It can sometimes be difficult to tell if they're absentminded or coy." She hesitated and then added, "Of course, we're talking about the later work. Not the Vietnam material. That would have been a more emotionally charged topic, but Rachel didn't discover that until after she'd brought all this here." She waved her hand across the pile of boxes.

Joe got to his knees and pulled one off the top, opening it carefully. Beverly joined him, holding back the flaps as he reached in and extracted a thick wad of eleven-by-fourteen-inch black-and-white prints.

"See what I mean?" she asked as he began leafing through the collection—all of it documenting a mesmerizing world of angles and objects, light and shadow, at once detailed and open, seductive and disturbingly harsh. He thought back to her comments about the unlikeliness of scrap metal being able to compete with artistically posed nudes as subject matter. Now he could understand what she'd been saying. In his eyes, Ben Kendall had become the undiscovered genius that fiction so often heralds, but which so rarely exists in fact.

Beverly crawled to one side of the pile to drag over another box. "Here is some of the war stuff."

Her description had prepared him for something unusual, but the close-up portraits, urban scenes, and vistas of Vietnam's eerily familiar countryside were arresting in their peacefulness. Cumulatively, they were testament to how a culture at war can at least in part maintain the appearance of normalcy.

But there were others—a few images of soldiers on patrol, their eyes wide and fearful, of a land mauled by past explosions and fire—which struck a deep-seated chord of pathos and sorrow for a combat veteran like Joe. They weren't numerous, or graphic. There were no likenesses of a napalmed child running naked down a road, arms outstretched, or of a South Vietnamese officer shooting a man in the head. But such icons echoed as distant memories nevertheless, and because of them, Ben's pictures of a nation and a people struggling to maintain a peaceful routine became all the more powerful.

Sensing as much, Beverly laid her hand supportively on his shoulder as he studied the sampling before them.

"Such a waste," she said.

He didn't argue the point. He'd once followed the orders of superior officers to fight for God and country, never questioning—at first—how either God or the country's fate were remotely being threatened by the enemy opposing him.

He thought of the costs, both immediate and long range, blatant and subtly corrosive. "And not one that's run its course yet, more's the pity."

CHAPTER FOUR

Philadelphia homicide detective Philip DesAutels logged in with the uniformed officer at the apartment's front door and stepped inside. His partner, Elizabeth McLarney—the so-called "up-person" for this call, or nominal lead—was already there, having responded directly from the unit's headquarters.

"You get to have dinner?" she asked. She was wearing a Tyvek suit, a disposable hospital cap, and surgical booties over her shoes.

He frowned as he struggled to match her appearance, variously pulling, grunting, and hopping on one foot as he spoke. "Girl had just taken my hoagie order, and—*bam*—the pager went off. It's like clockwork, every damn time."

Elizabeth reached out with her latex-gloved hand and patted his proud belly. "I think you'll live, Phil. Draw on your reserves."

DesAutels extracted gloves from his pocket and yanked them on as final preparation. "Very cute. What've we got?"

They were in a section of town just west of University City called Cedar Park—an early-1900s mixed neighborhood of two- and three-story row houses, apartments, small stores, a few restaurants, and a couple of churches. It was slowly undergoing a financial uplifting, stimulated in part by the muscle flexing of the nearby University of Pennsylvania, but its roots as a post–Civil War "trolley car" suburb of Center City were clear to see, as were the rail tracks still in use along Baltimore Avenue, the neighborhood's main drag.

Not the high-rent district, but not the kind of area where McLarney and DesAutels spent most of their professional time, either.

Elizabeth had him follow her past a small living room with bow windows overlooking the front porch, and down a narrow hallway. They were on the first floor of a three-story Queen Anne row house, once a family home, but since then chopped up into three separate apartments, cramped and made awkward by the need to accommodate a landing, a bathroom, and a kitchen on each floor.

"Came in as a 'welfare check,'" she said over her shoulder. "This woman's best friend supposedly called her every couple of days, as a routine. She got a run of no answers, got worried, and called 911."

"You talk to the friend?" Phil asked.

"Chelsea Kline. Not yet. She talked to someone from Detectives East, just enough to give 'em a name and number. I got a couple of guys driving her to the unit for an interview—also chasing down names of people the dead woman worked for. No alarm bells yet, and the BFF sounds like the real deal. See what you think."

With that, she entered a kitchen at the back of the house.

Phil stopped short. "Whoa," he said softly.

An older woman with short gray hair was lying spread-eagled on the floor, her wrists and ankles bound and attached by duct tape to four opposing, convenient anchor points. She was in the middle of a coagulated pool of blood, flanked by crime scene techs and a medical examiner, all busily at work like the curiously detached professionals they'd become through overexposure.

DesAutels joined his partner against a wall. "At least it doesn't look like she was raped," he said, relieved.

McLarney took in the woman's face—her eyes wide open, her expression agonized. It's true that her pants were still in place and fastened, but her sweatshirt had been sliced down the front, and her breasts exposed. Her many wounds made it clear that she had been tortured before dying, although not for any sexual gratification, if Elizabeth's years of experience were any guide.

"We know who this is?" Phil asked her.

She consulted her notepad. "Jennifer Sisto, age sixty-two. Worked as a bookkeeper for a couple of local docs, but from home. She was a bit of a hermit, according to Ms. Kline. There's a whole office set up in the other room—computer, fax, printer, shredder, the works. She handled billing and collections, as well as the day-to-day stuff."

"What kinds of docs?"

Elizabeth gave him a look. "I wondered the same thing. Ralph and Tommy chased that down from HQ. Right now, the doctors're looking as clean as the friend—couple of family medicine types. Marcus Welby and Dr. Kildare look-alikes."

"Who?"

She shook her head pityingly. "Phil. You gotta widen your horizons. TV characters from the old days. As famous as Lassie."

He smiled. "Who?"

Elizabeth crooked her finger at him. "Follow me to the office. It gets more interesting."

She led him down the corridor to the next room. It was filled with the equipment that she'd described, with a desk under a pair of windows overlooking the alleyway. Its most telling detail, however, was that it had been ransacked. Every shelf, drawer, and filing cabinet had been systematically emptied, and the contents heaped in the middle of the floor.

Phil was nodding as he looked around. "Okay," he said, speaking to himself, but so that Elizabeth could overhear. "First impressions? This was a more-than-one attacker."

"They found two sets of footprints in her blood," Elizabeth confirmed.

"Meaning they're either stupid and sloppy," he continued, "or don't care, because those shoes are already ashes. My little voice says the second. Another thing? She didn't give 'em what they wanted, which is why you have the double whammy of a torture and a tossing."

Elizabeth added her own opinion: "And what they wanted is small, and doesn't involve jewelry or drugs."

He cast her an inquiring look.

"I checked out the bedroom," she explained. "Rings, earrings, necklaces—untouched. It's been turned inside out, like here, but the bathroom? Just a once-over lightly, and all her scripts are still there."

"So maybe a document?" he mused.

Elizabeth expanded his earlier theory. "Here's an idea: If the torture didn't get them what they wanted, there's no saying that the tossing did, either. It could be their holy grail is still out there."

Phil didn't disagree. "What about a private life?" he asked. "Most people kill people they know."

Elizabeth returned to her pad. "Again, per Kline, Sisto lived alone, had no social life, liked to go to a movie now and then—either solo or with Chelsea—or maybe a museum or art show. But basically, she hung out here, worked, watched Netflix, and kept to herself."

"No kids?"

"Nope, and was divorced something like forty years ago, which to me rules out a pissed-off ex."

"Who was the ex?" Phil asked.

"Chelsea didn't have a name," Elizabeth said. "But she did say he lived up in Vermont and was a total but nonviolent whack job. Sisto and he hadn't spoken in decades, supposedly. Before it got bagged, I did have one of the scene techs check through an ancient-looking address book we found on the desk. There wasn't much to it, and the only Vermont name belongs to a Benjamin Kendall, who lives in some place called Dummerston, which sounds like the punch line to a joke."

DesAutels suddenly looked happier. "What's Vermont like right now? Not snowing yet, is it?"

Elizabeth laughed outright. "You think the boss is gonna let us do more than make a couple of phone calls up there? You *do* need to eat, Phil. You are losing your mind."

She surveyed the disrupted office and added, "Plus, I don't think we need to go to Vermont. My bet is that the City of Brotherly Love is the home base of these bastards."

Rachel Reiling and Joe met in Burlington the next day, as arranged by her mother, at the university's Fleming Museum just off Colchester Avenue. Beverly had to be at her office, and Joe had never met Rachel, but photographs of her on her mother's wall pretty much removed the guesswork.

Even so, any doubts vanished when the young woman greeted him as he entered the museum's glassed-in, modern entrance, clumsily tacked on to the rear of the 1920s Colonial Revival building.

"Mr. Gunther?"

He smiled and shook her hand. "I stick out that much?"

She was embarrassed. "Well . . . kind of, and Mom described you pretty well."

He patted her shoulder. "I was just ragging you. That was very PC. Thank you. Shall we?" He gestured toward the admission desk, where he paid for his ticket and she displayed her ID. She quickly led him through a tall, dark exhibition room, back into the building's startlingly bright, soaring Marble Court, complete with tiled floor, grand stair-case, and upper-floor balcony supported by a row of white columns.

Joe was caught by surprise. The court dominated the building's core, like an incongruously transplanted nineteenth-century ballroom from a Newport, Rhode Island, mansion.

The gallery housing Rachel's exhibition of Ben's work was located off the ground floor. In contrast to the Marble Court, it was bland, dramatically lighted, and conventionally laid out, feeling small enough to have been part of a tasteful downtown store. The two visitors didn't speak much as they traveled counterclockwise through the display, content for the moment to merely absorb what was before them.

In front of one of the few Vietnam photos, however, Joe softly asked his companion, "I realize Ben refused to talk about any of this—" he pointed to an American soldier yelling at a nearby peasant, "—but did you ever look into what he was doing over there? As part of your research?"

"I tried," she said. "My advisor helped, not that it mattered in the long run. It turned out his job was to go where he was told to by the Signal Corps. He didn't really belong to a particular outfit." She indicated another photo featuring Americans. "These two could have been different assignments, in different regions. There's no way to tell unless you can make out the insignia on the uniforms, and as you can see—" she pointed "—that's sometimes hard to do."

Joe saw what she meant. The yelling soldier's unit markings were blurred enough to make them unreadable. The same wasn't true in the neighboring shot, but Joe conceded that, some forty-plus years later, it probably didn't make much difference. All this was ancient history.

Which was a fact he found galling, because these were moments that Ben had preserved of a war that had fed on his soul forever after. It seemed to Joe that their history shouldn't be so dulled by time.

Of course, therein lay much of the compelling contradiction of Ben's artistic vision.

The Vietnam War had been a grinding, corrosive, nation-changing slog, forcing the United States to see itself—and to be seen worldwide—in a different light forever. However, that very spotlight on a stumbling superpower had all but eclipsed the conflict's host country.

By contrast, the Vietnam in these pictures had been captured in scenes that were missing from most images of the era, of people who, through all the mayhem, were simply struggling to exist. In his avoidance of conventional "war photos," Ben had, by haunting implication, documented either what was awaiting decimation, or what had barely survived so many decades of violence.

Ben had almost coyly documented a testimony to all the havoc—by placing most of it just outside each picture frame.

As a result, the interspersing of his more recent work—the cursive and flowing portraits of his cherished hoard—reflected a carefully thought-out balancing act by the curator. The modern pieces displayed a hard beauty that was present in the older Vietnam shots, if less obvious. Making the comparison, Joe could clearly identify Ben's evolution, as the people he'd photographed faded away in favor of their discarded belongings. In that fashion, his art reflected an aspect of his hoarding, in that the humans with whom he'd once readily interacted had been replaced by their stuff.

At the end of the tour, Joe escorted Rachel out to a bench in the sun-soaked Marble Court. "I really appreciate your meeting me here, and I'm sorry it's under these circumstances. Given all the years your mother and I have known each other, it's a shame it had to be this way."

The young woman smiled sadly. "I guess it's par for the course. Dead people are sort of the family business. What did you want to know?"

"Your mom filled me in on the basics," Joe began. "How you discovered these photographs as part of your video project. What I need to know is anything you can tell me about Ben as a human being."

Rachel thought a moment before responding. "I heard he died from an accident—like a cave-in or something. Are you and mom thinking something else?"

"Not specifically," Joe answered truthfully. "A couple of details aren't lining up the way we'd like, but that's standard for almost every death investigation. I remember once—years ago—looking into a supposed suicide where the man was on the bed and the rifle he used was neatly leaning against the far wall. Pretty unlikely, at first. It turned out fine—the first responder there had just moved the gun without thinking, and forgot to tell anyone. But the question needed to be answered. That's all we're doing here with Ben—and also because your mom asked me to."

She nodded. "Okay. Well, I don't know. He was a sweet man. I really liked him. I mean, he had problems—that's why the documentary, of course—but behind the weirdness, he was super nice."

"Was he ever violent in any way? Even verbally? Not at you, necessarily," Joe added quickly. "But at anyone or anything?"

She shook her head. "I wouldn't call it violent, or even angry. He could get intense. That's when he'd shut down or retreat. I had to watch out for those times, 'cause I didn't want to burn any bridges. Once, I drove all the way down there to shoot some footage, and he was in a mood. I just wished him well, turned around, and left."

"What would set him off?" Joe asked.

"It depended, and I wouldn't always know. At first, he was just protective of his stuff and shy about my seeing it. Later, it would be other things. I'd move something to get a better shot—that would get him worked up. I'd say something complimentary about one item or another, and he'd think I wanted to steal it. On the flip side, he'd give me things now and then, but I had to be careful about actually taking them, because while they were a gift, he hated to let them go. I'd get caught between looking ungrateful and getting him worked up."

"What kinds of things?"

"Small. Crazy, too, sometimes. He gave me a broken plate once. I thought it might be a museum piece, the way he handled it, but later, when I looked at it back home, it was like from a deli or something."

"What else might get him going?"

"He could be pretty paranoid. Planes flying overhead put him on edge—especially small ones, flying low. And I wasn't allowed to roam around unless he'd set out where I could and couldn't go. And I never stayed for too long. Maybe three hours, tops. He was kind of a neatnik, in an off-the-wall way. I mean, he was a slob—the place was a mess and it smelled gross, especially in some spots. But he treated it like a sculpture garden, almost. He knew exactly how one stacked-up pile related to everything around it—like the inner working of a living body. That's why I think he used to photograph it all the time, and why he hated me to move things, even after he gave up taking pictures.

"The most fun," she then said, changing the subject, "was when he had me join him on rounds. That's what he called them, like a doctor. He'd drive around the area, visiting people who seemed to know him well—old car graveyards, backwoods mechanics, a building salvage place he especially liked . . . you name it. He'd even stop at yard sales and pick up stuff that was slated to end up by the curb. It was just the reverse of when he was at home—he was outgoing, funny. People loved him."

"You must've asked him how all this started," Joe suggested. "As part of the documentary, maybe? Or just cousin-to-cousin?"

"I did, but he only said, 'It was the war.' You could tell it was a place he didn't want to visit. I thought I'd get more out of him after I found the Vietnam pictures." She indicated the exhibition again.

"But I had enough on my hands just getting him to let go of them. Did Mom tell you that I pulled this show off only because I already had them at her house? And that I'd promised not to use his name anywhere?"

"She did," Joe conceded. "Was the anonymity because of his personality, or something else?"

Again, she reflected before answering, "It might have been something else. I didn't think it was, at first—that it was just shyness. But when we started negotiating putting on the show, I realized his privacy concerns were second to his wanting the pictures to be universal, and not about who took them—kind of the way the Vietnam shots are about the country and not the war. That's one of the reasons I tried so hard to make this happen. The images are beautiful and haunting because of what they don't say."

She looked down at her hands. "I guess now that he's dead, that's even more true."

Joe gave her a few seconds before he reached out and laid a hand on her forearm. "Rachel?" he asked. "Would you do me a big favor?"

"Sure," she said immediately, looking into his eyes.

He smiled supportively. "Thank you. I'd like to see your video footage of Ben and his environment, but I'm hoping you'll also be willing to come down to Dummerston and give me a private guided tour. I think it would help me to see the place through your eyes."

She stood up, checking her watch unobtrusively. "I better get to class, Mr. Gunther, but I'd be happy to help. It's the least I can do after everything Ben did for me."

Joe stood also and thanked her again, shaking her hand in departure. After she'd left, however, he resumed his seat and watched the crowd slowly shuffling in and out of the gallery entrance.

His most nagging question had little to do with what he'd spoken about with Rachel. Rather, he was wondering why, while purportedly

conducting a simple favor for a friend, he was feeling the same adrenaline buildup that attended a regular case.

His unit, the VBI, represented the elite of Vermont law enforcement,
and its ranks were filled with the best, most motivated transplants from
almost every agency or department across the state. Scratching around
the edges of an apparently accidental death had nothing to do with his
mission.

Except that something about it was beginning to bother him.

CHAPTER FIVE

"Updating your porno?"

Joe looked up from the computer screen, where he'd been watching Rachel Reiling's unedited documentary footage on Ben Kendall. "Yeah. Found a flash drive in your drawer. Hope that's okay."

Willy Kunkle, one of the three other special agents on the squad, laughed outright as he hung his jacket on the coat tree near the door. "Right. You wouldn't stand a chance, getting into my desk. I've got it rigged to explode if anyone tries."

Joe believed him. Willy was a fellow combat vet—an ex-sniper, in fact—who embodied paranoia. Also, he was a recovering alcoholic, a transplanted New York City cop—although decades ago—and, most noticeably, the acerbic and blunt-spoken owner of a crippled left arm, which he kept anchored in place by shoving his hand into his pants pocket. It was an unlikely detail for a cop, but through the Americans with Disabilities Act, his own persistence, and—albeit never acknowledged—Joe's help, he'd fought his way back from being disabled during a case years earlier.

"You hear about the Dummerston hoarder they found dead at home?" Joe asked him, knowing how Willy tracked the police dailies.

"Yeah. Thought that was accidental."

"It is for now. I'm just making sure."

To Joe's surprise, Willy walked over and glanced at the screen, where Rachel's images were still unfolding. Kunkle was rarely guilty of such a companionable gesture.

What he said was even more unusual. "Interesting. Made me think about an old case in New York when I heard about it, dating back to the late '40s. Two recluse brothers named Collyer. Lived in a four-story brownstone. People smelled something bad, cops broke in, and found one of them dead in his own booby trap and the other dead of starvation. Supposedly the second one had been paralyzed for years and dependent on the first for food. Pathetic whacko's, of course, but famous for all that. For years after, the New York Fire Department used to call a hoarder's house a 'Collyer.' They're basically death traps. I'm not surprised your nutcase got himself killed."

Joe looked up in amazement. He was struggling to recall when he'd last heard Willy go on about any historical tidbit. Lester Spinney, another member of their four-person squad, indulged without the slightest provocation, but Willy?

"That was called in by a thief, right?" Willy asked.

"Yeah," Joe replied. "Jason Newville. You know him?"

"I know who he knows. I've seen him, is all. Too low on the totem pole. He steal anything before he found the body?"

Increasingly intrigued by Willy's interest, Joe told him, "No, but he made two prior visits before he fell over the body. I guess he was scoping the place out and building up courage."

Willy laughed. "That fits. You met him?"

"Newville?" Joe asked. "No. Why?"

"Total wimp, from what I know. Still, I can see the appeal of a hoarder house. The Collyer place had something like fourteen pianos, a car in the basement, maybe twenty-five thousand books—about a hundred and forty tons of crap, total."

"Why would any of that appeal to Newville?" Joe wanted to know.

"Because of the value of it all. The Collyers' estate was priced at over a million bucks, in 1947 dollars," Willy stated. "That's what sticks to these loonies: Every hoarder's somehow sitting on a pile of gold coins. Burglars circle these dumps like flies on shit. You been to a hoarder house, haven't you?"

"Sure," Joe conceded, recalling several without hesitation.

"You ever see anything other than a thousand stuffed teddy bears, or a million moldy newspapers, or the world's biggest stack of garbage bags full of clothes? Or all three?"

"No."

Willy returned to his desk across the small room, still speaking. "Well, there you have it. That's the truth of it. But I guarantee you that every chicken-headed, douche bag thief I know will swear on a stack of Bibles that all hoarders are just millionaires dressed by Goodwill. Dumber than hell."

He sat down and without another word began poking through some paperwork, his interest in Joe's research extinguished as quickly as it had caught fire.

Joe resumed watching the screen as Rachel followed the late Ben Kendall around his cluttered realm. Embarrassed to be counted among Willy's misinformed losers, he couldn't deny sharing the notion that there was something rational lurking beneath Ben's mania. After all, wasn't it smart to hide something in the midst of plenty?

Of course, in Joe's case, it wasn't necessarily jewels or money that he was envisioning. It was answers.

. . .

Rachel hesitated getting out of the car at the end of Ben's rutted driveway.

"You sure you're okay with this?" Joe asked her.

She nodded once sharply. "Positive." She pulled open the door handle. "It's just a little weird, coming back."

They entered the clearing side by side, Joe watchful, as cops tend to be; Rachel more introverted, her eyes straight ahead.

"I looked at the video you sent me," he told her as they approached the main house. "You could tell how Ben warmed to you, in short order."

"I think he was lonely," she responded. "He got along with everybody, but it was mostly on the surface. I noticed that when we went out collecting, he was great as long as he kept moving. If anyone talked too long, or tried to get closer than a couple of one-liners, I could see him tense up. He had these escape phrases, like, 'Well, don't wanna lose the day,' or 'Gotta go. Promised Wayne I'd get there by three,' even though there was no Wayne. I felt like the one exception."

"You mentioned how things improved between you," Joe said. "And also how you had to keep your eye on his mood swings. Was there any consistency there toward the end, as in a prolonged bad temper or a growing anxiety? I'm wondering if something was eating at him that he didn't tell you about."

She considered it, but her reply came as no surprise. "Nothing stands out," she said. "He seemed fine, last time I saw him. Really, the end of that footage says it all. He was more upbeat than usual. Off camera, he was even showing a little interest in the exhibition—even in maybe wanting to come see it. But he wouldn't really talk about it—not in so many words."

They had stepped around a couple of the larger piles in the front yard and were now standing near the main entrance, where they paused.

Joe indicated the mechanical "haystacks" around them. "The way he photographed these, and the stuff inside—obsessively, really—made me think of the Impressionists."

She laughed. "Monet? I guess you're right, only in black-and-white."

Joe nodded before asking, "Did you ever get a feeling that there may've been more to them than just scrap metal and junk? I mean, I understand he was a hoarder and that *everything* meant something to him, but was there maybe something of worth, in real terms?"

She shook her head. "*Truly* valuable? Not that I ever saw."

He still wondered if the modern photographs' so outnumbering the older ones wasn't in some way significant.

"Your mom tell you what's happening next?" Joe asked her after a moment.

Rachel was surprised, suddenly looking, to Joe's eyes, like a younger version of her mother. "No. What?"

"Well, since she's actually the legal owner here, and since we can't prove any crime took place, she and I were thinking she might pay to have most of this cleaned out."

Rachel was sympathetic, sentimentality aside. "I guess I can understand that. I didn't realize Mom inherited it."

"She bought it in the first place. She was the quote-unquote bank he paid every month. It was her way of helping him save face."

Rachel smiled. "That sounds like her."

"Anyhow, a clean-out crew will be coming soon, complete with heavy equipment. They may even open up one of the walls, for better access."

She looked mournfully at the tired house. "He would have hated that."

"I know," he suggested. "I have an idea: Would you be interested in filming the disassembly? It might supply some sort of conclusion for your project, and it would be handy for us as a document."

The idea seemed to lighten her mood, even though he'd been admiring her stoicism so far. "That would be cool. I was kind of lost about what to do now."

"Great," he said. "I'll mention it to your mom, to let her know we're all on the same page." He shoved the door open with his shoulder. "I gotta warn you, Rachel: You might not want to do this. It smells bad and it could bring back memories."

She joined him at the door, her nose wrinkling. "No, no. I'm okay. If it'll help you out, I'm game." She paused before admitting, "It is pretty gross, though, isn't it?"

His need to know overriding a protective instinct, Joe preceded her and turned on the flashlight that he'd brought from the car. He asked her over his shoulder, "Was it always so nasty smelling?"

She began looking around, her curiosity drawing her in and helping her down the tunnel of stacked paper. "Not this much. He didn't eat indoors hardly at all, and then mostly in one spot, way to the back. He called it his kitchen, but I doubt it was. You couldn't really tell what most of the rooms were anymore. He'd created his own miniature neighborhoods—where he slept, where he ate. He reminded me of an animal that way. I mean, in the best sense," she added quickly. "Anyhow, to answer your question, it was musty, but that was it. This is way worse."

She reached where the tunnel opened onto the waist-high, undulating field that Joe had encountered a few days ago. He kept playing the light around.

Her voice hesitant, she turned and asked, "Could I have the light? There's something weird. . . ." She left the sentence hanging.

He passed it over and watched as she not only shone it on various aspects of their view, but suddenly scampered up onto the pile in order to check out a few details.

"What're you finding?" he asked.

She looked back at him, resting on her knees, her expression baffled. "It's changed. It's not the way he had it."

Joe gazed across what looked like a sea of rubbish. "You can tell that?"

"I was here so often, studying it through a lensfinder. It sort of got in my head. Remember when I told you that Ben may not have been neat, but did have a sense of how things were in relation to each other?"

"Yeah."

"That's why he hated people messing with his stuff."

"Okay," Joe coaxed her.

"That's what I'm saying," she stressed. "It *has* been messed with. Almost everywhere, things have been moved."

"They did have to get him out," Joe said delicately.

But she wasn't deterred. "No. I thought I noticed it outside, too. It's like when somebody goes through a drawer of your private things, you know? Nothing's missing, but everything's been shifted a little."

Spurred on by her discovery, they proceeded to other parts of the house, including areas Joe had never visited. Rachel had the surefootedness of a seasoned cave guide, and shared her knowledge throughout. In the process, she helped Joe shape a better picture of the man who had once called this home.

Also, far to the back of the house, she found support for her earlier statement.

"There," she said, shining her light at a blank patch of wall. "He had some pictures there. They're gone."

"What did they show?" Joe asked, wiping his damp forehead.

"A woman. She was young and pretty. They were old black-and-whites. I asked him about her, 'cause there were no other decorations like them anywhere else, but he wouldn't say more than, 'A friend.'"

Joe looked around the room. "What did he use this spot for?"

"I always called it his bedroom," she said, adding, "Not that you can tell."

By the end, dirty and sweaty despite the cool weather, they found themselves back outside, wiping their hands on their pants and stretching out their kinks.

"That's what it was like every day," she said, almost happily. "It brought out the kid in you." Her expression grew somber again as she restated her earlier premise. "Except for that weird shifting thing. I think I know how I can prove it to you."

"Oh?" Joe asked.

"Compare how it looks now to what you can see in the video. Room by room, you'll see what I mean."

Joe considered the exploration they'd just completed, along with the hours he'd already spent on her video. "I'll take your word for it, Rachel. Still, what you're saying would've taken somebody a lot of time."

"I know."

He nodded. "Okay, then. All the more reason I'd like you along with your camera when we take the place apart."

Neil Watson was pissed. "It takes him a week to call a meeting, and now he wants it at two in the morning. What the hell's that about?"

His partner turned off the car's ignition. "Give it a rest. He was out of town. Why do you care, anyhow? You been dying to break the latest news to him?"

Neil stayed quiet. The other man, Frank Niles, opened his door and stepped out onto the street, instinctively looking around for any suspicious signs of life. This was Manhattan, of course, so that standard had to be flexible, but the time of night helped—there was little activity of any sort visible. And it was cold. Even the hotel's doormen were out of sight, probably smoking in the break room.

Frank leaned back into the car and looked across the front seat. "You coming?"

"I have a choice?"

Frank slammed the door, muttering to himself, "We should be married, for Christ's sake."

He waited for his sidekick to join him before they headed into the hotel lobby.

They didn't stop at the desk or pause on their way to the distant bank of elevators. They knew where they were going, even though they had never been here before. That was the whole point: to meet rarely and to do so in a new place—even a new state—every time.

They rode to the top floor. Frank gave that much to this particular client: He knew how to live.

The penthouse suites were in fact large apartments, so the room they were let into by a noncommunicative butler was a full-fledged lobby. Looking around, Neil let out a low whistle, which just further irritated Frank.

The butler gestured to them to follow him, which they did through a living room, past a bar and a small kitchen, and into a dark office lighted solely by a lamp on the corner of an expansive hardwood desk. Through the windows, they could see a panorama of the city's lights—the Milky Way brought down to earth and spread out for display.

At the desk sat an older man in a suit, watching them. "Jonathan," he demanded of the butler, who lingered in the doorway. "What the hell are you standing around for?"

"Will you be wanting coffee or anything else, sir?" was the bland reply, delivered with the slightest of bows.

The man shook his head with disgust. "I know to ask for something when I want it, for Christ's sake." He flicked his hand impatiently. "We're fine. Leave."

"Very good, sir." The butler disappeared, closing the door behind him.

His employer pointed to two chairs across from the desk. "Sit."

Frank nodded. "Senator," he greeted the man, and took one of the chairs. Neil remained silent as he joined them.

"Tell me about the woman," the senator ordered.

"She was a dead end," Frank reported.

"Is that supposed to be funny?"

Frank shook his head. "No. Sorry. I didn't mean it that way. She gave us nothing, and we tried everything we got."

The older man held up a hand. "Spare me. Overlooking that you came highly recommended and are costing me a fortune you aren't earning, what are you suggesting as your next step?"

Hoping that Neil would keep quiet, Frank said lightly, "We have a plan, but I thought you didn't want details, unless that's changed."

"They only change if you feed me a line of bullshit."

Frank sharpened his own tone a bit. "You asked us to find the lost ark. If it was easy, it wouldn't be lost. We're working our way up the line and we're making progress. It's not like this little project hasn't cost us, too."

"You are doing your best to reduce the population, from what I understand."

"Senator—"

But the latter cut him off. "Yes, yes. I get it. Fine. All I want to hear is that you're getting somewhere. I'm sure you'll find a way to bill me for all your inconveniences. Listen to me, Niles. This is very time sensitive. Will you get the job done?"

"Yes," Frank told him.

Neil remained silent.

The senator watched them without comment for a couple of ponderous seconds, and then dismissed them by looking away. "That's all, then."

The two men filed out, led by the impassive butler.

CHAPTER SIX

Joe turned off the table saw and sighted along the edge of the board he'd just cut. He'd added a woodworking shop to his small rented house, which itself was attached to the rear of an old Victorian residence on Green Street in Brattleboro. This was in large part to accommodate his late father's tool collection, but also to give himself something to do outside work. He'd been married only once, briefly as a young man, and never had children. Now, a widower for decades, he had Beverly as a romantic partner, his squad as a surrogate family, his love of reading, and this shop to balance out the rest.

All in all, especially given some of the lumps he'd encountered reaching this stage, life could have been far worse. The only problem recently was that he'd run out of recipients for birdhouses and jewelry boxes, which had forced him to move on to picnic tables and lawn benches.

"That one ours?" a woman asked from the door between the house and the shop. Most people knew to simply enter his place and seek him out. Joe lacked the distrust of most cops, and usually left his door unlocked.

Joe glanced over to see Sammie Martens leaning against the door-jamb. The squad's sole woman, and, like Willy, a cop who dated back to before the VBI's existence—to when the three of them had worked as detectives for the Brattleboro PD—Sammie occupied a special place in Joe's heart. Small, spare, and intense, she'd survived a dysfunctional childhood, fled to the military, joined law enforcement, and become a bull terrier on the job. She'd made of her boss a mentor, to the point where he'd once sensed that, if the cards were down, she would've taken any bullet heading his way.

But that field was now more crowded. She had fallen in love with Willy Kunkle—of all unlikely people—and had a daughter with him named Emma. To everyone's surprise, most of all Sam's, she and Willy had moved in together and begun to approach normalcy, albeit one fit-ting their own quirky needs. For Joe, that development had demanded tricky navigating. He'd come to see her as a surrogate daughter, almost. Much as he championed Willy to most detractors, Joe was still strug-gling with seeing him as a virtual son-in-law.

Joe held up the board. "Yup—one picnic table, in the making."

"You know there's no rush," she said. "I heard there might be snow coming next week."

"I'll believe it when I see it," he said. "But you won't be getting this too soon anyhow. In the spring, guaranteed." He propped the board against the table saw. "What brings you to the neighborhood? You want some coffee?"

She shook her head. "I'm on my way to pick up Emma at day care, but I'm early. I wanted to drop by and ask about the hoarder case. Willy said you had something cooking."

"Not really. It's a favor for Hillstrom. The guy was her cousin, and there're a couple of odd details about it. I said I'd look into it."

"Sounded like more than that."

Joe laughed. "Got Willy's nose twitching, did I? That's cool. Drive him crazy."

"Thanks a bunch," she said. "I have to live with it. He thinks you're pulling a fast one—working under the radar."

"He would. No," Joe reassured her. "In fact, crack of dawn tomorrow, a crew is coming to clean out the property. Backhoes, Cats, Dumpsters, the works. Might take a couple of weeks or more."

"Wow," she said. "What're you hoping to find?"

"Nothing," he replied. "Although you always wonder. I'll just be there for a while, keeping Hillstrom's daughter company. She's videotaping the whole thing for a thesis or something. Turns out Hillstrom's the home-owner, so she just wants it back to sell."

Ever the investigator, Sam referred to his earlier comment: "A couple of odd details?"

Joe came clean. "There's something about how he was found that doesn't quite fit—the position he was in, some of the marks on his body. It's not enough to punch a case number, and the autopsy gave us nothing except accidental death, but I don't see the harm in poking at it a bit."

She nodded and half turned to go. "Okay. I was just curious. You want company tomorrow? I got a light load on my desk."

He admired how she wasn't letting this go. "Absolutely. I'll be leaving the office just after eight."

Sam and Joe arrived at Ben's the following morning in the midst of a truck convoy, making Rachel's diminutive, two-door Mini Cooper look like an imperiled eggshell.

Resembling an amphibious invasion, the flatbed trucks fanned out around the house, ready to unload the heavy equipment Joe had de-scribed earlier.

Joe, Sam, and Rachel met to one side to exchange introductions and avoid being run over by the men in hard hats who were scattering to their respective posts.

"You got all you need to start shooting?" Joe then asked the young woman.

Rachel pulled a surprisingly small camera from her bag.

"That's it?" he asked.

"They make 'em smaller than that, boss," Sammie said softly. Having taken an immediate shine to Rachel, she added, "I'd love to get my hands on one of those, especially the way Emma's coming along."

Joe shook his head. "Okay. Rachel, your mom told me the cleanout crew knows you'll be lurking around."

"I already signed the death and injury waiver they faxed me last night," Rachel said cheerily. "All I need is a hard hat." She turned to Sam and told her, "I bet I can get you a camera cheap. I got this through the school."

For his part, Joe thought that a hard hat might be the one missing touch. Rachel was already dressed in a pair of oversized work boots and an insulated Carhartt jumpsuit with a T-shirt over the top of it, boasting, I SHOOT PEOPLE, and featuring the picture of a camera. That aspect of her made him think of an exuberant kid who'd wandered by accident onto a construction site.

With the ignition of several diesel engines, all conversation became challenging, so the three of them migrated to the foreman to receive hard hats and instructions on where not to stand. Rachel stepped away to film as the first of the crew began exposing the building's interior by pulling down a wall while simultaneously driving props under the roofline to maintain the structure's integrity.

In short order, they were confronting a second barricade comprised of Ben's belongings, as shaggy and disheveled as the wall containing it had been bland and smooth.

"Jeez!" Sam shouted into Joe's ear. "It's creepy—like the inside of a body."

"It is, in a way," he replied.

They moved back as two Bobcats approached to wolf down large mouthfuls before twisting around to deposit them into a waiting truck. Rachel continued darting around, following the action.

Slowly, attended by men with bags and shovels, the Bobcats crept into the wound they'd created. Joe and Sam approached the ragged edge of the hole to watch the room before them gradually regain definition.

This wasn't the same section that Joe had entered earlier, with the entrance tunnel leading to the large expanse of waist-high debris, but another one, more clotted and filled. The stacks reached virtually to the ceiling, and the Bobcats—in order to create more manageable divots—occasionally crashed into the piles to make them collapse like crumbling cliffs of shale, revealing more strata of paper beyond.

Joe was drawing just this comparison, when, with the abruptness of a magic show's apparition, a newly exposed cross section revealed the curled-up body of a man encased about three feet up from the floor. He resembled an oversized beetle, snugly fitted into an elaborate casting.

Joe and Sam simultaneously sprang forward amid the moving machines and men. "*Whoa!*" Joe shouted. "*Stop your engines!*"

But the operators didn't need telling, nor did Rachel Reiling, who stood stock-still in shock, her camera running.

In the sudden, complete quiet, the two cops clambered across the broken field to where the body lay exposed in the slanting daylight.

"That explains the smell," Sam said, noting the level of decomposition.

Joe was crouching down, trying to figure out the mechanics of the body's peculiar positioning, which was suggestive of a burial.

"Yeah," he replied. "It also makes this a whole new ball game." He glanced up at his colleague and added, "Looks like we're officially on duty."

"Hold it," Rachel said. "There. Back it up a couple of frames."

Lester Spinney gave his computer key a few jabs.

In silence, they watched Ben Kendall move in reverse, concentrating on the background just under his left arm.

"There," Rachel said again.

Lester froze the screen.

"See it?" she asked them.

Joe, Sam, and Willy pressed in to better see the image.

Joe tapped his finger on what appeared to be a small opening in the stack of boxes beside Ben. "Doesn't look like much."

"Maybe not, but he had at least a couple of them."

"How tall was he?" Willy asked, seemingly at random.

"Ben? Not very," Rachel said. Despite her youth and the squad room's austere setting, Joe couldn't not notice her maturity and poise in their midst.

"Five-eight," Sammie said, having recently consulted the autopsy report.

"Why?" Lester asked without turning around.

"Small guy—small hole," Willy replied. "Reminds me of the tunnel rats they had in Nam—crawling through the VC underground systems to see what they could find, like punji stakes, land mines, and grenades on the fly."

"Ben Kendall was a photographer," Joe reminded him.

"Everybody knew about the tunnels," Willy shot back. "He would've, too." He tapped Rachel on the shoulder. "Were his little rabbit holes booby-trapped?"

"I don't know," she answered. "He told me to never-ever go into one. I figured it was because they were dangerous."

"That's no lie," Willy muttered, stepping back, his point made.

"This new dead guy was small, too," Sammie said.

Joe looked at her. "We have anything on him yet?"

She answered, "The crime lab'll be running his prints as soon as they're delivered from the ME's office. Something's bound to crop up."

"Yeah," Willy threw in, "unless Hillstrom finds nothing, the prints don't hit, or whatever files there are have been eaten up by some stupid computer."

"No, no," Spinney said, reaching for his smartphone. "I told them to text me as soon as they got something. I bet it's in already."

Joe smiled to himself, seeing both men's outlooks in a nutshell— Spinney: upbeat, positive, supportive, a happy family man; and Willy: downcast, pessimistic, sarcastic, and the suspicious member of a family he seemed to orbit more than inhabit.

"Yeah," Spinney said, having scrolled to the proper screen. "Here it is, fresh off the presses: Tomasz Bajek. At least that's what his driver's license says. The ME's office extracted it from his wallet, which was covered with yuck and shoved into his underpants, for some reason. The lab ran the name through NCIC and got nothing, but the license says he lived in Philadelphia."

"That it?" Willy asked.

"For the moment, yeah, but I'm sure we'll get more. If nothing else, I bet the Philly PD has a file on him. Stands to reason, given what we think he was up to. There's a lot of data that hasn't made it to the national data banks, especially if it's local, older stuff."

Joe kept quiet for the moment, given the presence of their young outsider, but Ben Kendall and this Bajek having both originated from the same city seemed an unlikely coincidence.

He returned to the earlier topic. "Rachel, before we let you go, tell us more about these tunnels. You must've asked him what they were for."

As it had been throughout, her response was quick and enthusiastic. "I did, but I never got a straight answer. Also, it's not like there were a ton of them. I think I saw two or three. I always thought at least one might lead to his version of a den—just from things he used to say about 'burrowing in,' and 'being as snug as a mouse in his hole.' Remember what I said about how sometimes he reminded me of an animal that way? I actually thought it was kind of cool, and fantasized that at the end of one of them was a large cave with a TV and a pool table and all the rest. I know it wasn't true, but that's how I saw it in my mind's eye."

"God knows what it was really like," Willy said in a low voice, a man well known for his lack of possessions.

"Speaking of nooks and crannies," Joe said. "You mentioned some pictures that were missing from his version of a bedroom. Did you happen to shoot those with your camera, or were they off-limits?"

Rachel smiled shyly. "They were, kind of. But I shot them anyhow, when he wasn't looking." She gave Lester an idea of where to find the footage on his computer. A minute or two later, they were all looking at a trio of snapshots of a smiling young woman, thumbtacked to one of Ben's walls.

"Pretty," Sammie murmured.

"And he never identified her?" Joe asked again.

Rachel shook her head. "Nope. Like I said, just a friend. That was it."

They asked her a few more questions about Ben's living habits, getting little more in return, before thanking her for the video and her help, and escorting her to the door of their second-floor office.

"Was that tunnel booby-trapped?" Lester asked once the door had closed.

"I think so," Sam answered. "After they got the body out, Joe and I gave what was left of the tunnel a pretty good look. You could see how the stack spanning that part of the passageway had been built off balance, with a massive hunk of metal positioned right over it."

"The top of a welding table," Joe filled in. "Course, that kind of heavy equipment was all over the place. But Sam's right about it looking built to collapse. It seemed like the tunnel was narrower at that point, too, so the user would have to shove his way through to keep going, thereby triggering the cave-in."

"Why?" Willy asked succinctly. "Was there something worth protecting down the line?"

"I wondered the same thing," Joe admitted. "But we'll have to keep at it. There was no more excavation after that. We sealed the scene and sent the crew packing. From what we could tell, there wasn't anything to see beyond where Bajek's body was found."

"It was like the trap was the whole point," Sam added.

"Curiosity killing the cat," Willy said.

"Maybe so," Joe agreed. "If Ben was aware of the rumors that he was hiding secret loot, he might've built it solely for that purpose."

They'd each returned to their respective desks by this time, except Spinney, whose computer they'd been using to watch Rachel's footage.

It was he, therefore, still manning his keyboard, who said, "Wow. That's a double whammy." He looked up at Joe. "Boss, you may not love computers, but when they work, they're hard to beat. I was just checking e-mails and found a message from the Philadelphia PD—a Detective Elizabeth McLarney. She contacted the sheriff's department with an inquiry a couple of days ago, which they then put onto the intel Listserv. But she's not asking about a missing person named Bajek—she's asking if anybody up here has ever heard of Benjamin Kendall."

"You're kidding me," Willy reacted.

"Apparently it's in context with a case they got down there," Lester finished. "Here's the contact info." He recited McLarney's phone number, which Joe took down on a pad.

He looked up at his squad members. "Any reason not to jump on this now?"

No one bothered answering, as he was already dialing.

The voice over the speaker phone was brusque, urban, and fast-spoken. "Detective McLarney."

"Detective, this is Special Agent Joe Gunther of the Vermont Bureau of Investigation."

"You gonna talk to me about Benjamin Kendall?" she asked. "What the hell kind of name is Dummerston?"

Everyone in the room laughed.

"Detective," Joe told her, "I was about to tell you that you're on a speaker up here. I'm with members of my squad."

"Hey, guys," she said, unconcerned. "So, who's Kendall?"

"Why're you askin'?" Willy asked from across the room.

"You're no Vermonter," she shot back. "Even I know that."

"He's ex-NYPD," Joe explained. "A long time ago."

"Apparently not long enough," Sam threw in.

"Apparently not," McLarney agreed. "Look, you're calling me 'cause I got the ball rolling. You show me yours, I'll show you mine. Not the other way around."

Joe could see that Willy was about to argue the point, so he spoke quickly, "Ben Kendall was a local hoarder, originally from your fair city, but up here for decades. We found him dead in his house a few days ago, of undetermined causes, and he wasn't fresh. In the process of cleaning out the hoard, we found another body, also decayed."

"Jesus. Don't you people have noses up there?"

Willy could no longer keep silent. "No—we have houses, with things like trees and grass between them. Ya oughta try it."

"He lived in the boonies," Joe filled in. "But there's another wrinkle to it: We just found out that the second body also has ties to Philadel-phia. We got a name of Tomasz Bajek." He spelled it out for her. "That's all we have, though, and apparently the national data bank didn't cough up any criminal history, which strikes us as unlikely. So, any help you could give us from local sources down there would be appreciated. You willing to share now?"

"We found his ex-wife, Jennifer Sisto, tortured to death," she answered bluntly.

The air in the squad room instantly electrified. Joe felt his face redden. Beverly had told him that Ben had married before going to Viet-nam, and divorced upon being discharged from the hospital. He'd had it in his notes to chase that angle down, to see what the ex-wife might have to offer, but he hadn't done so. Now, not only had Bajek's origins com-pounded the oversight, but Rachel's missing photographs of the pretty young woman on Ben's wall also suggested a sickening, coldly logical connection to what they'd just been told.

"Why was she tortured?" he asked, covering his embarrassment.

"We have no clue," McLarney reported. "Right now, our theory is that the bad guys didn't get what they were after, 'cause they ransacked her place from one end to the other. We figure they came up empty. And no," she added without pause, "there was no record of a safe deposit box, or any alternate hiding spot. We're still checking her background, coworkers, neighbors, and so on, but right now, it's not looking good. Would you be willing to send me what you got on Kendall?"

"Sure," Joe readily agreed. "Would you do the same with Sisto and whatever you can find on Bajek?"

"You got it."

"When was Sisto worked over?" Willy asked, having reached the same conclusion as Joe.

McLarney gave them the approximate date, prompting Willy to say, "That sounds like it was after our guys got killed." He glanced at Joe, but without criticism, and added in a quiet voice, "And after those pictures disappeared from Kendall's house."

"We'll include whatever the medical examiner found out about Bajek," Joe said, keeping on task. "Given the hometown coincidence, it may be useful."

"Hey," McLarney said, "you never know."

"Okay," Joe concluded, his finger poised above the speaker button. "Any full face shots of Sisto would be greatly appreciated. Thanks for your help, Detective."

"No problem, Hon," she said. "Talk to you later."

The line went dead and Joe looked up at his colleagues. "What did she call me?"

Willy shook his head. "It's a Philly thing."

CHAPTER SEVEN

"I'm sorry. I know all this field and stream crap is supposed to make me feel good, but I think it's . . . I don't know . . . unnatural."

Frank Niles took his eyes off the road long enough to cast his partner a look. "You sure that's the word you're looking for?"

Neil Watson pointed vaguely at the passing Vermont countryside, admittedly not at its best—stark branches stripped of colorful leaves, grass killed by night frosts, all ready for a face-saving blanket of snow that had yet to arrive. "Cute. Come on. Look at it. It's a butt-ugly waste of space. Even worse than the last time we were up here, poking through that sick bastard's House of Shit. They should *do* something with this real estate."

"You'll like Burlington," Frank ventured. "It's got thousands of people. Traffic jams, pedestrians getting in the way, exhaust fumes. Maybe even manhole covers, just like New York."

"You're a funny guy, Frank," Neil grumbled. "I'm just sayin', ya know?"

"Yeah."

"How much longer till we get there?"

"Burlington?" Frank asked, checking the dashboard GPS. "Another forty-five minutes."

Neil unholstered his gun and checked to see if a round was chambered. A nervous twitch, of course. He never carried it empty or uncharged.

"I do like that they don't have gun laws here," he said. "I guess they're not total losers."

"They're hunters," Frank told him. "Or at least that's their culture." He added cautiously, "Still, I don't think it would be a great idea to be seen packing heat."

Neil replaced the gun angrily. "No shit, Frank. I got that. How long you think we'll be stuck here, anyhow?"

Frank tilted his head philosophically, personally enjoying what was parading by their windows. He liked mountains and sloping meadows and quaint farmhouses leaking plumes of chimney smoke. But unlike Neil, he also enjoyed reading and listening to music and even going to a museum now and then. "You know as much as I do. Kendall gave us diddly before he croaked. The museum Web site said nothing about him or who was behind getting his pictures on the wall, except for that 'anonymous donor' bullshit I showed you. Maybe it'll all be printed on a plaque on the wall when we get there."

"And if it isn't?"

Frank smiled pleasantly. "Then we do what we do. Find out who's got what we need and have a chat with them, too."

"That's done us a lot of good so far," Neil groused.

Frank shrugged. "We'll get what the customer wants. That's what we get paid for."

Lester Spinney awoke from his nap and sighed at the long line of traffic stretching ahead of their temporary hilltop vantage point. To him, it looked like an oversized boa, its scales comprised of shimmering blotches of colorful automotive paint. They were in New Jersey, on I-287, driving south at fifteen miles an hour.

"Who *are* all these people?" he wondered aloud. "And why're they out here, in the middle of the day, in the middle of the week? It doesn't make sense to me."

"I ask myself the same thing every time I come here," Joe replied. "Rough night?"

"Total waste. As a favor, I helped out a pal at the Springfield PD last night. A no-brainer, but it took forever." Resigned to the wonder of so much traffic, Spinney reached into the back seat of the car to retrieve their case file, speaking as he did so. "Sam told me that McLarney had sent up something from Philadelphia, but you sprang this trip on me first thing this morning. I'm not complaining, by the way. But *why're* we going there?"

"Sorry 'bout that," Joe said, keeping his eyes on the bumper four feet ahead. "I was planning to tap Sammie for this, figuring she'd like to stretch her legs a little, but I think she saw it as a chance for her and Willy to get a little private time in, away from us. Was Sue okay with the short notice?"

"Oh sure," Lester told him. "The way the hospital throws extra shifts at her, she'll probably barely notice. It's more Dave who's on my mind right now."

"Oh?" Joe knew that Lester's eighteen-year-old son had recently joined his local sheriff's department, so the concern was meaningful. Lester was in some ways his most dependable teammate. Also the unit's only traditional family man, he was steady, reliable, good-natured, and smart. Hard qualities to beat.

"Yeah," Spinney said. "He got into the academy."

Joe looked at him. "But that's great." He hesitated before asking, "Isn't it?"

Lester burst out laughing, setting his boss at ease. "Oh, yeah. He's totally psyched. But nervous, too. He's never been away from home, and he's all worked up about being a wimp. Everyone at the sheriff's department is telling him what ball busters the instructors are. You know the routine."

Joe waved a hand at the manila folder now in Lester's lap. "Compare the pictures of Ben Kendall with the ones of Jennifer Sisto, from the Philly PD. Tell me what you see."

Les leafed through the pictures and pulled out the appropriate ones, as instructed. "Damn," he said, half to himself, pausing over Sisto's. "They sure worked her over. Thank God it doesn't look as bad as I thought it might."

"Difference between inflicting pain that shows and that which doesn't," Joe suggested. "Look at her forearms and especially that mark on her side, near her abdomen."

"Okay."

"You could argue that those could've gotten there any number of ways, but look at the same spots on Ben Kendall."

Les pulled up a roughly similar shot of their case subject. "That's not so easy. He's pretty far gone."

"Give it a hard look. See the similarity?" Joe asked.

Lester took his time. "That's weird."

Joe nodded. The traffic was beginning to pick up slightly. "There are others. Some are subtle—or hard to see, like you said—but I think they're telling."

Lester studied one anatomical region at a time, shifting back and forth between pictures. "It's like they were handled the same way," he concluded.

"Exactly," Joe agreed. "But she's spread out and tied down, consistent with a torture/murder, while he was found under a supposed avalanche of his own making, looking like an accident."

"And he has a lot fewer marks on him overall," Les added.

"True, which I think ties into the other guy we found at his place," Joe said. "Check out the rap sheet McLarney sent us for Tomasz Bajek."

"How's he play into it?" Lester asked, scanning the referenced document.

"My guess is, Bajek getting killed screwed things up, at least in part," Joe answered. "It would help explain why Ben's place wasn't more disturbed, and why Ben doesn't show all the torture marks that his ex-wife does."

"Because Ben's interrogation was interrupted by Bajek getting entombed?"

"In part," Joe ventured. "I also think Ben died prematurely. Hillstrom couldn't pin his death to trauma, maybe because his heart caved under the strain first. He wasn't getting any younger and his eating habits must've made mine look like a health nut's."

Spinney looked up from his paperwork and gazed at the urban landscape around them. "What a crazy deal."

"And there's something else," Joe continued. He reached out and tapped on some documents toward the back of the file. "Pull that out—it's a printout from Rachel's video, of the pictures of that young woman he had on his bedroom wall. Compare them to Jennifer Sisto."

Lester did as urged, holding the glossies side by side. He shook his head sadly. "Lotta years in between, but definitely the same woman. That's bad."

"It's also another reason I think Ben was left to rot," Joe explained. "Once he died in their hands and Bajek got crushed in the tunnel, they still weren't necessarily staring at a blank wall." He indicated the printout. "They had Jenn in reserve. We may never get to see the originals that were on that wall, but I'm betting that if we did, we'd see her name on the back—or *something*, in any case, that made the connection between Ben and the ex-wife he still clearly loved. That's why we're heading to Philly—'cause I think it's what they did."

They were silent for a while, the traffic flow now back to normal.

"What I'm hoping," Joe kept going, unasked, "is that since we're assuming Bajek wasn't alone, we can maybe help Detective McLarney identify his local playmates, and from that find out who was with him in Vermont. That'll help us with our case and, with any luck, help her figure out who did in Jennifer Sisto."

He glanced at his colleague. "Assuming crossed fingers still work."

Frank, after considerable effort, found a parking place slightly west of the hospital, off Colchester Avenue, in Burlington's northeast quadrant, where the combination of the University of Vermont and the Fletcher Allen Health Care campuses overwhelmed the neighborhood—and the available parking. It was colder than it had been in New Jersey, where they began this trip after meeting with the senator in New York. Both men adjusted their coats as they stepped away from the car and made their way across the broad street, toward the museum housing Ben Kendall's exhibition.

The setting struck Frank as being at odds with itself, given his usual stomping grounds and the conversation he'd just had with Neil in the car. Considering Burlington's size and urban presence, Frank still couldn't shake the feeling that, in this far northern, thinly populated state, reputed for its independence, mountainous isolation, and hardy, terse inhabitants, nature was the ruling force—patient, benignly dominant, and passively lethal to the unprepared.

He removed the scarf from his pocket and looped it around his neck.

They passed a group of laughing students upon entering a pedestrian path, prompting Neil to comment, "Good-lookin' girls. Might be worth a return trip in the summer, when they're not wearing so much."

Frank didn't respond. Neil's verbal patter was like background noise to him by now—not much different from distant freeway traffic, or the ticking of a small clock. He certainly never bothered the man with the kinds of ruminations he'd just been entertaining. It would have been akin to discussing philosophy with a hammer.

He led the way around the corner of the museum and walked into its narrow atrium-style lobby. There, without uttering a word, he approached the ticket counter, purchased admissions for himself and Neil by holding up two fingers, and proceeded toward one of the museum's ground-floor galleries, following a sign reading OUTSIDE THE FRAME— ONE PHOTOGRAPHER'S VIEW OF REALITY, and ignoring the exhibitions through which they walked.

Given the day of the week and its now being midafternoon, there was virtually no one in the gallery.

Neil, inattentive to the building's vast and imposing Marble Court at his back, peered across the threshold, pausing by the large plaque by the door.

"Frank," he said in a low voice, "I thought you said there'd be a name we could chase down."

Frank glanced at the signage. "I said there might be."

He scanned the text and found only a jumble of verbiage addressing the era of the war, and the fact that this "remarkable, hitherto unknown" collection of anonymous photographs had come to the museum's attention through the generosity of a "thoughtful and generous member of the academic community."

"Could've been the night watchman," he murmured before walking farther into the quiet gallery and looking around.

"You think?" Neil asked, following.

Frank ignored him, moving from image to image. "Nice stuff," he commented.

Neil was still looking around vaguely. "Whatever. Looks like a bunch of dumb snapshots to me."

But Frank was clearly in his element, as Neil saw it. "Look at them. They're great. Each one of them pretends to show one thing, while revealing another."

"Of course," Neil faked, slapping his forehead. "Now I totally get it."

Frank nodded as if Neil had said something encouraging. He began pointing out examples of an evolving theme, ignoring Neil's eye rolling. "Look at the framing, how the camera's angled. The richness of the detail. Especially in the Nam pictures. It's the absence of action that makes it all stand out. If he's not showing the war, what *is* he showing? Right? There's real beauty there, regardless of the setting. And the guy was all about how to use light. It's almost like it didn't matter what was in the foreground. Like those soldiers there—they're basically irrelevant." He traveled to one of the newer, abstract portraits. "And here it is in stark isolation—all action gone, all distracting human eye candy. All that remains is the essence of light and shape. Wonderful. The curator really got it."

Frank paused, shook his head, and sighed slightly, his fun over. "Okay," he said, pausing before one of the few images featuring American servicemen. "Look at that."

Neil stared at the photograph, of members of a squad on the edge of a clearing and a cluster of huts. "Okay."

"See anyone familiar?"

Neil glanced at him quickly. "Frank, I wasn't alive back then. You weren't, neither."

"Go on. Look carefully."

Now mildly intrigued, Neil stood with arms akimbo and scrutinized the shot. "The big guy, maybe?" he said finally.

Frank laughed. "Beats me."

Neil scowled. "You are such an asshole. What the fuck're we doin' here?"

Frank shrugged. "I dunno. Maybe it's got something to do with one of these guys."

"They're not *doin'* nuthin'," Neil complained.

"Nope," Frank replied thoughtfully, moving down the line and studying the rest. "I noticed that, too. Could be it's one of the junk piles that's got the senator all worked up. Maybe he's after a thing, not a person."

Neil scratched his head. "So, what're you sayin'?"

"Nothing in particular. *'Theirs but to do and die.'*"

"What?"

Frank pointed toward the exit. "We need to find out who's behind this. Let's have a chat with the young lady at the admission counter."

The Philadelphia Police Department headquarters is a 1960s-era stained, concrete, curvilinear monster. Designed to be hip and progressive in its time—despite resembling either a pair of handcuffs from the air, or a woman's reproductive organs—now it is neither legitimately antique nor useful for its original purpose, stimulating a vigorous public debate concerning its fate. In the meantime, the city leaders had pragmatically if ironically chosen an almost ninety-year-old building to be the PD's new home, and were currently readying it for occupancy.

As Joe and Lester negotiated traffic to enter the building's parking lot, Joe could only sympathize with the structure's occupants. As large as it appeared from the outside, he'd read that the building bulged with twice its designated population, and had proved hopelessly ill equipped to handle new technology.

He and Lester located the homicide unit on the second floor, in jammed-together quarters whose wear and tear made the exterior seem sparkling by contrast. The desks and chairs looked fresh from a massive curbside "free" pile, the odd computer screen was as out of context as a *Star Wars* light saber, and the linoleum had been worn down to the subflooring under each mismatched desk.

That being said, the expressions greeting the two out-of-towners were universally pleasant and welcoming, including from the woman who approached them first, her hand extended. "You the Vermonters? Elizabeth McLarney. We spoke on the phone."

The obligatory formalities were invoked, with introductions and more handshakes all around, Lester issuing the standard joke that there'd better not be a quiz at the end. It was one of the happy conventions of law enforcement that, much to the consternation of movie screenwriters fond of turf tension, most cops tended to recognize a hardworking counterpart when they met one.

"So," McLarney addressed them, after she, Phil DesAutels, and their guests had settled around a small, cramped table with one wobbly leg. "This is pretty old-school, you two driving all the way down to deliver what could've been e-mailed and/or Skyped in seconds flat."

"I suppose," Joe admitted. "I'm not big on the modern stuff."

"He still refuses to text," Lester threw in.

"Of course," DesAutels suggested in a neutral voice, toning down his partner's cheery welcome. "Or maybe you didn't trust us to do your legwork."

"Not true," Joe countered. "Our legwork's the same as yours, as I see it." He laid out the photos as he'd had Lester do earlier. "Compare the injuries on the two bodies. Tell me there're not enough similarities to make you wonder."

Phil and Elizabeth leaned in together and exchanged a couple of murmured comments before she looked up and asked, "Was Ben Kendall stretched out with duct tape restraints?"

"Not when we found him," Joe replied. "But the marks on his body are consistent with a manhandling. We just didn't go there initially, because the circumstances didn't suggest it—a hoarder's landslide could've caused the same injuries. The new working theory, though, is that whoever did this was warming up on him when he died of natural causes, after which they covered him up with a pile of stuff to make it look like an accident."

Les slid over the photograph of their second dead body, saying, "The same working theory has it that Bajek got crushed while he was trying to ferret out whatever it is they were after."

Joe spoke to Phil's suspicion directly. "I hear you about stepping on toes, but unless I read your report wrong, you're about where we are with our case, which is close to nowhere."

"I wouldn't say that," Elizabeth said. "But Bajek is a detail we didn't have before you brought him to us."

"Did you get anything out of the people in Sisto's life?" Joe asked.

Elizabeth shook her head. "She was pretty retiring. Worked at home for a couple of docs, doing their bookkeeping, and basically only had the one friend, Chelsea Kline. We checked them all out. They were useless."

"We also tore apart what was left of her apartment," Phil added. "Which is how we found out about Kendall and you guys. But otherwise, it gave us nothin'."

"Unless you see something in it that we missed," his partner mentioned. "We have a complete inventory, including the address book listing Kendall. Maybe some of the other names there'll ring a bell—not that there's much, period."

"We could give it a look," Joe said agreeably.

"You want to see her place?" Elizabeth asked. "It's still sealed."

Joe glanced at Lester before replying, "I don't think we need to. You clearly went over it with a microscope. From our perspective, the best lead is Bajek."

Phil made a face. "What else we got?"

Elizabeth rose from her chair. "Up for a field trip?" she asked. "First stop is lovely, scenic Port Richmond—Tommy Bajek's last known address."

CHAPTER EIGHT

Frank had put on his most disarming face, even telling Neil to stay in the basement lobby near the restrooms so staffers wouldn't associate the two of them. All for naught. He'd walked down the untidy subterranean hallway housing the museum offices, introduced himself to the curator in a golly-gee manner—using a bogus name, of course—and gone on and on about how "blown away" he'd been by the exhibition, and especially the originality of the Vietnam photos. He'd told how his dad had been killed there, devastating the family; how, as a result, Nam had become a pivotal event in Frank's life; and how this show had therefore struck him to the core.

Could she—maybe—share with him how it had come about? Who the photographer was? Who'd been responsible for bringing his work to the gallery?

Nothing. Not a damn thing. Sandy Corcoran—according to her name tag—had sat at her desk, a smiling lapdog, and told him that while she was delighted to hear of his moving experience, there was no way in hell she was giving him one single iota.

At least, that's how he'd interpreted her.

She'd offered to take his contact information, to pass it along to the relevant people. He'd demurred, of course, but he'd still felt a modicum of gratitude. After all, she'd just implied that she held the keys to the kingdom.

And now, eight hours later, he and Neil were about to get those keys handed over—or take them outright—thanks to a "people finder" page on the Internet.

They were seventeen miles north of Burlington, in the uninspiring commuter town of Milton, watching Corcoran's home on a dead end dirt road within earshot of a spillway gushing from a small concrete dam containing Lake Arrowhead.

Neil, as usual, was unhappy. "Crank the heat up, Frank. Freezin' my butt off here."

Frank reached out to the control, but didn't actually adjust it. He was comfortable, and knew that Neil's complaint was largely psychological. Despite the amount of surveillance their job entailed, Neil had never cottoned to it. He preferred to keep busy, which meant he'd be happier soon.

Frank brought up the binoculars and scanned the front of the house again. Frank wasn't pleased, either. In the best of worlds, if you wanted to move on someone, as he and Neil were planning tonight, you did several days of prep work. You established a household's habits and patterns, you got to know the inhabitants and their schedules. You let your comfort level dictate the mission—not the client's impatience.

But the senator believed otherwise, and Frank, despite his inborn independence, could recognize when he was up against it. Not only were he and Neil being highly compensated for this job—to where Frank's retirement plans had been advanced by a decade—but it had been made perfectly clear that, were they to fail, the senator had other people as close as his speed dial whose assignment it would be to make that retirement immediate and permanent. And considering how the man had treated them at their meetings—and apparently his pathetic butler all the time—he was not big on human kindness.

So, the job was on for tonight, with no more preparation than a quick reconnaissance of the home and its surroundings, which they'd conducted two hours ago.

There, at least, they thought they might be in luck. Sandy Corcoran appeared to live only with an older woman and a cat, from what they'd seen through a few unobstructed windows. There were no dogs, no alarms, virtually no traffic along the dirt road, and enough cover supplied by the surrounding trees and brush to hide Frank's rental car. The constantly rushing water from the river downstream of the dam was good for muffling noise, and as a final bonus, the Corcoran household—as was often true in rural environments—didn't seem to be compulsive about using curtains or blinds.

He and Neil had constructed a rough floor plan from their observations, as they'd done in prior home invasions. Ideally, they analyzed entrances and exits, pathways and obstructions, locations of light switches, how doors swung open and whether they had locks, and number and proximity of phones.

In this case, there were gaps. Given his druthers, Frank would have waited for the house to be empty, gone inside, mapped it with precision, arranged a way to quietly enter once it was occupied, and maybe even placed a few tiny remote cameras for later monitoring. This time, they had sections of their layout that were completely blank—either the lights had been out in a room, or a single curtain had in fact been drawn, denying them visual access.

All such snags acknowledged, their combined experience and level of expertise gave them enough confidence to proceed.

Frank saw a sudden variance in the lighting seeping out from the house. He raised the glasses again and said, "TV got turned off. Time to rock 'n' roll."

They donned throat mics and earphones for covert communications, watch caps that could be pulled down to form face masks, and gloves for warmth and anonymity, and left their vehicle, heading off in different directions, according to plan.

As he closed on the building, Frank saw a shadow cross the nearest window and recognized Sandy Corcoran reaching for one of the living room lamps. As the light died, he traveled the length of the building at a slow pace, between the building and the river beyond, matching her progress as he saw it through a succession of windows. He was close enough that he could actually see her speaking with the older woman as she presumably wished her good night.

"Bedroom light just went on for the old lady," Neil's whispered voice announced over Frank's earphones.

"Roger that," he replied. "I'm with Sandy, heading for the back bedroom."

"Let's hope they aren't big bedtime readers," Neil said.

It was a pertinent remark, given that they'd decided to wait in their respective spots for a half hour after lights out before making a move. One reward they'd earned from their earlier surveillance was that the house had only the single TV set. At least there would be no hours of Jimmy, David, or Conan to contend with.

"Grandma just pulled a curtain," Neil announced. "I got no eyes."

"Roger," Frank acknowledged, positioning himself outside Sandy's window. She was not inclined toward the same precautions as Granny, given the lack of neighbors, which allowed him to watch her walk back and forth across the bedroom, entering and exiting the bathroom, disrobing in stages as she prepared for bed.

He'd layered up for the weather, as had Neil on the other side, and found himself now comfortably perched on a nearby log, with a full view of the room's interior, admiring a relatively attractive older woman as she slowly revealed herself.

It was not sexual satisfaction that he derived from this. His sex life was acceptably active and varied, and he entertained no particularly unusual fantasies. The pleasure that he was experiencing now was purely acquisitive. He watched Sandy Corcoran for the style and color of her underwear, for the presence of a particular mole or the shape and size of her nipples. He drew conclusions about her diet and exercise regime based on her muscle tone and the tautness of her stomach. Frank Niles was an archivist, as he saw it—a collector of facts and memories. His job went beyond the killings and mayhem it occasionally required, making him a traveler of sorts through other people's lives—absorbing, cataloging, often admiring. It was a fringe benefit that somehow supplied him with an aesthetic balance to the nature of his work.

He doubted that Neil shared any of this with him. Neil was more basic in his needs—a sturdy associate, and one he curiously enjoyed working with, unlike the occasional stringer like Tommy Bajek, whom they'd lost beyond retrieving in the hoarder's house. But Frank was not so foolish as to share his pastimes and insights with Neil. "Keep it simple" was one of his philosophies—people should know what you chose to tell them, and nothing more.

So, like the contented member of an exclusive audience, Frank studied Sandy's preparations for bed until she pulled the covers up to her chin, reached out, and killed the last light.

"Is Grandma making Zs over there?" he asked through his throat mic.

"I guess so. It's dark."

"I got lucky," he admitted. "Sandy opened her window a crack."

"Gotta love those fresh-air freaks," Neil responded.

"Okay," Frank concluded. "Get comfortable. Thirty-minute countdown."

Neil had once complained that this was when they earned the big bucks, sitting still in utter silence for sometimes hours at a stretch, in the cold or the wet or in considerable discomfort, waiting for the right time to move—in this instance, until the two women inside had fallen thoroughly asleep.

All that considered, this was looking like a cakewalk.

"Welcome to glorious Port Richmond, gentlemen," Elizabeth McLarney announced as she drove her unmarked green Ford Explorer off the interstate, onto Aramingo Avenue, and under a railroad overpass at East Lehigh. "Once home to shipyards, coal dumps—and nowadays, teen gangs, the Polish Mafia, and a dash of Irish hoodlums to spice things up."

Phil took over. "The Mafia, we call the Kielbasa Posse," he said. "Out the right window is the east side—upwardly mobile, getting gentrified, complete with photo-op cute streets, hipsters, and parks with kids playing ball."

"And out the left window"—Elizabeth played along—"is the west side—heavy on rentals, abandoned buildings, shooting galleries, and gang fights. Bipolar Town is what I call it."

"Of course," Phil explained, "It's not that simple. At night, the whole area can get dicey, especially when the summer heat kicks in. The parks become staging areas for scumbags looking for trouble. Old-time residents are making inroads—neighborhood patrols and what have you—and I think the place is looking better. Campbell Square used to be nicknamed 'Needle Park.' It's improving, but it still has a ways to go." He cocked an eye at Joe. "Bet you don't have much of that up in Vermont, huh?"

"Not in the quantities you have to deal with," Joe agreed.

He and Les took in the buildings to both sides, a blur of glued-together two-story row houses interspersed with block-house commercial structures, all of it crisscrossed overhead with a visual spaghetti bowl of taut electrical lines, making Joe feel as if they'd just been trapped under a screened lid, like bugs in a box. The first floors of dozens of the narrower buildings advertised an assortment of minuscule restaurants, markets, and stores, many having hard-to-pronounce—mostly Polish—names, and with a smattering of everything from Asian to Irish.

Partway along, Elizabeth took a left into Port Richmond's western half, and then a right a couple of streets down. Here, the street was narrow, closed in, and far from quaint—house after beleaguered house, scarred and stained and sometimes boarded up, crammed together and festooned with the predictable mushrooming of weather-beaten TV dishes. Where a porch had been worked into the building's plan, an occasional bundled-up figure sat, sometimes smoking, staring out at the desolation. Joe had seen worse—in Chicago, Newark, and New York, to name three—but none of that made this neighborhood upbeat by comparison.

"Here we go," Elizabeth said cheerily, parking by the curb. "Home sweet home to the late Tomasz Bajek. Everybody out."

The four of them stepped into the trash-strewn street and looked around. Each was aware of people watching from nearby—a stoop, a parked car, or behind half-drawn blinds. The neighborhood buzz that cops were on the street was like a small electrical impulse.

McLarney crossed the cracked sidewalk, bounded up the three steps of one of the row houses, tried the door, hoping for the best, and successfully walked inside, the rest of her entourage following.

In the claustrophobic entryway, she pounded on the nearest door.

An older woman appeared after three minutes, the view of her face transected by the security chain she'd left in place. "What?"

McLarney showed her badge. "Police. We need to get into Tommy Bajek's place."

"Be my guest. I'm not his mother."

"Which one's his?"

"Upstairs. To the right. But he's not here."

"And he's not gonna be. He's dead."

The woman frowned, said, "Shit," and closed the door with a bang.

"Oops," Lester said.

Elizabeth smiled at him. "She's already forgotten we were here."

They headed up the dark, narrow, evil-smelling stairs, stepping lightly out of habit, their eyes on the shadows.

Joe recognized the faint traces of what had once been a family home, before the building was transformed into a cramped multi-dwelling. Old architectural details had been painted over or crudely remodeled. He could see where prior doorways had been Sheetrocked, if not taped and floated, in an effort to divide the house evenly, and he saw water pipes and wiring supplying bathrooms and outlets that—a hundred years earlier— hadn't existed.

It all made him wonder if anyone from the city's building codes enforcement branch had the slightest idea of the place's current function.

At the door to the right of the landing, Phil gently tried the knob, which caused the door to swing open before them. Instinctively, all four flattened against the wall, their hands on their guns.

"Police," Phil called into the apartment. "Comin' in."

He eased the door wider with his toe, staying where he was. Opposite him, Elizabeth extracted a small flashlight, shone it into the darkness, and quickly bobbed her head into the opening to check for any threats.

"Looks clear," she said softly.

That observation applied to people only, for the cramped, stinking, lightless near-hovel they entered was far from clear otherwise. As they spread out and opened filthy curtains or attempted to roll up petrified blinds—having found the lights inoperative—they discovered a messy, one-room den. Or, as Phil put it, "What a shit hole."

Joe agreed privately, although, having been to Ben Kendall's, he was jaded. Still, almost everything that could have been placed on a shelf or a counter, in a closet or a fridge had been deposited in a heap on the floor—including the remains of discarded meals stretching back into history.

As a result, the place was alive with insects scurrying away from the intruding light.

"Wow," Lester admired, studying his shoes and socks for invaders. "It's a whole ecosystem."

"It's also been tossed," Joe said.

"I agree," echoed Elizabeth. "Look at the dresser."

"The dresser," Joe went on, "the mattress, the closet, the cabinets over the stove, even the freezer. All open and emptied."

"Someone connected to the Kendall B and E?" Lester asked no one in particular.

"Dropped by after his death?" Phil joined in. "Maybe."

"It would make sense," Elizabeth said. "You said they didn't try digging him out of that booby trap. Next best thing would be to come here afterwards and erase any and all trace of his connection to them."

She extracted her cell phone and hit the speed dial. "I'll get the crime scene folks to sort things out, and have 'em grill Ms. Hospitality downstairs, along with whoever else lives in the building, not that I'm holding my breath."

As she was talking on the phone, Joe and Lester convened with Phil.

"How familiar was the PPD with Mr. Bajek?" Joe asked.

"From what I read," Phil replied, "he was a Kowalski. You ever see *Combat!*—that old TV show?"

"Sure," Joe admitted while Lester looked blankly at them. "Had Vic Morrow as the sergeant. Never smiled."

Phil laughed. "Right. Whenever they had a new guy join the squad, he'd be the one who bought it. We used to laugh 'cause his name was always Johnson or Kowalski. It became a thing, you know? 'A real Kowalski.'" Phil then looked at them seriously for a moment. "Neither of you is Polish, are you?" he asked.

Joe shook his head before inferring, "So Bajek was a perpetual number two man?"

"Yeah, and usually the guy left holding the bag. I checked him out when you first brought him up—before you got here—and it looks like he was the doofus we were left with, more times than not. Not too bright, but maybe good in a pinch. We had him for fights, store robberies, vandalisms, stuff like that."

"Smart enough to hold a bat," Joe suggested. "But too dumb to run away?"

Elizabeth had ended her phone call. "You talking about Tommy?"

"Yeah." Phil smiled like a proud father.

"We go after his family and past associates now?" Joe asked.

Elizabeth sighed and checked her watch. "That's the drill. Let's hope we get luckier than here."

Frank enjoyed entering people's bedrooms when they were asleep. It didn't really matter if they were male or female, although the females were an added attraction. And it wasn't as if he did it all that frequently. But the pure pleasure of it hit him every time, akin to reversing the standard nightmare—instead of fearing what might come bumping in the middle of the night, he *became* that something.

Sandy Corcoran's window slid open without a sound, and he'd stepped inside like a passing shadow on the wall. Now he settled on the bed beside her sleeping form, simultaneously placing his gloved hand across her slightly gaping mouth.

She awoke with a full body spasm, her limbs trapped under the covers, her eyes as round as marbles.

His face masked, he leaned in close and spoke softly. "Sandy, Sandy. I'm not here to hurt you. Stop moving. Just lie there and breathe through your nose."

Her breaths came in gasps, understandably, so he let her situation sink in for a few seconds before adding, "Good. Now, listen carefully. I have an associate with . . . Who is that? Your mother? Anyhow, she's fine and you'll be fine, if you cooperate. Will you do that? Either nod or shake your head, although I wouldn't recommend the latter."

Her eyes above his gloved hand were watching him with astonishment.

She nodded.

He smiled under his mask and moved his hand slightly. "Now. No shouting or screaming, okay? No point making a lot of noise for nothing."

She nodded again and he removed his hand entirely, only to rest it, an implied warning, across her breasts—a gesture from which she tried to recoil into the mattress beneath her.

"Okay," he said gently. "Let's talk."

CHAPTER NINE

"Wit or witout?"

Joe looked up, startled. "What?"

"Onions."

He shook his head, already half regretting the invitation to be taken out to dinner and introduced to Philly cuisine. "No thanks."

Phil DesAutels turned back toward the man at the crowded counter and finished ordering their cheesesteaks.

"Geez, Hon." Elizabeth leaned toward Joe to be heard. "Live dangerously. I can't introduce you to the local culture unless you stick your neck out a little."

"I think I am," he told her, pointing at a dark rectangular slab of something resembling a breaded, oversized domino tile—without the white dots. "What's that?"

"Scrapple," she said happily. "You never had that?"

"Not knowingly." He poked it with his finger and found it slightly spongy. "What's in it?"

"Pig," Phil explained. "Everything but the squeal. Eyelids, intestines, organs, boiled-down bones—technically it's called offal, but don't let that stop you. It's really good. It's meat loaf meeting a hot dog."

"Yum," Joe murmured.

Elizabeth laughed. "Aren't you glad you asked?"

They gathered up their meals and drinks and muscled outside to where the SUV was parked by the curb. They were on Chestnut Street, west of Center City, across the Schuylkill River, having driven across town solely for Joe and Lester's benefit. Supposedly.

Although Lester was a believer. "I can't wait to tell Sue," he said to no one in particular, taking a cell phone picture of the gleaming, dripping concoction within the bag he was holding. "The Philly cheesesteak is like an icon."

"You better hope it won't be iconic around one in the morning," Joe said, thinking that they were sharing a motel room.

"No problem," Lester assured him, slapping his middle. "Iron stomach."

"Wait till we put some Tastykakes in there for dessert," Phil told him. "That'll break you."

"What's next?" Joe asked their guide as she headed back east across the Schuylkill, using the Spring Garden Street Bridge.

"Well," she said, "like I was saying at Tommy's, if you can't get a guy one way, there's usually another. You mentioned his friends and family. I figured we could do worse than to talk to a man who knows a man, so to speak."

Joe nodded silently, understanding that this would make better sense later, and concentrated on eating, discovering at last what all the commotion was about.

"Christ," he said around his first mouthful. "This is terrific."

Elizabeth pointedly took them on the tourist roundabout, passing before the city's art museum, and worked her way back toward the general direction of Port Richmond, ending up somewhere on the edge of Kensington, near Frankford Avenue, where she pulled over, engine running, to make her own inroads into her meal.

Joe glanced back at Lester, who merely shrugged, as the door beside him opened suddenly enough to make him almost drop his cheesesteak, and a rough-dressed man with long hair and a beard ordered him, "Shove over."

Lester did as he was told, while Elizabeth said with her mouth full, "Yo. Gents—this is Peter Kindler. Pete—the Vermonters I told you about."

"You get me one?" Kindler asked.

Phil dug into the bag at his feet and passed a sandwich over, across Lester's lap.

Kindler murmured, "Ahhh," as he unfolded the wrapper on his knees and took an inaugural bite. "Okay," he finally said after taking a swig of soda to wash down the food. "What can I do you for?"

"Tommy Bajek," Elizabeth said. "What can you tell us about him?"

Kindler seemed surprised. "Tommy? You interested about him in Vermont? We barely give a shit about him here. He move or something?"

"He died up there," Joe explained.

Elizabeth went further. "Could be he was part of a hit team. Ended up on the short end of the stick."

"There's a shock," Kindler said, taking another bite.

"You know who he's been hanging with?" Phil inquired.

"Not hired killers. He was more like the guy you leave outside to watch for the cops. You get any fries?"

Another oil-stained paper bundle was passed along.

"How 'bout his regulars, Pete?" Elizabeth asked. "If some outsiders were looking for somebody like that—driver, bagman, doorman, whatever—they'd ask around before they found Tommy, right? I mean, since he didn't normally rent himself out to the killer elite."

"Yeah. I see what you're sayin'," Pete replied. "I didn't know Tommy 'cept in passing, but I know the crew he hangs with—or hung with. And you're barking up the right tree there. The Kielbasa Posse has its bad boys, for sure, but Tommy's bunch is bigger on what you might call the illegal jobs business—you wanna be an electrician or a Sheetrocker or whatever, but you're not union and you're maybe not squeaky clean under scrutiny, these boys'll set you up. They take a piece of your action, and later, ya gotta take who they offer under your wing, assuming you get big enough to start hiring yourself, but who cares? It's all about the money."

Phil paused to eat again and then added, "Not Tommy, of course. He was more of a permanent filler." He tapped the side of his head. "Not terrific in the brains department. Still, a solid worker."

"His crew cool enough for us to approach them solo?" Elizabeth asked. "Or should you be along to make the introductions?"

Pete raised his eyebrows at her. "Very classy, girl. Nice of you to ask. Smart, too, 'cause I'd doubt they'd say diddly to any of you. The guys I'm thinking about don't know I'm a cop, so we'll play this kind of discreet, if that works for you."

"You call it, Pete," she replied easily.

"Listen to this," Sam said, her eyes on her computer screen.

Willy looked up from what he was reading at his desk.

"There's a BOL been issued from the Burlington area for an unidentified man—"

"Don't tell me," he said. "Medium height, medium build, hair light or dark, unless he was bald."

She ignored him out of habit, continuing, "—who's wanted in connection with a home invasion and assault on Sandy Corcoran and her elderly mother."

"Sucks to be them," he stated unsympathetically.

Sammie persisted. "The old woman is a widow, while Sandy is an administrator of the Fleming Museum."

Willy immediately recognized where this was headed and went silent, absentmindedly watching their small child, who was fast asleep in a portable crib that they'd brought to the office as a way to give them all a bit more midweek family time.

"While the man at the time of the attack," she continued interpreting from the BOL, "wore a mask and gloves and spoke in a low voice so as not to be recognized, Corcoran said she suspects he was the same one who entered her office earlier that day and inquired about the source of the photo display currently at the museum."

Willy crossed the room to read over her shoulder. "Nice."

She looked up at him. "Thought you'd like that part."

He pointed at the screen. "They say why this guy came at her?"

"Nope. They pretty much left it at that. No doubt the local PD's case narrative will have it. I can probably access that."

He walked back to his desk, saying, as she'd expected, "Nah. Let's do that ourselves, face-to-face. I don't trust other people's reports. They never ask what I want 'em to." He checked his watch and glanced at the baby again. "Louise good to watch Emma if we take a trip up north? I can stay put while you fly solo, too. It's fine with me, either way."

Sammie worked to control her reaction. The double whammy that he'd both stay behind to babysit *and* trust her to run an interview was virtually unprecedented. From the start of their relationship, everyone—except Joe—had warned her against getting too close to Willy's quills. Nevertheless, in his uncomfortable, spasmodic, but dogged way, he was struggling to make her proud.

She reached for her phone. "I'll give her a call, but I doubt there'll be a problem."

. . .

Sandy Corcoran looked up nervously at the man who entered Milton's police station, one wing of a modern, multi-building municipal complex that included the town library, town offices, and fire and rescue squads. The duty sergeant had placed her in a small meeting room, along with a cup of coffee that she hadn't touched, and asked her to sit tight for the arrival of two agents from the VBI. He'd sounded impressed by this, emphasizing how the VBI was a major-case squad only, but she'd simply been baffled—and a little frightened. Now, eyeing this intense-looking, angular man with what appeared to be a nonfunctioning arm anchored to his left-hand trousers pocket, her apprehension escalated.

She was tiring of being cornered by strange, domineering men asking weird questions.

Fortunately, on his heels came a slight, athletic, if equally focused, young woman whose overall looks delivered a curious sense of comfort— her accompaniment of the man somehow legitimized his presence.

Sandy stood nervously as the woman closed the door behind them.

The man waved at her to resume her seat, speaking in a voice belying the scary authority in his eyes. "Please, don't get up. We really appreciate your meeting us at such a time. How're you holding up?"

Sandy regained the edge of her chair.

The man opened his jacket to reveal a badge on his belt, saying, "I'm Special Agent Kunkle. This is Special Agent Martens, from the VBI. Just to confirm, you are Sandy Corcoran. Is that correct?"

She nodded. "Yes."

Both cops shook her hand in turn and sat on either side of her, since she was seated at the head of the table.

"We're sorry about the circumstances that've brought you here," Sammie said, her eyes directly on Sandy's, making the latter look down at her hands.

"We read about what happened," Kunkle explained. "And we hate to make you relive it all, but we're very interested in what you and this man talked about."

While he spoke, Sam pulled a small recorder from her pocket and laid it on the table, her eyebrows raised questioningly. "This okay?" she asked.

"Sure," Sandy answered, further comforted by her tone. "I guess." She then looked at Willy. "You want to know what we talked about? It wasn't like a conversation," she told him.

"I got that," he replied, the hint of an edge to his voice. "But you did speak together, which seems to have been the major reason he was there. What about?"

Sam murmured encouragingly, no doubt used to her partner's effect on people, "It's okay."

Sandy was beginning to wake up to the fact that these two were here for the content of what had happened to her, not the assault itself. "It's what made me think he was the same man who came into my office that day. He asked about the photo exhibition. It's a display we've—" She was stopped by Kunkle's raised hand.

"We know about it," he said, his voice encouraging despite its abruptness. "What did he want to know?"

"How we got it," she explained, adding, "Not so much who took the images, but who brought them in for display. Everyone else has been curious about the photographer, but not him."

"Okay," Sammie said supportively. "Now the harder part: Can you tell us about what happened at your home? Step by step—what he did, what he said. Try to include every detail, every gesture, even."

Sandy's eyes welled up, her hopes dashed, realizing that she would have to go over it all again. Taking a breath, and trusting to an overall numbness, she forged ahead. "I woke up with him sitting on my bed. His hand was on my mouth, and he was telling me not to make a sound. He said he had someone else holding my mother and that she'd be hurt if I didn't cooperate. It wasn't true, I found out later. Mom never knew anything about it. She slept through the whole thing. I don't know if the man had a confederate or not, but he did know Mom was in the house, so I believed him."

"Good," Kunkle said patiently. "That was the right choice. Keep going."

"Okay," she said, feeling her face redden as she continued. "He asked me if I'd scream—no, I mean, he said something about not screaming. Anyhow, I got the message because that's when he told me that he had someone in with my mother, and then he . . . moved his hand."

Willy shifted his head so slightly that it barely moved, but Sandy sensed in the gesture his complete knowledge about everything that had happened.

"He put his hand on my breast," she said, her modesty overwhelmed by the sense of Kunkle's clairvoyance.

"On top of or under your clothes?" he asked.

She pressed her lips together before answering, "On top at first, then underneath. But he didn't do anything. He just rested it there. I was so scared."

Sam removed a tissue from her jacket pocket and handed it over so that Sandy could catch the tears that were traveling down her cheeks.

"Thank you. I was so sure I was about to be raped, and that Mom was already dead. I was angry for not having locked my door, or done a better job of protecting my house. It was all a little crazy, thinking things that made no sense."

"That's very common," Sam said.

Willy confirmed, "We hear that a lot. What did he do or say then?" he asked.

"He pulled the blanket off me—all the way down—so I was just lying there, and he put his hand inside my nightgown, like I said, but all he asked about was the show."

"Details, Sandy."

"Right. He said something like, 'I'm going to ask you again: Who brought you the photographs?'"

"Again?" Kunkle almost interrupted, "Because he was the same man who came to your office?"

"Yes. The voice was the same. He was whispering, but I'm sure of it."

"What did he look like?" Sammie asked.

Sandy blinked. "He had on a mask."

"I'm sorry. I meant when he was at the museum—earlier."

"A baseball cap, beard, dark glasses, medium height. His jacket made him look kind of beefy, but it was hard to tell."

Sammie leaned back in her chair. Whoever it had been, he knew how to run himself. What Sandy had rattled off were accessories—not human characteristics. And Sam didn't doubt for a moment that the beard had either been fake or was now down the drain somewhere, accompanied by some shaving cream.

"What did you tell him, Sandy?" Willy was asking.

"The truth. At the office, I was happy to follow policy, but at home? Being threatened that way? I wasn't going to risk my life and Mom's, both. I told him that one of our students approached her faculty advisor, and that—between the two of them—they'd written an application to have the work displayed at the museum."

"You gave him the names?"

"I didn't have the student's," she said. "That was the agreement between him or her and the advisor. I was told it was because of the anonymous standing of the photographer, who I gathered was still alive and pretty eccentric. The student didn't want attention diverted away from the artist, and wanted the anonymity to be across the board. But the advisor was Nancy Filson. She's in the art department."

Sandy hung her head before admitting, "I did give him her name." She looked up suddenly and added quickly, "But I called her right after he left, and told her what happened. I told her to get away, to hide, that she didn't want happening to her what I'd gone through."

Willy frowned and placed his palm flat on the table, leaning toward her. "The guy in the mask just walked away after you told him about Filson?"

Her face flushed and she reached out to grab his hand pleadingly, her earlier comforting numbness stripped away by the question. "He didn't know how well I knew her. He didn't know we were friends. I pretended to barely recall her name. He'd threatened me that if I ever told anyone, he'd be back to get me and my mom." Her voice escalated. "I didn't know what to do," she cried. "It was either me and Mom right then, or Nancy later. It was an impossible choice."

"That makes you an incredibly brave woman," Sam stated, adding, "How did Nancy react when you told her?"

Sandy calmed a little, blowing her nose and dabbing at her eyes. "She thought I was kidding at first—for a second, at least. Then she heard how emotional I was. She told me to go to the police, which I did, and she agreed that she'd be careful." Again, her voice grew anxious. "I told her it would take more than that. I told her how scared I'd been— what that man had done to me."

Sammie heard what she interpreted to be a deeper meaning there. She reached out and touched Sandy's shoulder to get her full attention. "What *did* he do to you? Finish telling us what happened."

Sandy stared her in the face, her cheeks damp, her eyes bloodshot. "He ran his hand down my body after I told him what he wanted— slowly—feeling everything. I tried to freeze, to not feel it, but it was horrible."

"Did he do anything more?" Sam pressed her.

Sandy hesitated, said, "No," and then curled up on herself, crying convulsively. Sammie leaned over to rub her back as she glanced at Willy and raised her eyebrows.

He rose and left the room, returning moments later with a box of tissues and a glass of water. He placed both before their witness and waited for Corcoran to regain her composure.

This she did after several more nose blows.

"We're very sorry to put you through this again, Sandy," he then said supportively. "But we need to get it all."

"I understand," she said from behind a wad of tissues.

"After he touched you that way," Willy resumed, his manner dramatically softened from before, "what did he do or say?"

"Just that I was to keep my mouth shut and not tell anybody, or he'd be back and it 'wouldn't be so pleasant.' Those were the words he used."

"So it's your feeling that he really bought the story that you could hardly remember Nancy Filson's name?"

"Yes," she said, revealing her face to show her conviction on this point. "He even got a little frustrated with me because of my so-called faulty memory. I'm positive he thought I barely knew her."

Sammie slid a pad and pen across the table before her. "You did well, Sandy. Write down every address, phone number, Facebook page, e-mail, and anything else you have on Nancy. We need to get hold of her fast. Did you tell the local police the same thing you told us just now? In other words, might they be looking for Nancy, too?"

She shook her head. "No. I reported the assault and the fact that the man wanted to know about the show, but I didn't mention Nancy. It was kind of chaotic when I first came here—I think there was a big accident across town or something—and by the time they got to finishing up with me, one of them had already called you. I think that's how it worked. Anyhow, they pretty much stopped asking questions, saying that you were on your way."

Neither Willy nor Sam had any trouble believing that. There wasn't a cop working that hadn't had nights when it seemed nothing more could go wrong—before it did. Times like that, you counted yourself lucky just to cover the bases, much less tend to the finer details.

Willy waited for Sandy to finish writing before asking, "Now, this part is really important: Where do you think Nancy is now?"

Sandy, however, looked at him helplessly. "I have no idea. I've tried calling her cell phone since I warned her, but all I get is her voice mail. And this morning, her office said that she never showed up for work."

Sammie spoke with as much confidence as she could muster. "Well, of course. She's following your directions. Keeping off the grid. What about other friends or family she might be staying with?"

"I don't know. Nancy's pretty private. I know she has family, but she's never mentioned them by name, and she doesn't seem to like people asking, or at least she changes the conversation. As for friends, I can't say. We hang out, but on campus, mostly during lunch. I really don't know what she does or who she sees when she's not at work."

"Sandy," Willy asked her, keeping any criticism out of his voice. "When you warned her about the man, why didn't you tell *her* to call the police, like she told you? I understand why you didn't tell these guys—you explained that. But the police could've protected her. Now she could be anywhere."

Sammie cut him a look, but Sandy took it in stride, responding, "I did. But she didn't think the police would do anything if a crime hadn't been committed. She said it was like a rule or something."

Both cops got up, gathering their possessions. "Okay," Willy addressed her, stifling his frustration and handing her his business card. "Well, a crime's definitely been committed against you, so we'll make sure the local police keep an eye on you, for protection. Those numbers are how to get hold of us, day or night, if you need to."

He took a breath and added, "You did great work here, okay? I know cops that wouldn't have kept their heads so well. Take credit for that. You deserve it."

They said their farewells to both her and the officers waiting in the foyer, stressing to them that the man in the mask might return. But once they were alone in the parking lot, heading toward the car, Willy couldn't resist concluding, "Don't know if you're taking odds, but I say her pal Nancy's fucked, somethin' royal."

CHAPTER TEN

Joe had no notion of where he was. Somewhere near or in Port Richmond—where most of Tommy Bajek's short life had been spent, before his unfortunate trip to Vermont. But as for a specific location, Joe was lost. You could put him most anywhere in the wilds of Vermont, and he could give you his approximate whereabouts. In an urban locale like Greater Philadelphia? He might as well have been standing in a desert. In the middle of the night.

It was close to the middle of the night now. They were parked slightly down the street from the Philadelphia equivalent of one of the social clubs Joe had seen in Newark a few years earlier, on a different case. It was a bar in some respects, with minimal signage—in Polish, in this case—and no doubt with all the proper paperwork, but crossing its threshold, straight off the street, would've gotten you only a room full of cold stares, and certainly not the tall one you might have been hoping to order. This was a members-only establishment and, to the cops' advantage, Peter Kindler was a member.

"So, what's Kindler's story?" Lester asked, in part to pass the time as they waited. "Has he been undercover long?"

Elizabeth this time was working on a large, oddly shaped pretzel—thick, soft, white-cored, and heavily salted—which even Joe had passed on when she offered to treat them all. Phil DesAutels answered instead. "It's not that kind of undercover—not like in movies. This branch of the Kielbasa Posse's not a major felony outfit, like he was sayin', so Pete can pretty much come and go as he likes. He fits in like that anyhow, pretty much wherever he goes. He's an old-school guy, which probably means that he's on the endangered list, as a cop."

Joe nodded sympathetically. He was without question the oldest warhorse in the car, and knew too well how law enforcement had evolved in recent years. Personally, he had no idea what he'd do with himself if he could no longer wade in among other people's troubles, sorting them out. He only hoped that he wouldn't have to find out anytime soon.

"Here he comes," Elizabeth announced, wiping bright yellow mustard from her lip, her eye on the bar's front door. She fired up the car's engine, leaving the headlights off, and pulled away from the curb slowly, heading for the far end of the block. There, under cover of near total darkness, they waited for Kindler to draw abreast, and—with the slightest of gestures—open the rear door and slip inside beside Lester.

"How'd it go?" the latter asked.

"Everybody on their best behavior," Kindler said. "Even if they were poundin' down the beer pretty good. It was hard keepin' up." He noticed what Elizabeth was still holding in her right hand. "You got more of those?"

She handed the remains of the pretzel to him. "Didn't know when you'd be getting out. Feel free." She fumbled in her lap and gave him a small container, as well. "Mustard," she said.

Joe smiled to himself, wondering how McLarney and Kindler managed not to look like blimps, given eating habits that Joe could only envy.

"Any luck locating Bajek?" he asked as Kindler tore at the tough white dough and dipped a piece of it into the mustard.

Pete chewed and smiled happily. "Kinda. I think I got a girlfriend's name, or at least someone he was hangin' out with before he disappeared."

"Meaning, they're saying he did disappear?" Lester asked.

"Yeah," Kindler told them. "At least nobody's seen him lately. Course, Tommy's not a standout in this crowd. Anyhow, the name I got is Natausha Greenblott. They call her Tausha for short."

"That's not Polish," DesAutels blurted out.

Kindler looked at him. "Phil. I'm shocked. This is America, you lunkhead. You can screw who you want here."

He laughed at his own joke, pulled out a pen and what turned out to be a gas station receipt, and wrote on it, handing it to Elizabeth. "That's her address, near as I can figure. It's probably an apartment building, and I didn't get a number, so you'll have to ask around, but that should do it."

He lifted the remains of the pretzel as he popped open the door and prepared to leave. "I steal this?"

"Go for it, Pete," she said, reading the note. "And thanks for the help."

Joe echoed that as Kindler slipped out and slammed the door behind him.

Elizabeth addressed her remaining passengers: "It's not far from here, surprise, surprise. We can roust her now, or wait till tomorrow. Preferences?"

"You good with now?" Joe asked in turn, seeing Lester shrug.

Elizabeth put the SUV into gear. "Hi-yo, Silver."

Frank Niles got back into the car, removed his sunglasses and the goatee/mustache combination that he favored over the beard he'd worn at the museum, and tossed his ball cap onto the back seat. He rubbed his face with both hands. "Hate the way that itches."

"You get a line on her?" Neil asked.

"Got an address," Frank told him, starting the engine. "Amazing what's available at your local library. Course, it's handy when you're named Nancy Filson and not Jane Smith. But I can see why librarians are calling themselves information technologists nowadays. Makes them sound like the CIA, but they ain't wrong."

Neil wasn't interested. "She live near here?"

"Yeah. South Winooski Ave. Just across town." Frank leaned toward the dash and punched an address into the car's GPS unit.

Neil checked his watch. "You think she'll be there?"

Frank pulled into traffic. "Beats me. She didn't show up at work, and the woman on the phone said she was supposed to. So, either she's sick or she hit the road."

"'Cause of us?"

Frank grinned. "I hope so. I like to think I'm a scary guy."

"The other broad tipped her off—Corcoran?"

"That surprise you?" Frank asked, his eyes on the road. He always drove with two hands on the wheel, never broke the speed limit, always signaled his lane changes, and regularly checked that all his car lights functioned, even if it was a rental. He was not a man to make it easy for a patrol car to pull him over.

"I thought you told me she barely knew this one."

"Everybody lies, Neil. Haven't you heard that? All the cops know it. I'm not saying Corcoran necessarily called Filson, but it's a small town, they work for the same college, and are in kind of the same discipline, more or less. Stands to reason they know each other. I'm betting old Sandy kept her cool about telling me how buddy-buddy she was with Nancy. Gutsier than I thought she was."

Neil wasn't so admiring. On his own, he would have returned to Corcoran's house and exhibited his irritation. Not that it would have been necessary, since he wouldn't have left her alive in the first place.

Still, Frank was the boss, and while he may have been the weirdest guy Neil had ever worked with, he was also the most successful and the most generous—not a bad combination in a line of work renowned for its generally poor benefits. Neil would put up with a difference in style for that.

Burlington is the largest city in the state, numbering roughly forty-two thousand people, and surrounded by a metro area containing a third of Vermont's entire population. But it retains some aspects of a close-knit community, at least within its tree-shaded neighborhoods. South Winooski Avenue captured that mixed identity well, with dozens of homes looking straight out of a Rockwell painting, while located on a heavily traveled connector road between downtown and South Burlington's commercial Route 7.

The worst of that traffic was understandably at the end of the business day, however, and it was far from that now. As a result, Frank took his time both scanning the numbers on the houses, and circling the block twice to analyze the lay of the land. Eventually, he found an available parking spot almost directly opposite Nancy Filson's address.

Both men got out and looked around, flipping up their collars and lowering their hats. The snow had held off, but it was cold and gray, and the radio had warned of precipitation in the forecast. Their sunglasses were not against the sun.

Frank joined his partner on the sidewalk. "Might as well try the easy way first. You never know. Maybe she is home, sick."

Neil merely nodded and started toward the entrance of an odd-looking, white-painted brick building. "Looks like the Alamo turned into a college dorm," he appraised.

Frank laughed outright, surprised and impressed. "Very good, Neil. I like it."

It was a three-story structure, seemingly designed by a committee of architecture historians, with four or five distinct and conflicting styles

stuck to four ugly walls and crowned with a row of rounded crenella-
tions.

"What floor?" Neil asked, in the lead and heading for a central
doorway equipped with several mailboxes.

"First," Frank answered, eyeing the windows ahead of them for
movement. He saw none.

Thankfully for their purposes, the door opened without resistance
onto a shared lobby and a staircase, allowing them to leave the exposed
sidewalk. Unlocked doors were not a given in Vermont, but still surprisingly common.

There was only one oak door on the ground floor, labeled FILSON.
Without hesitation, Frank rang the bell, which they heard faintly through
the thick wood.

It was to no avail. After several attempts, Neil asked in a low voice,
"Now what?"

"We break in," Frank said simply. "Best way of finding her is to toss
her stuff."

"Not through that, we don't," Neil countered, indicating the door.

Frank agreed. "Wouldn't want to anyhow. Too much noise and too
much risk of being interrupted." He looked around and followed the
hallway beside the staircase to the back of the building. There, they
found a rear entrance. He pushed it open and brought them into a rear
alleyway lined with trash cans and shielded from view by shrubs and
trees.

Frank looked up at the wall above them, again scanning the windows.
But here, most were small and covered with pebbled glass, indicating a
preponderance of bathrooms.

He nodded with satisfaction, walked over to the nearest window associated with the Filson apartment, checked to see if it was locked and,
without pause, extracted a glass cutter from an inner pocket and ex-
pertly sliced four lines to form a box. He then donned a glove, punched

at the window sharply, and saw a neat hole appear before them, accompanied by the barely audible tinkling of the glass breaking on the floor within.

They waited a full minute for a response from any quarter, at once calm and fully attentive, before Frank reached into the hole, flipped the window's lock, and pushed the unit open to gain them access. They were inside the apartment in less than a minute.

The interior made a lie of the building's bizarre outer shell, and encouraged Frank to think that perhaps the people responsible for its design had merely been more interested in the living spaces. Nancy Filson's apartment—as Frank thought appropriate for a college professor— was open, airy, nicely furnished, and adorned with countless playful and attractive architectural details that made of the whole place a hidden jewel of a home.

As even Neil put it admiringly, "Holy crap. Not bad."

Slipping on latex gloves, they started by checking that they were alone, and then, room by room, began their specialized archeological search.

Most people's homes reflect their owner's tastes, enthusiasms, personal habits, sexual orientation, living arrangements, and even background and education. In the choice of decorations, the equipping of kitchens, the cleanliness of bathrooms, and many other indices, people mark where they live with their personalities, their passions, and the things they choose not to have, like books or exercise equipment or music CDs. They also salt every room with their histories, from the arcane— such as cherished mementos whose meanings are obscure—to the obvious, such as address books and computers.

Frank and Neil were on the hunt for it all. They paid heed to everything in Nancy's private environment, from the vibrator beside her bed to the family photos lining the hallway to the styles of clothing and shoes in her closet. They also noted what wasn't there—the empty slot alongside two suitcases, the suspiciously clean rectangle on her desktop—the size of a computer base—and the way her nonbusiness attire had been picked from, leaving telling gaps behind.

To these two veteran searchers, all were signs of a hurried departure for a destination in which some element of rough or casual living played a part.

The next challenge became determining that destination, which they set about doing with the same perseverance. Files were gone through, the trash rifled, drawers checked for letters, postcards, and documents, and books opened for personal inscriptions. The phone's memory was read for recent incoming calls. Even photographs were removed from their frames so the backs could be checked for legends.

By the end of it, two hours later, they sat down comfortably in their borrowed living room, still wearing gloves but enjoying a couple of microbrewery beers from the fridge, and compared notes.

"So, what I got," Frank began, "is a middle-aged single woman with no kids, no boyfriend, and a life consisting of her job, her sports—which include swimming, sailing, hiking, skiing, and tennis—her friends, and a fondness for French cooking. Although from the pictures I've seen, she either doesn't eat much or works it all off."

"She was married once," Neil said tersely.

Frank raised his eyebrows.

"Divorce papers," Neil explained. "Other legal stuff, too. They stuck it out for six years."

"Any mention of other property in that paperwork?" Frank asked.

"Like a weekend place? Nope."

Frank pushed his lips out slightly, muttering, "That would be too easy." He took a swig of beer and crossed his legs. "You think maybe she and the ex got along well enough that she'd camp out with him in a crisis?"

Neil smiled. "Beats me. Depends on how big a crisis we are."

Frank nodded. "Good point. We have no idea, do we? Corcoran claimed to barely know the woman, although"—he leaned forward to hold up a photo—"here we have a picture of them, arm in arm. So, let's say old Sandy called her right after we left and told her the Big Bad Wolf was comin' around. What do you do as Nancy?"

"Me? I call the cops, just like Corcoran probably did." Neil added, since he couldn't resist, "Which is why I wanted to kill her."

"Right," Frank agreed dismissively, "but we don't think Nancy did that, do we? We checked for surveillance before we parked out front. As a cop, wouldn't you stake this out as the perfect place to nab us? I would."

Neil remained silent this time, knowing better than to chime in. Frank was at it again.

"That being said," Frank continued, "I think she's playing ball with her friend, but only up to a point. She grabs her computer and work stuff, she takes a couple of days' vacation from the office, and she lies low without making a big fuss about it."

"And she keeps in touch with Corcoran by phone," Neil threw in.

"Nice," Frank agreed. "Which, if she does, lessens the probability that she'll call the police, since she's got Sandy doing that already, and it allows her to put the whole thing behind her faster.

"Because," he emphasized, holding his finger up, "we don't represent much of a threat to Nancy. This is Sandy's deal, and while what she told Nancy is alarming, it's not the end of the world. As far as Nancy's concerned, we're a disembodied threat. We'll go away with time, like a bad dream."

Neil disagreed, but as he often did in such cases, remained quiet, waiting.

"Okay," Frank went on, as if his partner had concurred. "That then suggests a different possible scenario, more psychologically nuanced: Maybe Nancy has cut off communications with Sandy, making it appear as if she's following her pal's orders to disappear, but in fact because she thinks Sandy's a pain and wants to put some distance between them. It's a colder version, but—" And here he waved his hand to include their surroundings. "—I think we've discovered this woman is way stronger than her friend-who-lives-with-mom."

He widened his eyes inquiringly at Neil, asking, "What d'ya think?"

Neil finished his beer and slipped the bottle into his pocket, so that it would leave the premises with him—along with his DNA. "What I think," he replied, "is that half the time, I don't know what the fuck you're saying."

Frank smiled, proud of the way he could use language. "No problem. Let me put it to you this way: You're Nancy; you're a little worried—at least, you don't want to be stupid. You have some time off due from the job, along with a little homework you wouldn't mind doing quietly in a corner, and you want to throw your friend Sandy a bone. Question is: Where is that quiet corner? Where do you go to drop out of sight but not deprive yourself of the daily comforts?"

Frank wasn't expecting Neil to respond. He usually didn't during these sessions. But Neil surprised him by bending over the scattered items on the coffee table between them and extracting a photograph that he'd removed from its frame earlier.

He held it up so that Frank could see a smiling couple posed before a handsome log cabin surrounded by trees. "You go visit Mums and Pops," he said. He flipped it around and showed what was scrawled across its back, quoting, "'We always have a room for our sweetheart, in our hearts and in our home.'"

Frank reached out for the picture and studied it and the handwritten sentiment. "I like it," he said softly. "I like it a lot." He replaced the photograph on the tabletop and looked at Neil. "Do we know where this room and these hearts might be?"

Neil smiled. "We do. They bought the place about a year ago, and mailed her directions. She had 'em filed under 'Mums and Pops.'"

Frank raised his beer bottle to his colleague. "Here's to the compulsively organized."

"There is one thing, Frank," Neil felt obliged to mention.

Frank was halfway to his feet, ready to wrap things up. "What's that?"

"I know how crazy you are about playing Russian roulette, and how you don't give a rat's ass about what happens to me, but don't you think we ought to head out? I mean, you could be right about Filson not calling the cops, but Sandy sure as hell did. Why wouldn't they be beatin' feet here right now?"

Frank laughed, always cool under pressure. "I would be if I were them. Really wanna go? Okay, but let's mess with their heads a little, and remove the more helpful items."

Neil made a face as he also stood. Much as it was thrilling to watch Frank skip rope along the cliff top, the bitch was that the two of them were tied together—not so great if Frank went over the edge.

CHAPTER ELEVEN

Sam waited patiently by the car as Willy stood on the sidewalk, slowly scanning the neighborhood—cars, windows, doorways, trees. He did it almost every time they arrived anywhere. She didn't fault him. It reflected his complicated history, and was further supported by the disability that he owed to a marksman's bullet. Plus, she knew his caution protected her as well.

"All set?" she asked after he was done.

"I know people think I'm nuts," he said as they walked toward Nancy Filson's apartment house. "And most of the time, I'm happy to agree with 'em." He glanced up at the building's ugly façade and shook his head slightly, adding, "But this time, I just got that feeling somebody was watching. Gave me the creeps."

"You got good instincts," she told him. "I wasn't criticizing."

They entered the hallway and stood to either side of Filson's door before Willy pressed the bell while he looked up the staircase and down the hallway toward the back of the building.

There was no answer.

"Too bad we don't have a warrant," she said.

"Too bad we never had a chance in hell of getting one," he replied sourly. "At least in this Goddamn state."

She didn't respond. Every cop bitched about the liberal laws of Vermont. To her, the restrictions didn't mean much. It was what it was.

"What's our next move?" she asked him.

He shifted to the foot of the stairs. "We're not done with the first one yet," he answered, and headed up.

The second floor was like the first—a single apartment door and, instead of a rear entrance, a custodian's closet. For the size and appearance of the overall structure, this was a little surprising. It meant that the triple-storied building had only three residents. Each apartment had to be enormous.

Willy's pounding on the door here resulted in a bright-eyed elderly woman opening up. "Yes?" she asked.

Both cops showed their credentials as Willy said, "Police, ma'am. We're trying to locate Nancy Filson."

The woman looked surprised. "She's not home?"

Willy was about to answer in his usual style when Sammie quickly intervened. "No, ma'am. We just tried her bell."

"Well," she said, "she must have stepped out, then. I know she was there. I heard her just a while ago. I thought she might be cleaning. She does that quite a bit. Very neat girl."

"How long ago?" Willy asked.

"That she stepped out? I wouldn't know."

"No," Sammie spoke again. "How long since whatever it was you heard?"

"Oh. Not ten minutes. That's why I was surprised that you missed her."

Willy was already heading back downstairs.

"Thanks," Sammie spoke over her shoulder, following him. "We may check it out, just to be sure."

"Is she all right?" the woman asked. But neither cop answered her.

Willy headed directly to the back door and out into the alleyway. There, he turned and looked straight at a window with a square hole punched out of it.

"I knew it," he growled. He pointed at the hole. "That exigent circumstances enough for you?"

"Yup," Sammie replied.

Inside the apartment, they took in the disarray of the large living room and—visible through the nearest doorway—the pictures and files scattered about, the drawers hanging open, the closets emptied. Willy made to advance when Sammie grabbed his right arm. "They may've left prints, other trace."

He kept going. "Not these guys, and we're gonna find out just how good and fast they are if we fuck around waiting for a bunch of lab rats to tell us what we already know: They don't screw up. We need to find out what they know and head 'em off at the pass." He stopped abruptly to face her, indicating the surrounding mess. "Because," he continued, "I guarantee that they got something out of this, and they've gone for it like dogs after a rabbit."

"If that's true, you think what they discovered is still here for us to find?" she asked him.

"I doubt it," he replied. "But I got an idea." He walked past her back out into the corridor and took the stairs up two at a time.

The woman was still home. "Did you find her?" she asked through her half-opened door.

"No, ma'am," he said as Sammie joined them. "What's your name?"

"It certainly isn't 'ma'am,'" she said with a slight smile. "But you didn't give me much time to tell you that earlier. It's Millicent Jarvis."

"Yeah," he apologized, "sorry 'bout that. But we're in a real hurry."

"So, Nancy is in trouble."

"Not trouble, Ms. Jarvis," Sam corrected her. "We're trying to help her out."

"Of course."

"If she was to go anywhere," Willy proposed, "like somewhere off the beaten track, where do you think she'd go? A particular friend, maybe? Or a family member?"

Jarvis didn't hesitate. "Her parents. They're very close. I'm afraid I don't know their names. She just called them Mums and Pops. Not very useful."

"Do you know where they live?"

She frowned. "No, I'm sorry. It's supposed to be beautiful. Nancy's spoken of it that way, which made me think it was out in the countryside somewhere. And I believe they moved there recently."

"You think it was in Vermont?"

"Yes, but I'm not sure why I say that."

Once again, Willy was backing toward the stairs. "Okay. Got it. Thanks."

Millicent Jarvis reached out and touched Sam on the forearm. "He's a little high-strung, isn't he?"

Sam laughed and followed Willy's lead.

Back in Filson's apartment, Willy was dialing his cell phone.

"Going for her phone records?" Sam asked.

He nodded. "Not just. I'm puttin' out that we better muckle onto Rachel Reiling, too. The way things're going, we may not be able to stop these two before they figure out she's the one they're after." Someone came on the line and he began talking. Sam left him to it and began exploring Nancy's home, hoping Willy was wrong and that their predecessors here had left something relevant behind.

But she wasn't confident. He had a good instinct for these things, especially about bad people.

. . .

Tausha Greenblott was not pleased to see them. "What the fuck do you want?"

Elizabeth McLarney opened her coat wide enough to show the badge clipped to her belt. "Don't be nasty. We just wanna talk."

"What about? I know my rights."

Phil pushed by her and entered her apartment uninvited, saying in a low voice, "Like we care."

"*Hey!*" Tausha yelled at him. "You can't do that."

"We can if we're not here to arrest you," Elizabeth said, looking around the dark, shabby space like a disappointed Realtor. "Take it as a good sign. Wow. I thought *I* lived in a dump."

Joe and Les exchanged glances over their colleagues' aggressiveness and walked in as well, as Tausha complained, "Fuck you. This is my home. You're not allowed in here."

"You got anything to drink?" Phil asked, going to each door off the living room–kitchenette and glancing inside the bedroom, the bathroom, and the sole closet to make sure they were alone.

"Up yours," their hostess said resignedly, and flopped down in an armchair covered with an old, patched blanket.

Elizabeth chose a hard-back chair from near the kitchenette's card table, twisting it around so that she could rest her arms on its back as she addressed Greenblott conversationally. "So, Tausha. Tell us about Tommy."

"Who?"

Elizabeth laughed. "There is nobody in the whole city who doesn't know somebody named Tommy—it's right up there with Bob. But you say, 'Who?' like I'd asked you about Rumpelstiltskin."

She moved the chair closer, so that Greenblott had to shift her knees to avoid being rapped by it. "Where's Tommy Bajek, Tausha?" she asked, her face suddenly hard.

"I don't know," Tausha conceded with a pout.

"He dump you?" Phil asked, still wandering around, looking at her possessions.

"Screw you," she spat at him. "More like the opposite."

"You broke up?" Elizabeth asked.

Tausha's anger shifted briefly to a look of hurt. "That's bull."

"We heard he went up north on a job," Elizabeth suggested.

"For good pay," Joe added quietly.

"Yeah," Elizabeth picked up. "Money that might've helped you get out of this hole."

"Or at least kept you in dope for a month," Phil contributed from his less hopeful view of reality.

Surprisingly, Greenblott didn't have a comeback. She merely sat sprawled in the chair, looking deflated.

Joe took that as a good sign, at least for them. Since McLarney didn't seem to mind other people chiming in, he said, "Tausha? We've got bad news. Tommy's not going to come back."

She looked up at him. "You locked him up?"

"I wish we had," Elizabeth said, matching Joe's tone. "It might've saved his life."

Tausha drew her knees up to her chest. She wrapped her arms around her shins and buried her face until she was curled into a tight ball. Her muffled wailing was the only sound in the room.

Phil looked bored and moved to the room's one window to look out. He made Joe think of how some outsiders inaccurately viewed Willy Kunkle, writing him off as callous and uncaring. Only here, Joe sensed that the caricature was more accurate.

As if setting a contrast to her partner, Elizabeth turned her chair around and sat so that her hands rested on Tausha's feet as she spoke. "I'm really sorry. I know you had a thing going—dreams you shared."

Joe was suddenly struck by something in the girl's reaction, combined with aspects of her appearance that he'd overlooked until then—in particular, her loose clothing. He crouched by her chair and joined Elizabeth by asking, "When's the baby due?"

It could have gone either way—not that they had much to lose. But she looked up at him tearfully and admitted, "Four months."

"I'm so sorry," he sympathized.

"What happened?" she asked meekly.

"You know the people he was with," Elizabeth said. "You can guess what happened."

Tausha's eyes widened. "I never met them. Tommy just came home and told me about them."

"What did he say?" Joe asked.

"That he'd hit it big. That if this went good, he'd be part of a team and pull in regular work."

"Did he mention names?"

"No," she said, drawing the word out in a moan.

"What did he make them sound like?" Elizabeth asked.

"Just this guy and his partner. He didn't say who he was. He even joked and told me to call him Mr. X. It was stupid, but he said the guy was real private. That's what made him so good. And that the two of them only used special people, once in a while, and that Mr. X treated them super good."

"It was a test, then?" Joe asked. "Like an entrance exam?"

"Yeah, yeah. Like that."

"And what was the test?"

"They had to go up north somewhere. Talk to a guy—that's what Tommy said: 'Talk to a guy.' I mean, I know he meant other stuff, but he didn't say."

"When did you last hear from Tommy?" Elizabeth wanted to know.

She looked confused. "I don't remember. A while ago. He said they'd be unreachable. I asked him what the fuck that meant, and he said he couldn't call from the road. I been waiting ever since."

She scowled suddenly and demanded, "What's gonna happen to me? I'm totally up a creek now. Goddamned Tommy. I thought he'd dumped me, the bastard."

Joe took her hand. "He didn't, Tausha. He was working for you. Help us set this thing right. How did Tommy hear about Mr. X? He didn't know him before he was hired, did he? Meaning somebody introduced them?"

"Yeah," she said, but her voice revealed her growing lack of interest. The truth of her situation was beginning to take hold, and their concern with Tommy's fate at the hands of Mr. X was fading in comparison with her own predicament.

"Who was it who put Tommy together with Mr. X, Tausha?" Elizabeth asked.

"I don't know," she said. "I think maybe Jarek."

"Jarek who?"

Tausha blinked and looked at them as if she'd been awakened from a dream. "I want you to leave. You're trespassing."

"Jarek who, Tausha?"

She jerked her feet away and struggled to sit up, putting her hands on the arms of the chair. Elizabeth pulled back and Joe quickly took Tausha's elbow to help her up, muttering, "Steady. Wait for the feeling to come back to your legs."

He shifted his position to cut her view off from the others, putting his face close to hers and smiling sympathetically. "You gonna be okay? Do you have any family or friends to help you out?"

She blinked at him a moment before asking, "Who are you?"

"Joe," he said. "I'm from Vermont. I found Tommy."

Her face slackened at the reminder. "Oh."

He took one last shot: "What's Jarek's last name, Tausha, and we'll be out of your hair."

"Sroka. Get out."

Joe glanced at Elizabeth, who nodded. They left.

Nancy laughed at her mother's doubtful expression. "Trust me, Mums. I've done it before. It works like a magic trick."

"The magic'll be if we end up with any salad at all," the older woman said skeptically.

Nancy seized the head of iceberg lettuce firmly and smacked it forcefully down onto the carving board's surface, separating the core from the surrounding leaves and presenting a perfectly symmetrical globe.

Her mother marveled, "Well, I'll be darned."

"What're you two doing in here?" a male voice asked from the kitchen door. "Sounds like you're swatting each other."

Nancy turned to her father. "You think you're kidding, Pops, but that's something else I just learned: You know that sound you hear in the older movies when someone punches somebody else? Well, they used to make that noise by smashing a head of this stuff." She held up the lettuce.

"Oh, honey," Mums said, taking it from her daughter in order to prepare it for dinner. "That's too much."

"Like they used coconut shells for horse hooves," her father added, rhythmically slapping his open hands against his thighs in parody.

"Right," Nancy agreed. "You heard about that one, didn't you, Mums?"

Her mother was chopping the lettuce as she spoke. "I suppose I did. And something about a nail being dragged across a sheet of glass to make screechy sounds. I remember seeing those scary movies as a young woman." She glanced at her husband. "Hank, you used to take me to those so I would hold your hand."

He laughed. "You held more than that. I thought you'd leave bruises a couple of times."

"Oh," she protested. "It wasn't that bad."

"Where's Jackson?" Nancy suddenly asked, holding a slice of sausage she'd cut up for the spaghetti sauce they were fixing.

"I let him out," her father said. "A half hour ago. He should come back in. It's getting late."

"I'll get him," Nancy volunteered, handing Pops the knife she'd been using. "You finish up."

Wiping her hands on the apron around her waist, Nancy went to the kitchen door and stepped out onto the back deck, closing the door behind her to keep the heat in. St. Johnsbury was located in Vermont's northeast quadrant, just over an hour below the Canadian border. What might have been deemed "a little nippy" elsewhere in the state at this time of year was downright cold here.

Nancy wrapped her arms around her chest as she whistled into the dark, also calling out Jackson's name. He was an old retriever—steady, loyal, and no longer very adventurous. Normally when he was let out, he wandered no more than twenty feet from the house and lay down.

Tonight, he was nowhere to be seen.

Having anticipated a twenty-second excursion, Nancy was by now getting quite cold. Adding to her discomfort was something beyond concern for the welfare of the family dog. In the silent darkness opposing her, on an overcast and moonless night, she couldn't shake the chilling notion of some menace lurking.

As she turned to reenter the house, she thought again of the reason she'd come to spend a few days with her parents, and considered the man that Sandy Corcoran had warned her about.

She paused with her hand on the doorknob, and instinctively glanced over her shoulder, as if the mere thought of the threat would project a light into the night and cancel all cause for worry.

But once more, she saw nothing, and continued into the house.

A hundred yards from the deck, hidden by that very darkness—a dead dog at his feet and Neil by his side—Frank Niles stood by a tree with a pair of binoculars in his hands, through which he'd been studying Nancy's range of emotions.

"You got it, girl," he barely whispered. "Trouble's about to come knockin'."

CHAPTER TWELVE

The room Willy and Sam entered was filled with police officers in tactical gear, their bodies bulked out with armored vests and equipment, their faces watchful, their uniforms reflecting not just the St. Johnsbury PD, but the state police and county sheriff's department, as well.

"People," their host, the chief, announced, "These are VBI Agents Martens and Kunkle. This may be their show, and it may be the St. J PD's turf, but all of us are responsible for the final outcome. You will all act as if you are the lead here. More importantly, there will be no mention of it to anybody afterwards. This is considered a covert op. We will all rise or fall with the honor and integrity of every one of you on these points. Do I have your attention on that?"

Sam glanced at Willy, wondering about a sarcastic one-liner, but her partner's expression remained inscrutable despite the theatrical overtones of the speech.

The chief turned to Sammie. "Agent Martens, they're all yours."

Sam walked to a wall map of the town and its immediate environs, paused for a moment to get her bearings, and pointed to a spot not far from the center of St. Johnsbury before facing her audience. "This is the location of the residence of Henry and Abigail Filson, parents of Nancy Filson. We have intel that Nancy is staying here to avoid a couple of men who are threatening to do her bodily injury. Without going into details of an ongoing case, what you need to know is that these two men—who have occasionally employed others to help them—are armed, dangerous, and from out of state. The last three jobs they've pulled involved the torture/murder of a woman in Philadelphia, the likely killing of a man in southern Vermont, and the terrorizing of another woman outside Burlington. That's why the chief just told you that there's an informational lid on this operation. If any of this leaked out, we'd have every news outfit in the state down our necks."

She stepped away from the map to look at them more directly. "These men are lethal. They don't make mistakes; they don't get excited; and if one of their team gets in trouble, they just walk away. Make no assumptions that they'll be like anybody we bump into regularly in Vermont. These boys are pros."

One of the men in the group spoke up. "Can you brief us on what we're doing?"

"Time is of the essence," Sam said. "They want information, and they're torturing people to get it—basically going up rung by rung until they find what they're after. Our job is to break that ladder at the Filsons'. We will brief you on our planned approach and move out ASAP to make it happen. There is a good chance that things are in motion as we speak, so we have no time to waste."

She returned to the map and gestured to their host. "The chief and I will tell you how and who we're deploying, so listen up. This is gonna move fast."

A similar, if less adrenalized, conversation was occurring in Philadelphia, with Elizabeth McLarney instructing Joe, Phil, and Lester on what she'd learned about Jarek Sroka. "We've obviously moved up from the likes of Tommy Bajek."

Again, they were in the nondescript SUV, pulled over by the curb. "Sroka," she continued, "is a lieutenant, if you want to call him that— richer, more dangerous, better connected, and with people at his disposal. He's responsible to his own bosses, but he's got turf and autonomy. As long as he keeps his nose clean and meets the expectations of the higher-ups, he can pretty much do as he likes."

"Easy to talk to?" Lester wanted to know.

"Yes and no," Phil contributed. "The rules of engagement get trickier as you move up the ranks. It sort of depends on the question and who's asking it."

"True 'nuff," Elizabeth agreed. "Which is why, as with Pete Kindler, we're meeting another of our people who hangs out with this crowd, and who might be able to get us a one-on-one. Unlike before, this'll be more like a business meet. No barroom loose lips this time."

"It'll either happen or not," Phil threw in unnecessarily, "depending on Sroka's mood."

Elizabeth pointed through the windshield to a man in a long woolen coat and a cashmere scarf, who was strolling toward them like a suburbanite taking in the sights—except that the sights were no better than they'd been throughout this trip, Port Richmond being a far cry from Center City's historic district. "Here he comes."

The man openly stopped by Elizabeth's window and rested an elbow on the door. "Hey. How're tricks? I heard you were after me."

Elizabeth made the introductions, which her contact—whom she only named Ralph—barely acknowledged. "The Vermonters're lookin' to have a short chat with a mid-level Posse member," she told him.

"With no strings attached," Joe added. "We're trying to identify a couple of people who might not even be connected to the local scene, but who've just done some recruiting."

Ralph looked doubtful. "I guess it can't hurt to ask," he said. "But unless you got something to trade, I wouldn't hold my breath. Who's supposed to know these guys? Maybe he's one of the chatty ones."

"Jarek Sroka," Elizabeth answered.

Ralph straightened and smiled down at her. "That makes it easy. You can talk to him all you want. He's in a coma. And they're saying he'll stay that way."

Joe leaned forward to make eye contact. "Are you kidding me? What happened? Did somebody get to him?"

Ralph considered him without comment for a slow few seconds. "Interesting you should ask," he said finally. "He wasn't the worst-off specimen in the gene pool, so a coma was a surprise. You know something I should?"

"They never even heard about him till an hour ago," Elizabeth said supportively. "We're just following a line of inquiry to help 'em out."

"Well," Ralph said, "you hit a brick wall. Sroka ain't talkin' and his crew's twitchier'n hell, tryin' to figure out if it was Mother Nature or somebody with the right cocktail that conked him out."

"Is there a police investigation, as well?" Lester asked from the back seat.

Ralph raised his eyebrows. "On Sroka? Nope. No sign of foul play, and enough on our plates anyhow. Why make work?"

There was an awkward silence at the finality of the comment, which prompted Ralph to lean in again and ask them all, "That suit you? Anything else I can help you with?"

Elizabeth glanced at Joe, but he shook his head and said, "Guess not, other than to let us know if he comes out of the coma. Thanks for the help. Keep safe."

Ralph pushed away from the car. "Back at ya," he said, and resumed his stroll down the sidewalk.

Elizabeth was still studying Joe's expression. "What're you thinking?" she asked.

"*How* I'm thinking," he told her, "is suspiciously. We've followed this thread all the way to where Sroka might've given us the name or names of whoever hired Tommy and killed Ben Kendall. So far, that 'whoever' has been a careful, unemotional planner—he's left people alone when they posed no real threat, as with Sandy Corcoran, and he's killed only to get information, or to seal a leak."

"As with Jarek Sroka," she finished.

"It may be that some bad habit of Sroka's caught up to him and put him in a coma. But I prefer that our guys came back, once they knew we were tracking them, and put an end to our inquiries. But not—" Joe held up a finger, "by knocking him off outright and stirring up a bee's nest. Instead, by silencing him ambiguously, they've left us with no proof of a crime, and the Posse has nowhere to go for revenge."

"Which to me implies a local connection," Lester suggested.

"Why's that?" Phil asked.

"Why would they care otherwise about disturbing the local Mafia?" Les asked.

The rest of them considered the notion. "I still think they're outsiders," Elizabeth concluded. "Maybe local, but not from the Posse. I don't argue against their knowing to recruit from Posse ranks. I do see your point there."

"It still doesn't get us to who they are," Joe said mournfully. "Maybe Willy and Sam'll have better luck finding that out from the hunted, than we've had chasing the hunters."

"White leader to base."

Willy keyed the mic from the control van they'd parked a half mile from the Filson home. "Base."

"We're in position."

He glanced at the map mounted to the interior wall of what was in fact a converted ambulance. There were three teams, predictably Red, White, and Blue. White was the last to check in, being located at the tree line, west of the large field behind the house. They'd have the most open ground to cover when the time came to close in on the target.

If there was any reason to close in, of course. Their opening gambit was to send in a decoy to knock on the front door under some plausibly innocent pretext, to see if any of this military-style orchestration was needed. For all they knew, the Filsons might be simply watching television, having not seen their daughter in weeks.

Sam and Willy had made a point of not revealing much of their investigation, but in fact, they were here solely on the basis of Nancy Filson's having called her folks often and lately, which suggested that she might have come here to avoid staying in Burlington.

That was it. A far cry from hard evidence.

Willy readied the mic to notify the decoy that it was time to approach the house.

"White leader to base. We may have a problem."

"Go ahead," he replied.

"We found a dead dog at the edge of the woods. He's been shot. The dog collar identifies his owners as the target residence."

"Damn," Willy said under his breath before keying the mic again and saying, "Plan B is now activated. All units go to Plan B. Acknowledge."

All three teams quickly responded, prompting Willy to stare at the map again, imagining them closing in from all three sides, ready to return fire if necessary. He shouted to the driver of the van, "Get rolling. I wanna be there when they hit the door."

As the command vehicle lurched forward, the speakers resonated with radio cross talk between Red, White, and Blue, each of them reporting no movements, sightings, or sounds from the house. For an instant, Willy's mind wandered to Sam, in the Red team, hoping she'd be all right. From childhood, he'd been overly trained by disappointment and deceit. Love had always been, "I knew it," when it came to betrayal or loss. It put him on tenterhooks to be so dependent on Sam and Emma, especially at times like these.

"It's just around the next curve," his driver told him.

"Keep going," he said irritably.

Over the speaker, he heard Red leader report that they'd reached the front door.

"Ring the bell first," he recommended. "They may know nothing about the dog."

The van came to a stop just as Red leader announced, "No response."

Willy threw open the back door and stepped into the cold night air. "Force the door," he called out.

He followed the group of five across the threshold, the fingertips of his extended right hand barely touching the back of Sam's ballistic vest as he tailed her down the central hallway to the modern log cabin's cathedral-ceilinged living room, where they met the other two teams, arriving through other entrances.

"All clear?" he asked in general.

There was a moment's pause as they all looked at each other, some of them quietly securing their weapons. One of the team leaders said, "We found nothing. Nobody."

Sammie had entered the kitchen almost immediately, and now appeared at the doorway, saying, "They were here, and they left in a hurry, obviously against their will."

Willy and several others went to her. She pointed into the kitchen. "There's food on the ground, the fridge was half open, and the spaghetti was still boiling on the stove, although it's mush by now and the water's mostly gone. I turned it off." She indicated a smear on the floor. "I don't think that's tomato sauce by the back door."

Willy gave it an appraising glance. "It doesn't look arterial. More like somebody got mouthy and got handed a split lip."

"A kidnapping?" one of the men asked.

"They weren't running late for a potluck," Willy grumbled, pulling out his cell phone. "I'll update the boss. And we better put out a BOL and order up roadblocks."

CHAPTER THIRTEEN

Beverly Hillstrom was waiting for Joe at the VBI's Burlington office on Cherry Street. He had driven there directly from Philadelphia after receiving Willy's news about the disappearance of the Filson family and catching only a few short hours of sleep.

She gave him a hug as she asked firmly but without anger, "What the hell is going on? Your people grabbed Rachel out of class late yesterday afternoon, supposedly for her own safety, but won't give us an explanation. According to them, *you* have to do that. They told me where you've been, so I didn't call, and they've been very accommodating, but was that entirely necessary?"

He asked the nearest agent, "Where'd you put Rachel Reiling?"

"Down the hall, third door on the right," he was told.

"I could have told you that," Beverly said. "We've been keeping each other company for hours."

Joe wrapped his arm around her waist and escorted her down the hallway, explaining, "I want to tell you both what's happened."

She took advantage of the interlude to assess him quickly. "You look like hell. How was Philadelphia?"

He laughed. "Interesting, and you look terrific, as always."

He turned the doorknob and entered the indicated room to find Rachel sitting by the window, staring out at the overcast morning sky.

Rachel stood as they both entered. "Oh," she said. "Hi."

He waved her back into her seat, positioned another one for Beverly, and sat on the edge of a desk that had been shoved up against the wall. The room was someone's office, complete with family photos and knick-knacks scattered about. He guessed that its occupant was temporarily bunking with a colleague—probably as a courtesy to Joe. The cot in one corner testified that the place had been turned into a bedroom.

"First off," he began, "are you both okay? Have they been feeding you well?"

Beverly resumed her severe tone. "Joe, none of that is of any interest to us. Please explain what's going on."

He did not mince words. "My squad and I, working here and in Philadelphia, have been chasing the men we believe killed Ben. But not just because of that. We also think they're now hunting for some-one who can tell them about Ben's photos, which means you, Rachel, whether they know it yet or not."

"What?" she murmured.

"So far," Joe continued, "several people have been killed and/or ter-rorized, and we think three more have been kidnapped." He stared straight at the young woman. "That's why we're protecting you. As for why we didn't tell you what was going on, or for any other oversights we may have committed, I can only apologize and take full responsibility. Cops are not always great at either sharing information or making people comfortable in times of turmoil. Please accept my apologies for any distress. Their actions were all well intentioned and on my orders, but I took off for Philly pretty abruptly and left a few things hanging. I am sorry."

Rachel was staring at him wide-eyed, but her mother responded,

"That's the least of anyone's worries. What can you say for sure about this threat to Rachel? Why do they care about a college student's project?"

"We don't know why and we don't know who," Joe admitted. "It does seem to have something to do with the photographs, like I said, but we're not sure what. We interviewed Sandy Corcoran, who was questioned by one of these men—there may or may not be two of them—and she said that he wanted to know specifically about the source of the pictures. Not who took them, but the person or persons who brought them to the museum's attention."

"Why?" Beverly repeated.

"We don't know," Joe said. "We can dream up scenarios till the cows come home, but we got nothing to back them up. One of the more obvious possibilities is that the pictures show something these two men think you know about." He pointed at Rachel.

"Was the man who was discovered during the excavation of Ben's house one of these men?" Hillstrom followed up. "Mr. Bajek?"

"Maybe. A hired hand. We traced him back to Philadelphia. We went to his apartment, talked with his girlfriend, and tried to contact the man we believe introduced him to these killers, but there again, all we ended up with are suppositions. We only *think* he may have been hired to help chase Ben down in Vermont, which, after he and Ben both died, *seems* to have led to the murder of Ben's ex-wife—"

"Jenn's dead?" Beverly interrupted.

Joe rubbed his eyes. "That was tactless. Not enough sleep. I shouldn't have told you that way. Yes, she's dead, and it looks like she was questioned beforehand. That's what prompted us to drive down to see if we could get a lead on some of this, since Bajek also came from Philly. But we don't know why she was killed, except that it may have been for the same reason: to discover who had access to the photos."

"But, as far as I know, Jennifer Sisto hadn't been in contact with Ben or the rest of the family in decades," Beverly protested.

"We know that," Joe reminded her. "But these guys may not have. And Bajek's death in that booby trap, combined with Ben suddenly dying of natural causes, probably cranked up everyone's adrenaline and made things uglier—'specially for Jenn."

In the pause that followed that image, Joe tried to bring them back to the issue at hand. "Anyhow, that's why we yanked Rachel from class. If we're right about any of this, we need to keep her safe."

Beverly rose and moved to the door. "I totally agree. Can you show me where the ladies' room is, Joe? We've been cooped up here drinking coffee for quite a while."

"Of course." Joe rose and opened the door, telling Rachel, "We'll be right back."

In the hallway, however, Beverly placed her hand on his arm. "I don't need a bathroom. I need to know what you haven't told us."

He glanced back up the corridor, having spotted a small conference room earlier. "Come with me," he said, steering her by the elbow. "I should've known you'd see a few holes in all that."

As they entered the room, she said, "If these people went as far back as Jenn Sisto, and from that, you concluded that Rachel was in danger, I'd have to be an idiot not to notice a gap or two. Rachel's never even *heard* of Jenn. And I'm also assuming that your euphemism about Jenn's being questioned beforehand means that Jenn was tortured."

He closed the door behind them and conceded, "You're right. They also grabbed Sandy Corcoran and got her to give them Rachel's advisor."

"Nancy Filson?"

"Right."

"They tortured Sandy, too?"

"They only scared her half to death."

"How's Nancy?"

"We don't know. Sandy called and warned her that she might be in trouble, so we think she went to hide out at her parents' home, outside St. Johnsbury. But we aren't sure. The team we sent there found only an empty house, a dead pet dog, and signs that everyone at the house had been forcibly removed."

Beverly's eyes grew round. "Kidnapped?"

"We think so. But again, we don't have much to work with."

"My God," she said. "What could be so important?"

Joe reopened the door. "Let's get Rachel back into the conversation, 'cause I clearly don't know."

They returned to the borrowed office, where they resumed their seats before Joe asked the young woman, "You want to use the facilities, too? Or are you all set?"

"I'm fine," she said.

"Good," he continued. "As you can imagine, your mom and I were chatting outside about what these guys might be after. Have you been able to think of anything, either from your research into the pictures or your conversations with Ben? Anything—no matter how small—might be important."

"I *have* been thinking," Rachel said, almost complaining. "I can't come up with anything. Ben was so . . ." She paused before saying, "Eccentric, you know? So touchy about almost everything, that I couldn't really tell what was important and what was just sort of crazy."

"Early on, you told me that while he finally got comfortable with the documentary, it was a harder sell to get him to support the photo exhibition. What was it about the stills that he objected to? They fall into two distinct categories."

"I couldn't tell," she replied. "I know you'd think it was the Vietnam stuff, what with all the trauma he suffered, but he was much twitchier about the junk he photographed than he was about old war pictures. I told you that he was almost vague about those at first, as if they'd slipped his mind. I know it sounds funny, but when he finally agreed to the show—and to my including the war shots with the others—it was like he could only see them in an artistic way. He never referred to their contents. I asked him a couple of times—things like, 'Wow, that must've been scary,' or 'What's happening here?' but he never answered, beyond maybe an 'I don't remember.' It got to be enough of a thing that I stopped asking."

Joe pressed her for more. "A couple of them look like they were taken at the same time—American soldiers near or at a Vietnamese village. You can see an officer giving orders, maybe men fanning out. Was there any discussion about that? They're the only pictures showing Americans."

The girl was still looking dumbfounded. "No. I never felt those particular ones meant anything special—just that the war in total had been a bad thing."

"Okay," Joe conceded, straightening. "One last question. Then we'll figure out how best to keep you safe and still allow you to have a life. Your mom has shown me the extra pictures you stored at her house. Are there more? For example, how did the college go about reproducing them? I've never seen anything bigger than Ben's original eleven-by-fourteens, but the ones on display are four times that size."

"Normally," Rachel told him, "they'd just print from the negatives, and there was a negative stuck in an envelope on the back of each print. But they decided instead to digitize the process and scan the negs, so it's all on the art department's computer—or at least the ones that caught their eye. I've got the originals of what's in the show, including a few that didn't make the cut."

Joe blinked once, absorbing this detail. "Where?" he asked calmly while feeling a surge of hopefulness.

"In my dorm room," she answered guilelessly.

Joe exchanged glances with Beverly. Without hesitation, she gave him the dorm's name and Rachel's room number, adding in an aside,

"Sweetie? You have your key on you? I think Joe would like to retrieve those."

"If it's okay," Joe threw in to downplay his growing sense of urgency.

"Of course," the girl replied, digging out the key and handing it over.

Joe stood and moved to the door. "I'll be right back. We're almost at the point of tucking you away somewhere more comfortable than this. I just have to do a couple of things first, okay?"

Rachel smiled wearily. "Of course—as long as it's okay with my profs."

"We'll get that covered," he answered without knowing anything of the kind. He walked quickly to the squad room near the front, where he found a haggard Lester Spinney, as ever sporting a lopsided grin.

"Hey, boss. Figured you'd want company."

"Sue must be loving me right now. I thought you were heading home."

"She's cool," Les said simply. "In fact, she's the one who told me to stay with you."

Joe shook his head, appreciating how the dedication of his entire team extended beyond what even he had imagined, and motioned to the agent he'd addressed earlier to join them—a recent state trooper transplant to the VBI named Tom Wilson.

"We need to go to the UVM campus immediately," he said, and repeated the dorm address and room number he'd just received. "If this thing is rolling the way we think it is, Tommy Bajek's friends have either been there or are about to be." He spoke directly to Wilson: "Which means we better round up some backup, too. Tell 'em to meet us there. I'd sooner be safe than sorry, having company where these crazy bastards might suddenly show up."

Wilson set to work as Les and Joe headed out at a trot toward their car, Spinney asking along the way, "Why the dorm? What's there? They after Rachel or something else?"

"Rachel's got some of Ben's photos there—including a few that didn't make her show. It may not be anything, but given that we think these guys are killing people to get those pictures, I figured we'd better get there ASAP."

They'd reached the car. Lester slid into the passenger seat, saying, "Sure. What the hey."

Fifteen minutes later, six of them were gathered around the same car, now parked on campus, near the dorm's out-of-sight loading dock and Dumpster area. Joe, Les, and Tom Wilson had been joined by representatives of the UVM and Burlington police departments.

"We have no reason to think this threat is necessarily alive and well," Joe was explaining. "But no point being foolish. The hope is that we get in there, secure the items we're after, and get out without a hiccup."

Joe looked inquiringly at them all. "That seem reasonable?"

The two uniformed cops keyed their radios to start issuing orders.

"How're we selling this to the public?" Wilson suddenly asked. "If it comes up? We're gonna be pretty visible."

Joe waited for the UVM rep to finish his radio transmission. "You hear that question?" he asked.

The man nodded, replying, "The kids are used to us running around, practicing training exercises or drills."

"Okay," Joe told them all. "When asked, give my name as the contact for any questions." He glanced at Wilson. "Sound good?"

"It'll do."

After another five minutes of coordinating details, they went to their separate assignments—Joe, Les, and Tom Wilson joining a UVM patrolman and heading directly for Rachel's room on the building's third floor.

Much of UVM's student housing is located in a cluster on the south side of Route 2. It doesn't get the attention received by the cen-

tral campus, with its eye-catching, high-end architecture. Most mo-
torists pay little heed to the brick-clad, multi-storied, barracks-like
buildings across the road. Joe was hoping that Wilson's concerns about
attracting attention might be helped by their being on the campus's
fringe.

Also, although Joe had personally set this course of action in
motion—and for good reason, as he saw it—he couldn't avoid feeling
somewhat odd by how mundane everything appeared all around
him. Young adults by the cluster, still enjoying the cold for its novelty,
and not yet oppressed by months of freezing wind and snow, spilled
out of the dorm ahead. They were laughing and without concern on
their way to morning classes, despite many having seen the cops spreading out.

It didn't last. The shared radio channel they were using, which had
been muttering nonstop with the various units announcing their status
and progress, suddenly stopped them in their tracks.

"All units. We have activity on the third floor—" As the four of them
began running upstairs, the interrupted transmission returned with,
"Officers down, officers down. Need assistance."

It was too early. And, Joe realized, he'd been too lax. His presump-
tion had been that backup might come in handy, but he'd tempered the
thought because of the lack of any real threat against Rachel personally.
He was kicking himself now.

"Suspects're coming down the back stairs," the radio announced
frantically.

By now on the second-floor landing, but to the building's front, Joe
ordered half his number to race down the length of the hallway in support of the pursuit team, while Joe and Tom Wilson turned tail and
headed back downstairs in hopes of an interception.

It almost worked. They burst out onto the concrete walk just in time
to see two figures mirror them from the building's far end, sprinting

toward the adjacent parking lot. Tom took off like a jackrabbit, with Joe hot on his heels, yelling at him to be careful and giving a breathless update on his portable radio.

Joe also took note of the suspect in the lead. He seemed to be watching Joe directly, almost calmly, his running gait loose and steady, with a menacing, self-confident air—despite wearing a beard, hat, and dark glasses. The body language suggested that he was calculating his next move.

Joe picked up speed, alarmed by what he was interpreting, trying to catch up to Tom Wilson. "Tom," he called out. "Watch him. He's up to something."

As soon as the words left his mouth—not that Tom had paid them heed—the man in the beard reached under his coat and smoothly extracted a long-barreled weapon that he pointed and fired without a sound at the two of them.

Joe saw the muzzle flash just as he threw himself onto Tom's back, sending them both sprawling as a bullet whined overhead.

"Under the car. Under the car!" Joe yelled, rolling for cover.

But there were no more bullets. The shooter had gotten what he wanted, which was to break their momentum. By the time the two VBI men, guns drawn, returned to their feet and looked out over their barricade, all they saw was the last glimpse of their quarry ducking into a sedan and squealing away toward the Spear Street exit and Route 2 beyond. The other cops exiting the dorm, their weapons ready, slowed their running or stopped altogether, realizing that direct pursuit was out of the question, as was returning fire. The radio in Joe's hand filled with orders to other units to close in on the area, along with a full description of the fleeing car.

"Think they'll get 'em?" Wilson asked, staring intently at where the two men had once been.

"Maybe," Joe replied without confidence, catching his breath. "My guess is that we'll find the car empty, wiped down, and rented out to a John Doe."

Wilson nodded and slowly holstered his weapon. His voice was quieter as he said, eyes averted, "Thanks for saving my butt."

Joe gave his shoulder a soft punch. "Too much paperwork otherwise."

"I didn't see it coming," Tom continued.

Joe waved it away. He looked around at all the cops milling about the parking lot, feeling the cumulative embarrassment rising off them like heat from fresh tar.

"You're in good company," he added quietly.

CHAPTER FOURTEEN

Bill Allard didn't get up or offer to shake hands as Joe entered his office in Waterbury. As the head of the VBI and, technically, Joe's only real boss, he generally treated his field force commander as an equal. Indeed, Joe was senior in terms of years served. But Bill remained the director, appointed by the governor, and as such, on rare occasions felt it necessary to play the role.

Like now.

"What the hell is going on, Joe?" he demanded.

Today, however, he wasn't the only one feeling irritable. Joe sat down uninvited and said shortly, "You've been getting reports."

"This you imitating Willy Kunkle?" Allard asked. "Not a good move. No report I've seen explains why homes are being invaded, families are getting kidnapped, cops are getting shot at, and people are getting killed from here to Philadelphia, all because of a museum show."

Joe opened his mouth to reply. Bill cut him off by waving a sheet of paper in the air. "This says that an unidentified man, fleeing the scene of a break-in, fired a gun in the middle of the UVM campus, in broad daylight, at a cop. That is correct, is it not?"

"I was one of the cops," Joe answered simply.

"Good for you," Bill countered without sympathy. "And do we know where that bullet ended up? In some student across campus, maybe? Or better still, in the windshield of a *Free Press* reporter driving by?"

"There's been nothing reported," Joe said calmly. "It didn't hurt that the guy used a silencer."

"Are they making students that stupid nowadays?"

Joe allowed for the hint of a smile. "Blame it on texting. Kids no longer look up. So far, it's worked."

"What about the two cops that were bushwhacked in the dorm? How're they doing?"

"They were treated and released, one with a stiff neck, the other some bruised ribs. At least they weren't shot at."

Allard remained unamused. "What about everything else? Where's the entire Filson family?"

"We don't know yet."

"Concerned relatives haven't started asking?" His tone was incredulous.

"That *is* the relatives. Nancy's a single child. They all originated from California a long time ago."

"I am seriously pissed off," Bill warned him. "You know who I'm talking about: friends, neighbors, colleagues, whatever. People do not live in isolation anymore—especially normal-sounding people like these. What about Sandy Corcoran? She warned Nancy in the first place. What does she think of her friend suddenly disappearing?"

"Lucky for us," Joe told him, "Sandy told her to disappear. As far as she knows, Nancy took her advice."

"And Hillstrom's daughter," Allard continued. "Where're you going to hide her? And for how long? Her generation no longer breathes without being told to by the Internet; you gonna tell me she hasn't already tweeted her friends about this?"

"Rachel's not that kind of kid. She's on board."

Bill rose from his desk and crossed to the window, where he looked out sightlessly, regaining his poise. Joe stayed quiet, waiting patiently.

Calmer after a few moments, Allard turned and faced him. "All right, break it down for me, and stick mostly to the political and PR ramifications."

Fighting his own exhaustion, Joe thought a moment before responding, and began with: "From the top, Ben Kendall is looking like a natural death stimulated by the stress of an interrogation."

"Sounds like a murder to me."

"True. But the death certificate will read, 'Undetermined.' So, as a topic of media attention, he should slide under the radar."

"What about the other guy you found there?"

"Tommy Bajek is being listed as a Philadelphia bad boy who got caught up in one of Ben's booby traps. Accidental death."

"And he came all the way up to the house of a near recluse in Vermont to do this, why?"

Joe shrugged. "They both hailed from Philly. Who knows? Criminals work in mysterious ways. Right now, we can stare any reporter right in the eye and honestly tell them we don't know. Since Ben's body was called in by the thief, why couldn't that apply to Bajek? That tells the media nothing about what we might be suspecting."

Bill held up a hand to stop him. "Let's stay on that for a moment. Why were you and Spinney down in Philadelphia? I'm talking cover story."

"Same as above," Joe told him. "We were curious about Bajek. We were trying to be thorough, but we hit a brick wall. Chances are that Jennifer Sisto won't even come up in any press conference."

Allard moved on without comment, despite a sour look. "Sandy Corcoran?" He was looking for ready responses here, Joe understood. Fortunately, they could both take comfort from Vermont's media resembling the kinder, gentler journalism of the 1950s more than the current feeding grounds of New York or L.A. Nevertheless, this entire mess was becoming a potential news bonanza by anyone's standard.

"Corcoran's agreed to keep quiet for Nancy's sake," Joe explained. "And as for Nancy and her folks, we've put the confidential word out and enlisted everyone from Fish and Wildlife to the state police to traffic enforcement to keep their eyes open for anything unusual. That's probably the lid that'll blow off first. You're right there. Somebody's gonna wonder where they went."

Allard returned to his desk and sat down heavily. "Who the hell are these guys, Joe? And what're they after?"

"I think they're hired help, but hired to do what, I don't know. The easy assumption is that it has something to do with what's in those photographs, but we've looked at all of them—the old ones and the modern stuff—till we're blue in the face, including the ones we got from Rachel's dorm room. I have made an appointment with a contact who works at Norwich University and who served in Vietnam at the same time as Ben Kendall. But the wrinkle is that the war pictures at the museum number under half a dozen and don't show anything particularly relevant. There are a couple or so shots showing U.S. troops, but they're not really doing anything. Most of the exhibition consists of the close-ups of the hoard in Dummerston. That may be the key to what's not making sense to us: The Vietnam angle is a pure distraction."

Bill stared at him incredulously. "People getting killed over snapshots of a scrap pile? I don't think so."

Joe tilted his head. "We don't know, Bill. And we have to leave that door open till we do. The war was a long time ago, and the people in those pictures are now easily in their sixties. Isn't it likely that something in that supposed junk pile is worth killing for? Plus, the answer we're after can't be in what's already hanging on the wall. That's out in plain view. It must be among the shots that didn't make it in, or in something that Rachel is forgetting she saw or knows."

Allard looked disgusted. "Whatever. What's your plan?"

"There are several. The first is to take each of Kendall's pictures and analyze it down to the smallest detail—including the ones in the show and in Hillstrom's archive, which we've moved to our office. The second is to squirrel away Rachel, and then set up a decoy to see if we can't get these guys to stick their necks out to where we can grab 'em. The third involves the Filson family, of course. We'll keep quietly beating the bushes for any sign of them. That's where the biggest effort will go, and most of the manpower, but I want to keep my team focused on the first two."

Bill had been listening quietly, and now nodded thoughtfully, his earlier irritation replaced by some inner meditation.

"What?" Joe inquired.

"It's like standing in a minefield during an earthquake, wondering which one's going to go off first," he said. "When it does—which you know it will—and we end up on the front page, it won't take long for the rest to blow up like fireworks in a bonfire."

"We've been there before," Joe commented.

"And I hate it every time."

Joe stood up and looked down at his boss sympathetically. "It doesn't have to happen that way. We might get lucky. We just need to tilt the table in our favor."

Bill leaned back and waved toward the door. "Then tilt away, Joe, and best of luck. Needless to say, you get anywhere, be sure to let me know. In the meantime, I'll give you guys all the cover I can."

"You know?" Frank began philosophically. "A guy could get to like a town like this."

He stood before the floor-to-ceiling window of the condo he'd leased overlooking Lake Champlain, enjoying the sight of a cutter slightly north of him, leaving its berth on its way to Port Kent, New York—barely visible on the distant shore. Leasing condos, even for brief periods, whenever they were staying in far-flung towns, had become a more private alternative to a motel room. And much more comfortable.

"You sayin' that 'cause the cops didn't shoot back?" Neil replied. "Call me crazy, but I don't think they like us here." He was sitting in an armchair, facing the large-screen TV and a muted recording of a NASCAR race. "I don't like them, either," he finished, talking to himself.

Frank looked back at him and smiled. "Hey, we're making progress. Don't get negative on me."

Neil's mouth opened as he stared at him. "Making progress? Are you kidding me? They almost got us, Frank. I know you have all this weird shit goin' on about fate and Zen and whatever the hell else, but I'm not nuts about cops breathin' down my neck. This is not cool, and it sure as hell ain't progress."

"I disagree," Frank said conversationally, turning away from the view and taking the armchair beside Neil's. "We know what they're doing, and they think they know what we're doing, which puts the advantage with us."

"Right," Neil agreed facetiously. "I totally get it. *Not.*"

Frank was used to this. Neil's role as a foil was one reason he enjoyed his company. It forced Frank to occasionally think out loud. "Let me lay it out this way," he began. "You get two people sneaking around in a house with no lights, there's a dumb-luck chance that one'll find the other first. On the flip side, if one of them catches sight of the other and sneaks up behind him, then he can not only figure out what's goin' on, but he can either get the drop on the guy, or slip out a side door anytime he wants. That make it clearer?"

Neil did make an attempt. "A little, 'cept we're not sneaking around a house."

"No," agreed Frank. "But we *are* trying to tag Rachel Reiling, thanks to the suddenly talkative Nancy Filson. The cops know that's our goal, since they were heading for Rachel's dorm room at the same time we were, complete with backup. By doing that, they showed us their hand."

Neil was again confused. "Showed their hand? We're the bad guys, Frank. It's their job to catch us. That's no mystery."

"Yes," Frank resumed patiently. "But how? Our all bumping into each other was just bad luck. They were actually there to either stake out the room, or take something out of it, like we wanted to before we were rudely interrupted. Either one tells me they have Rachel in protective custody."

"Okay," Neil said slowly, still trying.

"Well, if you were them, wouldn't you take advantage of seeing the so-called bad guys' cards and set up a decoy to lure them out? To use a different image, it's like Rachel's the cheese and we're the rats and they're gonna try to catch us by putting out a piece of cheese that looks just like her."

"You think they'll dress up a cop for that?"

Frank laughed. "I have no idea, but I'll almost guarantee that we'll somehow be allowed to hear about quote-unquote 'Rachel' being hidden by the cops in such-and-such a location, with them hoping we'll take the bait."

"But we won't, right?" Neil asked.

"Right. We might tease 'em just for fun, but that depends on the setup."

Neil scratched his neck. "Okay, fine. I still don't get why we care. If they're gonna plan a trap and we're not gonna bite, what do we gain?"

"What we gain," Frank told him, his eyes bright, "is that once they think the trap's failed, they'll retreat to consider what to do next. That's when we'll follow them—just as if we'd spotted them in the dark and snuck up behind them."

Neil looked at him, his expression cleared. "But they won't know we're right there, doggin' their heels. That's cool, Frank. You think we can maybe grab the real Rachel that way?"

Frank sat back and crossed his legs contentedly. "I do."

At that same moment, less than a mile away, Joe Gunther also stood at a window, enjoying a far more restricted view of Lake Champlain—in fact, barely a sliver between two of Burlington's downtown buildings. Still, the allure of the water's ever-changing leaden hues, along with its pure enormity, never failed to impress him.

"Special Agent Gunther?"

He turned at the voice—having been told of its owner's arrival at the VBI office—and replied in a neutral tone, "Daniel Reiling?" He approached the man with his hand outstretched. "Glad to meet you."

Beverly Hillstrom's ex-husband was dressed in an upscale lawyer's three-piece, pin-striped version of a uniform, which to Joe seemed ostentatious for a place like Burlington. This was a town that—despite its major-city status—encouraged a more off-the-rack look. Of course, Joe had heard—including from sources other than the man's disaffected ex-wife—that Reiling had the reputation of being a big fish in a small pond. He was very bright, very good at his job, and very successful at attending to the legal needs of Vermont's movers and shakers. This was a man who consciously hobnobbed with the mighty, with no apologies, and had by now earned his place alongside them in both status and income. Gunther had honed a talent over the decades of keeping his body language and expressions neutral, but he was the first to admit that the entitled rich aggravated a prejudice that he'd never bothered explaining to himself.

He was also ill inclined to like anyone who'd ever mistreated Beverly Hillstrom—as this man had by cheating on her before abandoning her and his two daughters.

It actually embarrassed him to be thinking all this as he motioned Reiling to a chair, and made him more mindful to treat the man first and foremost as the father of a young woman in danger.

"I am sorry to be meeting for the first time under these circumstances, Mr. Reiling," Joe therefore began. "Your daughter has been extraordinarily helpful, and we are committed to her safety until we bring this case to a successful conclusion."

Reiling crossed his tailored legs, revealing expensive tasseled loafers, and gave Joe a frown. "Spare me, Special Agent Gunther. I hand out one-liners like that for a living. I want to know precisely what is going on."

Joe ignored the rudeness. "Feel free to call me Joe. We've placed Rachel into a protective setting, based on certain evidence that leads us to believe that she may be in jeopardy."

"As in someone taking a shot at you after rifling through her dorm room? I happen to know about that," he said sarcastically, not returning the courtesy about how to address him. "You take a lot of believing if you're calling that 'certain evidence.' In my language, that constitutes a lethal threat. What are you doing to safeguard my daughter?"

Joe felt his face warm and hoped the reaction wasn't apparent. "We've got her under wraps, Mr. Reiling, with her full understanding and cooperation. And while I know this may be awkward to hear, as part of that protection, we are not releasing the details of the arrangement, even to her parents."

Now it was the attorney's turn to get hot under the collar. The elegant legs untangled as Reiling sat forward. "You can't do that."

"Actually, we can. Your daughter's becoming of age a few weeks ago legally makes her an adult. All we need is her blessing."

"This is bullshit. I bet you told Beverly. You people are always playing favorites in these things. I've seen it before."

Joe had calmed considerably, now that the man's true measure had surfaced. He'd morphed quickly in Joe's mind from being his lover's ex-husband to just another pissed-off member of the public—a creature with which Joe was all too familiar.

"I would recommend that you call your ex-wife," he therefore counseled, "and discuss that with her. You'll find her as ignorant as you, and by her own preference."

Reiling maintained what he hoped, no doubt, was an intimidating expression, but his accompanying silence revealed an underlying hesitance. Joe remained quiet to see what developed.

Reiling took a breath, and his shoulders sagged slightly. "I'm being an asshole," he said softly. "Sorry."

"You're under stress," Joe suggested, relieved. "I'd react poorly if my daughter were being targeted."

Now torn between gratitude and lingering suspicion, Reiling studied Joe before saying, "You're being kind."

"Maybe," Joe admitted. "Which doesn't mean it's not true. I will promise you," he said with more meaning than he guessed Reiling knew, "that your daughter will receive the protection I'd give my own child. This is not routine to me. I can't grant what you asked for just now, but I will give you that much."

The lawyer considered it briefly, as if he had options, before getting to his feet and shaking hands once more. "I'll hold you to that."

The Willy Kunkle part of Joe's brain was tempted to respond, *Whatever*, to match Reiling's own tinny bravura, but instead he kept it to, "I expect nothing less," and escorted him out of the office.

He was still standing in the lobby, reviewing his impressions of the man who'd shared Beverly's life for almost twenty years, when a soft voice asked behind him, "My dad gone?"

He turned to see Rachel standing with the inner door held open in her hand, the look on her face hovering between quizzical and vulnerable.

He ushered her back into the office, surprised by the emotional lurch he felt in his chest at her appearance. "Yeah. Did you want to talk to him? I should've asked."

"I'm fine."

They walked over to a small side room where the squad kept the coffee machine, a microwave, and a fridge.

Joe poured them both coffee. "You two get along?" he asked lightly, guiltily hoping for a negative response.

"Okay," she said. "We're not buddy-buddy. Anne and I aren't important enough."

Joe silently stirred in his usual startling amount of cream and sugar.

"He was never around much," she told him.

Joe stated the obvious as they returned to the room where they were keeping her until they set up alternative quarters. "He was building a pretty big career."

"So was my mom," she said simply.

That was true. Beverly had turned the medical examiner's office into an enviable institution—to the point where she and members of her small staff were often asked to share their methods and practices with other state OCMEs across the country.

"She was home every night," Rachel finished as they reached her door and entered. "Close enough, anyhow."

They sat opposite each other as they had hours earlier, when her mother had been with them.

"Did the guys bring you everything you asked for from your dorm room?" Joe asked. "Clothes, books, iStuff?"

She finished sipping her coffee. "Yes, thank you."

"We've almost set up where you're going to be staying. We're just putting the final touches on the security. I hope today hasn't been too wearing."

She didn't answer, and the makeshift bedroom became awkwardly quiet. Joe considered what to say next.

"I know about you and my mom," she said.

He focused on her face. "I'm sorry?"

She smiled, holding her mug in both hands. "It's okay. I'm happy she's found someone. So's Anne. We talked about it."

Joe rubbed his cheek. "Thanks."

"You're a nice man."

"So are you," he replied, and they both laughed as he tried to cover with, "for a girl, I mean. I mean, a woman. A young woman."

"Thank you," she said. "You're very smooth."

"Enough." He waved at her. "I surrender. But I appreciate the vote of confidence. I'll do everything I can to keep earning it. Your mom totally floats my boat."

CHAPTER FIFTEEN

Norwich University is the nation's oldest private military college, created in Norwich, Vermont, in 1819 as the American Literary, Scientific and Military Academy, and since moved to Northfield. Its founder—Joe always relished this fact—was a local man who'd been thrown out as superintendent of West Point for advocating a citizen soldiery over the aristocratic officer class favored at the time. It was yet another indicator for Joe of his beloved state's stubborn devotion to common sense and pragmatism over trendiness, fashion, or elitism.

But he'd not traveled to this hilly, austerely designed campus to pay homage to tradition. He was here to see Marcus Perry, who, according to Lester, had served with Ben Kendall's outfit in Vietnam and at about the same time. In a team discussion earlier, they'd agreed that interviewing Perry might be a stab in the dark, but better than losing more time searching for other Signal Corps alums farther afield.

Based on every statistic available for similar kidnappings, each hour that passed ate into the Filson family's chances of survival.

Joe parked near the library and began heading uphill on foot toward Jackman Hall, where, during a phone call an hour earlier, he'd been told to meet Perry in his office. Jackman anchored one end of a large, green, rectangular commons that formed the campus's primary parade ground on top of a mesalike hilltop. The parade ground was lined by two severe if photogenic rows of opposing buildings. It was built to impress—and succeeded, if your tastes ran to authoritarian. As Joe trudged nearer to the building blocking the far end, with its columns, cupola, and carillon tower next door, he easily imagined the cadenced display of cadets across the central green expanse, wheeling in lockstep to shouted commands. On the basis of that memory alone, he drifted back in time to his own days at boot camp, and being hectored and disciplined into becoming an integral part of a fighting force.

He finally reached Jackman Hall, passing several cadets who were saluting a professor in passing, and climbed the interior staircase. He came to a large, dark, wooden door labeled COL. PERRY—HISTORY, knocked, and entered without waiting for a response.

The white-haired uniformed man who looked up at him from his desk fixed him with a disapproving stare. "And you are?" he asked.

"Joe Gunther. VBI. We spoke on the phone."

Perry nodded once, stood, and circled the desk to greet Joe as an equal, ushering him into one of two leather guest chairs and taking the other for himself. The office appeared airlifted from central casting, its walls lined with battle flags, portraits of men in uniform, assorted weapons of yore, and boxed awards and medals. Every flat surface was littered with military paraphernalia, from dummy hand grenades to scale models of jeeps, cannon, and even a motorcycle. It was comfortable, lived-in, and as male as an old sleeping lion.

"Thank you for meeting on such short notice," Joe began.

"Not a problem," Perry replied. "I've accommodated the spontaneous all my life. It's part of the job and something I like anyhow. Keeps me on my toes."

"The plaque on your door says 'History'," Joe continued. "That what you do now? Teach history?"

"Not military history, like most people think," Perry explained. "U.S., although I admit that my students don't have much difficulty derailing me into telling war stories when they think I'm getting boring. I get my revenge come exam time. It balances out."

Joe pointed to several decorations and insignia on the wall. "And you were in Vietnam," he said.

"I was. Three tours. You serve?"

Joe nodded. "Not there."

The tone of his response ended further inquiry. Old combatants have an instinct for whether fellow vets want to talk or not. This was clearly a case of the latter.

"You said you had a problem," Perry said instead. "How can I help?"

"My research told me you served in the Signal Corps."

Now Perry nodded. "Yes. It's called COMCAM nowadays, for Combat Camera. Very catchy, and it gives them another acronym to abuse, so who could resist?"

"But the unit's duties were to photograph the war, is that correct?"

"Basically, yes. But it didn't usually consist of taking the fancy portraits we saw in *Life* and *Look* magazines. Those were mostly shot by photojournalists, not that we didn't contribute a few. First and foremost, we were the eyes and ears of theater command. That meant a million pictures of buildings, facilities, roads and railways, basic infrastructure—you name it.

"Not," he added suddenly, Joe thought almost defensively, "that we didn't regularly get our asses shot off. We were supposed to be in the gunfire and we all carried weapons. It was up to us to choose between shooting a picture or a bullet in a crisis, and woe be it for the poor bastard who chose wrong. You'd catch hell from the brass for missing the photograph, and even worse from your buddies for being a shutterbug at the wrong moment. It was tough sometimes."

"Sounds it," Joe said supportively. "Were you permanently assigned to the same unit?"

"Oh, no. They moved us around. That was part of the problem. No time to bond and build trust. We'd get dumped into a bunch who treated us like the plague—our cameras might as well have been beaming a direct signal to Command. It took time to show we were just like them—grunts who could take a beating and watch their backs when it came to it. But we usually weren't given the chance to prove that."

"Did it ever really get bad?" Joe asked, getting closer to why he'd come. "Did the troops ever get pissed off enough to do something?"

"Like a fragging?" Perry countered without hesitation.

"I suppose," Joe hedged slightly, not wanting to move too fast.

"While I was over there, we never lost a man, one way or the other—which I guess is a bit of a miracle. There were close calls, and I won't say that a couple of them might not have been friendly fire situations. Passions can run hot in a combat zone, especially a politically charged one like Nam."

"Did you ever know a man named Benjamin Kendall?" Joe finally asked.

"Slightly," Perry said readily. "I saw him at Fort Meade more than I did in-country. That's where we trained. But we never buddied up. Interesting you should bring him up, though."

"Why's that?"

"He took a bullet and was shipped out. He came the closest to jinxing that stat I gave you a minute ago, about not having lost a guy while I was over there."

"Do you recall the details?" Joe asked.

"Of how he got shot? It wasn't fragging or friendly fire, if that's where you're going. He was part of a patrol. I don't remember where. Somewhere in the Delta, I think. It was the same old story: A platoon comes up on a village, maybe suspected of harboring VC, maybe not. Shots are fired, all hell breaks loose. Kendall caught a bullet in the head." He reflected briefly. "Talk about bad luck. He was the only platoon member hit."

Joe looked at him closely. "Hit, period? Or hit, seriously?"

"Period, as far as I know. The only one. That was pretty common—a low casualty count. Don't get me wrong, it was a pisser of a war—bad to fight, impossible to win, and high casualties overall. But the number of dead compared to other conflicts we've been in, like the two world wars and Korea—I'm talking pure statistics here, involving the years committed versus casualty rate ratio—wasn't as bad as some people think. All I'm saying is that there were many hostile encounters where our casualties numbered in the single digits."

Joe considered what he'd said—and more, how he'd said it—before observing, "What happened to Kendall seems to have left an impression. What's it been? Over forty years? Concerning a man you barely knew? You pegged on his name right off."

Perry's already ruddy complexion darkened. "What're you implying?"

Joe decided to use a little body language, and so stood to be near one of the wall-mounted flags. He looked down at his host. "It's not an implication," he said, hardening his voice. "It's a straight question: Why the instant recall? You may not have known Ben Kendall personally, but you do know something, Colonel."

Perry glanced at his hands and scratched his jaw before responding. "It was a stand-out event for our unit. Ben's injury was a shock, and there were questions."

"What sort of questions?"

He crossed his arms. "We mostly wondered. Ben had a reputation."

"So you did know him more than just in passing."

Perry looked up. "I knew *about* him. A few of us had started carrying second cameras—off the books, officially. The fancy photographers were getting big bucks for their stuff. We were way more in the thick of it than they were, and getting squat—same pay as everybody else and shit from our own people for being Signal Corps. It ticked us off. We started selling shots on the side. The brass didn't care," he emphasized, again as if Joe had said something. "They were dealing with so much other crap—drugs, wholesale theft, smuggling, prostitution . . . murder, even. People have no idea what was going down in those days."

The reviving memories stirred the colonel to rise as well, and stride back and forth across the room as he spoke. "An army of teenage draftees in the middle of a foreign country where, from basic training onward, you've been programmed to think, 'Gook, gook, gook.' Can you imagine? And in the middle of the '60s? The drugs, the rock and roll? These guys were getting shot at and blown up by people they'd been told to hate, didn't understand, and who didn't identify themselves as combatants."

He stopped and held his forehead for a moment, gathering himself. "I'm sorry," he said quietly. "I haven't thought about all that in quite a while."

Joe moved to the windowsill and sat on the ledge. "I do understand."

"Yeah—well, you're one of the few. Everybody else? Damn. Vietnam might as well be the Crimean War, for all they care. I feel like I saw hell on earth. And now?" His chin dropped and he shoved his hands into his pockets. "I don't know. I can't figure out how to put it in perspective."

He cast a look at Joe. "That's why I became a history teacher. I'm either trying to find some anchorage, or maybe I'm just hoping it'll fade away and leave me alone."

"I'm sorry to have churned things up," Joe said. "But I still need to know about Ben."

Perry's tired, creased face turned plaintive. "Why, for Christ's sake? Who gives a good goddamn?"

Joe briefly considered how much to divulge. "I do, Colonel, because Ben's been murdered, and I'm wondering if his time in the military played a role."

Perry's mouth fell open. "Murdered? Recently?"

"Yeah."

The old colonel returned to his chair and sat down heavily. "Jesus. It just never goes away."

Joe stayed where he was. "What can you tell me? You said he had a reputation."

"I told you about how some of us were freelancing, selling shots to the magazines. Ben had something else going. Like I said, this is all secondhand. I wasn't lying about not knowing him. But the word was that he never sold a thing to anybody. He was building an archive."

"Why?"

Perry rotated both hands palms up. "Who knows? Given the times, my bet was it was political. That was the scuttlebutt when he got shot."

"You ever see any of these pictures?"

"No one did that I know of."

"So, an American may have shot him?" Joe asked.

Perry scowled. "Rumors were flying. I heard he was a blackmailer, or an agitator for the peaceniks back home, or that he'd attacked a villager and wouldn't stop until he was shot. Who knew what to think? Most likely, he was doing his job and caught a bullet from some VC running away. But because he was such a weirdo, so wrapped up in himself and isolated, no one would give him that much credit. It had to've been about something underhanded. But what, nobody knew." He sighed. "And now you tell me it's still going on, and that he's been killed because of it."

"We don't know that any of it's connected," Joe tried to make clear, choosing not to disclose that all of Ben's work showed peaceful countryside vistas and gentle portraits of locals. "What happened to him over there changed him forever, so we don't know what he may or may not have gotten into. But somebody needs to be held accountable for his death. I understand that you have no memory about where he was assigned when he was shot, but there have to be ways to find out—"

Perry interrupted him. "I can do that. I still have contacts." He reached over to grab a pad off his desk.

"Can you go further and get me everything you can about him?" Joe persisted. "Reports or summaries about his getting wounded?"

Perry was making notes. "Sure."

Joe rose, returned to the chair, and handed Perry his business card. "I'm sorry to say that time's of the essence. What happened to Ben might happen to others if we don't get a leg up fast. I can't go into details, but the ball's still in motion."

"I understand. I'll get on this as soon as you leave," Perry assured him.

Joe paused before saying, "Colonel, I do apologize for being pushy. But what you're doing could be key."

Perry rested the pad on his lap and sat back in his leather chair. "I hope so. There hasn't been a night that I don't go back there in my dreams. And I'm not talking about the bloodshed, although that was bad enough. I used to think God existed to bring us redemption for times like these—to make it bearable. But after what I saw there, I can't believe He had anything to do with the creation of this terrible world—or at least with creating us."

It struck Joe as an eyebrow-raising statement, especially within the confines of Perry's red-white-and-blue office, and considering the calmness with which it had been made.

Joe rose and placed a hand on his shoulder, at a loss for any comforting response. "Take care, Colonel. I can't thank you enough."

But as he headed back across campus to his car, he only hoped that his thanks wouldn't prove premature. Perry's crisis of faith, as shattering as it had to be for the man himself, mattered little to Joe.

He had less philosophical examples of evil to combat.

CHAPTER SIXTEEN

Later that night, Joe, Lester, Tom Wilson, and Willy gathered around the dining room table of the apartment they'd rented across the landing from Rachel's new home. They were still in Burlington, for convenience, and had taken over the top floor of a four-story building, which they'd rigged with cameras, keypad locks, and other security. Sammie, yielding to the temptations of her hard-won domesticity—and with Joe's encouragement—had opted to go back to Brattleboro to stay with Emma. Where the standard refrain in emergency services was always, "Families first," Joe knew Sam's situation to be trickier—for years almost beyond counting, law enforcement had been her family. Absurd as it might seem to an outsider, therefore, spending time with her daughter could be a real test of loyalty for Sam.

"You really think Marcus Perry can bird dog that kind of information from the army?" Tom asked skeptically.

"He wouldn't have asked him otherwise," Willy answered in Joe's stead.

"I think he can," Joe said more civilly. "He's spent his entire adult life working for the military, in one form or another. Man like that tends to learn the system and keep his contacts updated. I definitely think he'll have better luck than we would."

"Okay," Tom said. "Then what do we do in the meantime?"

"I've been thinking about that," Joe replied. "I even talked to Sam about it."

"Stop right there," Willy cut in. "I can smell another of your harebrained schemes a mile off. You want her to impersonate Little Miss Shutterbug over there." He jerked his thumb in the direction of Rachel's place.

"She had no problem with it."

"Of course she has no problem with it, Joe," Willy said. "She'd jump off a cliff if you suggested it. You know that goddamn well."

Tom looked at both men in alarm, not used to their style with each other.

"It's not really your call to make," Joe said quietly.

"The hell it's not. She's my kid's mother."

"You'd do this in a heartbeat," Lester reminded Willy.

Willy pointed at him angrily. "You stay out of this."

"Except that he's right," Joe said. "And it's not like we're asking Sam to stand in front of a firing squad."

"She doesn't even look like that kid," Willy kept pressing.

"Exactly my point," Joe came back. "We can only use her from a distance—set up an apartment, have her turn lights on and off, move around, just show signs of activity. They do have the same build, and we can fix Sammie's hair."

"It sounds reasonable," Tom suggested.

Willy glared at him, and seemed about to vent all his rage on someone with whom he didn't have to work on a daily basis. Instead, he stood up abruptly and walked over to the kitchen. "You guys are so full of it. Why pick on Sam all the time?"

Joe watched him pretending to fiddle with the coffee machine while not actually pouring himself a cup. "She volunteered," he told him. "I was suggesting one of the Burlington PD's younger officers."

Willy turned away from the machine and stood in the kitchen doorway, his hand against the frame, as if steadying himself. "That figures," he said resignedly. "She is such a tool sometimes."

"She's a good cop, just like you."

Willy shook his head. "She's an asshole, just like me. No wonder we're an item."

Vermont Game Warden Caitlin Holt was working her pickup truck slowly along Lewis Pond Road, north of Route 105 in the state's Northeast Kingdom, under ten miles from the Canadian border. This region was as remote as it gets in New England—a smaller version of Maine's hundreds of square miles of wilderness farther east. Surrounded by mountains, forests, lakes, and ponds, it offered few of the farms, resorts, quaint villages, and sweeping vistas that made Vermont so attractive to outsiders. Here was simply woods, allowing for only the occasional seasonal camp, and known primarily to loggers, hunters, fishermen, and the rare smuggler—the last of whom might be inclined to pursue their trade covertly and heavily armed.

Which is what brought Caitlin to the area. Once every week or so, as part of her routine, she swung up into this abandoned piece of real estate and slowly patrolled its narrow, overgrown roads, trails, and pathways to metaphorically take its pulse. Her efforts were aided by the area's hypersensitivity to the passage of any visitors—and her own ability to spot signs of them. The packed dirt surfaces could hold the telltale traces of ATVs for days, and things like footprints, cigarette butts, beer cans, and abandoned fire pits stood out as they didn't in more populated spots. Caitlin had been in such environs all her life, had hunted here with her father and two brothers throughout her teenage years, and to this day, far preferred the company of trees and wild animals to anything she'd ever met among her own species.

All of which helped her to notice a fresh set of tire tracks stamped on a thin layer of snow coating the edge of an opening to a narrow road just ahead.

She slowed her truck to a stop, resting her hand instinctively on the butt of the .40 in her holster.

She radioed dispatch that she was exiting the vehicle to investigate on foot, and gave her GPS coordinates rather than any physical address—privately thankful that she could do either, given that her predecessors had enjoyed neither good radio coverage nor fancy satellite-linked mapping devices. Times were slightly better than when one of her ilk stood a chance of simply disappearing into the wild during what had begun as a routine patrol.

The tracks belonged to a large vehicle, as broad and heavy as a truck, and had entered and departed the trail, most recently the latter, which heightened her hopefulness that she was still alone. Less comforting, however, was that the signs were fresh. The regular hunting season had concluded weeks earlier, there was no local logging going on that she knew of, and it was becoming far too cold at night for people to be camping recreationally.

She walked alongside the trail, keeping her prints among the underbrush. So far, there had been no indicators to make her specifically wary, but she defaulted to caution by nature, and always tried to leave wherever she was with minimum evidence of having been there.

A half mile along a gentle, uphill curve, Caitlin caught her first glimpse of a cabin tucked deep into the woods like so many of its type. It appeared to be the standard one- or two-room structure, built to last a decade at best, and now probably much older than that. It had a rusty metal stovepipe protruding from its mossy roof, showing no smoke, and a single, small window.

She paused by a tree that matched her dark green uniform, and trained her binoculars on the building—especially on the footprints marring the fresh snowfall on the closed doorway's lip.

"What've you been doin', people?" she whispered, letting the barest wisp of vapor escape from her lips. She remained motionless for ten minutes, studying, before finally easing away from the tree to venture forward, slipping her weapon into her hand.

Her own family's backwoods cabin was substantial, solidly built, and afforded a wide view of a pond and distant mountains. Most of the ones like this—which Caitlin had always considered hovels—had the romantic appeal of an outhouse. Their advantage, however, was that the walls and nearest trees were often at arm's length. As a result, Caitlin managed to keep cover all the way to within a few feet of the front door.

There, she could distinctly see multiple sets of footprints heading inside—and two leaving.

Moving soundlessly, she sidled up to the dark window and attempted to peer inside, half suspecting that all she'd see would be a pair of ragged curtains or a smear of impenetrable grime. Instead, she discerned two bodies sprawled out on the floor, each with one wrist handcuffed to the wall.

She hesitated a moment. She knew she should call dispatch immediately, possibly even retreat and wait for reinforcements.

But that wasn't going to happen. At least one of those bodies belonged to an elderly female, and before her shift, Caitlin had read the law enforcement–only BOL listing an older couple and their daughter as missing.

This was no time to wait.

After a quick tour of the cabin's perimeter—to ensure she was dealing with only one door and a window—she steadied herself behind a tree opposite the entrance and shouted, gun extended, *"Inside the house, this is the police! Come out with your hands in plain view."*

She waited, straining to see or hear anything, before repeating her order—to the continuing accompaniment of only the faint creaking of the trees, far overhead.

Again, she considered retreat, and again rejected it, driven by excitement, determination, and a young officer's too-common fear of calling for help prematurely.

She slowly stepped free of her cover, crossed to the door, breathing quickly and with her gun slightly trembling, and rested her free hand on the knob.

This she turned, fully expecting the sudden explosion of a shotgun or rifle.

What she got instead, as if to mock her apprehension, was the door yielding easily to reveal the two bodies she'd glimpsed, along with the third of a younger woman propped up in a far corner. All three were alone and handcuffed to heavy cleats driven into the wooden walls— and all three appeared dead.

Letting out a relieved puff of air, Caitlin twisted around to see no one outside, sneaking up behind her. She then moved to the side of the first body.

There was a pulse. She pulled out her radio.

"Getting bored, Frank."

"Patience, my man. Just keep your head in the game."

"Got nowhere else to put it. That's my problem. How much longer're we gonna do this?"

"Not much. Sooner than later, they're going to lead us somewhere weird. That's when we'll know."

"Cops go to weird places all the time," Neil argued, his voice sounding thin over Frank's earpiece. "How're we gonna know which weird is *our* weird?"

"Bear with me, Neil," Frank reassured him calmly, adding two seconds later, "Okay, I got another bogey hitting the sidewalk and heading for his car. Tan four-door Ford, the usual oh-so-subtle antenna sticking out of the trunk. Listen up for the plate number."

He rattled it off, turned on his ignition, and slipped into the light Cherry Street traffic driving by the VBI Burlington office, taking position a couple of vehicles behind the Ford. Frank didn't know whom he was tailing—that wasn't important. He only knew the man was VBI, and his fingers were crossed that this time, they'd be led to where Rachel had been tucked away.

"East on Cherry," he announced on his hands-free cell. Neil was in a car one block over, ready to swap positions to lessen the chances that they'd be spotted.

"Roger that."

"South on South Winooski Ave," Frank relayed. "He may be going for Route 2 East and the Interstate."

"Got it."

He was right. The Ford kept wending its way east, until it entered I-89, heading north.

"Neil, take over for me. I'm dropping back."

As the three cars left the on-ramp and picked up speed, Neil passed by and swung in behind their target. Frank allowed half a dozen vehicles to come in between them.

It was well planned. Two exits later, Neil spoke up. "He's signaling, Frank. We're getting off here."

Frank kept his position, buried in traffic. He was able to see the Ford's taillights as it pulled up to the intersection at the bottom of the ramp.

"Goin' right on Route 7," Neil announced.

"I see you." Then Frank was caught by the red light and rolled to a stop, losing sight of the other two.

"Whoa. Hang on," Neil said almost immediately. "Left onto Mountain View."

Frank didn't respond, trying to recall the area from his studying of the map earlier.

"Oh, for Christ's sake," Neil groused, his voice losing its tension. "He's pulling into the Shaw's lot. Shit."

The light turned and Frank headed after them. "That's good. What cop goes grocery shopping in the middle of the day? Could be he's making a supply run for the girl."

"Do I follow him in?"

"No. Keep his car in view. I'll find you. Let me know when he heads back out."

"Got it." Neil's voice sounded happier, if marginally, which was enough for Frank.

"So far, so good," Neil said about fifteen minutes later. "He's comin' out with a couple of bags."

"Paper or plastic?" Frank asked, feeling heartened. They'd been at this—tailing VBI personnel around town—for several days, and it was getting old.

"What?" Neil asked, not much given to humor.

"Nothin'." Frank started his car and waited.

"All right. Headin' out," Neil radioed.

"Turning left, back to Route 7," he then said, and a moment later, "North on 7."

Frank craned to look up through his windshield, trying to locate a familiar chopping sound. He saw a National Guard helicopter pass overhead at an angle, probably aiming for its base at Camp Johnson, near the Burlington airport. He watched it carefully for a moment, wondering, but saw nothing unusual or suspicious. He also took comfort in its being military, knowing that cops and soldiers traditionally don't play well together.

Their small caravan continued toward Colchester, one of the cluster of satellite communities bordering Burlington, until it reached the junction with 2A, where they all veered right. By this time, both Neil and Frank were hanging far back, traffic having thinned considerably.

"You sure that's them?"

Willy didn't bother responding over the chopper's rhythmic chatter. He merely gave his boss a pitying look and returned to studying the traffic below through his binoculars.

Given the man's years of sighting in targets through rifle scopes, Joe was content to take Willy's reaction as a yes. He tapped the pilot on the shoulder and said over the intercom, "Keep going as you would. If you alter your flight pattern, they'll know we're watching. You can start dropping down to the rendezvous with our vehicle."

The pilot nodded without comment, and Joe watched the slowly vanishing topography behind them. As was typical with him, he took time to look around and appreciate the mundane along with the job at hand. They'd asked the National Guard for the use of a helicopter, as cops had to in Vermont, there not being a single police chopper in the state. Compliance had been immediate and friendly, as usual. The pilots needed the flight hours, and the Guard could tout such interagency cooperation to Washington when annual budget negotiations came up.

They hadn't wanted to push their luck by overusing their eyes in the sky, and so had worked hard to figure out how their nemesis was going to identify Rachel's hiding spot—or false hiding spot, as was the case. Joe and Sammie had finally won over Willy to her impersonating the girl at a dummy safe house located in Colchester.

They'd had their choice of buildings, too, Joe mused, looking down. It had taken no time at all to fill the former farmland on Burlington's edges with ever-expanding blooms of housing developments, which from the air made Joe think of undulating oil blots, spread across green water. But merely building such communities didn't necessarily make them successful, as a recent economic slump had made clear. Joe's team had easily located both a house and a neighborhood that they hoped would reel in the murderous twosome that Willy was calling Mutt and Jeff.

"We should've borrowed an Apache helicopter instead of this thing," Willy now half shouted over the intercom. "We could've just blown the fuckers up from the air."

"Except that we don't know for sure that they *are* our fuckers," Joe replied.

"Yeah, yeah, yeah. I got the memo."

Joe pulled out his cell phone and adjusted the plug-in device he'd been instructed to use with his headphones to overcome the ambient noise. He dialed Sam's number.

"Don't tell me," she answered. "You're not on the ground yet."

"You should be a detective. Your keen-eyed other half is telling me that you have two vehicles tailing Tom Wilson right now, and he's about to deliver your groceries. So you might want to check the monitoring equipment to make sure we get a shot of 'em."

"Give me the details," she requested.

Joe recited the make, model, and registration of the two cars they'd spotted on the ground earlier and from the air just now, adding, "Of course, the cars may be hot or just in use today. These two seem smart enough to mix things up regularly, and we already know they like disguising themselves. Try to get face pictures if you can."

"Got it. Tom's coming into view right now."

She hung up to get to work. They'd mounted high-definition cameras—again, borrowed from another department—onto the roof of Sammie's two-storied tract home, and hidden them among a false TV dish setup. They were hard-wired to a laptop that Sam controlled from inside the house. Joe knew that this entire ploy was a long shot, but they'd almost caught Mutt and Jeff once. It wasn't unreasonable to hope that the two might stumble again to the cops' advantage.

Lester was waiting in a field where they'd earlier agreed to meet up with the car. "Success?" he asked.

"Hope so," Joe told him, walking quickly away from the helicopter in order to allow it to take off and head home. "I just gave Sam the heads-up that she and Tom had company. With any luck, she'll get some pictures."

"I wish we could've just loaded the neighborhood with cops and jumped 'em, instead of all this razzle-dazzle."

Joe laughed and turned to watch the chopper fly away. "You sound like Willy," he said. "If we'd done that, I doubt these boys would've showed at all. Plus, a neighborhood like that? How do you realistically seal it off without showing your hand? We'll put people in after we think the bad guys are satisfied they've found Rachel's hideout. Besides, for a surveillance like this, who's to say the drivers of those two cars are even our guys?" Joe shook his head before adding, "Let's just play this out. So far, so good."

Lester accepted it, just as Willy would have argued the point, and changed subjects. "So far, so good for the Filson family, too, by the way. About five minutes ago, we heard Fish and Wildlife found them in an abandoned camp in the Northeast Kingdom. They're half dead with exposure and dehydration, but it looks like they'll pull through."

Joe was genuinely relieved, remembering the family photos from Nancy's house. "Where did they take them?"

"Dartmouth-Hitchcock," Lester told him. "They thought about taking them to Burlington by air, but wouldn't risk it because of the old lady; she's in the roughest shape. Plus, they didn't want to break up the family."

"No, no," Joe agreed. "That was right. After we're all set with Sammie's situation, let's head over there and see what they've got for us."

In major cities, hospitals are as common as the neighborhoods they serve. In northern New England, the top-level centers are few and far between. Fortunately, for tricky cases like what Spinney had just outlined, Dartmouth-Hitchcock in nearby Lebanon, New Hampshire, was one of the best.

The three men reached the car. Between the cool weather in general and the prop wash from the departing aircraft, they were grateful that Lester had left the engine running and the heater on.

Once inside, Joe used his phone again. "Anything?" he asked Sammie when she answered.

Her voice was flat. "No. Only one of the cars came within view, and I never got a look at who was driving. When Tom came up, I flashed the wig and that bracelet she wears at the door and kept my face in the shadow. I think it worked. But I guess it's just watch and wait now."

Joe pursed his lips. "Okay," he said. "I'll move a few people in a little closer, just so you have company."

"What's your guess on when they'll make a move?" she asked.

He paused before answering, "God only knows, kiddo. You're going to have to keep on your toes."

In the rearview mirror, he saw Willy glowering at him.

CHAPTER SEVENTEEN

The Dartmouth-Hitchcock Medical Center is nicknamed the Emerald City by the medevac pilots that return to it like moths to a light, using its ethereal glow and its trademark green-and-white paint job as a beacon. In Joe's mind, it remained "Mary Hitchcock," which was its name when it was located in nearby Hanover, and a far humbler affair than the sprawling, forest-girdled complex it had become. Then as now, however, it was the preferred destination for those hanging on by a thread, as it had been for him when colleagues or family had come in need of its services.

As a result of those memories, Joe entered the facility's lofty, multistory atrium with a relatively light heart, if only because this time, he didn't know the people he'd come to visit. His life had been so punctuated over the years by loss and grief, through death or trauma, that to visit a hospital to see strangers was almost a relief.

He was alone, having left the others to coordinate the trap, and so decided that he'd speak with Henry Filson first—the paterfamilias. Reportedly, Henry was conscious and in the best shape, Joe having heard that Abigail, his wife, remained unresponsive, and Nancy, although awake, had apparently been seriously traumatized.

The hospital had put Henry in a room by himself, although adjacent to his daughter's. Joe glanced through the entrance of her room as he walked by, and saw her staring sightlessly out the large window overlooking the trees. Henry, by contrast, had both the TV on and a magazine spread open. Joe noticed that the magazine displayed an ad only, however, and that the older man's eyes were fixed on a point between both distractions.

He looked over as Joe entered.

"Mr. Filson?" Joe asked.

"Yeah," he said, almost regretfully.

Joe circled the bed and sat in the guest chair near the window, by instinct putting the light behind him. He reached out and proffered his hand in greeting. "Joe Gunther. I'm a cop. Probably the latest in a long string of them."

"At least you're no spring chicken."

Joe laughed. "Nope. That I'm not. You feel like you've been grilled by kindergartners?"

"Not that so much. More like they don't ever talk to each other."

Joe couldn't disagree. That's what he was doing here, after all. "A case like yours gets kicked around some—state police, Fish and Wildlife, local guys, special unit people. I have no idea what you've been subjected to."

Henry smiled tiredly. "The first one was cute, at least."

"The game warden?" Joe smiled. "We nickname them the Fish Cops, but they're really good. From the report I read, there was no way that young woman should have paid attention to the tire tracks leading to that cabin."

Henry's words belied his sad expression. "I'm glad she did."

Joe took the opportunity to ask, "How's Abigail doing?"

Henry idly fingered the saline IV taped to his forearm. "I can't tell from what they say. Sure as hell, she's hasn't come to."

After a moment, Joe asked him, "Can you tell me what happened, Henry?"

"Hank."

Joe nodded. "Got it."

Hank thought a moment before speaking. "Nancy had come to visit. It wasn't planned. She said she just felt like it—needed to get away for a while. I thought it was funny, but I didn't question her. She didn't seem troubled, so I thought maybe she was just tired. For a while, it was fine. Then, we were all cooking dinner one night, and the next thing we knew, they were there."

"You had a dog," Joe prompted him after he lapsed into silence.

He seemed to come out of a dream. "Yeah. Jackson. He'd gone missing earlier. Nancy went looking for him. I guess they got him."

"I'm afraid so," Joe confirmed.

Hank accepted the news stoically. "I hope it was quick. He was too old to have done any damage, but they wouldn't have known that. Or cared."

"How did they deal with you?"

"It was rough. Abigail overreacted when they came in. They had guns and masks."

"There were two of them?"

"Yeah. She screamed and yelled at them." He chuckled unexpectedly. "I'll give her that much—she actually grabbed a pan to hit one." He stopped abruptly before adding, "That didn't go so well."

He rubbed his face with his free hand, his voice raspy. "I just stood there."

"Hank," Joe tried easing his guilt. "They had guns. You reacted rationally. She didn't. You never know till it happens to you. What did they do?"

"The one she swung at smacked her hard. She hit the back of her head against the doorknob. That's why I think she's in such bad shape now."

"And Nancy?"

He sighed. "She's like both of us combined. A thinker like me, but emotional, too. She kept apologizing, which didn't make any sense until she told me why she'd come to visit in the first place—because of the threat to her friend. I still don't know what that had to do with anything—why we had to go through all this. . . ."

"Did the two men say anything when they broke in?" Joe asked.

"No. They were in a hurry. They gave us orders to leave through the back door, to drag Abigail between us—stuff like that. One of them kept saying, 'Speed it up, speed it up.' It was hard, with Nancy apologizing and crying, and the length of the walk. I finally stopped, so Nancy and I could coordinate with Abigail. The one who'd hit her was pissed by that, but the other one—I guess he was in charge—he saw the sense in it."

"Where did you have to go?" Joe asked, surprised.

"They'd parked down the road a ways, off to the side. I guess so no one would notice. It's not bad if all you're doing is walking the dog, but . . ."

Joe got the point. "What happened then?" he asked.

"They handcuffed us and put hoods over our heads and they drove. I kept asking them to take care of Abigail. I even suggested they drop her off, since there wasn't anything she could've done to them. There's a small hospital right in St. J that might've helped her. They could've just dumped her in the driveway, for Christ's sake. It's not like they had to fill out a fucking insurance form."

He stopped to take in a deep breath. "Sorry."

"It's okay," Joe reassured him. "Totally understandable. Did they respond to that at all?"

"The mean one told me to shut the hell up, if that's what you're talkin' about."

"Where did they take you?"

Hank stared at him, his face flushed with anger. "I don't know. I don't know a goddamned thing, no matter how many times you people ask. We were grabbed, given the third degree, and then dumped, okay?"

Joe gave him a moment before saying, "And they're still out there, doing the same thing—in fact, killing people. You want that to continue?"

"Fuck you," Hank said angrily.

"Then help me out," Joe snapped, his tone matching the old man's. "Your wife and daughter are safe and being treated. It's the best we can do. Tell me what happened."

Hank tucked in his chin slightly at the rebuke, but when he spoke, the resolve was clear in his voice. "I'm sorry. You're right. They drove us somewhere—I don't know where because of the hoods—but it was about half an hour. Maybe more. When the hoods came off, we were where you found us. That cabin. Handcuffed to the walls. Abigail was still out, but they did the same to her anyhow. At least they put me next to her so I could reach her with one hand. That's how I knew she was still alive. Nancy, they moved to the far end."

"How were the cuffs attached to the walls?"

"They looked like oversized metal drawer pulls—like a ship's hatch handle, maybe. I don't know. But they were solid."

"And had clearly been set up beforehand?"

Hank nodded thoughtfully. "Yeah. You're right. They must have been. I hadn't thought of that, but the place had been prepared for us."

"Okay, keep going. They had Nancy located on the far wall."

"That's when the difference between the two men really came out," Hank went on. "The mean one started taking off Nancy's shirt without saying a word, and the other one stopped him."

"Go on."

"But he played on it," Hank explained. "He told us, 'You can see how this can go, can't you?' Or something like that. He told us that if we gave them what they wanted, they'd just walk away, and leave it at that."

"What did you have to give?" Joe asked.

Hank's eyes widened. "That was the crazy part. Sure as hell Abigail and I didn't know. And even Nancy kept asking, 'What do you want? What do you want?' It was totally nuts."

"But they told you," Joe suggested.

Hank lay back against his pillow, spent. "Yeah," he conceded. "It was the kind of thing you could've asked over the phone. 'Who brought you the pictures?' That was the question."

"And what did Nancy tell him?"

Hank pressed his lips together for a moment, his expression dark.

"Hank?"

"She didn't, at first. She told him that was confidential." His eyes had dropped to studying his hands.

"Talk to me," Joe prodded him. "What're you holding back?"

"I yelled at her," he whispered.

"What?"

"I yelled at her," he repeated loudly, his voice resonating off the walls of the small room. He blinked before repeating quietly, "I yelled at her to tell them what they wanted. That her mother was dying. That she needed to get her fucking priorities straight."

Joe imagined the scene. The tension in the air. "And?" he asked.

"She gave them what they wanted. Rachel Somebody. I don't remember the last name. They asked a few details, like where did this girl live, was anyone else involved, where were the original negatives—stuff like that. And Nancy told them that she really didn't know. That the arrangement between the photographer and this Rachel person was confidential. She did say that the girl lived in a dorm on campus, and gave them the address."

"What was the nature of the interview?" Joe pressured him. "Was it conversational by now? A free exchange?"

"No. They wouldn't believe her at first. At least the mean one wouldn't. He pulled out a knife at one point and held it to Abigail's throat, threatening to kill her if Nancy didn't spill the beans. This time, the boss didn't stop him."

Joe was surprised. "Did he cut her?"

"No. I was shouting, Nancy was crying and screaming. I guess they finally believed her. Eventually, they packed up and left."

"And that was it?"

"Except for the cold and the lack of water. After a while," Hank admitted, "I couldn't make sense of it. I think I went in and out. I don't know. I felt light-headed. I have a bit of a problem with diabetes. . . ." His voice trailed off.

"Hank," Joe addressed him quietly. "Is there anything you can tell me about the two men? Their accents, movements, any scars or tattoos? Anything at all."

But the older man was already shaking his head. "Their masks never came off, they kept their gloves on. The accents weren't local. They were city guys, but I don't know from where. Just away."

"How 'bout any expressions they might've used? Or did they call each other by name at all?"

"No. I've already thought about all this, since the first cop who asked me. But they were really careful."

Joe stood up, preparing to leave. "And the things that Nancy told them? Anything you might've forgotten?"

Hank looked hapless. "It was so stupid. Just the girl's name, where she lived. Nancy didn't have any more to give them."

Almost as an afterthought, Joe returned to an earlier part of the man's story. "In the car, I know you said you were blindfolded, but did you hear anything? Notice something that might be useful?"

Filson stared at him for a moment, his face registering surprise. "I'll be damned."

"What?"

"There was something. Well, maybe. Anyhow." Here, he twisted in his bed and reached for a crumpled scrap among some tissues on the rolling table designed to hold meals. "I could see just a little, out of the bottom of the hood—at my feet, really, and the car's floorboards. I saw this, so I picked it up. It was an impulse, I guess. I'd forgotten all about it. I just crumpled it up and kept it."

He handed Joe a slip of paper.

"I thought you were handcuffed?" Joe asked. "How could you reach anything?"

"They cuffed us with our hands in front. That was for Abigail, to make it easier to carry her."

Joe studied the item, a hardware store receipt. The date was a few days prior, and the address was Burlington. It wasn't clear what item had been purchased, however, since the description had been reduced to an inventory code.

He extracted an empty evidence envelope from his pocket and slipped it inside. "This is great, Hank. It may be really helpful. Thanks."

He laid his business card on the night table and extended his hand for a second time. "I'll get out of your hair. That's how to contact me if you think of anything else. Otherwise, take care and best of luck. We'll do our damndest to get these two."

Hank gave him a hard look, as fueled by guilt as by anger. "You can shoot 'em, as far as I'm concerned. Bastards."

CHAPTER EIGHTEEN

Beverly Hillstrom opened the passenger door and slid into the front seat, a box of pizza in her hands. The heat of it immediately fogged the inside of the car. It had begun to snow at long last, and her coat was glistening with beads of melting white flakes.

"You are redefining the meaning of eating out," she said, loosening her scarf and opening her collar. It was evening, and dark, and Joe was parked inconspicuously by the side of the road in Colchester.

Joe laughed. "When it comes to some of the things I eat and where I eat them, you better be prepared for worse. I'm just happy you're providing something that's been cooked within the last two days."

"And well cooked at that, if my staff is any judge," she said. "I found this place through their recommendation." She handed him a couple of napkins and began rummaging through her shoulder bag.

"How's Rachel holding up?" he asked, spreading out the napkins and placing one of the Cokes she'd extracted onto the dash.

"The novelty's worn off," Beverly conceded. "Now she's just bored."

"She's still doing her work online, isn't she?" he asked. "She's not falling behind?"

"Not in the least," she said brightly. "Besides, if all this effort results in her being released back into the wild, I will be happier than you can imagine."

"She calling you a lot?"

She rolled her eyes. "If I had any doubts about equipping youngsters with cell phones—or anyone under thirty, for that matter—they've been settled. She's even got me texting now."

Her preparations completed, she asked, "What, exactly, is going on? You just mentioned something about hoping to spring a trap."

"That about sums it up," he replied, opening his can of soda. "We figured that in addition to putting Rachel under wraps, we ought to see about offering a substitute for these two sharks—draw them out, if we're lucky."

"Sammie?" she asked.

"Oh, God. Don't start. I already had Willy beat me up about that."

She spoke through a mouthful, an unusual breach of decorum for her. "No, no. That's not what I was saying. I assumed that she'd be perfect for it—still young and athletic enough to pass for a student. What was Willy upset about?"

"That I constantly expose the mother of his child to danger."

"Good Lord," Beverly exclaimed. "How sweetly old-fashioned. I don't suppose I should be surprised."

Joe's cell phone began buzzing where he'd placed it on the console between them. He reached for it, explaining, "We decided to keep off the radio on this. Just to be on the safe side."

"Joe?" It was Sam.

"Go ahead," he said, putting it on speaker so Beverly could hear.

"We're thinking we've got some action here."

"Is everyone in place?"

"Yeah. That's all set."

"What've you got?"

"It's hard to say. The same car's been by twice, driving slowly. Tinted windows, rolled up. Can't make out who's driving. Willy wants to launch an RPG at it, of course. The others go from wanting to stop it to assuming it's a decoy to draw us out."

"That's what I'm thinking."

"You want to ignore it?"

"Not ignore it, but don't jump on it. What do your instincts tell you? You're in the thick of it."

"I think it's a diversion," she answered without hesitation, which helped him believe that she wasn't simply agreeing with him.

"What kind of car?"

"Dark red Ford Focus. Not a rental. Vermont registration." She rattled it off quickly.

"You run it?"

"Yeah. Came back to some local yokel from the Old North End, in Burlington. Multiple arrests. Mostly petty stuff; nothing major."

"All right. This may be it, or it may be he's just lost. Keep me posted."

"Really?" Beverly asked after he'd hung up. "Lost?"

"No," he said, taking another bite. "They're circling the bait. Anyhow, it would be dumb not to think so. I just wanted Willy to think for three seconds before he blows it up."

"He *wouldn't*," she exclaimed, never having been completely sure of Kunkle's mental balance.

"No," he agreed, "he wouldn't. But he'd like us to believe it."

She was no longer eating. "What are you going to do?"

"Eat," he replied cheerfully, sipping from his can. "They don't want Rachel harmed—they want to know what she knows. More immediately, given what we've learned about how they operate, they want to find out if this isn't exactly the trap it is. A large part of me doesn't believe we'll catch 'em tonight, unless we get very lucky."

"So why are you doing it?"

"To stir things up," he answered simply. "When the dust settles, we may be in a whole new ball game." He raised his pizza slice as if in a toast. "At least, here's hoping."

The phone went off again. "A diversion—no doubt about it," Sammie started right off. "The car just came by for a third time."

"What's everyone else seeing?" he asked, his mouth full.

"Nothing."

"Okay." He hung up.

"You want to drive out there?" Beverly asked, not actually knowing where the trap was located. The development they were near was older, dating back a few decades, and consisting of three interconnected circular drives, tethered to 2A via two feeder roads. The houses were a mishmash of plastic-clapboard, cookie cutter boxes, and more individually built, traditional suburban homes.

He pointed with his chin. "It's only a couple blocks away. We're good." He narrowed his eyes then and told her, "Slump down in your seat."

They both tucked their knees up—he as best as he could, given the steering wheel—and made themselves invisible to a pair of slowly approaching headlights. "Considering the speed," he proposed, "I'd bet that's the same car, widening his surveillance circle."

The car drew abreast. Just as it slipped by, Joe risked a quick glance. "Yup. Same car. Red Focus. Interesting."

"How?" she asked, still tucked down, uncertain about whether to straighten as he was doing.

"You're okay," he said. "It just displays more caution than I'd expect. Makes it almost guaranteed they're smelling a rat." He was looking into the rearview mirror as he spoke, and now said, "Watch it. He's heading back."

She quickly slid back down as Joe flopped almost into her lap, his face inches from the pizza. "Good God," she burst out. "Is this routine?"

"Sometimes," he laughed, speed-dialing the phone's preset conference call setup so that the entire team could hear and join in. "He's coming back at you fast," he warned them.

Beverly and he saw the car's brake lights flash quickly, making the falling snow around them ignite like tiny bulbs, just before the Focus took the corner into Sam's street with its tires squealing. They were close enough—and the car traveling fast enough—that they heard it crash, even through the closed windows.

"He T-boned a parked car about half a block away," Sam reported.

Over the distant wailing of a disturbed car alarm, Joe replied, "Everyone sit tight. Watch and wait."

"No movement from the Focus," Sam continued her running commentary. "Lights are coming on up and down the street; people starting to come out."

"You upstairs, Sam?"

"Yup."

"Keep your eyes on the monitors," Joe warned her. "But get to the window with a backlight and pretend to look out, so they can see you're home and acting normally. But not well enough to see your face," he added as an afterthought.

"Already doing it, Boss."

"Everyone else," he went on. "Look for the person not watching the crash, or not acting like the rest of them, or anyone studying Sammie's place."

Being distant from the street itself, Joe could hear approaching emergency sirens in the far distance. "Somebody called 911," he reported. "EMS and fire are on the way."

He turned to Beverly, who leaned into him before he could speak and said quietly, so as not to be overheard, "Don't tell me. Date's over. You do know how to entertain a girl."

She was already opening the door as he said, "Thanks, sweetheart. I'll call you later."

She looked back at him, her door almost closed. The pizza rested in her seat. "You do that, Joe. No matter what time of night. Okay?"

"Right."

She smiled. "And enjoy the rest of that." She slammed the door and was gone—back to her own car, and home.

The snow was falling harder. He looked longingly at the pizza, knowing that part of the evening had come and gone, and truly missing the woman who'd suggested they share it.

The first of the emergency trucks swept by, followed by a cruiser, just as an explosion shook the neighborhood and threw a bright orange flash up against the low clouds.

"Joe," Sam shouted. "The parked car just blew up. The driver got out and is just standing there."

He started his engine, all pretenses evaporated. "Eyes on the monitors, Sam, and listen for any breach downstairs. Remember the drill. Everybody, look around. If you see something out of whack, photograph it, follow it, whatever. These guys are testing us. We need to turn the tables on 'em. Sam, they may come for you. Don't rule it out."

He pulled away from the curb and raced to the corner, coming upon a block dancing with flames, flashing strobes, and even a few bright cell camera winks as bystanders took photos.

"Goddamned Facebook," he muttered, thinking that they'd have to round up all the phones later to get what they were capturing.

On the second floor of the Colchester house, Sam crouched beside the broad table they'd set up as a command post, which was cluttered with a bank of small closed-circuit TV screens, and trained her shotgun on the room's door. Megaphoned shouts, diesel engines, people yelling all drowned out any sounds within the house that she might have been able to hear otherwise, lending credence to Joe's caution that the noise and commotion were to disguise an assault on her position.

Periodically, she'd glance at the screens, but of the cameras aimed at the property perimeter, most revealed either a milling crowd or debilitating lens flaring as a result of the flashing strobe lights, exacerbated by falling snow. By contrast, the interior cameras showed nothing moving at all.

"Anything, people?" Joe asked over the open phone line.

"Like we wouldn't tell you?" Sam recognized Willy's blunt rejoinder.

She saw a firefighter, his features blocked by his helmet and its visor, walking away from the blaze and carrying an ax and a canvas bag. She almost dismissed him, until she considered his context: He had no hose in hand, wasn't headed toward a lighting unit, a hydrant, or the fire, and didn't seem attached to any squad or truck.

"Check out the firefighter at my northeast corner," she recommended. "I can't figure out what he's doing."

She did seconds later, when on another screen, she saw his outline at a back window, followed by the ax coming through the glass and a grenade-like, cylindrical object bouncing across the rug.

"He's thrown something into the house," she called out.

The subsequent explosion whited out the camera and shook the building. Sam ran to the door and threw it open to see a thick cloud boiling up the stairwell from the first floor.

She worked to keep her voice calm as she reported, "Stairs are blocked. Can't tell if it's a smoke grenade or an incendiary. Anyone see that firefighter?"

The exchange of replies almost jamming the line revealed only confusion. She did note with comfort, however, no reaction from Willy, who as usual had gone silent and was presumably hard at work. Backups and pre-plans were fine and necessary in these situations, but for Sam, there was no substitute for a Willy on the loose, her best interests foremost on his mind.

She stepped back inside the room and closed the door as the smoke began lapping up and over the landing's top edge.

Joe stopped partway down the street, listening to the chatter on the phone. He could see the crash site ahead, the staged fire trucks and ambulances, and—as it happened—the bright flash of the explosion inside Sam's supposed safe house, followed by smoke oozing out of its lower windows.

And, of course, the people. They were running, gawking, talking on radios, taking pictures, hauling fire equipment—firefighters, police officers, EMTs, and civilians. He even saw the driver of the red Focus being questioned by Colchester cops.

The possible goals of this chaos were simple enough: either to assault a legitimate safe house in order to grab Rachel Reiling, or throw a staged police trap into turmoil for the pure hell of it. With the latest addition of the bomb, Joe was seriously doubting the first. Whoever his opponents were, they had not fallen for the trap. This mess was their way of stating that.

There was pride at play here, and flagrant braggadocio.

And there was intention: to reverse the police plan, flush the cops out of hiding, and force them to save one of their own.

It was this aspect of the situation that drew most of Joe's focus. He began watching for people dressed for the weather, acting with purpose, but perhaps not to any constructive end. Sammie's identification of an ax-wielding firefighter wandering on his own was an example. Joe therefore forced himself not to think of her—she was being helped by others, after all—and to determine instead the exit strategy of his enemies.

If any of this reversal was to be of benefit to them, now was the time for at least somebody to step back and take note overall.

Which is why he noticed a car with its lights out—beyond the scattering of trucks and their tangle of fire hose—leaving the curb at the far end of the block and slowly retreating toward the scene's rear exit.

Joe threw his own car into reverse, to head the other way.

Upstairs, Sammie was running the shower in the adjacent bathroom, soaking towels and herself in preparation for a worst-case scenario. She also ran to the room's door and laid a long, drenched towel at its base, where smoke was beginning to trickle in. The air was as hot as a sauna's.

"Sam," she heard Tom Wilson update her. "The bomb was an incendiary. The fire department is working to get it out and extract you, but it's stubborn and the fire's right under you. They can't get ladders in place till they knock that part down. How're you doing?"

She was standing at the door of the bathroom when its window smashed open, accompanied by a blast of cold air and the face of Willy Kunkle.

"Hey, babe. How're ya doin'?"

She burst out laughing. "What the hell?"

"I stole one of their ladders," he half explained. "Wanna get outta here?"

One street over, Joe killed his lights and drifted to the curb. Far ahead, a man in a fire coat, minus his helmet and ax, stepped out from between two homes, a block away from the action, to be met by the dark car Joe had seen quietly slipping away.

As the car then gathered speed and turned on its headlights, heading in Joe's direction, he once more flopped onto the passenger seat, resting his cheek against the warm pizza box, and let it pass by.

Then he pulled into the road, executed a quiet U-turn, and followed from a distance.

CHAPTER NINETEEN

It was long past midnight, and the storm had finally arrived. Vermont's largest city was looking like an empty Christmas pageant soundstage, where someone had forgotten to switch off the artificial snow machine. Joe topped the hill with his headlights out, hoping to preserve his relative invisibility, and headed into downtown and toward the mesmerizing black hole of Lake Champlain beyond. It was a neat trick, however, driving in the dark, barely keeping the car ahead in view, and relying solely on passing streetlamps to guide him. The heavy snow made every overhead bulb appear like an isolated, smudgy beacon, shrouded as if by fog and barely extending to the roadway.

In the end, Joe's ambitions proved unrealistic. Despite his best efforts, circumstances overwhelmed him. Just shy of the water's edge, the tenuous visual link between pursuer and pursued finally snapped, and he lost sight of the taillights that had transfixed him since Colchester. Idling in the middle of the intersection of Main and Battery, without another vehicle in sight, he searched in vain for any movement whatsoever.

His cell, which he'd hung up after leaving the fire scene, vibrated again.

"Gunther," he answered distractedly, still turning his head to and fro.

"Nice leadership," came Willy's flat voice. "Leave one of your own behind in a burning building."

He ignored the taunt. "She okay?"

"No thanks to you."

"I got that part."

"Where the fuck are you?"

"Downtown. I picked up on the two who torched the place and followed them as far as I could."

"You lost 'em?"

"Finally. Yeah. But I don't think they made me."

True to Willy's character, he dropped the bitterness of his opening comments without further thought, as Joe trusted he would. When he spoke next, his voice was solely that of a co-investigator. "You think they were heading home after a hard night's work?"

"I hope so. It might give us at least a notion of where to concentrate a search."

"Cool. We need a break with this stupid case."

Joe returned to what would be tomorrow's headlines. "You get anything like a lead from the fire scene?"

"The Focus driver was a predictable dead end. Fire marshals haven't started yet, but you know they won't find shit from that bomb. You get the car's registration?"

"Yup. Might help. Where's everyone right now?"

"Heading back to the office."

"Sam doesn't need someone medical to look at her? Bill Allard will have us for lunch if we don't cross that *T*."

Willy laughed. "Right. Sam in the hospital for anything short of a bullet? Good luck. We got her looked at by EMS at the scene. You'll have to live with that."

Joe had expected as much. "Okay. See you at the office."

He brought the rest of the cold pizza to share when he entered the front room, his hair and shoulders covered with snow. The office elsewhere was mostly dark, lending an oddly intimate air to their small group consisting of Tom Wilson, Sam, Willy, and Lester.

Joe crossed straight over to Sammie and kissed her on the cheek. "God, you're a sight for sore eyes. How'd you get out?"

She smiled at Willy, who was rummaging through the pizza box, not listening. "My hero. He stole a ladder when they weren't looking and climbed to my window to rescue me."

Joe laughed. "Really?"

Willy turned with a slice in his hand. "That's bullshit. She was fine upstairs and they were just following protocol, making sure the fire wouldn't come back around and cut them off. I just got impatient."

"You?" Joe exclaimed. "Impatient?"

"Kidding aside," Tom said, "the fire chief will be reaching out to you tomorrow—well, I guess later today," checking the wall clock. "He's pretty pissed."

"And for once not about me," Willy added. "You know firemen and cops. Somebody blabbed from our side, so now he knows we had an undercover op going, and he's all worked up about how we put one of his neighborhoods in danger."

"What *is* left of the house?" Joe asked.

Willy looked slightly rueful. "Not much, which means the people we borrowed all the video stuff from'll want to tear you a new one, too."

Joe ran his fingers through his hair. "I can't blame them. Not that we saw any of this coming. I'll dump the whole mess onto Allard."

Unusually, Willy then offered a bit of moral support. "It wasn't a total bust. You followed the bad guys pretty far. Main and Battery? That must be close to where they're holed up. There aren't too many options down there."

That was true, but it nevertheless involved at least three major hotels and hundreds of apartments facing the water. Still, they were drawing closer, as Joe revealed by removing an envelope from his pocket and holding it up. "And let's not forget the receipt that Hank Filson picked up from the floor of the kidnap car. It traces back to a hardware store in the same neighborhood."

"You talk to them yet?" Willy asked.

"Nope, but I will. When Hank gave it to me, I wasn't sure of its value, since Mutt and Jeff move around so much. But now I'm thinking maybe they've found a home base, at least for while they're in this neck of the woods."

"Why did they do it?" Sammie asked, her face and blouse still damp and smeared with soot. "If they were coming for Rachel, they've got one hell of a weird way of running a kidnapping."

"They were flipping us the bird," Joe told her. "Telling us they were onto our game. What did we get from the driver of the red Focus?"

"What you'd expect," Lester reported. "I coordinated with the locals when they interviewed him at the scene. He's just a dirtbag homeboy who was paid to do what he did. He don't know nuttin', didn't see nobody, and has no idea."

"So he never met his contractor?" Joe asked.

"Nope. It was all by phone, the money was cash, and the delivery by dead drop. Like Tomasz Bajek, once removed—disposable labor."

"Except that he's still alive," Joe mused. "Might as well put him under the hot lights later at the PD, just to see if he remembers anything else."

"And what do we do in the meantime?" Tom asked. "Canvass the neighborhood around Main and Battery to see if we get lucky?"

"Kind of," Joe replied. "But let's start with the hardware store. We've been hoping they'd make a mistake." He held up the envelope again. "Maybe this is it."

Hardware stores had been a favorite haunt of Joe's for as far back as he could recall. His father, a quiet, introspective, gentle farmer from the Thetford area, had taken Joe and his younger brother, Leo, to hardware stores when they were kids, as if passing along his appreciation for mechanical things through a form of educational miming. The three of them would wander the aisles, weighing a succession of tools in their hands, the boys watching their father's expression and learning the values of durability, precision, and craftsmanship by how their teacher winnowed through the offerings to his final choice. An odd, near-silent ritual, cherished by the boys and guaranteed to make them nostalgic every time they entered such a place forever after.

Of course, it couldn't be a huge building center so common across suburbia. The setting was as key as whatever crowded its shelves. In Burlington, the store that had issued Joe's receipt fit the bill to perfection. It was older, had creaking wooden floorboards, and smelled of sawdust, varnish, and what Joe could only think of as old iron. It also looked as if the merchandise jammed into every nook and cranny was merely what they'd been able to fit in, implying a gold mine of much more, somewhere just out of sight.

"Can I help you?" a white-haired woman asked as Joe and Sam passed under the small bell that jangled softly above the front door's upper frame.

Joe glanced about, taking in the tight aisles and loaded bins, shelves and cubbies, noticing with pleasure that some items were even hanging from the pressed tin ceiling and looked about as old as the clerk.

"Yeah, if you've got a minute."

"All the time in the world. People aren't knocking down my door anymore," she said, with no tone of complaint.

"Too bad," Joe said. "I'm from the other side of the state, otherwise I'd be here weekly."

The woman smiled. "I know the feeling. What can I do for you?"

They both showed their credentials as Joe continued, "We're from the police, and we're working a case where one of your receipts cropped up."

She nodded. "Nothing too bad, I hope."

Joe took out the receipt and laid it on the scarred wooden counter, facing the clerk. "This one of yours?"

The woman bent at the waist and studied it without picking it up, as if it might be tainted with something catching. "Sure is."

"We couldn't figure out what was purchased."

She left her station at the counter and headed toward one of the aisles as she spoke. "We call them harness cleats, but basically, they're super-rugged staples you can attach to a barn wall to hold heavy gear." She stopped at a bin, reached in, and extracted an example. "Pretty beefy. You actually drill all the way through the wall and attach the cleat from the other side with a couple of bolts. I suppose if you had enough of them, you could make something like a metal ladder going up to a loft—like what you see on some of the older utility poles, you know?"

Joe held it for a moment before handing it to Sam. "You can't sell too many of them, I'd guess."

The owner headed back to her counter. "Nope."

"You work here all the time?"

The woman turned and extended a hand in greeting. "I own the place. Sande Snyder—Sande with an *e*. If I didn't work here, the sign in the door would say, 'Closed.'"

"But you sold a few of these lately," Joe stated, more as a fact than a question.

"The receipt says three," Snyder responded laconically.

Sam laughed. "Right."

Joe smiled. "You remember who bought them?"

Snyder placed both hands, palm down, on her counter and eased her back slightly by leaning forward. "I do, not that that'll be of much good to you. I'd have a hard time describing my own husband's face to you, even if he was still alive. I never can figure out how they do that on TV."

"Tall, short, fat, skinny? Nothing?" Sam asked.

"Medium on all counts, and mean in the face," Snyder told her. "Struck me as a city man, born and bred." She shoved away from the counter and crouched down briefly, adding, "But you don't have to take my word for it. I got surveillance here, ever since I was broken into a few years back."

She reappeared with a plastic case containing a CD. "I don't have, like, a nonstop movie system. Too expensive." She twisted around and pointed at what resembled an old hurricane lamp, placed at about eye level on a shelf. "It's hard to see, but it's sort of a camera with a stutter, rigged to a motion detector. Takes about a picture per second when it's running, so a single CD can hold a bunch of time. Lucky for you, I just swapped over to a new one. You want to find who you're after, check toward the end. Like I said, he's the mean-looking one, the cleats'll be on the counter in front of him, and he's wearing one of those Russian-type trooper hats with the ear flaps snapped up over the top. Looks pretty dumb, if you ask me, but I guess they're warm enough."

Joe distributed the prints of the hardware store customer to the people around the table—the assembled VBI squads of both Burlington and

Brattleboro offices, and Bill Allard, who had driven up from Waterbury to be in on the meeting.

"With many hours of work from several of you here, and help from the FBI and others," Joe began, "we now know this to be Neil Watson. Date of birth: 7/30/76. He is known as an enforcer for hire, and has multiple arrests for aggravated assault, battery, use of a deadly weapon, and so on, but nothing in the last ten years. At first glance—" Joe paused long enough to hand out a summary of Watson's past charges. "—you'd be forgiven for thinking that he either died a decade ago or has been locked up in prison. As the surveillance photograph proves, you'd be wrong. It seems that either Mr. Watson got smart, which I personally doubt, or he finally associated himself with someone possessing a better sense of self-preservation."

"Any idea who that someone is?" Allard asked.

"Not a clue," Lester chipped in.

"Tommy Bajek wasn't so well preserved by him," Willy commented.

"Apparently not," Joe agreed. "But look at what happened right after Tommy died. Jennifer Sisto was tortured to death, which—when you combine it with the fire bomb attack on the Colchester house—hints at a leader both shrewd and with a seriously violent revenge instinct. That could make the Neil Watsons of the world pretty loyal, I would think."

"Sure," Willy picked up. "All the best bosses are secretive psychopaths with a penchant for killing people."

A suppressed wave of laughter circled the room as Joe bowed slightly and said, "Thank you, William."

"But you're saying they're here in Burlington, aren't you?" Allard asked. "Even if we don't know the alpha dog's name."

"Correct," Joe said, placing another picture on the table. "This is the car I followed on the night of the fire. It was found abandoned in a downtown parking garage near where I lost it. Tom contacted the firm that rented it out two days before the fire, and got zip for his effort—the same as with the two cars that were used to tail Tom to Colchester and Sammie last week."

Tom explained a bit more for Allard's benefit, "Bogus name, credit card, address, the works. They must do identity theft on the side. I showed the counterman Watson's picture, but it didn't ring any bells, and unlike the hardware store, there was no closed-circuit camera in use."

Allard nodded in response. "What's the plan, then?"

"We have three options, as we see it," Joe replied. "One is to keep Watson's identity to ourselves and put every VBI agent we can on the street, hoping we'll bump into him by accident. That'll almost guarantee keeping a lid on it and, by extension, a lid on the headline screamers that we've been trying to avoid with the Filson and Sandy Corcoran and Ben Kendall cases. The second option is to circulate Watson's mug shot—if not his name, maybe—to every cop in the Greater Burlington area, with instructions to report any sightings to us, but to otherwise take no action. In other words, a red-letter, police-only, highly sensitive BOL, where we keep all details to ourselves except our need to catch the guy."

"I like that one," Allard muttered.

"And the third," Joe wrapped up, "is to release everything we have to the media, complete with that picture, and turn everyone who sees it into our eyes and ears."

"And guarantee that Watson and his boss and whoever else might be working with them will disappear like a bat fart in a high wind," Willy cracked.

"Probably," Joe acknowledged.

Bill Allard didn't hesitate, restating, "Let's go for Door Number Two. Cops get enough BOLs every week that another one isn't likely to get leaked, especially if we keep our cards to ourselves. And I like the idea of a red alert, or high priority, or whatever they use up in this area, to make Watson stand out from the average jerkwater deadbeat dad."

Joe scanned the assembled faces for dissent and found none. "All right," he said. "That's what we go with, then."

CHAPTER TWENTY

"Special Agent Gunther?"

Joe had been standing before the window of his borrowed VBI office, once again admiring the snow outside. As with the region's yearly foliage change, the annual advent of winter never ceased to impress him. He'd heard the grumblers among his friends say that retirement could only be enhanced by moving to where the word "snow" had no meaning. But Joe was a dyed-in-the-wool New Englander, and had no problem with an environment that could reach out and kill him half of every year. He felt that it added to the character of the region—and its inhabitants—even if they chose to also live in Burlington.

He immediately recognized the voice on the other end of the phone line. "Colonel Perry," he acknowledged. "What's up?"

"I wanted to get back to you about Ben Kendall. You asked if I could find out more about how he was injured—maybe medical records or a combat injury report of some kind."

"That's right."

"Well, I got a bit more, but better than that, I think I found someone who was there."

"Where do you mean?" Joe asked.

"The village where Kendall was shot. His name's Robert Morgan. He's living just outside Peterborough, New Hampshire."

"How'd you find him?"

"He's listed on one of the forms—as one of the men who helped get Ben to a medevac. The contact who supplied the report said, out of the blue, that he actually knew him, although they'd since lost touch. So I got his current address, as a result. I didn't call him. I figured I'd leave that to you."

"Thanks, Colonel. I appreciate it. You mentioned a report. Did you get a copy of that?"

"I got a summary. It's basically a letter from one office to another. It doesn't say much, to be honest, but I can fax it to you. The full-fledged incident or battle report seems to have disappeared. My guess is that this Bob Morgan may be a better bet anyhow, given how much was being shoved under the rug in those days."

"And was there a medical file on Ben?"

"Yes. Sorry. I forgot to mention that. Again, what I found was a problem list and a narrative overview—what looks like a cover sheet, except that it's a couple of pages long. The original document was probably about a foot thick, given that the VA had him for most of a year. Lord knows where that is. But, again, I can fax you what I got."

"You have a pencil?" Joe asked, and gave him the office fax line. "Just to kill the suspense," he then said, "what's the summary say?"

"Only that he was shot in combat. There's nothing detailing how it happened."

Joe wasn't surprised. Being ex-military himself, he'd been expecting results that would have made a mime seem like a chatterbox. He now knew not to be disappointed when the faxes appeared.

But Robert Morgan sounded promising. Before thanking Marcus

Perry and wrapping up the conversation, Joe made sure to get the man's contact information.

Neil Watson scowled at the snow up and down the street outside the condominium. "What the fuck," he muttered under his breath. "These assholes *live* up here. Why the hell don't they shovel this shit? Even *we* do that much in the city. Jesus H. Christ."

Ruing that he hadn't brought a pair of boots—or at least purchased a pair, since in fact he didn't own any—he headed up grumpily toward the small market at the north end of the block.

He wasn't impressed by the expansive view of the lake beside him, or—as Gunther had been earlier—by how the snow had softened the city's harder edges. He just wanted to get this job over and return home.

It wasn't only the weather, although, as his smooth-soled shoes slipped slightly on a small patch of compacted snow, that definitely wasn't helping things. It was how this whole assignment had turned into some kind of chess game. Frank was in hog heaven, of course, getting off on how the cops were engaging "brain to brain," as he put it, instead of just reacting to whatever mess Frank and Neil left in their wake. But Neil was getting antsy.

He was also stumped. While he'd enjoyed blowing up that lame-assed trap the cops had set for them, he was hard-pressed now to figure out a next move. The girl was still out there, and Frank was all hot and excited to discover who her friends and relatives might be so they could cook up a variation on how they'd treated Nancy Filson and her folks. But Neil had had enough. He'd even suggested that he head back to the city until Frank figured out what to do next. He had a life, after all, despite Frank's opinion. It maybe consisted of bars, hookers, and watching sports on TV with his mom at the old folks' home, but it supplied him his version of normalcy. He was due for a break.

Instead, Frank had sent him out for groceries. Typical.

And what about the three Filsons? What the hell had that been about? Leaving them alive? What had Frank been thinking? Neil didn't give a damn about masks and disguises. You kill witnesses. That's how it was done. This was where Frank's eccentricity started to look stupid.

Neil saw a police cruiser turn the far corner and roll toward him, moving peacefully, the cop visibly checking both sides of the street as he went. Neil reached up, slid his trooper-style fur hat farther down on his forehead, and then propped his foot up against the base of a streetlamp, as if tying his shoelaces, thereby hiding his face entirely.

The cruiser slid by without pause. But Neil's inner rant was over. Never let your guard down; never get distracted. There are rules.

Lester swung into the doorway like an excited kid, one hand hanging on Joe's doorjamb. "The guy in the videotape—Watson—was just spotted on the sidewalk one street up from the lake. He tried hiding his face, but he's wearing the same dumb hat."

Joe was already halfway to his feet, coat in hand, heading for the lobby. "They sure? Those hats are a dime a dozen."

Lester fell in beside him as they jogged toward the stairs down to the garage. "Everything else fits—location, stature, general appearance. They're pretty sure."

"Any response?" Joe asked.

"Only from us. Willy already headed out. I did alert the PD to the threat, though, in case this is the big one."

"Let's hope it's not too big," Joe countered, reaching the bottom of the stairwell and yanking the door open to enter the garage. "I want a nice, quiet, non-eventful arrest. I want a conversation at the end of this; not another shit storm with a hundred cameras all around."

He twisted around to fix Lester with a stare. "Does Willy know that? So typical that he just headed out without waiting."

Les answered with a tilted head. "You've known him longer than I have, boss."

Joe pulled his keys out and opened the car door. "That I have," he murmured dolefully.

Just shy of the corner market, Neil noticed a second patrol car, this one approaching from a side street. He stepped into the store's entrance, hesitating long enough to watch the vehicle's behavior, its driver blocked by the reflection off the windshield. But again, he saw no cause for alarm. The cruiser passed by, came to a full stop at the light, turned on its indicator to head away, and slipped into the sparse traffic to drive off. Neil grunted to himself and entered the market, pulling out his short grocery list.

Joe drew up to the curb, two blocks from the market, and approached the rear of the unmarked panel truck ahead of him, Lester by his side.

He knocked on the door after letting a couple of pedestrians pass by.

The door opened a crack, revealing an unsmiling man's face.

"Gunther and Spinney," Joe said. "VBI."

The door swung back and they climbed into a stuffy command center jammed with electronics, computers, and TV monitors, along with a couple of grim-faced men.

"Kunkle not here?" Joe asked immediately.

One of the men reached up and tapped the monitor showing the front of the market. "He's in there."

"The store?" Spinney blurted out. "With the perp?"

"You got it."

"That's fine," Joe soothed them both, inwardly irritated. "He knows what he's doing."

Of course, Joe could only hope that was true. On the other hand, of all the people he might have chosen to be on the inside, Willy would have been his preference. Along with his bum arm and an ability to blend into his environment, Willy wasn't a man to draw attention to himself—until it was necessary. It had proven to be a handy range of attributes in the past.

"He wired?" Joe asked, moving on, watching the screen for activity.

"Kind of," the same technician replied. "He's on open mic, on his cell phone." He reached out and twisted a knob before him to fill the van with the market's ambient sounds—along with the scratchiness of the phone's mouthpiece rubbing against the interior of Willy's overcoat.

"We can't talk to him?" Lester asked.

"Not unless you want to blow his cover."

"Perfect," Spinney said under his breath.

The side door to the van flew open, inundating the small space with light and cold air. A tall, slightly disheveled man in a coat and tie stepped in and slammed the door behind him.

"Captain," one of the techies greeted him without turning around.

The newcomer fixed both VBI men with a glance followed by a look of recognition. "Joe," he said, extending a hand. "I heard you were causing problems up here. You about to make another mess?"

Joe introduced Lester. "This is Michael McReady, of Burlington's finest. You here to coordinate this?"

McReady was consulting the array of monitors now, getting his bearings. "As best as I can, given your sorry excuse of a heads-up," he said pleasantly. "I've been working the phone for the past twenty minutes, shuffling troops."

He pointed to a screen displaying an electronic map of the area. The market was highlighted, along with several brightly colored dots, most of which were moving along the streets.

"These are our vehicles, marked and unmarked. We're still getting sharpshooters into position, and we've rallied our TAC people, but we're scrambling." He eyed Joe and added, "Of course, there are a few small details missing, like, who the hell is this guy?"

"Neil Watson, urban bad boy," Joe replied. "The abridged version is that he's a hit man working for somebody we don't know. His primary assignment at the moment is to kidnap the state medical examiner's daughter and extract information."

McReady took his eyes off the equipment to stare at him, a startled smile on his face. "Are you kidding me?"

"Nope. He's armed and dangerous and he's killed before. This is the real deal. He's also not alone."

McReady scowled. "In there?" He pointed at the image of the market.

"Kunkle's with him, undercover, but Watson has a partner in the neighborhood. We think they've holed up within walking distance, but we don't know where. Could be a hotel, a condo. Could be they even pulled off a home invasion and have some family in their own back bedroom, bound and gagged, while they play house in the front. They're capable of any of that."

"I hear this all started because one of our people spotted him on the street," McReady commented.

"Correct, and for the record, my apologies for landing on your turf like a bunch of uninvited Navy Seals. You have a preference for how to bring this guy down? Without killing him, I hope?" Joe asked.

McReady tapped his finger on the map. If he was in any way aggravated that the VBI had brought a potential gunfight into his backyard—especially following the embarrassment on the college campus earlier—he showed no sign of it. "That'll be up to Watson. On this short notice, we'll work on the assumption that he'll retrace his steps with whatever he buys in the store. That puts him on this street here, heading south, with at least one hand occupied. I put together something quick and dirty, which is a mobile unit here and there; men with sniper rifles here, and here, and here; and backup teams at this location, and over here." At each step, he used a special stylus to circle points on the interactive map, like a football coach outlining a play.

"Finally," he concluded, "we blocked the streets out of sight of the market. To compensate, we'll have a couple of unmarked vehicles pass back and forth to simulate normal traffic. The idea is to close in on him mid-block—right here—where his flight options are limited, and to display enough firepower that he'll get the hint and give up."

He straightened as much as possible in the low-ceilinged space and tilted his head at Joe. "It's the best I can do, with such minimal heads-up."

"It's great, Mike," Joe reassured him. "And point taken. We appreciate what you can give us."

"No problem," McReady said. "Can I propose an alternate scenario?"

"Sure."

"No potential shootout, no bullets flying across town. Just follow this guy home to his buddy, organize a calm and carefully thought-out plan of attack—including a neighborhood evacuation—and grab both dudes while they're chowing down and enjoying TV, or whatever."

Joe nodded sympathetically. "Normally, I'd totally agree. Considering the threat, the way they keep vanishing, and the fact that we don't know the nature of their hideaway, I want to nail what I can, when I can."

McReady pursed his lips before saying, "You know how VBI is big on letting local agencies take all the headlines?"

Joe could see where he was headed. "I know. I know. This one's on us, especially if it goes sour. I will personally state that we kept you in the dark."

McReady wasn't entirely placated. "Easy for you to say. It's our citizens that're gonna get caught in the crossfire." He returned to the map. "I know about your cowboy Kunkle," he said. "One of the reasons we're setting up this ambush the way we are is because right here—" He tapped where he hoped to stop Watson on the sidewalk. "—there's a stretch of concrete wall, giving us a good backstop, and opposite it an overlook onto the lake. It cuts down on the chance of a round going haywire. Please, for everyone's sake, could you tell Kunkle to leave this to us?"

Willy Kunkle watched Neil approach the short line at the checkout counter, his arms full of grocery items, and faded back until he was tucked behind a bank of refrigerators. He pulled his phone out of his pocket and reported, "Looks like he's about to head out."

"Willy," he heard Joe say, "stay put and let him go. The block's been sealed off and the PD plans to take him about halfway down the street, toward where he came from."

Without responding, Willy shut off the phone and joined the same checkout line with his own few items, emphasizing his disability by moving awkwardly and acting as if he were slightly mentally challenged, as well. As he fell into line, Neil glanced back at him without interest.

Willy was pissed. While the Neil Watsons of this world were precisely the types he felt most charged to combat, he never sold them short as predators. And Watson and his unknown pal were clearly a cut above the competition. Why Joe and his idiot local colleagues thought that Neil wouldn't notice the difference between normal traffic and a sealed-off city street was beyond him.

Willy knew as sure as he was breathing that whatever plan had been constructed to catch the man ahead of him was doomed, leaving Willy as the only chance of reversing the inevitable. He had no actual evidence of this—it was just the way it always worked out.

While Neil busied himself paying for his purchases, Willy surreptitiously abandoned his basket on a nearby shelf and presented only a pack of gum to the clerk when his turn came, along with a dollar bill, in order to cut down the processing time. As a result, he reached the store's front door just as Neil stepped onto the sidewalk and looked around.

As Willy had expected, Neil came up short, studying the block in both directions. On cue, a bland four-door sedan rounded the corner with a single man at the wheel—the only vehicle within sight—and drove by the market at a leisurely pace, its driver staring straight ahead, as if he were concentrating on negotiating a slalom course.

For Christ's sake, Willy thought. *That's* the best they could do?

Immediately, Neil placed his bag of groceries on the ground near the wall and began quickly walking away from whence he'd come.

"Hey, buddy," Willy called out in a slurred tone, displaying his left shoulder crookedly for emphasis. "You dropped your stuff."

Neil ignored him. Willy fast-hobbled after him, hoping to head him off before he reached the corner and could see up the next block, to where there was probably a row of police barricades barring the road.

"*Hey.* Somebody's gonna steal your stuff, you don't watch out."

Neil waved at him without looking back, too busy checking every door and window within sight. "Doesn't matter. I don't care."

"You can't do that, man," Willy persisted, closing the gap. "That's littering."

Still walking, Neil relented and glanced over his shoulder. "Let it go, asshole. I changed my mind. You can have it."

In the corner of his eye, as they walked, Willy saw exactly what he'd been fearing. As the adjacent street came into view, a roadblock could be seen at its far end.

"I don't want it, man. And who're you calling asshole? You don't know me. I'm trying to be a good neighbor."

By now, Willy had drawn up to Neil's left side, away from the open street opposite. Neil moved slightly toward the curb in an attempt to keep his distance.

"I'm sick of people dumpin' on me 'cause I'm different," Willy continued.

Neil stopped in his tracks, facing Willy, his self-preservation briefly distracted, and shouted, "Fuck off, man! Leave me the fuck alone!"

He reached out to push Willy in the chest. Willy took advantage of the gesture to grab Neil's wrist and draw him forward while at the same time stepping back and bowing slightly to create a tripping fulcrum with his extended right leg. Continuing the motion to its conclusion, he pulled Neil completely off balance, upended him over the leg, and finished by throwing him flat onto the concrete. Willy then swiveled like a dancer and placed all his weight behind his other knee as he brought it down between Neil's shoulder blades.

"Don't move, you fucker," he ordered. "I'm a cop."

But Neil did move, twisting violently to one side while bringing up an arm in a scything motion, his fist closed.

He didn't catch Willy directly in the face, but close enough to make him pull back, which allowed Neil to roll free.

Willy, however, had taken advantage of Neil's efforts to go for his gun in the meantime, and now leveled it at him before the other man could do the same. "I said, don't move," Willy repeated.

Of course, he did, as Willy expected. Neil, still on his knees, swept open his coat, grabbed his weapon, and was bringing it to bear when Willy began a chopping motion intended to snap Neil's wrist and make him release the gun.

It didn't happen. A large chunk of Neil's head vaporized into a burst of blood and bone shards, showering Willy. It was immediately followed by the crack of a distant rifle shot. Neil's body collapsed like a dropped sack of laundry.

Willy stared at the body in stunned disbelief, his perfectly planned maneuver frozen in midmotion, before facing the empty street—along with the invisible sniper who'd acted to save his life—and screaming, "You fucking, stupid, son of a bitch. *I had him.* I had him *cold.*"

CHAPTER TWENTY-ONE

Joe burst out of the van's rear entrance and began running down the street toward the market, Lester in close pursuit. He'd watched in slow motion horror as McReady's best-laid plans fell apart—leaving Willy, as he was bound to argue later, in place to improvise.

He ran across the road to where Willy was kneeling by Neil's folded body, from which a thick flow of blood had already spread across the sidewalk and was dripping into the slush-clotted gutter.

"Willy," Joe called out as he drew near. "Are you all right?"

Kunkle was going through the body's pockets, and merely growled without looking up, "How the fuck you think? Right when I'm about to shut him down, some asshole blows him up."

"Are you hit?" Joe asked, now standing over them.

Willy looked up at him. His face was speckled with Neil's blood and there was a lump of pink brain matter caught in his hair. "He wasn't that good," he replied.

"Jesus." Joe shook his head. "And they say you don't have a way with people. What the hell're you looking for?"

"Anything," Willy answered as the thudding of approaching runners began filling the air around them. "Why do you think I was trying to take him alive? Where's his home base? Where's his buddy holed up? Now we got nothin', thanks to Annie Oakley, and your girlfriend's daughter still has a target on her butt."

"Hillstrom?" Joe said stupidly.

Willy scowled. "Oh, pleeeeze. If you two think you're being discreet, we kids are in the know. Get over it. Better still, help me with this asshole. I can't get into some of his pockets."

Joe blinked at having been simultaneously outed and caught leaving Willy to struggle in his efforts. He dropped to his knees and began using both hands to help.

McReady and Lester were now hovering as Joe had been. "What're you doing?" the Burlington cop asked.

This time, it was Joe who sounded testy. "Looking for a hotel key, a receipt—anything that'll tell us where he's living." He fixed McReady with a stare. "Mike, we need every cop we can round up—your PD, all surrounding departments, everybody you can think of. We need to seal the whole area within two blocks of where Watson was spotted a half hour ago. If we're lucky, his confederate didn't see this out his window. Even so, he'll be wondering where his groceries are in about ten minutes, and if I'm any judge of character, he'll be gone ten minutes after that."

McReady pulled out his cell phone without further questions. "I'll get on it."

Two hours later, Joe received a call.

"Gunther."

"It's Mike. We got something—fifth building we checked." He gave Joe the address and hung up.

It was a two-minute drive. Since the shootout involving Neil Watson, the entire neighborhood had been blanketed by cops in all forms. McReady had risen to the challenge and gotten responses from eight different agencies and departments. Traffic had been all but frozen, checkpoints established on all avenues, including back alleyways and hiking paths, and the media had been in a frenzy to find out why. Bill Allard and his counterparts at half a dozen agencies were going to have their hands full, coordinating and issuing press statements for the foreseeable future.

They had found a single key in Watson's pocket, but to a conventional door lock. That had both refined and deepened the complexity of the search, ruling out a nearby hotel, but implying everything else, including private residences.

The fundamental problem had remained the same since Watson and his cohort first became a presence: No one knew anything about the other player, aside from the fact that he was most likely a male, and—from what Joe had seen of the two fleeing Rachel's dorm—probably the team leader.

Joe parked near the railroad tracks that had once played a key role in Burlington's economic welfare—and now mostly stood in the way of its lakeside development—and took the stairs of the condominium building that McReady had identified, two at a time.

The Burlington cop was waiting for him in the third-floor hallway.

"What've you got?" Joe whispered.

McReady held up Neil Watson's key. "The lock this fits," he said.

"And?"

The other man smiled slightly. "Given everything you and your team's gone through, I thought I'd give you the honors. We started on the ground floor, quietly shoving this into every lock we could. Number thirty-nine proved the charm, but we left it at that. Didn't knock or anything else."

"Any ideas who's inside?"

"We contacted management. They leased the place to a Matthew Richardson a few days ago, for a cash deposit."

"They say anything about him or them?" Joe asked.

"It was all done by phone. I also talked to maintenance, to see if any of them had set eyes on either guy, and the answer—as usual—was Watson."

Joe had been walking down the hallway, toward number thirty-nine, as they'd been talking. A group of black-clad and heavily armed assault officers was grouped around the door.

"You hear anything from inside?"

"Classical music—sounds like public radio," McReady said. He nodded toward the other men, who were crouched and ready to take the door by force. "We also have people watching the windows. How do you want to do it?"

Joe was still holding the key in the palm of his hand. "Well, not to be a buzz killer, but let's at least start out conventional."

He reached around from the side of the doorframe, making sure everyone was clear of any potential shots coming through the door, and knocked loudly.

The answer was quick and laconic, if slightly muffled. "Come in. I'm assuming you have the key."

Joe readied the key as one of the TAC members held a small mirror up to the door's peephole, to check for any shadows that would betray a presence on the other side—possibly armed.

The officer gave Joe the thumbs-up. Joe fit the key into the lock, gave it a twist, and pushed the door open. It swung back on its hinges until gently bumping against the wall.

"Come in. Come in," said the same affable voice. "All's safe and sound."

Again, the mirror was used. This time, its operator spoke softly to

Joe. "He's sitting by the window, at the far end. No weapon in sight. Hands visible."

An option all along had been for a strong tactical entry, involving weapons at the ready and possibly flash-bang grenades. But now, Joe was inclined to follow his instinct. He led the way inside—slowly and cautiously—but with his own gun holstered. The rest of the team followed, quickly spreading throughout the apartment to make sure that they were alone.

They were, apart from the man in the chair, who sat with his legs crossed and his hands in his lap.

"Welcome," he said, greeting them with a smile.

That sparked the limit of McReady's team's tolerance. They swept around Joe, grabbed the man like a rag doll, and slammed him face down onto the rug, his hands behind his back. They then checked him for weapons, as roughly as possible.

Their leader then announced to McReady, as their nominal superior, "He's clear."

Joe crouched by the man's head, whose left nostril was oozing a drop of blood. "What's your name?"

"You can call me Frank Niles."

"That your name?"

"It'll do."

"Your colleague was Neil Watson," Joe said as a statement.

"I gather 'was' is the operative word," Niles replied.

"You got that right, asshole," one of the TAC members said in a low voice.

The sentiment caused Joe to straighten up and tell McReady, "Mike, let everybody know how we appreciated their help. If you wouldn't mind escorting Mr. Niles to the VBI offices, I'd like to continue this conversation over there."

McReady gave a quick nod. "Happy to be rid of him."

. . .

Joe entered the small, windowless room with a cup of coffee and crossed to a steel table secured to the wall. Opposite him sat Frank Niles, handcuffed to a metal ring welded to the tabletop before him. He appeared as unflappable as ever, despite also having been grilled for hours by Sammie and Lester, in turn. Their report to Joe had been that (a) he seemed fully aware of the scant evidence against him, (b) he wasn't about to self-incriminate by saying too much, and (c) he might be interested—for an unspecified consideration—in beginning a conversation addressing everyone's mutual advantage.

Joe placed a recorder on the table and asked, "You are Frank Niles?"

"You know I am."

"You've been read your rights and have signed them?"

"You know I have."

"For the record, this is Special Agent Joe Gunther of the Vermont Bureau of Investigation," he continued, sitting down and arranging his coffee cup and papers. It was not his intention to repeat what his colleagues had just done. He was more curious about Niles's supposed offer.

He therefore began in a less-than-orthodox manner, given most acceptable interrogation techniques. "Do you, Frank Niles, admit being directly involved in the deaths of Benjamin Kendall, of Dummerston, Vermont; and Jennifer Sisto, of Philadelphia; and in the kidnapping of Nancy, Henry, and Abigail Filson, of St. Johnsbury, Vermont; and in the assault on Sandy Corcoran, of Milton, Vermont, after breaking into her home? Also, in the firebombing of a residence in Colchester, Vermont, and the attempted murder of those within?"

Niles raised his eyebrows. "What interrogation school did you attend? I do not."

"Were you acquainted with a man known as Neil Watson?"

"I was." Niles began to smile.

"Were you acquainted with a man named Tomasz Bajek?"

"I was."

"Were you present when they were engaged in illegal activities, including some of the above-mentioned events?"

"I am familiar with the events."

"Were you present—?"

"I don't recall," Frank cut him off, now clearly baffled by Joe's almost disinterested laundry-list style.

Joe paused before continuing. "You think we don't know what you've been up to?"

"I have no idea what you think you know."

"Why did you ask to speak with us when you're not willing to say anything?"

"You haven't asked me the right questions yet."

Joe crossed his legs and made himself more comfortable in the metal chair. "So I've been led to believe. What're the right questions?"

Niles smiled. "Who am I, for starters."

"You're not Frank Niles?" Joe asked.

"You've run me through the system by now," Frank replied. "My fingerprints. My DNA, perhaps. It may be a little early for that. Any hits?"

Joe didn't answer, although the question was valid. They'd found nothing so far. It explained in part why Joe had put Sam and Les onto questioning Niles, while he and Willy had been digging fruitlessly into his background. "Are you saying you're working under an assumed identity?"

"I say what I say, Special Agent Gunther. It's up to you to do the interpreting—much as you have by putting me in this room, wearing these." He rattled the handcuffs briefly.

"What's that mean? You're innocent?" Joe asked.

"What proof do you have that I'm not?"

Ah, Joe thought, they were getting to the point. "As you know, being familiar with the system, it's not my job to lay out the substantial evidence that we've gathered against you—that's for the prosecutors to present to a jury later. My job is to help you help yourself in lightening the ton of bricks that'll fall on you if you don't cooperate."

Niles shook his head slightly. "Nah. Your job is to close this case and not get tainted by the bad smell that's going to go up when you let me loose without a scratch."

"Why would I do that?"

"Because, other than a sense of moral outrage, you've got nothing against me. You have evidence pointing at poor old Neil and pathetic Tommy, and witnesses who'll tell you about a man in a beard or some guy wearing a ski mask, either whispering or speaking in a funny voice. You've even got your own memories of running across a parking lot and being shot at by *somebody*. But when it comes to fingerprints or reliable witnesses or DNA or anything else, what've you got against *me*?"

Joe looked disappointed, choosing to play out his role. "You ever hear of the *CSI* effect?" he asked.

"As in the TV show?" Frank replied. "I've heard that juries are asking prosecutors why the cops didn't collect epithelials off of a doorknob, or whatever."

"That's it," Joe agreed. "But it runs both ways. Crooks like you think that unless we have a genetic link to your great-great-grandmother, we can't throw the book at you. But we're still putting people in jail based entirely on circumstantial evidence."

"People that are underrepresented at trial or lacking anything to barter."

Joe cupped his chin, happy to be getting to the crux of the conversation. Sociopaths had a way of looking at the world that was wondrous to people of integrity and character. The effect was like being confronted with a creature—often urbane, bright, and well mannered—but manipulative and evil to an extraordinary degree.

Like now.

It wasn't the kind of company that Joe sought out if he could avoid it.

"What do you have to barter, Mr. Niles?" he asked this prime example.

His prisoner's eyes widened with pleasure. "I thought you'd never get there. Ask yourself, Special Agent Gunther: What's this all about? All this running around? All these tortures and killings and kidnappings."

"We don't have to ask ourselves that, Frank," Joe told him. "That's another common misconception. People think we need to know the why of things before we can arrest you for the how and when. We don't. We just have to put you at the scene, doing the nasty. If we never find out why you did it, well . . . too bad."

"Except that in this case," Niles countered, "the 'why' of it will give you the puppet master you're after. We're not talking philosophy, after all. I'm not the endgame you want—or I shouldn't be. Who's pulling the strings? Who's the one whose needs are costing so many lives? If you don't want to know that, then you're not doing your job."

Niles sat forward for emphasis. "Ask yourself this, Mr. Gunther: Is throwing the book at me worth letting that man go, who set everything in motion?"

"Are they mutually exclusive?" Joe asked.

"That's the deal I'm offering," Niles stated. "They either are or you get nothing at all." He sat back again. "Who's prosecuting this? I doubt it's the state's attorney. This is a federal case now, is it not?"

"That's hardly good news for you," Joe told him. "They have the death penalty. We don't."

Niles made a dismissive gesture. "It doesn't matter. You go back to that prosecutor, do some more homework. Put me in a hole in the meantime. When you're ready, we'll meet again and I'll give you what you want. Letting me go in the end will only hurt for a while. You'll get over it."

Joe rose without comment, pausing to gaze down at Niles, who took the opportunity to stress, "In time, I'll barely be a memory."

Joe crossed back to the door and placed his hand on the knob. He considered a response, but then abandoned the idea. Gestures were going to speak louder than words with this man, and Joe was about to do his best to guarantee that his next move would be something Niles never forgot.

At least, he hoped it was.

CHAPTER TWENTY-TWO

"How are you, Mr. Gunther?"

Joe opened his eyes and took in the dark ceiling above him, dully flickering with the nighttime reflections off the lake's surface below the bedroom window.

He smiled and turned to face Beverly, who was curled up naked beside him. She'd greeted him at the door an hour earlier, put her finger to her lips for silence, and brought him directly here, where she'd undressed him and made love with him in a more soothing, restorative, and caring manner than he'd thought was possible.

"I've never felt better, Doctor. Thank you so much."

"I was hoping you'd say that," she said. "It's the least I could do."

He chuckled. "Oh?"

"You've returned my peace of mind and given Rachel back her life."

He kissed her at the hairline, enjoying the fresh smell she always gave off, and kept his concerns to himself—that in a reasonable world, anyone who would hire Frank and Neil would probably do so again with suitable replacements. For the moment, Rachel had been released to her dorm room and granted her freedom, albeit with a panic button around her neck and a bodyguard to keep her company, but as Joe saw it, this was a temporary reprieve only.

Not that Beverly didn't know of the hardware and the protection—and, more important, what they implied. But he was sympathetic to both women's sense of relief, which Rachel had exhibited by asking if she could return to Ben's house and resume her documentation of its excavation. Since it remained a crime scene and was therefore populated by police, Joe had been willing to oblige.

By the same token, the request had reminded him of a fundamental missing link in the entire case: What lay at the root of it all? What had stimulated such carnage? And what, if anything, might they find in the remains of Ben's hoard that might explain it?

And finally, what if they found nothing at all? Especially given the overdue media tsunami that had finally crashed down on their heads. Beginning with the ring of news trucks—from as far away as Boston and Albany—that had encircled the cordoned-off section of Burlington during the hunt for Frank Niles, every office of the VBI had been staked out by reporters ever since. The demands for even a marginal show of progress were heading their way already, from the governor's office on down.

As if sharing these same thoughts, Beverly suddenly asked, "What happens, now that you've rounded up these two?"

"That's what I've been discussing with federal prosecutors," he told her, limiting his response to what he could state with certitude. "All afternoon of back and forth. Frank Niles is offering us a deal: his freedom for the name of the man who hired him. They're inclined to consider it; I'm inclined to tell him to go to hell."

"Sacrificing your capture of the head man?" she asked, her tone at once incredulous and tinged with apprehension for her daughter.

"No," he admitted, thinking that he'd have to get used to such emotional responses. "Just the opposite. I'm feeling greedy, given everything

Niles has done. By the time I left them tonight, the legal beagles were willing to give me a little time for an experiment. I want to try an end run around Niles—see if I can wipe the smirk off his face, nail him *and* his boss at the same time, and maybe find out what this is all about." He propped himself up on an elbow to better make eye contact. "There are two pretty solid presumptions we can make right now: Whoever's behind this is convinced that Rachel has something worth grabbing her for—and it's probably something she doesn't even possess, except they don't know that till they talk to her. In any case, whatever it is, it's connected to Ben's photographs. The trick is to either identify the item or items, or the history behind it, or both, and then use it to pin the tail on the donkey. We do that, we'll be able to tell Frank Niles to screw himself and his offer."

"But you've had people studying Ben's photographs for days," she protested. "Do you have another angle in mind?"

He kissed her and smiled, his inner bird dog's instincts undaunted. "I think I do."

Peterborough, New Hampshire, is well known to visitors of the southern half of the Granite State. Half the size of Brattleboro and, strictly speaking, containing only about half its population—some three thousand people downtown—Peterborough exudes an appeal well beyond its physical appearance.

Whatever its charms, however, this time Joe drove through it without pause, aiming toward General Miller Road, in the township's hilly upper right quadrant. There, he found a split-level home, probably quite old, but built in a style made so popular in the 1970s that it now just looked kitschy.

He pulled into the short driveway and killed the engine. The oversized painted replica of a Vietnam service ribbon—green and gold and red—nailed over the garage door confirmed the address as belonging to Robert Morgan, as did the Purple Heart commemorative license plate on the Jeep parked ahead.

Joe slid out from behind the steering wheel, encouraged by the Jeep. He hadn't called ahead, not wanting to give Morgan time to prepare for his arrival.

"What do you want?" a woman asked.

The front door hadn't opened. He followed the voice to the corner of the house, where he saw a woman dressed in corduroys, boots, and a heavy wool jacket, holding three ice-encrusted split logs against her chest.

Joe smiled at her. "Sorry to disturb you. I'm looking for Bob."

She didn't move. "Who're you?"

Joe approached her. "Can I help carry that? I'm from the police, but I'm not here to cause any trouble—just doing some research."

She turned her body slightly away from him, as if protecting her load. "I'm good," she told him. "You have ID?"

He pulled out his credentials. "Vermont Bureau of Investigation," he added.

"Vermont?" she replied. "You can't do anything over here."

"Not looking to," he said. "Like I said, I just need some help. Is Bob around?"

"What do you want to ask him?"

"With respect, I'd like him to tell you that."

She gave him a level stare, considering her response. Fortunately for Joe, she was interrupted by a man appearing behind her, also from around the corner. He had a splitting maul in his hand and was similarly dressed for the outdoors.

"I'm who you want."

His companion gave him a scornful glance, deprived of her role as gatekeeper, and brushed by Gunther on her way to the garage, where he could discern a growing stack of cordwood piled against the far inner wall.

Morgan watched her leave and gave a small, appreciative nod. "My wife," he clarified unnecessarily. "Kind of a watchdog."

"Can't knock that," Joe commented.

"She came to it the hard way," Morgan said, tapping the side of his head. "Trying to keep my PTSD under control. Hasn't been easy."

Joe acknowledged the wooden sign over the garage. "So I guessed. One of my colleagues is in the same boat."

Morgan grunted softly. "Yeah . . . Well, what're you after?"

"Got a place we could talk?" Joe asked. After the heat from inside his car, he was beginning to feel the cold. Also, he was hoping for a long conversation.

"Sure."

Morgan led the way back to the rear of the house, down a steep slope, toward a large pile of newly split wood. "We got our load in late this year," he explained. "You know how it is—life always getting in the way. Our daughter had to have some surgery done, so that kind of got us distracted."

"She okay?"

"Oh, yeah. Just one of those things."

They came to the building's lowermost side, and Morgan escorted Joe into a basement workshop that opened onto the yard piled with logs. They both stamped their feet free of snow on the threshold, and opened their coats to the warmth of an ancient but effective cast-iron stove in the corner.

"Take a load off." Morgan gestured to a threadbare armchair, one of whose legs consisted of a chunk of two-by-four. He settled onto a much-abused wooden sawhorse, picking up a nearby screwdriver to fiddle with.

"So, what can I do you for?" he asked, his tone relaxed but his eyes watchful.

"I'm afraid I need to take you back to the source of your PTSD," Joe told him frankly. "Specifically, to the Delta, where Ben Kendall was hurt."

"Ouch," Morgan said, before lapsing into thoughtful silence for a few seconds.

Joe waited for him to find his bearings.

"Okay," he said eventually. "Go ahead."

"Kendall's name rings a bell, then?" Joe asked.

"Oh, yeah."

"What can you tell me about that day?"

Morgan let out a heavy sigh. "You know . . . It was like a ton of others, mostly. Ben getting hurt was really the only unusual thing about it."

"How?"

"On patrol," he said vaguely. "Shots from a village. Everybody opening up. Happened all the time."

"Except that Ben *did* get hurt," Joe prompted.

"Yeah . . ." Morgan drew out the word slowly.

"I read in the action report," Joe continued, "that you were the one who helped evacuate him."

"There were others, too. That's what you did."

"How were you made aware that he needed help? You see him fall?"

"No," he said quickly. "Nobody did. There were shouts. 'Man down.' Something like that. He was near a hooch with that head wound."

"Nobody nearby?" Joe asked.

"No. I mean, there were other guys who came running like I did. But not before."

"So what did you think when you came up to him? Did you wonder what had happened? Did you take cover?"

"I could see what happened."

Joe didn't say anything, choosing to stare at the man for a few long moments. Morgan dropped his eyes to study the screwdriver in his hands. The absurdity of a so-called combat situation where no one re-turned fire or took evasive action hung in the air.

"All right," Joe finally resumed. "Was Ben conscious when you got to him?"

"He was alive, but he didn't say anything."

"Tell me what you saw—every detail you can recall."

Morgan looked up and made a face. "It was years ago—"

"And it's glued in your head like it was yesterday," Joe cut in. "I've been there. I was in combat. What did you see? Not who. What?"

"He was lying there."

"What was around him?"

"His stuff. A bag, his cameras. His helmet."

"A hole in it?"

"Yeah. In the front—same place he had the wound."

"The cameras broken?"

"Nope. But both of them were open."

"What do you mean?"

Morgan shrugged. "Open. I don't know. Like when you take the rolls of film out. They were in two pieces, but not busted. Nikons. I'd seen Ben and the other photographers do it a bunch of times. They sort of separated the bottom from the rest to remove the film. Both cameras were that way."

"Were there any rolls?"

"No."

Something about his tone, or his expression, made Joe press harder. It felt as if Morgan had caught himself revealing too much, and was wishing that real life came with a rewind button. "But there was some-thing else. Was there film anywhere at all?"

Morgan put the screwdriver down impatiently, then immediately retrieved it. "No."

"Why're you saying that, Bob? You're leaving something out."

They stared at each other for a couple of seconds before Joe asked, "What really happened?" For the first time in this convoluted case, he was feeling like a dog at last on the right scent.

Morgan pressed his lips together without comment.

"I think you liked Ben," Joe suggested, lowering the tension.

Morgan conceded, "He was a good guy."

"Did you two hang out? Earlier?"

"We weren't buddies, if that's what you mean."

"But . . ."

Morgan returned to studying the screwdriver. "He cared. Most of them didn't. It mattered to him what we were doing over there."

"And it did to you, too," Joe stated.

His response was almost inaudible. "Yeah."

"Bob," Joe began. "I'm hearing what you're not telling me, filling in the gaps. Ben wasn't hit by any Viet Cong bullet. You weren't even on the lookout for enemy fire."

"I don't know."

Joe tried again, purposefully keeping his voice low and even. "What happened that day may have been routine, but it didn't begin with shots from the village, did it?"

Silence. The screwdriver kept turning.

"There was shooting, nevertheless," Joe said.

Morgan nodded.

"Wasn't this a case of an American unit taking out a village that posed no threat?" Joe asked, adding, "It was the Delta. There was a lot of that going on down there. Passions were hot. The brass wanted body counts. Ambitious colonels were moving up the ranks at your expense."

Morgan didn't react.

"Am I right?" Joe pushed him.

Another near whisper. "Yeah."

"That's good," Joe encouraged him. "We're on the same page. But Ben stepped out of line, somehow. He was squashed."

Morgan let out another sigh, but remained quiet.

"Tell me," Joe urged him. "People are still suffering from this. I'm working on two homicides, maybe three, including Ben's. Others have been tortured, kidnapped, almost killed—all because of what you know. We need to stop this, Bob—together."

The other man looked up. "Ben's been murdered?"

"Just a few days ago. Help me now like you wanted to help him. If I'm right, something started back then that's going on to this day. You know what it is, Bob."

Morgan moved his lips soundlessly at first, his eyes filled with tears. He managed to say, "I can't."

Joe got to his feet and gave him a stern look, changing tactics. "Think about that long and hard." He handed him a business card. "You get tired of what you've got on your conscience, call me. I'll meet you anytime, anywhere. In the meantime, consider yourself under a microscope. Whatever problems you think you have now have only just started."

He walked to the door, but paused to face his host once more. "What was your unit?" he asked sharply.

Instinctively, Morgan rattled it out as he'd once regularly recited his serial number.

"And the name of your commanding officer?"

Morgan hesitated.

"I can look it up," Joe said, maintaining the stern tone.

"Lieutenant Joyce."

Joe stood motionless, waiting.

"Jack Joyce," came the murmured follow-up.

Joe left without further comment. In the car, returning to Vermont, he called Sammie Martens. "Do me a favor," he asked her. "Get me everything you can on a Robert Morgan, DOB 6/20/1946. Go as deep as you can; pull out the stops on favors and contacts. We're not going for prosecution here. It's purely investigative, so use everything you can think of. I need leverage. The faster, the better."

"Got it," she said.

"Also, take this down," he said, and repeated the information Morgan had given him concerning his unit and its commander. "Maybe you can sic Willy onto that. I'm after what they did in Vietnam, before, during, and after the date that Benjamin Kendall was injured there. I need combat involvements, roster of names, anything he can find."

"Damn," she commented. "We are going back in time."

"That's the crux of this, Sam. It's all about what Ben Kendall knew."

"And what he photographed?"

"That's what I'm thinking."

CHAPTER TWENTY-THREE

"Any luck?" Joe asked Sammie as he entered their Brattleboro office, having silently run a gauntlet of reporters in the parking lot.

She didn't look up from the computer screen. "Not if you're looking for a smoking gun. You didn't tell me what you were after specifically, but so far, Mr. Robert Morgan is about as bland as his name. I found a minor speeding ticket dating back years. There seems to have been an alcohol problem a long, long time ago, after he got out of the service, that landed him in a little hot water—disturbing the peace, trespassing, evictions from a bar or two—but it's all ancient history. I had to make phone calls to get that stuff, since it predates computers. Lucky for us, he's lived in Peterborough his whole life, as has my primary source."

Joe removed his coat and hung it from the rack near the door. "How 'bout financials?"

She finished typing and pushed her chair back from the desk enough to cross her legs and fix him with a gaze. "Nice house, nice cars for him and the wife, no bankruptcies or lawsuits or lottery winnings, no sudden unexplained spikes in income, no official inquiries or audits from the IRS, no over-the-top insurance settlements."

"What's he do for work?"

"Custodian at the local elementary school."

Joe sat at his desk near the small room's only window. "That's it?"

"Far as I can tell. He may be up to something under the table, but I spoke with the chief over there, who's been with the PD for just under a thousand years, and said that he knows Morgan from the VFW and having gone to high school with him. He also said the guy keeps a really low profile. The chief thought it went back to Vietnam—that the war messed with his head. But he stressed that Morgan's just quiet and retiring. Not violent."

Joe stared thoughtfully at his desk top.

"What?" Sam asked.

Joe raised his eyes. "It's a disconnect. I just left him. Something's eating at him, big-time, but he's scared to let it out. Did you get anything on the wife? I should've asked you to look into her, too."

Sam smiled slightly. "I did, anyhow. Not much to find. She doesn't work, volunteers for their church, is a member of both the garden club and the historical society. They married about ten years after he got out of the army, have one daughter who lives in Florida, and seem like candidates for the world's dullest soap opera—*As the World Grinds On*. She's a homie, too—born and bred in Peterborough—with a background as humble as his. What did you mean by a disconnect?"

"They present like upper middle class," Joe told her. "Not like people making ends meet off a custodian's salary."

She raised an inquiring eyebrow. "Trust fund?"

"You find evidence of that?"

She conceded the point, partially. "No, just the opposite. Like I said, humble roots. The chief described the backgrounds of both of them, and it was pure poverty hollow. But unusual financial information is harder to find than the public record stuff. I'm just saying one of 'em might've gotten lucky somehow—legitimately or otherwise."

"Were you able to get Willy started on Morgan's military background?" Joe asked.

"Yep. I'm not exactly sure where he is, but he texted me that he was on it. What's going on, anyhow?"

"You read about my meeting with Marcus Perry? I posted it to the case file yesterday—the part where he mentions the official action report concerning Ben Kendall's injury."

Sammie scowled. "I thought it was missing—that there were only a couple of letters referring to the firefight."

"Right. One of which states that Bob Morgan was at the scene and helped load Ben onto the medevac chopper. That's why I wanted to talk to him, especially when I heard that he lived nearby. That conversation should've been simplicity itself, even with the passage of time. Instead, he was hinky as hell, doing everything he could to avoid laying out a straight story. I left with the distinct sensation that there *was* no firefight, and that Ben Kendall was shot by one of his own. It's got to have something to do with his photographs—Morgan admitted that both Ben's cameras were open and empty when he reached him. Morgan knows more than he's telling, and the additional wrinkle that he lives beyond his means and won't come clean strikes me as interesting."

Sam opened her mouth to speak, but Joe added, "Plus, I don't think it has anything to do with any trust fund, legit or otherwise."

"So he was bought off for what he saw there?" she asked.

He heard her incredulity, and didn't argue against it. "I know. When you say it out loud, it sounds like a stretch. But that's why I asked Willy to dig into the squad's background—to see if there's a context."

"Could be," said Willy from the doorway.

They both turned toward him.

"You do love that creeping-around shit." Sammie laughed at him.

"Hey." He smiled, entering and hanging his coat next to Joe's. "Old dog, old tricks."

"Did you mean that?" Joe asked. "About a context?"

"Yeah," Willy told them. "I been working my little black book, far from here," he gestured around the office. "And all the taps and wires that're hangin' off our phone lines."

Sam rolled her eyes but made no comment. Willy's obsessive distrust was at once famous and—nowadays—difficult to dispute.

"And?" Joe asked leadingly.

"I still got feeds comin' in," Willy explained. "So this is preliminary. But it is interesting." He settled in behind his corner desk and placed both feet on its untidy surface. Only here—as if in protest against the confines of an office—did his compulsive neatness abandon him.

"On the day Ben caught his bullet," he went on, "he was tagging along as part of a two-fireteam squad, or eight guys—including two sergeants—under a lieutenant. Not the standard setup, but they played fast and loose out of habit back then, and Ben being there as an official photographer probably helped. Not only that, but there was a civilian with 'em, too."

"A civilian?" Joe asked. "That's the first we've heard of that. Who?"

"A writer. Officially a reporter—at least he was attached to some bullshit newspaper from nowhere—but as far as I can figure out, he probably pulled strings to get out there so he could write the great American novel. Everybody I talked to so far says he never filed a single article, but scribbled in a notebook like he was writing *War and Peace.* Anyhow, he made the whole unit eleven men, total—the squad, the looie, Ben, and the writer."

"What was the writer's name?" Sam asked.

But Willy shook his head. "That's the damnedest part. Nobody remembers. We can find out—can't be that hard. But he obviously didn't make much of an impression. And," he added with a telling half smile—the cat with the canary—"he died that day."

It had the expected reaction. Joe and Sam exchanged glances as Sam said to her boss, "I thought you said there was no hostile fire."

"I said I thought so," Joe corrected her.

"And I think he's right," Willy added.

"*Two* friendly fire casualties?" she asked him.

"I don't know how friendly they were," Willy countered. "From what I know right now—and the reason I counted off how many guys were there that day—is that only six of the original eleven are alive today. Ben and the writer are dead, and three others that I got feelers out for."

"Is Jack Joyce one of the six survivors?" Joe asked.

"And how," Willy confirmed. "I don't blame you for knowing nothing about politicians, since they're all such assholes, but he's a hotshot senator, down in D.C.—has been for years. He's also a millionaire—or whatever they all are. A million's probably chump change now."

"So, not counting a follow-up with Bob Morgan—which will definitely be happening," Joe said quietly, "that leaves five more to interview, including a senator."

He checked his watch and stood up. "I better get out of here. Rachel wants to keep going on her project and record the last of the excavation of Kendall's house. I said I'd put her up for as long as that takes, rather than have her driving back and forth."

"I'd still have her under lock and key," Willy said bluntly. "You're playing with fire."

"Where there's one hit team, there may be more?" Joe asked before addressing his own question. "I don't disagree. I ran it by Allard, but he said we don't have the funding if I can't articulate a threat. With Niles under arrest, I don't have that."

Willy stared at him, incredulous. "You can talk the clothes off a nun."

"Charming," Sammie muttered.

"Say what you want," Joe insisted, "he still wouldn't play. The way I see it, we're kind of splitting the difference anyhow. The excavation's a crime scene, cordoned off and guarded around the clock, and she'll be in my care the rest of the time. Not to mention that only her mother knows she's down here."

"And everybody she texts and Facebooks and tweets and Christ knows what else," Willy groused.

"I asked her for radio silence," Joe told him. "She didn't screw around when we had her in the safe house."

He walked to the coat rack and paused. "Willy, keep the pressure on about those squad members. As much information as you can get, any way you can get it."

"Already rollin'," Willy said.

"And Sam? Dig into the writer. Who he was, what he was doing over there, everything and anything—any way you can think of."

She'd already returned to her computer keyboard. "Got it, boss."

Joe met up with Rachel Reiling and Lester Spinney at his home on Green Street, in Brattleboro. Lester had been heading back from Burlington to his family in Springfield, and offered to take Rachel all the way to Brattleboro as a favor—officially ducking Bill Allard's prohibition on more expenses relating to the young woman's security.

Rachel seconded Allard's opinion as she got out of the car. "This really isn't necessary, you know? I could've driven here myself."

Joe instinctively gave her a hug. "Yes, you could've, but thanks for catering anyhow. You have a nice way of making hopelessly old worrywarts feel better."

She laughed and pushed his arm playfully. "Oh, please."

Lester handed him a small overnight bag from the back seat, which Joe lifted easily into the air. "This it? Aren't you staying for more than one night?"

Rachel patted another bag hanging from her shoulder, holding her computer and camera gear. "My mom trained me well. I'm a very practical packer, if you don't mind seeing me in the same outfit for days on end."

"I do not," he reassured her, unlocking the front door to his small house. He ushered her inside, saying, "Make yourself comfortable. I'll be right in."

He turned to Lester after she'd closed the door behind her. "Trip okay?"

Les smiled. "As in, did I see anyone in my rearview mirror? No, Willy's opinion notwithstanding." He looked around them. "I'm impressed you don't have any reporters camped out here."

Joe sighed. "Either courtesy or ignorance on their part. Don't know and don't want to know. Willy's still hyper about the lurking forces of evil?"

"I see his point," Lester conceded. "There's no reason to think someone else won't come after her. I feel like we should hang a sign around her neck like they stick on car windows in New York: NO RADIO. Only, with her, I guess it would have to be: NO WHATEVER IT IS YOU SORRY ASSHOLES ARE AFTER. She is a trouper, though—upbeat the whole trip."

Joe extended his hand in thanks. "You're no slouch, either, Les. Thanks for tacking on an extra hour to bring her here."

Lester shrugged and returned to the driver's seat. "No sweat. Happy to make an end run around Allard."

Joe leaned in slightly. "Everything okay at home? How's Dave holding up at the academy?"

Spinney shook his head. "He's hangin' in there, I guess. I haven't been able to talk to him. Anytime he's at home, he's sleeping. I still think the academy's good for him," he added after a pause. "And so does his mother, more importantly."

Joe stepped back from the car and waved. "Well, give them my best, and thanks again for making the detour. Sorry I've been keeping you away from them for so long."

Lester started the engine. "All's good. Part of the job."

Joe watched him back out of the driveway before following Rachel inside. He found her investigating the contents of the refrigerator.

"Hungry?"

She straightened to look at him. "Can I call you Joe?"

"Of course."

She grinned. "Well, Joe, I don't know how you've lived this long." She gestured toward the fridge. "This makes dorm food look organic."

He returned the smile and reached for the phone. "Pizza—my treat."

A half hour later, they were sitting across his coffee table from each other, eating a pizza loaded with choices Joe never would have imagined, much less selected.

Rachel seemed as interested in his reaction as in the food itself. "Can you stand it, or are you just being polite?"

"Both," he admitted. "But it's much better than just standing it. It's not bad. Just a little . . . more complex than I'm used to."

She laughed. "Mom said you could be diplomatic."

"Uh-oh," he said. "That sounds like faint praise."

Her eyebrows shot up. "From *my* mom? Not hardly. She thinks you're wonderful that way. She's like the most undiplomatic person I know, so it's a good thing in her book." She paused before adding, "She thinks you're wonderful in lots of ways."

He felt his cheeks flush. "Really?"

"Oh, yeah," Rachel spoke guilelessly. "Anne and I talked about the effect you've had on her, and we're really happy. Not that she ever said it, but we think she was kind of lonely."

Joe scratched his forehead. "Thanks."

She tilted her head. "I didn't mean to embarrass you. I figured you'd like to know. People start dating, they're always driving themselves nuts, wondering what the other person's thinking."

"No, no," he said quickly. "I appreciate it. I just wasn't expecting it. Guess I'm kind of old school—less open about personal stuff—which isn't always so great. No, it's nice to hear."

"My dad likes you, too," she added.

This time, he laughed outright and sat back in his armchair. "Okay."

"No, really," she emphasized. "He knows Mom and he weren't a great match, so he's happy, too. You've done good work, Joe Gunther. The whole family approves."

He shook his head and gave her a hapless expression. "What can I say? I have ice cream for dessert."

"You do know how to seal a deal."

The following morning, he drove her to Dummerston and introduced her to the police officers securing Ben Kendall's home, making sure to impress how important she was to him. Progress on the house had been steady and fruitful, with well over half the rooms empty and the rest coming along. Part of the problem was that a former scoop-and-dump operation had become a forensic dismantling of painstaking proportions. Everything removed was now subject to scrutiny and cataloging, when relevant. Additionally, a real fear lingered that the booby trap so fatal to Tommy Bajek hadn't necessarily been the worst of Ben's surprises.

Along those lines, Joe made sure to stress to the girl how potentially dangerous this was, and how she was absolutely to keep her distance and mind the people in charge. In response, she showed him the telephoto lens that she'd attached to her camera.

Arriving at the office later, bearing a box of doughnuts and some coffee, he found Sammie in the same position he'd left her the night before.

"You go home at all?"

She turned in her seat to accept one of his gooey offerings. "Would I miss the chance to see my baby girl? No way. I left late and came back early—all the better to duck the reporters. Plus, I needed to reload this." She held up her cell phone.

"Reload it?" he asked, at a loss about most cell phone functions.

She switched it on and displayed a screen saver photograph of her daughter. "I take a new one every day. Helps me feel in touch. How's Rachel?"

Joe smiled at the picture. "Fine. I just dropped her off at the site. She's a good kid. Lot of her mother in her—nice combination of hardworking and funny."

Sam put her phone down and took a bite of doughnut before saying, "Only a man in love could say that Beverly Hillstrom was in any way, shape, or form funny."

Joe waved that away, embarrassed to have his personal life crop up in office banter. For all that he cared about what happened to his colleagues away from work, he remained a private man. "Anything new on your homework assignment?"

She patted her keyboard. "I know you don't want to hear this, but the Internet puts all sorts of miracles a keystroke away."

"Meaning, yes," he guessed.

"Yup. The writer who died the same day Kendall was shot was named Nathan Sievers. He was from Milwaukee and fancied himself a literary genius. In other words, he was impossible to work with and never got published. He conned an old college roommate, who edited a free weekly paper, to make him their overseas correspondent. With that, he got press creds from the government and paid his own way to Vietnam.

What you were told about him was right on the money. He was only there to write the next best thing to *The Naked and the Dead* or *Dispatches.*"

Joe was about to ask her a follow-up question when he was stopped dead by her literary references. "No offense, Sam, but what do you know about *The Naked and the Dead* or *Dispatches?*"

She laughed in reaction. "Busted. I used Google to drill my way down to the editor-slash-roommate and talked to him on the phone last night. He gave me that. I don't even know what they are."

"Worth reading," Joe said, smiling. "What did the editor say about how Sievers died?"

"Nothing. He said the military notified him that his correspondent had been killed by enemy fire during a combat exchange, and that was about it. Sievers had no family that my source ever knew, the weekly paper wasn't about to pay to have their so-called correspondent shipped home, so Sievers was buried over there. That's where it ended."

"*Lonely Are the Brave,*" Joe murmured.

"What?"

"Just another title. This guy didn't ask about how his friend died?"

Sammie looked rueful. "It wasn't *The New York Times,* Joe. And despite the favor, I think the editor did what he did to get Sievers out of his hair. From what I heard, old Nathan could be a moralistic, preachy pain in the butt. They weren't pals."

"Was he anti-war?" Joe asked.

"Big-time, but being holier-than-thou, he didn't want to be an armchair critic. He wanted to write from the trenches, like Hemingway." She smiled. "Again, I'm quoting, but I do know who Hemingway was."

Joe adulterated his coffee as always. "You hear from Willy?"

Sam reached for the phone. "Yeah. He said to call him when you were ready. He's having a father–daughter day at home—decided that he'd been away too long and needed an Emma fix."

Joe kept quiet, but was struck by how times had changed. Back in the day, before Willy and Sam became involved romantically, Kunkle had been the hard-drinking, dysfunctional survivor of a short and violent marriage that ended with his wife's escaping to New York, where she'd eventually died under violent circumstances. That was a long stretch from what he'd just heard, and gave him heart when he recalled not only Sam's cell phone décor, but also his own charming, if slightly disorienting conversation with Rachel the night before. Maybe there could be light at the end of the tunnel of love.

He motioned to the phone, smiling. "Put him on. I'm ready." He crossed to his desk and sat down as Sam dialed home.

"He there?" Willy's voice came over the speaker shortly thereafter.

"We both are," Sam answered.

"How's Emma?" Joe asked.

"You gonna give me shit about that?"

"Right," Joe answered him. "Six demerits for spending time with your daughter."

"Whatever," Willy said. "What d'ya want to know first?"

"You had five dead to check out from the original squad," Joe said, "and six survivors, including a U.S. senator. Give it to me any way you want, not that you wouldn't have anyhow."

"Getting to know me?" Willy snorted over the phone. "Okay, let's go with the dead, since that's where I started. Ben Kendall and the writer you already know about."

"His name was Nathan Sievers," Joe interjected.

"Good." Willy paused, as if writing it down. "That's a match. I was told Nate, by one of my sources, which didn't give me much. Anyhow, that leaves three. I checked those out and got one suicide, one accidental car crash fatality, and one natural causes—specifically, an undetermined."

"That sounds tame enough," Sam commented.

"'Sounds' is the operative word," Willy said. "These happened all over the U.S.—I'm writing a report when Emma goes down for a nap, and I've got documents and pictures coming in electronically or via snail mail, so I'll spare you the boring stuff right now—but I got hold of people in each place and grilled them pretty hard. Bottom line is, there's major wiggle room for doubt in every case."

"You smelling covered-up homicides?" Joe asked, his spirit sagging in the face of so much carnage.

"Yep. The car crash was under-investigated forty years ago by a rural department in Missouri with minimal training and equipment, leaving a bunch unexplained—like how some different-colored paint ended up on a part of the car that fit perfectly where it could've been smacked and sent flying off the road. That's just one squirrelly detail. Another is that the dead driver had an empty bottle of booze with him, his clothes reeked of the stuff, but his blood was clean when they tested it and there was never an autopsy."

"So, hit and run, with maybe a victim who was unconscious or dead just prior," Joe stated.

He expected a sarcastic comeback, but Willy missed his opportunity for once, responding instead, "Yup, and they're not saying I'm wrong, either. I'm not beating 'em up on it. This was back in the '70s, everybody associated with it is dead or gone, and the guy I talked to was relying on an old file and some Polaroids. He didn't like it any better than I did, but there's not much anyone can do about it now."

"Okay," Sam said. "That's one."

"Right," Willy resumed. "The suicide would've been an even more obvious set-up today, but again—way back when—they didn't catch a thing. It was a hanging—man found in his garage, complete with a 'farewell cruel world' note—but the note was typed. And—you'll love this—there was no typewriter in the house. It was right in the report.

The chair he supposedly used was still upright, and placed wrong, to my eye. And the rope marks on his neck didn't match how the rope was positioned when they found him, indicating to me that he was strangled first and then strung up. Oh yeah, and he had bruises on his knuckles, as if he'd put up a fight."

"Same kind of conversation with the local cops?" Joe asked.

"Pretty much," Willy admitted. "Not so friendly, but this one happened about the same time, in L.A., which was corrupt as hell back then, so it doesn't matter what their attitude is now.

"The last one," he continued, "was even more open-ended. Guy was found dead at home, in bed. Next to him were some heart pills, but just lying in a jar, with no prescription, like M&M's. Conclusion? Died of a heart attack. Any mention of a bad ticker in his military medical records? Nope. But his drunk wife liked the benefits, and everybody else was happy to let it lie. So, there you have it."

Joe trusted that he'd have the literature supporting all this soon enough, so he took it at face value and moved on. "You get anywhere on the living squad members?"

"Superficially. I got the Fusion Center to spit out generic intel reports on each of 'em, and did some once-over-lightly digging on the side. I didn't want to tip our hand, in case somethin's going on like a conspiracy, so I avoided any interviews by phone, or anything else too obvious. I'm just tellin' ya."

"Okay," Joe reassured him.

"Jack Joyce was the easiest," Willy went on. "Super rich from birth, lots of good press for going into the service in the first place, since he's both prep school and Ivy League, and of course a shoo-in as a politician for the same reason, even with all the anti-war crap back then. No one's been able to boot him out since, so he's one of the Grand Old Men of the Senate now, but not famous like the rest of the fogies, 'cause he doesn't do squat. From what I could get from articles, blogs, book digests, and the rest, the man's a manipulative prick who brings home the pork and otherwise lines his pockets.

"The other four," Willy began wrapping up, "came across like your pal Bob Morgan—underemployed underachievers with more money than their lifestyles can explain. Again, the details'll be in my report."

Joe and Sam could hear the sounds of Emma crying softly in the background.

"Uh-oh. Got an attack of the munchies," Willy said. "Gotta feed the inheritor."

"Quick gut reaction to it all before you go?" Joe spoke fast.

Willy chose his words carefully, given his usual breeziness. "There may be others, but one scenario that fits everything is that something happened out there that got five people killed—including one at the scene—and made the surviving six happy campers for life."

"Like a major haul of some kind?" Sammie asked. "A financial windfall?"

Willy hedged. "Anyone's guess."

Joe frowned. "Treasure Island? A trunk of drugs or doubloons? In the middle of the Delta? That sounds like a stretch."

Willy let out a short laugh. "What hasn't been a stretch so far? The dead hoarder with a corpse in one of his own booby traps? No . . . Hold it, maybe his ancient history, ex-wife found tortured to death five states away, with no apparent connection. Nah—that clearly makes sense. I got it. The daughter of Vermont's chief medical examiner gets stalked by two hit men, straight out of a bad movie. There you go."

Joe held up both hands at the phone in surrender. "Okay, okay. You made your point. So you're suggesting that eleven men in Vietnam maybe stumbled across something of value which made some of them dead and the rest of them rich."

"I said that *seems* how it wound up," Willy corrected him. "I have no idea what started it. On the flip side, I do know why my kid's crying."

"Ben Kendall knew," Sam suggested.

"And so do the surviving six," Joe added.

After a moment—during which they could hear him cooing to Emma—Willy asked, "Who d'you wanna start with?"

Joe smiled slightly. "Why not the proverbial bird in hand?"

CHAPTER TWENTY-FOUR

Paula Sagerman was a detective with the New Hampshire State Police whom Joe had met at a tri-state terrorism training several years ago. Such events served as much as meet-and-greet opportunities—or "networking," as Joe refused to describe them—as chances to learn things that common sense didn't already supply. Cops like him had regularly benefited from discovering worthwhile counterparts and keeping in touch. Sagerman's immediate agreement to meet in Peterborough and accompany him to Bob Morgan's house was proof of it.

She was smart, ambitious, and diplomatically canny—at once reminiscent of Sammie, while demonstrating how lucky Joe felt that Sam was not cut from the hard stuff that might eventually make of Paula a commissioner of public safety or a politician. Joe wasn't sure what in Sam seemed missing from Paula, but he suspected that it might be the self-doubt that he valued in the former.

That having been said, he genuinely liked Paula. She had a no-nonsense, pragmatic view of things, and enjoyed telling people exactly what kind of jackass she occasionally found them to be.

So . . . perhaps not a future politician.

"Wuzzup, Joe?" she asked as she settled into his passenger seat at the spot where they'd agreed to meet.

"I want your statutory muscle along for when I ask this guy what he's holding back," he explained.

"I thought you loved me for my mind."

He smiled and started the car. "Not this time, but feel free to chime in if you get the urge."

"What're we grilling him about?"

"Vietnam. He witnessed something he won't admit about a squad of men, deep in the bush. The Cliffs Notes version is that close to half of them are now dead under suspicious circumstances, while the rest are just as inexplicably well off. So what happened? Was it a My Lai without the headlines? Did it involve finding a cache of money or drugs and keeping it quiet? One of them—who just died—was a photographer. But we've seen his photos, and they tell us nothing. On the other hand, both his cameras were empty when he was found with a head wound. And why were the only people shot at the scene—one fatally and one almost—a writer and a photographer, respectively?"

Paula absorbed it all before asking, "You said this guy's named Robert Morgan. Is it just his proximity to Vermont that makes you want to milk him?"

Joe smiled as he left the parking lot and headed out of town. "You are good, Sagerman. Yes and no. Morgan's living nearby is handy, but it's not the only factor. The last time I talked with him—also the first time we met—I suspected he was starting to crumble around the edges, which is why I want you to look threatening in the background. I need to impress upon him that we can buckle him up if he forces us to."

Paula nodded. "Cool. I guess I'll figure out the rest as the conversation gets going." She paused before saying, "You know I wasn't even alive when the Vietnam War ended."

He sighed wearily. "Yes."

"Okay, then," she said, settled on the point. "Sounds like fun."

Which attitude reflected, in part, why Joe had called her in the first place.

There was no sign of Mrs. Morgan when they reached the house on General Miller Road, and the Jeep was missing, Joe noted gratefully. Bob answered the doorbell himself, ushering them into an empty living room after Joe had introduced Paula, and offered to fix them coffee.

Both cops turned down the invitation, and angled their chairs toward the sofa in such a way that Morgan, when seated, had to swivel his head back and forth to address them, psychologically undermining any sense of his being in control.

"You know why I asked Detective Sagerman to join me?" Joe asked after they'd settled down.

"Not really," Morgan hedged his reply.

"Last time I was here," Joe explained, "your wife pointed out that I couldn't act as a cop in this state. Detective Sagerman can." He added, almost as an afterthought, "Should it become necessary." He extracted a recorder from his pocket and turned it on. "Furthermore, I'll be recording what's said, just to ensure that nothing can be misconstrued or misunderstood. Is that all right with you?"

Morgan looked at them without comment.

"I need your permission, Bob. Out loud. I want it on the record that you're being frank and open with us, and that we haven't promised or threatened you with anything. Is that the case?"

"Sure."

"Because," Joe resumed, "it's my belief that you were less than candid last time."

"I answered your questions," Bob countered without much conviction.

"How do you make a living, Mr. Morgan?" Paula asked, almost

cutting him off, taking Joe's earlier cue about the squad survivors all being well off.

Morgan opened his mouth in surprise before answering with a stutter, "I'm a . . . a . . . a custodian."

She looked around. "No kidding? Your wife loaded? You have a trust fund?"

His face flushed.

The point made, Joe took his turn, laying a file folder on the coffee table and saying before Morgan could respond, "We been brushing up on our homework, Bob, since you chose not to cooperate." Joe stared at him. "Even though you felt guilty about it."

"What?" Morgan said.

Joe didn't address the question. "I told you I was investigating several felonies in connection to what happened in Vietnam, including Ben's death. Which makes me wonder: You keep in touch with any buddies from back then?"

"What?" he repeated.

"Simple question," Paula pressed him.

"Ian Faulkner, for example," Joe said, extracting a photograph and laying it face up on the table, oriented toward Morgan. "That's a picture of the car crash that killed him, soon after you all got home. No explanation of why he was covered in booze but had none in his bloodstream, and no explanation for the paint smear where the other car hit him and forced him off the road."

Morgan didn't touch the picture.

"Andy Weiss," Joe intoned, placing another picture between them, this one a close-up of an obviously dead man. "Found at home, around the same time. Ruled to be a natural—a heart attack. Did you know Andy had a bum ticker? Funny the army missed it during his physical."

Bob whispered mournfully, as if to himself, "Oh, Andy."

"You hear the question?" Paula asked.

"No, I didn't know about a bad heart," Morgan said quietly.

"That's because it was fine," Joe announced, although he had no proof of that. "His death was just too uninteresting to pursue at the time, and they found heart meds next to his bed, although not prescribed to him. Course, he was no Slim Jim, so why bother investigating? People weren't as thorough as they tend to be now."

"Bummer for you," Paula commented.

Morgan looked back and forth at them, as they'd anticipated with their seating arrangement.

"Bryan Cosselli," Joe said to recapture his attention. He laid down another picture. "That's him hanging in his garage—again, same time period. Suicide note and everything. You know Bryan to be down in the dumps when you served together?"

Morgan shook his head slightly.

"Yeah," Joe agreed. "His mother didn't think so, either. Still, hard to argue with a note."

Joe placed a copy of the short note onto the growing pile as Morgan murmured, "I guess."

"Except that this one is typed, and there wasn't a typewriter in the house."

Morgan rubbed his forehead.

"You connecting the dots here, Bob?" Paula asked.

Joe sat forward. "What did Bryan, Andy, Ben, and Ian have in common, Bob, that they all deserved to be murdered?"

Morgan remained silent, his hands clenched between his knees.

"You were friends with Andy," Joe said. "I could hear it in your voice."

"Yeah," he whispered.

"*What?*" Paula demanded.

He looked up at her. "Yes. We were friends."

"Well, somebody killed your friend," she said.

"And Bryan, and Ian, and Ben," Joe added. He placed a crime scene photo of Jennifer Sisto on the low table, tied spread-eagle and semi-nude on her apartment floor.

Morgan turned his face away.

"Look at it," Paula ordered.

"Focus on the face," Joe suggested. "That might make it easier. She's an older woman there. This just happened. But maybe something about her features rings a bell."

Baffled, Morgan took a closer look. But he shook his head.

"You know how it is in combat," Joe reminisced. "Guys show each other snapshots of their kids, wives, girlfriends. Ben Kendall ever show you a picture of his wife?"

Morgan blinked, caught off guard.

"That's her, after she was tortured to death. Recently. In Philadelphia. Ben ever talk about her? Or about Philly?"

"A little."

"Yeah, I know what that's like—shooting the breeze, talking about what'll happen once it's over, pretending that nobody's going to catch a bullet in the meantime, feeling guilty that you hope it's the other guy and not you. Am I right?"

Morgan nodded.

"And then something does happen, and it's not the way you figured. The wrong people die, the world stops being the same, and you're left with all this crap in your head—ghosts reaching out, accusing you of not having done the right thing. You still see Ben Kendall at night, Bob? You still see the hole in his head? All the blood?"

Joe reached out and tapped the stack of pictures. "And what about the others? They got home before they died. Did you know they didn't truly survive?"

Morgan stayed frozen in place, and Joe suddenly knew why. "You did know, didn't you, Bob? You've known all along. Maybe not how. Maybe not the details." He pawed through the images, spreading them out. "You didn't know they'd strung Bryan up like a dead deer. Or poisoned Andy. Or terrorized Ian, ramming his car as he fought to control it, their headlights blinding him from inches away. But you knew they were dead."

Morgan sat hunched on the sofa, his entire body like a closed fist.

"Didn't you?" Joe yelled, making Bob and Paula jump.

"Yes." It was barely audible.

"While the rest of you were taken care of financially," Joe stated.

"Yes."

"And you've been living with that ever since."

A tear ran down Morgan's cheek, and spilled onto the knuckles of his hand.

Paula's voice was soft when she spoke, completely at odds with her tone earlier. "Talk to us, Bob. Get it off your chest. It's not like it's a secret anymore. We just need a few details confirmed."

"What happened in Nam?" Joe asked.

Morgan looked at them haplessly. "If I tell you, I'm as dead as them, and so's my family."

Joe waved that away. "You've got it the wrong way around. You tell us what happened, and we'll get the guy responsible. We just did that with these two." He laid out mug shots of Niles and Watson. "One's dead; the other's never getting out. You ever see them before? A couple of hit men?"

Bob shook his head. "No."

"They came after a few folks in Vermont, like Ben." Joe reached out and tapped the photo of Jenn Sisto. "And they killed his ex-wife. But they're done for now. We nailed their asses."

"There'll be more," Bob said gloomily.

"We know that," Joe answered him. "They're just blunt instruments. We get the man winding them up, and it's over. And you and your wife and daughter get to live without fear."

Paula spoke in the same soothing tone as before. "We get it, Bob. It was a lousy choice—you either lived with the guilt, or died because of what you knew. But there were fringe benefits with the guilt, 'cause you got paid. That it?"

"Pretty much."

"Good," she said, almost happily. "Well, that gravy train's over, as of now, 'cause we know about it. You think that whoever's pulling the strings is gonna keep shelling out bucks when the cat's outta the bag? Think it through. You're screwed. If you were him, wouldn't you take care of this problem the same way you did years ago? Right after Nam?"

"I suppose."

"We can protect you and your family," Joe joined in. "Provided you help us out." He paused to let that sink in, before repeating, "Tell us what happened."

The request this time seemed to deflate him, almost as much as it had set him on edge earlier. He slumped in his seat, his eyes unfocused, his hands opened in his lap.

"I'll never know what life might've been like without that day," he began. He looked up for emphasis. "And not because of anything I did. That's the craziest part. I even talked about that with some of the others. We didn't *do* anything. We were just there, like we had been for months before and—for some of us, at least—for months after. But nothing was ever the same again."

Joe and Paula remained silent, letting him navigate through his own narrative.

"It was a standard recon," he went on. "We'd done them so many times, it was almost routine. We joked about how stupid it was—heading out, finding some village. Usually no more than a few hooches clumped around a fire pit. Sometimes, every once in a while, when we were part of a platoon or something bigger, there'd actually be some action—somebody really shooting at us."

He looked up and grinned incongruously. "They did do that, you know? They did fight, now and then, like crazy bastards. They won the fucking war, didn't they? It wasn't just us, wandering around in the bush killing people. People think that's all we did—murder innocent women and children before we were forced to quit by protesters back home. Well, we did murder people—both sides did—but it was a real war, with atrocities to spare."

He paused.

The cops remained quiet.

"The thing is," he resumed, "we did it a lot. We'd been conditioned like robots, from boot camp on up. It was 'slopes' and 'rice-eaters' and the rest, all the time. They hammered it into us. It didn't matter what happened once we got in-country. Every local was a suspect, if not out to kill us. What the hell did we know? And what the hell did the Command staff care? To them, it was all 'What's the body count?' 'Why're your numbers so low?' Shit like that. People like Lieutenant Joyce were just following orders."

"Talk about Joyce," Joe prompted.

"He was an ass-kisser," Morgan said without hesitation. "Always sucking up to the brass. Nothing they ordered was too stupid, and nothing they said afterwards was ever wrong."

"Sounds like the kind of officer they used to find dead in a ditch," Paula commented. "Killed by his own men."

Bob's eyes widened. "Not the lieutenant. He was a nasty piece of work. He may've been a suck-up to the bosses, but he was a real dictator to us. You didn't fuck with Joyce. Plus, he had his goons. If he didn't come after you, they did on his orders. He paid them to. He was a rich kid. We never could figure out what he was even doing there. . . . Until later, of course."

"Of course?" Joe asked.

"The Senate," Morgan explained. "That's what it was all about from the start—the military career, the money, the controlling everything all the time. He wanted power. Hell, he would've gone for the presidency if things had worked out better, but the Senate's all his kind of bullshit would allow. There're more than enough stupid, nasty people in Congress. He never even stood out. But running for president? Even he knew that would be pushing it. Too many buried bodies would've come up to bite him."

"Like the time you're describing?" Joe asked, quietly directing him.

"Yeah," Morgan agreed. "That was typical. We were stretched out, been humpin' for days, the mood was bad. Lieutenant Joyce had been chewed out upstairs for some reason, and he was taking it out on us. We came on the village feelin' ugly."

"Was Ben a part of that?" Joe asked. "The feeling ugly?"

"Not Ben. He would've been invisible if it hadn't been for that damn camera always in your face. The other guy, the writer . . ."

"Sievers."

"Yeah. He was definitely a problem. All attitude and argument. I'm amazed it took so long for one of us to kill him."

A pause welled up, as the statement floated among them. Joe quickly said, "Go on," to get past it.

"Anyhow, we were pissed, and Joyce was the worst. We went into that village like we owned the place. No feelers, no caution, no preliminary scouting. We saw it, and we went in." He snapped his fingers. "Like that. It was crazy. There coulda been a hundred VC in there. We wouldn't have known. That was the mood."

He hesitated, as if to catch his breath, and added, "And then he found the girl."

"Okay," Joe coaxed him.

Morgan glanced at Sagerman, as if for permission. "Well, he raped her. We were checking the hooches, she was inside the one Joyce hit, and he just went over the edge. He was on autopilot. It was like watching one of those zombie shows on TV. Without hesitation, he shot the old woman, the kid, grabbed the girl, threw her down—"

He stopped and placed his right palm against his forehead. "I think that's what Ben saw."

Joe felt his face flush, the scene suddenly coming alive as everything they'd been sorting through over the past several weeks came into focus. "And Joyce shot him," he said without thought.

Morgan narrowed his eyes. "Not at first. The hooch was open at both ends. Sievers walked in, same time as Ben, from the other door. Joyce saw him first, looking up as he was raping the girl. And again, just like with her, it was automatic. He just shot the guy, right in the chest."

"Ben saw that, too?" Paula asked.

"Yeah. That's when Joyce must've turned and shot him—in the head. I don't know how he didn't drop right there, but he ran. We were all running by then, toward the hooch. Everybody was yelling. A couple more shots were fired, Christ knows at what. Joyce killed the girl. I saw him do that. And then he went after Ben."

"How long had Ben been gone?" Joe asked.

"A minute, maybe two. But times like that always seem longer. It coulda been a few seconds."

"Go on."

"Joyce did up his pants, pushed through us, ran outside. We were just standing there, taking it in, and then a couple of us took off after Joyce. We were worried about Ben. We'd seen him running out, covered in blood."

"Who went with you?"

"Andy."

"Okay. Where did you find them?"

"Not far. Around the corner of the next hooch. Joyce was standing over Ben's body."

"What was he doing with his hands?"

Morgan looked nonplussed. "His hands? Nuthin'. I don't know. I don't remember him doing anything."

"And Ben's cameras?"

"Yeah. Like I said, they were on the ground, open."

Joe locked Morgan's eyes with his own. "Bob. I need to hear this directly from you: What do you think happened to the film? What do you think Joyce did?"

"I told you what he did. I don't know anything about any film. Maybe Joyce took it. He'd just shot five people. Maybe he was worried Ben had taken pictures."

"Had he?"

Morgan stared at him, helpless. "I don't know." He dragged out the last word into a half wail. "All we saw was him running away, all bloody, and the dead bodies in the hooch, and the lieutenant doin' up his pants with his gun still in his hand."

Joe nodded several times to calm him down. "Okay, okay. What did you do next, after finding Joyce and Ben together?"

"I just tried to take care of Ben."

"And you said that Ben never said anything."

"That's right. He was out of it."

Joe kept at him. "You said Joyce was holding a gun. Did you see him fire it?"

"It was his sidearm. He'd dropped his M16 to rape the girl. I saw him shoot her."

"But the thing about Joyce shooting Sievers and then Ben, that's what you pieced together later. Correct?"

Morgan hesitated, a growing doubt on his face. "Don't you believe me?"

"It's not a matter of that," Joe said quickly. "It's a matter of being absolutely accurate. People're going to try to poke holes in this."

"What people?"

"The people that'll be protecting you and working to put Joyce in jail for what he did. For that to happen, everything you say has to stand up. You know this isn't going to end here."

Morgan nodded miserably.

Joe then played his trump card, and laid out several photos side by side on the low table. They were the shots of American servicemen, on display at the Fleming Museum.

"Do you know who these people are?" he asked.

Morgan hunched over them, scrutinizing them. "Holy Jesus," he said. "It's us. That must've been the day." He looked up and tapped a blurry figure in the background. "That's Sievers."

"You sure?" Paula asked, frowning. "You can barely see him."

Morgan's voice was excited. "Yeah, it is. You think I'd forget that day?" He tapped on another figure. "That's Joyce yelling, as usual. Must've been earlier. The background isn't the village."

This was a mixed blessing for Joe, both a confirmation and a disappointment, as his next question revealed. "Bob, you said there was no film to be found. That Ben's cameras were empty. If these were shot the same day, where did they come from?"

But Morgan didn't hesitate. "Sievers," he said, as if that explained it. "He'd agreed to carry Ben's kit bag, since he was unarmed. It had a tripod in it, some other stuff, and it's where Ben dropped all his exposed film. When the medevac chopper got there, I threw it in with Ben." He gestured toward the pictures. "They must've been in there."

Joe let his words sink in before he asked, "What happened after you'd tended to Ben?"

"We called in the chopper."

"What about Sievers?" Paula asked. "He go, too?"

It turned out to be a pertinent question. Morgan took her in with an almost surprised expression. "That's where it started getting really weird, and why—" He looked at Joe. "—I didn't make this up. No. Joyce said to leave him. Then he got us together after the chopper left and started on this rant, telling us how everybody was out to get us, from the protesters to Command to the politicians to the gooks, and how we had to hang together, especially against people like Sievers."

"Sievers?" Joe said, caught off guard.

"Yeah. He sort of worked his way around to pinning the whole thing on him, saying that Sievers had 'almost got him' or some shit like that, before Joyce got him first. The implication was that maybe it was Sievers who shot Ben, even though he didn't carry a gun. It was totally crazy. He was walking back and forth, waving his arms around, talking fast. Still with the gun in his hand."

"Did he threaten you?" Joe wanted to know.

"We felt threatened," Morgan confirmed. "Andy and I talked about that after, but we all did. Nobody knew what to do. What happened to whistleblowers was no secret—that was a given. A bunch of guys were killed for shooting their mouths off about stuff happening in the bush. But we were sure Joyce had murdered someone in cold blood—an unarmed American civilian, not even counting the others. In a heartbeat, without thinking about it. He'd done it before to locals—lots of times—but never an American."

Bob paused to rub his forehead again. "And the way his little speech ended, we were pretty sure he wouldn't have a problem doing it again."

"How were things left?" Joe asked.

"We returned to base, on foot instead of by chopper, carrying Sievers in a bag. That was the lieutenant's choice, and I found out why. He took each of us aside on the way back and grilled us about what we were thinking. He made it real clear to me that if I kept my mouth shut, I'd never have to work again. He said that his family had more money than God, and that I'd never have to worry."

"Or what?" Paula asked.

Morgan made a face. "I didn't ask and he didn't say, but I knew it would be bad. That's why we were carrying Sievers, I always thought. As a reminder. And after we got shipped back home and he contacted me to make his offer formal, he even told me—no bones about it—how my wife and any other family would die if I ever ratted him out." He pointed at the small stack of photographs Joe had shown him. "After my daughter was born, that fucker sent me a picture of her, like you would to congratulate somebody. But it was a photo taken through a scope, with crosshairs, and it wasn't one we took that he'd doctored. We thought one of his people probably shot it through a window or something, as a warning."

He studied Joe and added, "Jack Joyce is a crazy man, and a stone-cold killer. I wasn't gonna fuck with a guy like that. I see him on TV every once in a while, and he still keeps in touch through his goons, now and then, and every time, it's to remind me of—as he calls it, 'the terms of our contract.' That's how I knew about Andy and the others." He pressed his lips together before adding, "And now I've told you, which means your promise better be better than his, or my whole family is dead."

"Did all the squad members compare notes after you reached base?" Joe asked, not addressing the man's dilemma. "It seems from what you're saying that not everybody chose like you did. Andy, for example."

"There wasn't that much talking. Joyce had told us not to, and we were already freaked out. You gotta remember, the stuff you see in the movies about soldiers all being best buddies? That's a crock. Andy and I were tight, but the rest of 'em? Some were okay, but others? I didn't give a rat's ass what they did."

"But you and Andy talked," Paula suggested.

"Yeah," he said sadly. "I told him he was nuts. I mean, not only was the offer good, but the guy was a psycho. It was a lose–lose to turn him down. But Andy wasn't interested. He didn't think it was that big a deal. We saw a bunch of pure evil over there. Joyce shooting two Americans was terrible, but it wasn't unheard of, and Andy figured he'd just go home and forget about it." He pointed to the photo stack again. "Looks like he chose poorly."

"Your wife know about any of this?" Joe asked.

"She thinks we have a trust fund, which—if you think about it—I do. Or did. What's going to happen to us now?"

Paula glanced at Joe, probably wondering the same thing. There was no question of an official offer of protective custody. Joe had no case to justify it, much less any evidentiary proof of Morgan's story. Nevertheless, he didn't hesitate saying, "It's up to you, Bob, but you're both welcome to come to Vermont, where the Bureau will arrange to keep you under wraps for however long this takes to play out. It won't be easy—just so you know. You'll have to cut all ties, follow our rules, and not do anything that'll make it possible for Joyce and his people to track you down. It'll be a rough path to follow."

"Better than dying."

Joe had to grant him that.

Senator Jack Joyce looked up from the note he was writing with a gold Montblanc fountain pen.

"Jesus, Jonathan. What the hell is it this time?"

"Mr. Smith, sir."

His butler stepped aside without comment and let a giant of a man step around him and enter the office.

Joyce waved his hand imperiously. "Fine. Get lost. And no more creeping around tonight, okay? Go do whatever you do somewhere else."

"Very well, sir."

He waited for the door to close soundlessly before asking without preamble, "What's this supposedly Dead-Eye Dick's name?"

"Chris Hadsel."

"Any reason I should think Chris Hadsel's going to be any better than the first two? Far as I can tell, those dummies screwed everything up."

The big man shifted his weight slightly, which, at two hundred and fifty pounds, could make an impression. Joyce was unmoved. He kept a steady gaze.

"I've never been let down before," came the qualified response.

Joyce let out a weary sigh—the executive saddled with petty details. "Christ," he said softly. "I guess that'll have to do. Let your latest dog loose and let's see if we can finally catch a break."

CHAPTER TWENTY-FIVE

"How's my girl?" Beverly asked.

Joe pulled over to the side of the road. There was no Vermont law against driving and using a cell phone simultaneously, but he avoided the practice in general.

"She's a happy clam, from what I was told. You didn't speak to her directly?"

"No service, of course."

Joe laughed. That was the other reason he always pulled over. All of northern New England had spotty reception, at best. "I spoke with Dispatch not fifteen minutes ago. Rachel's fine, and Ben's house is getting down to where they can see an end in sight, which suits me fine."

"Oh?"

"I'm hoping against reason for some gold nugget to appear at the bottom of it all, but mostly, I just want it to be done. How are you holding up?"

"Generally?" she began. "Very well. But I could certainly do with a little less attention from the press. It's now become a rarity around here when the phone rings and it's not a reporter."

They spoke a little longer after that, largely on other topics. It was slowly becoming a habit of theirs, especially given the distance between them, to get in touch at least daily, if only to exchange mundane activities. Joe enjoyed the reaffirmation he got from the practice, that this foray of the heart—once presumed to never be tried again—had become one of the smartest moves of his life.

Joe swung by Ben's place before continuing on to Brattleboro. The weather had steadied since the last snow, so the crew at the site had been able to ignore it, as most Vermonters did at this time of year—aside from donning extra layers and cursing more frequently as they worked.

On the other hand, the combination of aging snow and active heavy equipment did not make for an attractive scene. Ben's spread, even compared to how Joe had first found it—what seemed like so long ago—resembled a battlefield. The entire property was gouged with deep, muddy ruts and piles of disturbed earth. And the house—never an architectural showcase—now presented like a building caught in some artillery crossfire, with most of one wall missing and its innards fanned out to both sides on the ground.

He found Rachel moving about the periphery, video camera in hand, shooting through gaps and windows with her long lens—although at what, he couldn't tell in the bright outside light. She was clearly taking her double assignment, as historical recorder and evidence documentarian, very seriously.

"Getting good stuff?" he asked as he approached.

She finished her shot and lowered the camera, smiling. "Totally. I really want to thank you again for letting me do this. I mean, it's sad, in a couple of ways, but it's good, too, you know?"

"I do," he said, appreciating her lack of guile or pretense. "You know if they found anything useful?"

Her expression sombered. "I don't think so. Agent Martens is inside."

"They been cooperating with you okay?" he asked. "You been able to do what you came for?"

"Oh, yeah. They've all been great."

He didn't doubt it. Having someone of her age and level of enthusiasm was a rare occurrence at a crime scene reconstruction. He imagined that she'd lifted the team's spirits and helped refine their focus. He made a mental note to consider using her in this role in the future.

"Good," he said. "I think they'll be wrapping up for today pretty soon. If you want, I'll drive you home after I check in with Sam."

"Thanks," she answered. "I'll be ready."

He found Sam deep inside, dressed in her hooded Tyvek suit. He hadn't donned equivalent gear, since forensic contamination wasn't a problem here. He imagined she'd done so mostly to keep her clothes clean. Given the smell still clouding the whole house—and the dust and mildew that they'd disturbed—he could only sympathize.

"Anything?" he asked succinctly.

She pulled back her hood and stripped off her latex gloves so she could rub her face vigorously. "Odds and ends. Letters, papers. Nothing to write home about. How 'bout you? How'd it go with Morgan?"

"He spilled the beans. Gave us the complete background in a sworn statement. The squad leader—now Senator Joyce—apparently raped and killed a girl in a small village, along with a child and an old woman who were with her. Sievers caught him in the act and was shot for his pains, as was Ben. Joyce then told everybody that he'd either take care of them for life, or they'd suffer the consequences. According to Morgan, that's exactly what he did."

"And it worked for this long?" Sam asked incredulously.

"Must have," Joe said. "Until Rachel stumbled across the pictures

Ben had taken of them earlier that same day. Joyce probably had a coronary when he saw them in *The New York Times*. I'm thinking that he destroyed what Ben had in his cameras, right after he shot him, but didn't notice that Sievers had been acting as a pack mule, carrying Ben's equipment bag as a favor, complete with shot film. For Joyce, seeing anything associated with that day must've been like a red rag for a bull—he saw his entire career disappearing in a cloud of smoke."

"Does that mean we have a case against Joyce?" she asked, reasonably enough. "Did Morgan pin the deaths of the other squad members on him?"

"Not credibly. He didn't even see him shoot Sievers and Ben. He just put it together. Joyce supposedly told them that he killed Sievers after Sievers shot Ben and tried to kill him. Obviously, we're going to have to round up the surviving members and see if they'll corroborate Morgan's story, and dig like nobody's business into Joyce's past—which'll be real fun, given that he's a U.S. senator and therefore under the watchful eye of our federal brethren. Also, since Morgan told me of the deal he made with Joyce, we have to assume that his life is at risk, which," he added after a slight pause, "is why I've arranged to put him and his wife someplace safe for a while."

Sammie stared at him in surprise. "Oh, Allard's gonna *love* that."

"Yeah," Joe agreed, "tell me about it. On the other hand, it might push him into getting the U.S. Attorney's office involved, to combine this with the Niles case, both to get a cleaner shot at Joyce and to pay for little niceties like keeping the Morgans alive." He checked his watch. "Anyhow, I told Rachel that I'd take her to my place for the night, since I guess you're about done for the day. You agree?"

"Yeah. Although, given what you just told me, I'm going to make double sure this site is secure overnight. If Morgan turns out to be a straight shooter, Joyce is likely to pull out every stop he can to destroy everything and everybody connected to his past. It could get hairy."

She looked around them. "This pile of junk, for example, would make one hell of a bonfire."

She gestured toward the outside of the building. "And not to sound overly cautious, shouldn't we tuck Rachel away again? No reason to think she's not still a primary target, especially if Joyce hears you've grabbed Morgan. Being a senator doesn't seem to have curbed his appetite for having people killed or kidnapped. The man likes a clean slate."

"Maybe you're right," Joe agreed. "I'll make arrangements tomorrow. Where's Willy?"

She laughed. "You think I know? He is in town, but as usual, all he told me was that he had 'stuff to do' and not to wait up. You know our boy—he does love that ninja-skulking. I'll try reaching out to tell him the latest."

Joe let out a sigh and stared at the floor a moment.

"What?" she asked him.

"I was just thinking of the irony," Joe explained. "Here's Joyce running around, ordering people grabbed, killed, and tortured, going crazy over a bunch of harmless snapshots a half century old, and we can't even build a case against him. The most we could do is dent his reputation— maybe make him lose the next election."

Sam smiled ruefully. "I wouldn't even put much faith in that."

He nodded resignedly. "Guess we'll just keep plugging. Our advantage is that he doesn't know what we can't prove. Oh, well. See ya tomorrow. Give Emma a kiss from me."

Two hours later, Joe and Rachel were standing side by side in his small kitchen at home, he washing their few dishes and she drying them. Dinner, prepared by Joe, had consisted of grilled Velveeta sandwiches, canned split-pea soup, and vanilla ice cream covered with maple syrup for dessert. Rachel had praised his flair for practical and tasty concoctions, which he'd taken as a compliment.

"What's your mom's cooking like?" he asked as they neared the end of their labors.

"Dinner's either something French, unpronounceable, and five hours in the making, complete with opera music and wine," she answered, "or it's scrambled eggs and toast at eleven o'clock at night."

Joe laughed. "That a roundabout way of saying you prefer her eggs to her French la-di-dahs?"

She joined him. "It is, but I think her fancy cooking is more meditative than it's supposed to be successful. She doesn't necessarily have guests when she goes wild in the kitchen. Sometimes, she's all alone, just forgetting about work."

He drained the sink of its soapy water. "I can sympathize with her there. That's why I turn out more wooden birdhouses and picnic tables than I've got interested takers."

"I was admiring your wood shop earlier," Rachel commented.

"I love going in there," he admitted. "Most of those big old iron monsters belonged to my father. They just hum along, barely vibrating, solid like the engines on a ship from the 1800s. Dangerous as hell," he added, "but wonderful to work with."

She hung up her dish towel and eyed him thoughtfully for a moment, making him raise an eyebrow. "What?" he asked.

"I was just thinking how glad I am that you and Mom hooked up."

He reached out and touched her hand. "So am I."

The doorbell rang—an almost unique occurrence. Joe's small house was attached to the back of the property, and was often mistaken from the street as either a barn or an abandoned garage. No one came by who didn't know him, and if they did, they knew better than to ring the bell.

Plus, of course, there was the recently heightened concern for Rachel's safety.

Joe pointed to the narrow staircase leading to the bedroom/loft he'd lent her. It was a tiny low-ceilinged alcove that had been added above the kitchen, wedged into the corner of the adjacent living room's skylighted vaulted ceiling. He kept his voice relaxed but quiet. "Why don't you head up to your room while I find out who that is? Just to play it safe."

They split up as Joe passed through the living room to reach the tiny entryway and the door. Instinctively, his hand fluttered above his right hip, confirming that his gun was in its holster.

"Who is it?" he called out, standing to one side of the heavy door.

A young woman's voice answered. "Hello?"

"What's up?" he asked, hand on the doorknob.

"Sorry to bother you," she replied, barely audible, "but I was driving by and almost hit this cat. He's a little guy and doesn't have a collar, and nobody answered at the front of the building."

"I don't own a cat," he answered her. "Sorry."

"Hello?"

He cautiously peered through the peephole in the door, making sure there was no light directly behind him, which could give his motion away and potentially make him a target. Before him stood a young woman, eyes wide and pleading, cradling a young cat in her arms.

"I said: I don't own a cat. Sorry."

"Hello? I can't hear you. The poor thing's almost a kitten. I don't know what to do."

He could barely hear her any better than she seemed to be hearing him.

He opened the door a crack.

Of course, it was a mistake. The door flew open under the charging weight of the woman behind it, spinning Joe enough off balance to allow her to push all the way in. As he fell backwards, she launched the howling cat at his head and swiped his temple with a silencer-equipped pistol she'd been hiding, causing a lightning-like flash to blind his vision.

She then efficiently tripped him up with her leg and brought him crashing face-first to the floor.

In one smooth, well-practiced move, she stripped his gun from its holster, twisted his arm up behind his back, and shoved the barrel of her gun against his temple, all while straddling his lumbar.

"You move, you die," she said quietly, her lack of excitement as menacing as her weapon. "Nod if you understand."

He nodded. The cat had disappeared.

Above, Rachel heard Joe speaking loudly through the front door as she entered the bedroom loft. So far unconcerned, she crossed to the backpack that she used instead of a suitcase, intent on retrieving her camera's backup battery, when the house trembled slightly to the sound of a crash and a shout of surprise. Startled, she quietly returned to the top of the stairs and dropped to her hands and knees, hoping to see without revealing herself. She could just make out Joe's upper half, pinned to the floor by a woman holding a gun. The side of his head was bleeding.

"Ohmygod," she murmured, and retreated soundlessly.

She looked around fearfully, for the first time fully captured by the threat they'd been discussing around her for so many days. The room was a hopeless dead end. The bed took up most of the floor. The small window was too tight to fit through, and led to a ten-foot drop in any case. Otherwise, there was a closet, a dresser, and a small table.

She opted for the bed, dropping to her stomach and rolling under it to press up against the far wall.

"What do you want?" Joe asked, his face hard against the rug.

"Put your other hand behind your back," the woman ordered, maintaining her conversational manner.

He did so, feeling the gun's barrel like a pipe being drilled into his temple. She slipped a thick nylon zip-tie around both his wrists and pulled it tight.

"You know I'm a cop."

"I'm getting up now," she said, ignoring him. "I'll help you to your knees. Then you stand and move to the ladder-back chair in the corner, near the stove. Any sudden move and you get a bullet in the head."

He felt her weight ease from his back, followed by her free hand grabbing the thick fabric of his shirt and yanking him to an upright position. He coughed at the cutting pressure against his larynx.

"Stand," she ordered as he struggled awkwardly to his feet.

She marched him to the chair, which she moved away from the wall, and sat him down so that his arms were draped behind the chair's back. She then attached the zip-tie binding his wrists to the bottom chair rung, and strapped each of his ankles to a front leg. Still feeling dizzy and faint from the blow he'd received, Joe now knew he was more thoroughly trussed up than the proverbial turkey.

But his primary concern was Rachel. Was she aware of what was going on?

Rachel was feeling like an idiot. Under the bed? Really? Why not standing on a stool, with her hands clasped to her open mouth?

She began inching her way back out into the room, straining to hear over her rapid breathing, and rethinking how she could better position herself. If she had to go, she wanted it to be with a little more dignity than cowering on the floor in a ball.

She heard muted voices downstairs as she emerged and straightened, but chose not to return to the staircase to check it out. Joe would come find her if he gained the upper hand. Otherwise? Rachel checked around once more, this time in search of a suitable weapon.

Frustrated, she stealthily opened the closet door and began pawing through the clothes there, finally locating—much to her surprise—an old wooden baseball bat, leaning in the corner. She picked it up and weighed it in her hand, liking the feel of it.

Her spirits slightly buoyed, she calculated a position with some advantage built into it, settling finally for the same corner of the closet in which she'd found her weapon. She wedged herself in—off to the side of the door—awkwardly practiced lifting the bat over her head a couple of times, and settled in to wait.

"Where's the girl?"

Joe gave his attacker a quizzical look. "After all this, you don't know? You picked the wrong corner of the state. She's in Burlington."

The woman snarled at him. "I know she's here, stupid. I meant where, here?" She glanced over her shoulder. "Upstairs? That's where I'd put her."

Joe smiled. "You're guessing, or you would've killed me at the door. You're right that she's under wraps. We knew we'd stir up your boss when we flushed out Morgan, so we first made sure the girl was way beyond your reach."

The woman was surprisingly frank. "I don't know who Morgan is, and I don't care. As for killing you, that's your choice. My contract's to grab the girl. Where is she?"

Joe merely shook his head sadly.

She straightened, gave him one last look—as if considering shooting him now to get it over with—and moved to the foot of the stairs.

Rachel felt more than heard the woman's presence outside the closet door. The house was completely silent. She thought she might have heard a single stair tread complain slightly, moments earlier, but could no longer distinguish reality from her mounting fears. As much to concentrate as to prepare herself, she slowly raised the bat until she was holding it as high above her head as the ceiling allowed. Ever since she positioned herself here, she'd been second-guessing her plan, and finding it wanting.

The moment, when it came, was almost a relief. As the closet door trembled slightly, Rachel found herself solely focused on her grip of the bat, and on how to use it to her best advantage.

It never came. In contrast to Rachel's soundless, slow-motion preparations, the woman with the gun finished her approach explosively, yanking open the door, crossing the threshold, and—the gun steady in one hand—reaching up like a cobra striking and pinning Rachel's bat against the wall behind her. The effect was as if she'd been looking through the wall with X-ray vision from the start.

For a frozen fraction of a second, they stood face-to-face, the gun's silencer looking disproportionally huge between them. Then, a deafening bang and a flash of light burst the darkness from the side. Rachel blinked, uncomprehending, at the abruptly empty space before her, as instantly stripped of the woman as it had been filled a moment earlier.

She felt a motion at her feet and looked down in disbelief at the woman's body, collapsed and lifeless among the scattered shoes, a pool of blood slowly spreading around her head.

Tentatively, the bat still in one hand, Rachel bent at the waist and peered around the doorway. Standing four feet away, near the top of the stairs, was a man with a limp left arm and a gun in his hand.

"Hey," he said quietly, smiling slightly. "Remember me? I'm Willy."

CHAPTER TWENTY-SIX

"Her name was Chris Hadsel," Ron Klecszewski said.

Joe looked up from his conversation with Beverly, who had driven down from Burlington to be with Rachel. It was five thirty in the morning. They'd collected in a conference room adjacent to the Brattleboro PD's detective squad, of which Klecszewski was the head. The state police had just wrapped up its post-shoot investigation, as required by protocol. Through the ground-floor windows, they could all see the glare from the TV lights of a half-dozen camera crews. Thankfully, Bill Allard had dispatched a media-relations person from up north to deal with them.

"You ever hear of her?" the state police detective next to Ron asked.

Joe shook his head. "She local?"

"Not even vaguely," Ron answered, having monitored the VSP's activities, since the shooting occurred on his patch. "She seems to have mostly worked in the mid-Atlantic states and in Florida, as far as we can tell."

"All we can do is trace her through prints and mugs," the detective said. "Which means we only know when and where she was caught for anything, which wasn't much. There are years where her activities are completely off the radar."

Joe nodded. "Right. Well, thanks for all the hard work."

The man nodded as he turned toward the door. "You bet. Good luck with your case. Looks like you'll need it." He paused and looked at Willy, slouched in a chair in the far corner of the room. "Good shoot," he added, as a collegial one-liner.

Willy, of course, was having none of that. "Yeah," he answered. "Sorry you couldn't bust me for murder. Maybe next time."

The detective gave a last, pitying glance to Joe and left, no doubt to spread the news that Kunkle's attitude had survived the evening's activities.

Beverly, however, took the other tack, addressing him. "For my part and my daughter's, Agent Kunkle, I'd like to thank you—good shoot or no," she threw in with a smile. "You may be one of the most unconventional police officers I've ever met, but in this instance, I will not fault your methods."

Willy laughed. "Least I could do, given what happened to her babysitter."

"Sad but true," Joe acknowledged, raising a half-empty plastic bottle of water in salutation.

"How'd you figure that out, anyhow?" Lester asked. He'd joined them hours ago for moral support and was now reclined in a chair with his legs resting on the conference table, as if ready to nod off at a moment's notice.

Willy tapped the side of his nose. "I smelled a rat. Figured the Old Man could stand some backup. It never made sense to me that Joyce would just lay off the kid." He raised his eyebrows at Rachel. "No offense."

"None taken," she told him.

"So," he resumed. "I watched the house. Soon as I saw the crazy bitch approach, I figured what was up, but I couldn't move fast enough before you opened up and she ran you over."

Joe appreciated his usual delicacy.

"That means," Willy said to him, "you'll have to fix a window in your wood shop. Hope nothing freezes in there tonight 'cause of it."

Joe smiled ruefully. "Believe me, small price to pay for seeing you sneak in through the shop door and follow her upstairs."

"I locked the place up after EMS took you away," Willy added. "Didn't know what to do with the cat, so I set him up with some tuna and water and put sawdust from the shop in a pan on the kitchen floor. He looked like a good fit. I hear older people do better with pets."

Joe merely gave him a stare.

"What happens to me now?" Rachel asked in general.

Beverly glanced at Joe expectantly.

"I'm afraid we button you up, like before," he said. "The fact that we think we know who's behind this still puts us a long way from locking him up. While tonight's little surprise party was being dissected, I phoned the State's Attorney, and everybody's on board for bumping this upstairs to the U.S. Attorney's office, given Joyce's highfalutin' job. That means briefings, federal investigators, and God knows what else, before anyone threatens him with handcuffs—which also gives him more time to misbehave."

"Elegant choice of words," Beverly commented.

He nodded. "Thank you, Doctor."

Rachel was not looking happy. "Does that mean I don't get to finish my documentary? After everything that's happened?"

Joe glanced around the room before interpreting the unspoken consensus he saw there. "I would say that if you can wrap it up today, despite last night's excitement and lack of sleep, that would work for me. Joyce wouldn't have a Plan B up and running this fast after Willy's handiwork." He looked at Kunkle in particular. "Agreed?"

"Sure," Willy said. "Sam tells me they've almost emptied the house, anyhow. That right?"

"Yes," Rachel agreed, her expression clearing despite her exhaustion. "And one more day is all I'll need."

Joe caught Beverly's eye. "Okay with you?"

Hillstrom stroked her daughter's back. "You don't actually think I'd oppose this, do you, much as I'd like to?"

Joe stood up and checked his watch. "All right, then. We've got a few hours to catch some sleep. My house is off-limits right now, but we can put the two of you into a motel for a while—with a guard on the door— before reconvening at, let's say, ten o'clock."

They all rose and began heading out. Joe touched Beverly's arm as her daughter crossed over to say something to Willy. "How's she doing?" he asked quietly. "Having someone killed at your feet has got to rank above a fender-bender."

Beverly took the question seriously. "Long-term? I have no idea. For the moment, I think her own recipe for keeping busy and on task is correct. I'm going to stay with her. I've already spoken with my office."

Joe affectionately squeezed her hand. "Good. Glad to hear it."

They didn't get to sleep for as long as they'd hoped. At eight thirty, Sammie Martens, who'd missed out on the night's highlights, called Joe at the office, where he'd been sleeping in his chair, to report, "Boss, you better beat feet to the excavation. We just found a booby trap."

Joe blinked to clear his mind. "Everybody okay?"

"Oh yeah. It didn't go off, but it is explosive. I called JP 'cause of his expertise. He's already on his way. It's not fancy—I know that much— and it's small, but I still don't want to lose an arm finding out."

Joe rubbed his eyes. "All right. You sure JP'll be enough? You don't need the state bomb guys?"

"I don't think so, but JP's no cowboy. He won't do it unless he thinks he can. And I'm freezing the scene till you get here anyhow, so you can call in the big boys if you want to then."

"Right," he said, straightening in his chair and getting ready to dial the phone. "I'll make some calls and head straight out."

JP Tyler was an old colleague of Joe's—the Brattleboro PD's evidence and forensics man, who'd since been moved up to being Ron Klecsze-wski's second-in-command. As befitted his almost scholarly nature, he'd long ago become immersed in the study of bomb disposals, to where he'd become one of the highest-rated experts in the state.

Tyler walked up to Joe's car as the latter pulled into Ben Kendall's dooryard. "Hey," he greeted him as Joe swung out into the cold morning air. "Long time. You'd never know we worked in the same building, huh?"

Joe shook hands and laughed. The point had an extra poignancy— before the creation of the VBI, Joe had been JP's boss at the PD. "I guess that's typical." He gestured toward the sad-looking house. "You been in yet?"

"Nope. Figured I'd wait for you."

Three more cars appeared from the woods behind them—Willy leading Beverly and her daughter in their own vehicle, and Lester bringing up the rear.

Tyler focused on the two women. "That the medical examiner? Little premature, ain't she?"

Joe patted his back. "Breathe, JP. She's here with her daughter, who's documenting this for the record. In fact, if we can make it work, I'd like her to video the booby trap, and maybe even your dismantling of it, if it's as small as Sammie thinks. I'll get the appropriate releases signed, for liability, if that'll help."

Tyler shrugged. "Okay by me, at least in principle. We can probably rig a remote unit on a tripod. I've done that before. Let's find out what we got, first."

The excavation team had arrived at seven that morning, as usual, so they'd completed a solid ninety minutes of work before uncovering the trap. During that process, they'd carved a narrow trench into what had once been the living room, right up to the fireplace. It was there that they'd found an aberration in the floorboards, directly before the brick hearth.

The cops, tightly packed, squeezed into the tight space to see what had caught everyone's attention.

Sam served as their guide. "They called me as soon as they found it, given that we were looking for anything and everything unusual." She pointed at the floor. "See how the staining suddenly stops? It's as if something leaked a long time ago, probably spreading unnoticed under all the junk, but instead of leaving a circular spot, like you'd expect, it got absorbed into that crack. The guys thought it looked like a hiding place, and I agreed. So we pried it open, just like it is now, which is when we saw the wiring underneath."

She took them all in. "And when I called you."

"Glad you did," Joe murmured, dropping to his knees to better study the half-open board. He glanced up at JP. "You still interested?"

The small man smiled. "You bet."

He got down beside Joe and played a small flashlight into the opening. "This shouldn't be a problem. And Sam was right—it's designed to blow someone's hand off. No more. Chances are the charge is no longer volatile. It's really old." He hesitated before adding light-heartedly, "Of course, that introduces the chance of decay presenting a last-second surprise."

His laughter was met with polite smiles. Willy was the only one to say, "You can have that bullshit, JP, I'm outta it."

They set things up to suit them, including proper lighting brought to the scene, and with Rachel, Beverly, Sam, and Joe positioned behind a solid barrier, far down the trench. The camera was placed as JP had suggested, controlled remotely. That way, whatever was filmed would be captured directly onto Rachel's laptop computer, in case something went wrong.

That being done, JP remained confident, and set to work with a comfort built of long practice.

Anti-climactically, it took no time at all. JP fully peeled back the piece of floorboard, and the spectators around the corner saw him on screen probe the device a few different ways, cut a few wires, and then lift the explosive into a heavy box that he'd brought along for the disposal. The entire operation was over in ten minutes.

At which point, he looked up into the camera's lens and said, "You want to see what he was protecting? Looks interesting."

The restrictions of the passageway forced them to create a pecking order as they filed back down toward the hiding place. Joe got there first, followed by Sam, Rachel, and Beverly. Willy, as announced, chose to wait for the discovery to come to him later.

JP, still on his knees, leaned back to allow them a better view. Nestled under where the booby trap had been located was a faded manila envelope, wrapped in plastic.

"Do the honors," Joe told him.

JP reached in after donning latex gloves, extracted the envelope, stripped off the plastic, and peered inside. "Interesting," he said, and slid the contents out into his other hand.

Rachel let out a small gasp. "Those are just like the negative sleeves I found with his photographs. It's thirty-five-millimeter film."

"There's something else," Joe said, reaching for the package, also having put on gloves. He shifted the negative sleeve to the back, revealing a small selection of eight-by-ten photos of poor quality.

"What are they?" Sam asked.

"They're called positive proofs," Rachel explained. "I learned about them when I started this project. Photographers usually did contact sheets of their negatives, to better see what they'd taken, but sometimes they also did quick and dirty blowups, to get a bigger image. The other ones I have of Ben's look just like these."

Joe held them up, one at a time, for general viewing, saying, "Folks, this may be the proverbial smoking gun. Looks like Ben had an ace up his sleeve after all, which is what Jack Joyce's been sweating over since this whole thing broke."

Silently, they leaned forward to see. Rachel was right about the print quality—they were poorly exposed and had been inadequately washed following development, resulting in brown stains mottling their surfaces. But they unmistakably showed a man from the back, lying on top of a young woman, her bare legs thrust apart; the same man holding a gun on another, dressed in fatigues but sporting a beard; the bearded man then clutching his chest and falling; and a fourth, quite blurred, of the shooter's gun pointing around at the camera, as if ready to fire. The last picture didn't show his face—or least not clearly enough to distinguish any features. Instead, the camera had, like prey focusing solely on the eyes of its attacker, instinctively centered on the gun.

"Jesus," Lester said softly.

"Yeah," Sam agreed. "So much for corroboration. Ben must've emptied one of his cameras just before Joyce reached him, and maybe shoved the roll into his pocket. I bet there's an inventory somewhere in the bowels of the VA, listing a roll of film among Ben's personal belongings."

"It still may not be enough," Joe cautioned, his frustration clear to all. "Look at them carefully. It's definitely an extra nail in Joyce's coffin, but I doubt you could say for sure that's Joyce. We're gonna have to keep digging."

CHAPTER TWENTY-SEVEN

Deputy U.S. Attorney Frederick Rawlings frowned at the files and photographs spread across the conference table at his office back in Burlington. Appealing to Joe's sense of fashion, he was dressed in an off-the-rack suit, a shirt with a slightly frayed collar, and a pair of boots suitable for the city slush outside. "We still have Frank Niles, supposedly willing to cut a deal," Rawlings said hopefully.

Joe looked him in the face. "I don't want to do that. Plus, we have less against him than we do against his boss."

"I hear you, Joe," Rawlings said agreeably. "But if we don't get lucky soon, we may have to get practical."

Joe said in an even voice. "Niles is a sociopath. He tortured people to death."

They had just received word that Abigail Filson, Nancy's mother, had died in the hospital without ever regaining consciousness.

Rawlings let a few seconds elapse before asking, "What's the status with the Chris Hadsel investigation?"

"We've got analysts looking at her phone and background for any linkage to Joyce or anyone near him. So far, nothing. Like Niles and

Watson, it seems she erased enough of her history to make her unrecognizable to her own mother."

Fred smiled. "I have a hard time believing that any of their mothers would care, but I take your point. What about the people Joyce supposedly paid off to keep quiet? You talk with any of them?"

"We're working on it. But if they're smart," Joe reluctantly had to concede, "they'll keep their mouths shut. I think Bob Morgan was manna from heaven, and probably unique. Not only that, but if Joyce hasn't reached out to every one of them by now and had come-to-Jesus chats, I'd be very surprised."

Rawlings sighed. "So, if you don't want to trade with Niles, the other witnesses won't play, and you're not finding any connections between Joyce and his executioners—"he waved his hand at the messy tabletop. "—and none of the Vietnam photos can be used as rock solid proof, what *is* on your wish list?"

Joe looked at him carefully. "Am I supposed to read into that? Like, unless I come up with something, you're not going to prosecute?"

Rawlings shook his head. "No. I'm perfectly happy to go after a United States senator circumstantially—probably at the cost of my career. I'd just like as much ammo as you can give me."

Hardly mollified—since Joe knew that Rawlings acted only on the authority of his bosses, who could have a less generous take—Joe answered his earlier question. "I think I'll go visit the senator."

"To what effect?"

He stood up and walked to the door. "I'm an old-fashioned man, Fred. I like to do things face-to-face, if I can. Jack Joyce may be a bigwig politician and a rich guy with pals in the right places, but I want him to know who I am—and that a podunk cop from nowhere might have enough stubbornness to match his supposedly unbeatable muscle. You saying that's out of bounds?"

Fred gave him a gesture of surrender. "As long as you abide by the rules, it's fine with me, Joe. Happy hunting."

The meeting took place in Washington, D.C., but not at the senator's office. Instead, Joe, Willy, and their official federal investigator liaison met with Joyce and his lawyer on the top floor of a nearby apartment building. Consistent with everything that Joe had recently learned about the man, the place was vast, pretentious, and designed to impress the kind of people Joe wouldn't have wanted as friends.

All the way to the stiff-backed butler who opened the door.

"Special Agent Gunther?" the man inquired, fixing Joe with an impassive look.

Joe displayed his credentials, as did the other two. The butler faded back from the door and allowed them in, by that gesture handing them over to a slim, well-dressed young woman, who escorted them to an office at the end of a long hallway.

Joe resisted rolling his eyes at the set piece awaiting them: a long polished table, at the head of which sat a white-haired man in a dark suit, his legs casually crossed, attended by another, younger man standing by his side as if poised to run errands. Joyce, whom Joe recognized from photographs, had one arm resting on the table, the gold cuff link of its gleaming starched shirtsleeve reflecting off the polished wood.

"Agent Gunther, I presume?" Joyce said with false heartiness.

"Yeah," Joe said, and introduced Willy and the fed, who had agreed beforehand to remain an observer only, to allow Joe and Willy a free hand.

Joyce gestured toward his companion without turning his head. "Jeremy Littlefield, my attorney." He then waved vaguely down the table. "Sit, sit."

The liaison accepted the invitation, but the two VBI agents moved to where the windows were at their backs, disrupting Joyce's posed symmetry, forcing him to shift in his seat, and putting the daylight in his face.

Still, he angled to maintain control. "I gather," he said, "that you wanted to see me about certain matters that occurred in Vermont." He smiled before adding, "I should warn you beforehand that I've never been to your beautiful state—just for the record."

"You were in Vietnam," Joe began, ignoring him.

Joyce looked surprised. "Everyone knows that."

"You volunteered."

"That's correct. Nowadays, I'm willing to admit that I let my youthful patriotism get the better of political good sense."

"Word is that political good sense played a big role in directing that patriotism."

Joyce frowned. "You forget that they were sending us home piecemeal by commercial jet—no ticker tape parades for us—and to people who spit on us after we landed. To enter politics straight out of uniform in those days wasn't the no-brainer it is now."

"You see combat out there?" Joe asked.

"I saw my share."

"How 'bout on March seventh, 1971?"

"The date doesn't ring a bell."

"What about the name Nathan Sievers?"

Joyce paused to stare into the distance, murmuring, "Sievers, Sievers," before he widened his eyes and said, "Right. A journalist. Quite unstable, if I recall."

"And Ben Kendall?"

"The photographer," he said smoothly. "It's all coming back. I do remember him. A quiet, decent man. Tragic, what happened to him."

"Bob Morgan?"

Joyce smiled thinly. "You sure you don't mean Dan Smith or John

Doe? Agent Gunther, you're talking about a long time ago. There are moments from that time that will haunt me for life, as you can imagine, but individual names?"

"You remembered Kendall," Joe challenged him. "What can you tell me about what happened to him?"

Jeremy Littlefield bent at the waist slightly, as if ducking into the conversation. "My client has already addressed his faulty recall. I think it inadvisable to answer such questions without his being given more time to reflect."

Joe had anticipated such a tactic, and opened the accordion file he'd brought. He extracted two mug shots—one of Frank Niles, the other of the dead Neil Watson—and stepped forward to place them on the table, side by side. "This falls into the category of current events. You ever see these two men?"

Joyce peered at them without much interest. "No."

The door opened and the butler entered, bearing a small silver tray with five cups, an ornate coffeepot, and the usual accessories. He set it silently in the middle of the table and withdrew like a forgotten thought.

Everyone in the room ignored his offerings.

Joe tapped the picture of Frank Niles and bluffed. "This one says he knows you."

"Then he's mistaken," Joyce responded. "That being said, there are hundreds of people who may believe they know me, whom I don't know in turn. It's that kind of job."

Predictable, Joe thought. The definition of deniability.

Joe laid down a picture of Chris Hadsel. "She look familiar?"

"No," he said, barely looking.

Another photo, taken by Ben, of Joyce in uniform, issuing commands. "Is this you?" Joe asked.

For the first time, Joyce reacted, picking it up and sharing it with

Littlefield. "Quite a few pounds ago," he said. "God. And look at the hair."

"Do you remember the occasion?" Joe continued.

The senator replaced the picture. "How would I? I'm guessing it's the date you mentioned earlier. That would make dramatic sense, given your general line of questioning." He raised his eyebrows. "And I do sense a bit of theater going on here. Compensating, perhaps, for a lack of substance?"

"The day two men were shot under your command doesn't stand out?" Joe pressed him.

"Again—" Littlefield began.

"If you mean Sievers and Kendall," his client interrupted. "They were not under my command. The first was thrust upon me by the PR people, and Kendall was assigned by Signal Corps. I had no control over him."

"Sounds like you didn't like Nathan Sievers."

"He had a chip on his shoulder—very antagonistic to our mission over there."

"Did that cause problems?"

"The men disliked him more than I did. I had to play interference. It didn't make my job any easier."

"Jack . . . ," Littlefield warned him.

Joe kept speaking. "Are you implying that he was a friendly fire casualty?"

"I implied nothing of the sort."

"But you are saying that he made things difficult."

"That's what I said."

"Enough that you had to deal with him?" Joe asked.

Littlefield tried again. "Special Agent Gunther, I think we've said all we're going to say today—"

Joyce stopped him with an upheld hand, his eyes on Joe's. "I spoke to him several times."

"Your men have been quoted as saying that you considered Sievers a subversive element," Joe said.

"He was disruptive to discipline, which was never too strong at the best of times in those days."

"Did you have to take matters into your own hands?"

Jeremy Littlefield laid a hand on his employer's shoulder as Joyce opened his mouth to speak, and said firmly. "My client has already answered that."

But Joyce repeated blandly, "I spoke to him a few times, to no avail."

Joe reached into his file and pulled out a cropped blowup of one of Ben's photographs, showing only the shocked face of Nathan Sievers.

"Is this Sievers?" he asked, adding the picture to the growing pile on the table.

"It might be. Again, it's been a long time."

Joe added the full-frame image—no longer cropped—showing Joyce pointing his gun at Sievers. "What caused you to aim your service weapon at Nathan Sievers?" Joe asked.

At this, Joyce crossed his arms. "I—"

"My client has nothing to say," Littlefield drowned him out in an exasperated tone, seizing the picture and peering at it. "Besides which, you can't see this man's face. You can't tell who it is."

"Is that the same for this?" Joe asked, knowing that his one chance to confront Joyce was almost over. He quickly slapped down the next shot, of Sievers clutching his chest and falling, Joyce having fired.

Littlefield stretched out fast and placed his hand flat on the picture to block Joyce from seeing it. "That's enough, Agent Gunther. We are finished here. You may leave. *Now.*"

Joe began to slowly collect the contents of his file. He spoke with more confidence than he felt, grappling with the fact that this man might get away with what he'd done, virtually without a scratch, and that because of it, Frank Niles was in an even stronger position to work out a deal with the U.S. Attorney. "Senator," he said, struggling to ignore a spreading flush of defeat. "What I've shown you today is barely the beginning. We've got you in such a web of your own making that Mr. Littlefield here is going to need an army of expensive help. You cannot go around killing people—not years ago and far away, and certainly not now and in this country—and expect to get away with it."

He finished refiling the photos and retreated halfway to the door—held open by the quiet and ubiquitous butler—before turning to add, "Remember the names Nate Sievers, Ben Kendall, and Jennifer Sisto, Tommy Bajek, Jarek Sroka, and just recently Abigail Filson, Silencing them took a lot of planning, Senator, and involved hiding a lot of evidence. Too much, in fact. The loose ends we're picking up almost daily will be used against you before long. And I didn't list the men who died after returning from Vietnam—men who thought they'd seen the worst there was to see, until they met you."

His anger just shy of boiling over, he indicated their lavish surroundings, adding, "Enjoy all this while you've got it."

"Enough," Littlefield warned him.

Joe considered saying more, but surprisingly, it was Willy who took his upper arm and gently guided him toward the exit, saying, "Steady, boss. I think I got something."

The three of them, including the federal escort, followed the butler back down the hallway.

Joe could barely murmur through his fury, "It better be good, whatever it is, 'cause this fucker's gonna get away with it."

Willy was unusually even-toned, not even commenting on Joe's rare crude language. "You had me convinced in there. If I was Littlefield, I'd be worried."

Joe stared at him. "Are you shitting me?" he whispered harshly, keenly aware of the butler just ahead. "We don't even have a good case against Niles. He plays it right, he'll get off with next to nothing and still won't have to rat out this asshole." He jerked his thumb backwards. "We need a smoking gun—dates, names, a diary, or access to somebody's e-mail account." He paused to shake his head in disgust. "A frigging miracle."

"Maybe not," Willy said mildly, adding in a slightly louder voice, "Could be we haven't asked the right person for help."

They'd passed a string of rooms containing several staffers by now, and were almost at the front door. Willy touched the butler on the shoulder and asked, "What's your name?"

The inquiry seemed to startle the fellow. He slowed and looked at them. "Mine? Jonathan French."

Willy checked over his shoulder to make sure they weren't being overheard. "The invisible man," he said quietly. "Sees all, hears all."

Joe stared at him, his mouth half open, his corroding bitterness momentarily stilled.

"I saw how you looked at the pictures on the table," Willy said. "When you came in with the coffee. You knew those two men."

A long pause settled among them, during which French's expression slowly changed from his impassive norm to something approaching a relieved smile.

"Mr. Niles and Mr. Watson?" he then asked calmly. "Yes—them and much more."

"Son of a bitch," Joe muttered.

Turn the page for a sneak peek at
Archer Mayor's next novel

THE COMPANY
SHE KEPT

Available September 2015

CHAPTER ONE

"Pull over, Doug. I want to get a shot of this."

Uncomplaining, Doug Nielsen checked his mirrors, slowed down shy of the interstate crossover—marked EMERGENCY USE ONLY—and eased their rig across the empty northbound lane, to the scenic pull-off his wife had indicated. A cautious man, he was wary of any black ice that could launch them through the slender barricade and over the straight drop beyond it into Margie's planned panorama.

He didn't fault her artist's eye. The view from this ledge was vast, inspiring, and beautiful. The Connecticut River, far below, lined by glimmering fresh snow, sparkled in the late afternoon sun, which itself was the only object visible in a stark, freezing, ice blue sky. A few farms stretched out to both sides of the winding river, empty of crops or live-stock, until their fields bumped up against the opposing Vermont and New Hampshire foothills. Several homes sported thin plumes of woodsmoke from their chimneys, making Doug think of feather quills protruding from toy-sized inkwells. He thought it might have been the sheer antiquity of everything before him that stirred up such an old-fashioned image, since—barring a barely visible utility line and a narrow paved road far in the distance—he guessed that little before him had changed much in over two hundred years.

He and Margie had been vacationing for the past week in the Green Mountain State, whose famous mantle had been deeply powdered by a recent spate of snowstorms. This had been good news for them, since they'd driven up from southern New Jersey to exercise the two snowmobiles they were now towing back home. There had been trips to New England in the past where the cover had been less than ideal for dedicated so-called sledders. But not this time. This visit had been perfect.

Doug rolled to a stop and they both got out, the cold air tingling their nostrils and biting the backs of their throats. The lot was deserted, which suited him fine, considering the combined length of his car and trailer. He'd been able to ignore the row of parking spaces hashed into the cleared asphalt, and simply park alongside the barricade.

"Isn't this incredible?" his wife asked, pulling out her smartphone.

"Pretty nice," he answered briefly, no less impressed by the vista, but sensitive to the near-total stillness accompanying it. "Quiet, too," he added, encouraging his wife to take in more of what he was appreciating.

But there, she had her own style.

"I know," she said, ordering up the phone's photographic function. "Can you imagine how this would be next to the Jersey Pike? I'd have to hope the pictures wouldn't blur, from all the vibration from passing trucks."

He nodded and began walking the length of the extended pull-off, putting some distance between them.

"Don't go too far, Doug," she called out. "I want to take a selfie of us in front of the view."

Refusing to break his inner code of silence, Doug raised his gloved hand without turning and stuck a thumb up in acknowledgment. Margie went back to concentrating on her shot.

Doug had lived in New Jersey his entire life, in the city, amid people. He worked in a large building, at a desk in a room the size of a football field, under an endless stuttering of overhead fluorescent tubes and surrounded by an army corps of cubicles, all like his own. He and Margie had a good life. The house was almost paid for, and in good shape, compared to some on the street. They were all more or less of the same architectural model, which made any standouts that much more glaring. And Doug was happy. The kids had turned out okay, Margie and he were pretty healthy, retirement was looking feasible in another ten years or so—assuming the world didn't go to hell in a handbasket.

He stopped walking, Margie now much smaller in the background.

And last but not least, he had moments like this, when he could absorb the spectacular vestiges of prehistoric phenomena like glaciers, fluvial erosion, and the efforts of mankind to make a living off the land. It gave him a comforting sense of being in touch with what so many of his coworkers back home couldn't even imagine.

He turned from the view at the sound of a car speeding by on the interstate, attracted by how lonely it sounded, and how quickly the sound of it was swallowed by the surrounding immensity. It brought back Margie's comment about the Jersey Pike, which in turn made him think that he ought to get back to her to pose for that photograph.

He paused a moment longer, though, his eyes not on the hundred-foot rock wall across the pavement, looming as high above them as the cliff dropped off to his back. Instead, he found himself drawn to a sharp but distant twinkling of gold, perched on the edge of the roadway, bordering the southbound lane.

Intrigued, he went up to the edge of the parking area's barricade, and climbed atop one of the short wooden posts there to get a better angle on the distant object.

"I'll be damned," he said to himself, recognizing a large handbag, its clasp reflecting the sun's blaze.

"What're you looking at?" his wife asked from surprisingly nearby.

He wobbled briefly on his post, turning and laughing. "Whoa. Honey. You snuck up on me." He pointed across the double lanes. "That thing caught my eye. Probably fell out of a car."

She squinted in the direction he was indicating. "That purse? Why would it fall out of a car? We're miles from the exit. Stuff like that only happens when you're leaving—like when you forget your coffee cup on the roof or something."

Doug was scanning the road up and down, as much for an explanation as in preparation for a quick sprint over to retrieve the purse. Margie, however, had tilted her head back to take in the towering cliff above.

Several years earlier, the Department of Transportation had been delivered some bad news: As a by-product of the construction of Vermont's two interstates back in the sixties, rocks from the cliffs alongside the roads had begun breaking loose. Most of the overhangs had been expensively angled back with drills and blasting. A few, like the one facing the Nielsens now, had been deemed too daunting and had received the alternate treatment of a steel retaining mesh, dropped before the rock face like a chain-link curtain, to prevent any debris from bouncing onto the pavement.

"Oh, my lord," Margie whimpered softly, her gaze halfway up.

The distress in her voice caught Doug's attention. "Holy Mother," he said.

Some forty feet up, hanging from a rope, was the body of a woman, dangling before the retaining screen like a talisman on display.

Margie, acting instinctively—her reflex as modern as her surroundings were primordial—snapped a picture.

CHAPTER TWO

Joe Gunther was studying Gilbert's face from inches away, watching for any indicators of what might be going through his mind. But Gilbert was a cat, and fast asleep on Joe's chest at the moment, so the challenge was probably insurmountable, even for a veteran cop.

Joe had never been a pet owner, not since leaving the family farm as a young man, where his father had kept dogs. Gilbert had been thrust upon him. Actually, thrown at him by a woman trying to distract him as she drew a gun. That had worked, in the short-term, even though she'd then been bested by one of Joe's colleagues. In any case, Gilbert had ended up in permanent residency, no worse for the adventure.

Which Joe had found surprisingly to his liking. His young roommate had settled in without a ripple, greeting him when he came home, sleeping peacefully with him at night, and snuggling unobtrusively whenever he had a moment to sit and read late at night.

Gilbert Gumshoe—as Sammie Martens, Joe's sole female squad member, called him—had become a gentle grace note at this point along an eventful, sometimes tumultuous life.

Of course, as Willy Kunkle—another member of the team, and

Sammie's "other half"—had put it in cruder terms, older people need pets as they get decrepit.

Joe smiled at the memory of the line. He did like his ragtag family of eccentrics. Just as he liked Gilbert.

The phone rang beside the couch, where Joe and the cat were stretched out. Gilbert half opened his eyes, assessed his chances of remaining undisturbed, and decamped for the floor in a graceful leap.

"Gunther," Joe answered.

"Susan's dead," a woman's distraught voice said.

"Gail?" Joe asked, recognizing his long-standing romantic partner of several years ago, now the governor of Vermont. Still a friend who called periodically—although usually not so dramatically—Gail Zigman had become an enigma to him, at times longing and sentimental, at others imperious and borderline ruthless. He had sadly found himself watching his choice of words with her—a caution he'd never practiced in the past.

"She was murdered."

"Susan *Raffner?*" he asked, sitting up, noticing at the same time that another call was coming in.

He ignored it for the time being. "Tell me what happened."

"I don't know. I just got a phone call. They found her dead near the interstate. I don't understand what that means, but they definitely said she'd been killed. They told me they called because she was my friend."

"Of course," he said soothingly, not adding that it was also because of Susan's being a state senator. The two women had begun in politics together, decades ago, when Susan had backed Gail for a place on the Brattleboro selectboard. She had been Gail's political adviser and trusted sidekick ever since.

"Did you get the name of the cop on the case?" he asked out of habit.

"I didn't talk to him," she said, sounding surprised. "They called the governor's office, not me directly. Rob told me." There was a sudden

catch in her voice, and when she resumed, she was choked with emo-
tion. "What does it matter, Joe? Who cares?"

"You're right, you're right," he said, ignoring her flash of irritation.
Rob Perkins was her chief of staff. "I'll get that later."

"You'll do this, Joe?" she pleaded. "You'll find out who did it?"

"I'll do my best," he promised.

"I already gave orders that VBI was to have the case, no questions
asked, but I want you leading them. If you get any shit from anybody,
you call me, okay?"

"Of course, Governor," he assured her. "I'll get on it now. I'll keep
you informed. Promise."

His use of her title seemed to steady her, transcending their past
intimacy to introduce a stabilizing formality.

Following a moment's hesitation, she said, "Thank you, Joe. I'll wait
to hear from you."

"I am sorry, Gail," he told her.

He heard her sob as she hung up. He checked his phone to find out
who'd called. It was Bill Allard, head of the VBI—the Vermont Bureau
of Investigation—of which Joe had been the field force commander
since its inception.

"You calling about the governor?" he asked as soon as Allard
picked up.

"I'm calling about Senator Raffner," Bill replied, sounding nonplussed.

"I was on the phone with the governor. She called to say she'd asked
us to look into this."

"Asked is hardly the word," Bill corrected him, not a fan of Gail. "But
it does look like our kind of case."

"With me as lead?" Joe asked.

"Ah," Allard reacted. "She told you that, too, huh? Yeah. That's what
she wants."

"I understand if you have to conflict me out," Joe told him. "Having the governor's old boyfriend running the investigation into her closest ally's death might get sticky."

"Not for me, it doesn't," Bill countered. "Raffner was a sitting state senator. I want my best team on it. We can't sacrifice quality to play politics—we don't have the manpower. Handpick whoever you want. We'll shift personnel around to cover, if need be."

The phone indicated a third incoming call. Joe said, "Roger that. Just thought I'd float the question. I'll call you back when I got something."

He hit a button on the phone. "Gunther."

"It's Sam," said his second-in-command, the weekend's on-call officer. "You hear yet? Hell of a way to start a sunny Sunday."

Her natural intensity reverberated over the line. She had a perpetual level of commitment—whether to him, the job, her baby daughter, or the acerbic Willy Kunkle—that radiated like a heat source.

"I just hung up on the governor and Allard," he told her. "Nobody's told me much beyond that Susan Raffner was found murdered."

"That's how it's looking," Sam said. "Unless she took herself out in the weirdest suicide I ever heard."

"*What?*"

"She was found hanging from one of those steel-mesh retaining nets they dropped across the cliffs lining the interstate. A couple of tourists called it in. It almost sounds like when a farmer hangs a dead fox from his fence, to warn other foxes. Totally crazy."

"But it's not a suicide?" he asked pointedly.

"VSP is guarding the scene," she reported, using the familiar initials of the Vermont State Police. "They're keeping everything as clean as possible for us, but it looks like a homicide, unless you know something I don't. For one thing, they're saying there's no car parked nearby. It could be a suicide combined with a car theft. Stranger things have happened."

Joe shook his head at the phone. "Okay. It's not like Raffner and I hung out. I barely saw her over the years. But suicidal? I never got that—she was way too full of piss and vinegar, protesting every cause under the sun. You did hear we've been assigned to head this up?"

"Yup," she said, sounding happy. "I'm at the office right now, packing stuff up. Who do you want to come along?"

"The way the cages are being rattled," Joe said, "everybody, so we start on the same page."

He could almost hear her grinning. "Cool. I already got Willy calling the babysitter, and Lester said we could pick him up at the gas station off exit seven."

Which is one of the many reasons Joe had made her his Number Two. "I'm headin' out," he said gratefully. "See you in a few."

Joe had once imagined that if you took a sheet of paper, crumpled it up into a ball, and then flattened it out—creased lengthwise, like a small, rectangular tent—you would have the rough approximation of a 3-D map of Vermont. The mountains run down its middle, the right and left edges are calmed and flattened by water—the Connecticut River and Lake Champlain, respectively—and the rest of the state's surface is as bumpy, irregular, and furrowed as the Ice Age relic that it is.

He loved every square foot of it. As he sat in the passenger seat of the unmarked car, with Sam at the wheel and Willy and Lester in the back, he watched the Connecticut River come into and out of view in the valley below them. The interstate this far north was never heavily traveled—certainly not by urban standards—and had been declared by various magazines as one of the country's most scenic byways.

And yet, he mused . . . There was always a flip side, as his long career attested: For all its sylvan beauty and apparent tranquility, despite its sparse population and square miles of emptiness, Vermont was also poorly financed, nonindustrialized, and far off the beaten path for everyone except tourists, and—more recently—drug dealers. None of that made it a crime magnet, but this very trip north was proof enough to Joe of humanity's chronic inability to live as peacefully as these calming environs suggested.

The VSP had sealed off an entire section of the road between two exits, rerouting the scant traffic to a parallel two-lane highway. Sam maneuvered their vehicle between the cones manned by a young trooper who waved them through, and continued for four miles along a pavement now as empty of traffic as an abandoned movie set.

"Spooky," Lester commented from the back. "It's like some spaceship beamed up everybody but us."

"I doubt it beamed up the people we'd like to see gone," Willy said sourly, grabbing his withered left arm and shifting it so he could sit more comfortably. They were all dressed for the outdoors, in addition to carrying their standard tactical gear. "Be typical if only the good guys got zapped."

The other three smiled at the comment, typical of the speaker. Willy's arm—a reminder of a career-threatening encounter with a bullet on a case many years earlier—was a testament to both the one-liner and Willy's overall Eeyore outlook.

Any humor vanished, however, as the car rounded the next wide curve, and a cluster of vehicles came into view, most of them sparkling with various combinations of blue and white and red strobe lights against the craggy backdrop of a dark rock wall.

Lester hunched forward, craning to see up, which his great height and the car's low roof made all but impossible. "My God. That's awful."

No one argued with him, including Willy. The sight of a single human body, hanging high and small and lonely halfway to the cliff's top, struck them all with its melancholy.

There was no need to pull off the road—trucks and cruisers were parked haphazardly, as if their drivers had subconsciously enjoyed not having to follow the rules.

"We're in the wrong place," Willy said as they got out, still staring at the mesmerizing vision overhead.

A state police sergeant proved him correct as he approached, saying, "They're waiting for you up top." He gestured with his thumb, continuing, "The next exit's a few miles north, but we cut a snowmobile path just past the cliff that connects to the road above. You could go that way if you don't mind one of my guys driving your car around the long way. We got sled operators standing by."

"Sounds good," Joe told him. "What about the people who called this in?"

"They're in their car." The sergeant pointed to the scenic pull-off and an SUV hitched to a trailer bearing two snowmobiles. "We got a video-recorded statement, but you're free to talk to 'em yourself, if you want."

Joe watched the man's bland, impassive face, looking for any signs that this was a dig. "Uniforms" versus "Suits" was a well-known rivalry within law enforcement, although less so in Vermont, given the small numbers involved. But VSP versus VBI was an additional factor, since the creation of the latter had seriously depleted the ranks of the former's Bureau of Criminal Investigation—and had eroded its influence.

The sergeant, however, appeared to be either totally lacking in such prejudice, or a skilled poker player.

In any case, Joe didn't care. "I'm good," he replied. "They tell you anything interesting?"

The man smiled and visibly relaxed. "Not really. They had the sense to keep their distance, but except for the obvious, they didn't see anything, didn't hear anything, and don't know anything. Our BCI guys called for the crime scene truck." He glanced upward. "They just arrived upstairs, so everything's looking pretty secure."

Joe shifted his gaze once more to the reason they were here. "This is going to sound a little screwy, but are we sure she's dead?"

The sergeant chuckled. "Not screwy to me. First thing I asked when I got here. She's dead, all right." He indicated an athletic young trooper in the distance, talking with a couple of his colleagues. "The tall one there was first on scene. He called it in, checked her out with his binoculars—so far so good—and then the crazy bastard climbed the netting and checked for a pulse."

Joe stared at him. "He climbed up?"

"Like a goddamned monkey. Wished I'd been here to see it. It's got to be forty feet. The female tourist took pictures. You should see 'em. I gave our boy a big thumbs-up, and then told him that if he ever did a thing like that again, I'd have him on desk duty for a month."

Joe shook his head, thinking that he would have pulled the same stunt a couple of decades ago. "I heard something about a purse," he asked.

"BCI took it. It was over there, looking no different than if you'd just put it down. The clasp was still closed, which is a miracle if it was dropped from that height."

Joe nodded without comment, and turned to face his team. "Okay. Let's go sledding."

They found five snowmobiles waiting by the side of the road, as the cliff tapered off to become a shallow, snow-packed gully that aimed back toward the hilltop. They divided up among four volunteer drivers and hitched rides to a two-lane dirt road above. Contrasting with the view they had been enjoying—and despite being higher up—here the road was screened by trees on both sides, with only glimpses between the evergreens of the Connecticut River valley.

They were met by a VSP van that took them to a second cluster of cars, including a large truck from the forensic laboratory. As usual at such scenes—which were blessedly few in this rural state—Joe was impressed by the number of people gathered. Besides the state police and the crime lab civilians, there were representatives from Fish and Wildlife, the local sheriff's office, EMS, a couple of local municipal cops, and even what appeared to be a town constable—most of them muttering and watching the very few people who were actually processing the scene.

He couldn't blame them. A cop in Vermont could go through most of a career without witnessing a homicide scene. A banner year in Vermont might produce twenty murders—fewer than he imagined New York City racked up in a month.

From inside the yellow tape enclosing a generous semicircle, a plainclothes detective they knew from past encounters caught sight of them and invited them over. "Oh, boy, here come the big guns. Can we all go home now?" he cracked.

Joe identified himself to an officer with a clipboard before ducking under the cordon. "Rick," he said. "Long time. How've you been keeping?"

"Can't complain. I'm happy to be the lowly BCI guy on this one. This is gonna be a nightmare before it's done."

It was a custom-designed moment for Willy to say something insulting, but Joe knew his man. Kunkle was ignoring the chatter, his eyes darting around the scene as he submitted his ID in turn, instinctively cataloguing every detail around him. A trained military sniper and a PTSD-plagued paranoid, he was someone who focused fast and hard.

Joe looked around as Sam and Lester took their turns at the checkpoint. The ice-hard dirt road was only twenty yards from the edge of the cliff, beyond the thin line of trees and the remnants of a dilapidated chain-link fence. Embedded in the otherwise pristine crust of snow, between the tarmac and the first tree trunk, were a set of tire tracks and some footprints. Joe saw a tied-off double loop of taut white rope around that first trunk, leading straight toward the cliff.

"You find any witnesses to anything?" Joe asked his BCI counterpart.

Rick frowned. "Not yet. I got guys pounding on doors, but it's pretty isolated up here. The road is rarely traveled, given both the interstate and the paved highway they're using for the detour."

Joe pressed his lips together before saying, "Makes you think. Whoever did this had to have been familiar with the area—the backwoods road, the broken fence, the proximity to the cliff . . . Even the trees being handy so the rope could be tied off."

He watched as the lab techs laid out a narrow sidewalk next to the tire tracks, giving them access while preserving the evidence. "We were having a conversation on the way up here about whether this could be a suicide."

"With no car?" Rick asked.

"It could've been stolen afterward," Sam contributed, crouched down with her small backpack and unloading her camera equipment.

Rick didn't laugh. "Great minds and all that," he said. "We thought the same thing, especially after we sent a unit to her house in Brattleboro and found her car missing. Problem is"—here he pointed at the tracks in the snow—"those belong to a pickup or an SUV. Raffner's registered to a Prius."

"Of course she is," Willy muttered, and moved away, shadowing the techs.

Rick and Joe ignored him. "You put out a BOL for the car?" Joe asked.

"Yup. Nothing yet."

"Curiouser and curiouser," Lester said, trailing behind Willy and now Sam, as they started coordinating with the crime lab team.

Because of the aging day's ebbing light, the protocols of how best to deconstruct a scene like this had to be altered, and provisions made to secure the area overnight. Fortunately, the weather was forecast to hold steady, making this an easy decision.

Less easy was choosing how to remove the body from its perch.

It couldn't be a simple matter of reeling her in by the rope from which she was dangling. Any tastelessness of doing so aside, the practical consideration remained of how the stressors of such a maneuver might play out. As Willy indelicately put it, "You don't want her head coming off."

As a result, after everything obvious had been thoroughly documented and the evidence gathered, a high-angle extraction crew was summoned and dropped over the cliff and the remains placed inside first a body bag, and then a lightweight wire litter to be pulled to the top.

Nevertheless, for Joe, who'd known Susan for decades, the shock of seeing her dead after the bag had been partially unzipped—the rope still around her neck—hit him harder than he'd expected.

Raffner had been Gail's friend, not his. He'd been open to some kind of relationship, given her importance in Gail's life, but he'd always felt that Susan didn't like him much. She'd respected him—both Gail and his own inner radar had told him as much—but he'd sensed that she'd viewed him as the loyal opposition.

That being said, he'd seen her laugh and cry and had shared meals and drinks with her for years—if always in the company of others. She'd been bright and smart and tough and good at getting things done—as well as devoted and dedicated to Gail. To see the source of such vitality so pale, stiff, and silent drove home what he knew Gail must be experiencing.

Her best friend—certainly her most steadfast one—had been reduced to a broken vessel, its vibrant contents emptied.

"You want to take a better look at her?" one of the climbers asked him, undoing the straps that held her pale corpse to the litter.

Shaking off his musings, Joe came alongside the device, asking, "How stiff is she?"

"Not rock solid. It's more than the usual rigor, 'cause of the cold, but she's not like some of 'em—straight out of the freezer."

Grateful to hear that, Joe slipped on a pair of latex gloves and crouched in the snow, a small crowd looking on. They'd all dealt with bodies that had truly frozen stiff. Not only couldn't you make them conform to anything, like a doorway or the inside of a hearse, but they took days to thaw prior to autopsy.

"Let's make sure," he announced generally, "that when she gets transported to Burlington, the hearse is heated to where the driver can barely stand it. We've got to do what we can to get her warm enough that they can open her up."

As Joe began helping with the straps and the bag's zipper, they all noticed how her underlying sweater, blouse, and bra had been sliced down the middle, exposing her bare chest.

"Damn," someone said.

Crudely cut into the flesh was the single word, "Dyke."

Follow Special Agent Joe Gunther through New England in what the *Chicago Tribune* calls **"the best police-procedural series being written in America."**

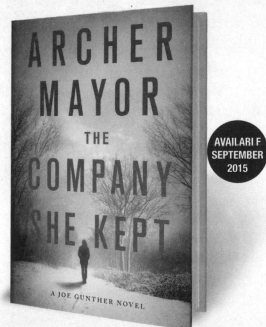

AVAILABLE SEPTEMBER 2015